D1077004

When We Were Romans

Sweet Thames

NON-FICTION

An Atheist's History of Belief
Rome: A History in Seven Sackings

PILGRIMS

Matthew Kneale

atlantic·*fiction*

First published in hardback in Great Britain in 2020 by Atlantic Books, an imprint of Atlantic Books Ltd.

This paperback edition published in 2021

10 9 8 7 6 5 4 3 2 1

A CIP catalogue record for this book is available from the British Library.

Paperback ISBN: 978 1 78649 239 5
E-book ISBN: 978 1 78649 238 8

Printed and bound by CPI Group (UK) Ltd, Croydon, CR0 4YY

Atlantic Books
An imprint of Atlantic Books Ltd
Ormond House
26–27 Boswell Street
London
WC1N 3JZ

www.atlantic-books.co.uk

For my mum

CONTENTS

PART ONE – 1264
CHAPTER ONE – Motte   3

PART TWO – 1289
CHAPTER TWO – Tom son of Tom   13
CHAPTER THREE – Constance   50
CHAPTER FOUR – Warin   66
CHAPTER FIVE – Lucy de Bourne   95
CHAPTER SIX – Tom son of Tom   146
CHAPTER SEVEN – Matilda Froome   164
CHAPTER EIGHT – Iorwerth   202
CHAPTER NINE – Tom son of Tom   238
CHAPTER TEN – Constance   261
CHAPTER ELEVEN – Motte   300
CHAPTER TWELVE – Tom son of Tom   316

NOTE OF THANKS   337
NOTE ON LANGUAGE   339
    Glossary of Middle English   341
    Medieval place names   343

PART ONE

1264

CHAPTER ONE

Motte

I should remember everything that happened that morning, every tiny jot, but I can't. I'll just have to imagine. My mother-in-law Licoricia would've been sat in her big green chair like usual, waving apples at my little boys, Leo and Hame, to steal their eyes from me. Not that I'd have minded as I'd have been glad to have a rest from them. Or she'd have started on about what a good man her husband Elias was, going off to work before the sun was up. That had a barb in it like most of Licoricia's talk did, and meant 'my husband's a far better man than any of the idle lollerers in your family'. Which was a black lie. Just because mine weren't rich like hers didn't mean they were idle.

Then came one thing that I do remember. Besse the maid was about to go out and get our morning bread when my sister Rosa told her no, she'd go as she felt like taking a little walk. 'Une petite marche,' she'd have said. I might have wondered about it, I probably did, but I didn't say anything. Then I'd have been distracted. Leo was new on his feet, running and squealing till he'd fall down and cry, Hame was two years older and they were like two fish hooks, snagging my attention. Or I'd have been fretting about Benedict, my husband, who was up in Lincoln, where he'd gone to make new silver ends for the synagogue scrolls. He'd left just before the new troubles, we'd had no word for weeks and my heart missed a beat every time someone came knocking at the door.

All the while I'd have felt the moments passing by, till I thought Rosa's taking her time. It's not far to the baker's so she should be back by now. Then I'd have told myself, stop worrying, Motte. There's probably a big crowd in the bakery, as there often is at this hour, and she's had to wait. Until so long had gone by that even if all of Pharaoh's army were in there getting loaves she should've been back. Then I'd have said, lightly like I wasn't much bothered, 'I wonder where Rosa's got to? I might go out and take a look.' Of course Licoricia would've seen through that clear as through a pane of glass. 'Let's hope your sister hasn't run off again,' she'd have said, casting me a woeful look, as if to say, your family's nothing but trouble. In her heart she'd have been pleased, as with me out of the house she'd have my boys all to herself to spoil. And then there's the one thing that I wish I remember so bad that it burns me. When I went to get my cloak and my purse, did Hame run up and grab me, like he sometimes did when I was going out, squealing and laughing and saying I must stay, and did Leo, not wanting to be left out, totter over and do the same?

After that I remember it all better. That would have been from my anguish I dare say, as there's nothing like fright to keep something in the mind forever. I walked over to the baker's, thinking I was a daft fool for worrying, and sure I'd see Rosa walking back through the crowds towards me, a loaf under her arm, giving me an aggrieved look for chasing after her. But no, here I was by the baker's and there wasn't a hair of her. There were only one or two bodies inside, and when I asked, 'Have you seen my sister Rosa?' the baker shook his head. So Licoricia had been right and she'd run off again. I was breathing faster then, scared and angry for her both at the same time. What if someone knew her face from the Jewry? I just hoped she hadn't gone all the way outside the city again. But she probably had. Last time she'd gone to Camberwell so I set off south across West Cheap.

The way took me past Everard the candlemaker, who was one of my father-in-law Elias's borrowers, and who knew Rosa, so I went in to ask. Everard was stirring a big steaming pot of fat that made the walls shine and filled the place with stink, while his boy was beside him ready to chuck in some more. Everard wasn't the friendliest so I suppose I should've known how it would go. 'Yes?' he said, giving me a look. 'There's not a farthing I owe as I paid up yesterday.' When I said I was looking for Rosa he gave a shrug. 'I haven't seen her.' But then his boy, who was milder, said, 'I think I did. Just now. I saw her through the door, walking by outside the shop.' When I asked which way she'd been going he pointed south, like I'd hoped he wouldn't.

Damn her, I'd have thought. That pitiless, singular child looking only to her own self. I pressed on to the bridge, which, like always, was tight with folk squeezing by. I wasn't halfway across when I heard someone call out, 'Look who's coming down the river,' and people started pushing into a space between the shops to peer down. Though it made no sense, as how could it be her, just for a moment I thought, what if it's Rosa, and I squeezed through them to see. But no, thanks be to God, when I looked over I saw there were a pair of them, just about to slip under the bridge, both so swollen that they looked almost like playing balls. One had half his face gone and another had no head. 'I wonder whose they are,' said one of the crowd, 'Montfort's or the king's?' 'The king's,' said another, 'see how fat they are,' which made the rest laugh. 'Some of his Frenchmen,' said a third. 'Or his Jews.' Which got another laugh. Somebody had found a big piece of stone and he lobbed it over, catching the headless one on the chest so he vanished under for a moment before bobbing up again, which got a cheer. No one was looking at me, thank heavens, and I edged back out of the crowd.

Reaching the Tower at the far end of the bridge I asked the guard, 'I'm searching for my sister. Have you seen her go out? Black hair, green eyes, pretty-looking.' Some of them can know you from half a mile off, don't ask me how, it's like they can smell you, and this guard was one. He gave me a look, not friendly, to show it. 'See how many people go by here? As if I'd know.' When I was small my father used to tell me, 'Motte, when things look bad, as they will some days, remember this. For every unkindness there's a courtesy, and for every wicked man there's a good one too,' and so it was that morning. I got out of the stream of folk and was standing there, wondering what to do, when I saw that a beggar, who was sat in a niche just out of the throng, was waving me over. He'd have heard me talking to the guard. 'I saw her,' he said. 'A pretty thing. She had a funny look to her, sort of dreamy. I wondered if she was drunk.'

That was Rosa all right. I gave him a farthing and my thanks and then looked out through the gate towards Southwark. Just because she'd gone out there didn't mean I had to go after her. But of course it did. I couldn't turn my back on my own sister, however undeserving. So, though every ounce of me hungered to go back the way I'd come, I walked through the gate and into Southwark. I just hoped she'd chosen the same spot she had last time, as otherwise I'd never find her in a hundred months and I'd be risking myself for nothing.

At least there shouldn't be many who'd know me out here, or so I hoped. Back in the house they'd be wondering where I'd got to, as I'd said I'd only be gone for a short while. I'd never forgive Licoricia if she got my little mites in a scare, which I could see her doing, just to make me look bad. I started down the Kent road. The way was crowded with walkers and riders, most of them going back towards London, and I could see the care on their faces. They'd be Montfort's, frightened they'd be caught by some of the king's. Montfort's were worse. Not that the king's were much better. I kept my face low, looking down at the ground, in case one of them might sniff me out like the guard on the bridge.

It was further than I remembered but finally I saw the tower of Camberwell church and then there she was. I swear she was in the very same spot she'd been the last time, sat on a tree root by the pond. For a moment I felt joy that I'd found her but that soon slipped away. I stepped up behind her and, not loud but hissing out the words, I said, 'Vous truie.' She twisted round then, her eyes open wide, at the vous, at being called sow, there being nothing worse, and most of all at the cold sound of my voice. 'How could you?' I said. 'And now of all times.' She gave me a pleading look. 'Motte, please. I meant to get the loaf like I said, but then. . . I just can't stand that house. I miss our home.' 'Come on,' I told her, tugging her arm hard so she winced. 'Let's get back.'

Even then she was slow. I'd take a few paces and she'd be straggling behind me, looking at a cat lying on a wall or at some ducks flying by, or a tree in blossom. 'I never see any green,' she moaned, like I was being unfair making her hurry up. 'You won't see anything at all if you don't come on,' I told her. Finally we got to Southwark but I'd hardly had a chance to feel joy when I saw there was a crowd up ahead and I heard shouting. Rosa was in her dreams like usual and didn't notice till we'd almost reached the Tower. 'I don't understand,' she said. 'Why's the gate shut?' 'Because you're slow and only think of yourself,' I answered. Then I wished I hadn't as she started crying and people were looking at us, which was the last thing I wanted. Someone called out to the guards on the Tower asking them to open up but they didn't even bother to answer, and then I heard someone saying there was talk of conspirators with a secret purpose to let King Henry's men into London and that was why the gates had been closed.

That didn't sound good to me. Sure enough, we waited through half the day, but when the light began to fade and the gates were still closed I cursed my sister for the tenth time and led us back into Southwark to find an inn. And though they doubled their prices, like they always did when a crowd was locked out, I had just enough in my purse for us both, thanks be to God. The place was dirty like they were and as we ate our sops I was sure some of the other eaters at our table were casting us looks, as if they knew us. That night I got hardly a moment's sleep. Every time I nodded off I'd come awake with a start, hearing voices in the street below, or someone riding by, and then I'd be waiting for the sound of footsteps thumping up the stairs. I prayed to God seven score times, not aloud but just opening my mouth without making a sound, please preserve us, I beg you. Or I beseeched Hame and Leo, please forgive me for being such a fool and going out of the city after my sister, and I entreated God, don't let them lose their mother when they're still just babies.

I must've dropped off in the end, though, because I found myself awake, it was fully light and looking round I saw half the beds in the dormitory were already empty. I got up and leaned out of the window and saw people hurrying by below, and sure enough when I craned my neck I saw the gate to the bridge was open. 'Come on, up you get,' I said to Rosa, giving her a smile, as my anger at her was all gone now. Down we went and as I stepped through the gateway, for the first time since I'd left the house the day before I felt my breath come out slow and calm. There was the same beggar in his spot so I pointed to Rosa and said, 'See, I found her.' He just looked at the ground like he hadn't heard. Still I didn't think anything of it. But then, just after, I passed the same unfriendly guard whom I'd asked the day before and I saw the look he gave us.

'I'm hungry,' said Rosa. 'There must be somewhere we can get something?' I got her wrist and pulled it sharp so she let out a little cry. 'Why d'you do that?' she bleated. I didn't answer but pulled her again. We'd hardly started over the bridge when I smelt smoke. The further we got, and the closer to Jews' Street, the stronger it was. It was strange, though. As we walked, I could feel my heart beating fast, but still things felt so usual. I thought, just keep going and do what you must. When I turned the corner to our street and I saw it was all gone, and that where our house had been, where they'd all been, there were stumps of timbers, fallen beams and the stubs of stone fireplaces, all black, I just thought, well, that's no surprise. It's what you thought it would be. It was still smoking and I could feel the heat. In the road there was a heap of things – a stool missing a leg, a broken mirror, a dead dog. Rosa let out a kind of whimper. 'But. . .'

Do what you can, do what you must. Don't ask me why but I thought, Everard the candlemaker, he'll know. So back we went. The door to his shop was open but he wasn't boiling fat today. There was no sign of him and I had to call three times before he and his boy came in from the back. When they saw us they stopped still for a moment like we were a pair of ghosts. Then Everard righted himself. 'Yes?' he said, unfriendly like usual. His boy had a black eye and was looking at us as if he might cry. Another thing was their clothes, which I'd never seen them wearing before. They were too good for work clothes and they didn't fit right. Everard's shirt was long in the sleeves as his hose were too big. 'Where are they all?' I asked. Now Everard was almost friendly. 'They'll be over in the Tower,' he said. 'That's what I heard.'

So Rosa and me started out for the Tower. We'd only gone a couple of streets when I sat down on a doorstep, dropping down heavy like a sack. 'Why have you stopped?' asked Rosa. 'They're not there,' I said, not crying because it was like there was nothing in me, even to cry. 'I know they're not. They're all gone. I saw it in Everard's eyes.' Rosa sat beside me on the doorstep. 'You can't be sure,' she said. 'We have to find out. Come on, get up.' And so I did.

PART TWO

1289
Twenty-five years later

CHAPTER TWO

Tom son of Tom

In the village they called me Simple Tom as they thought I was a witless dotard and they thought it twice over because I was so lovesome for my Sammy. Then you never saw another like him. Others were standoffish, going their own way, but not Sammy and wherever I went he'd follow. If I was in the field picking weeds he'd be there beside me come rain or snow. If I was up a ladder slapping daub on the wall where the damp got in, as our little house was so old we should've let it rot as an outhouse except we didn't have the money to build a new one, then Sammy would be lying on the grass looking up and watching me work. And it was this that took him, sad to say. One day I went to fetch some water, he ran after me like usual and then jumped onto the ledge of the well, which was slippery from the wet, and though I reached out to stop him so I almost went over myself, in he dropped. The bucket was down and I pulled it up quick as I could but he must have hit his head falling and it was no use.

If anything sent me as a pilgrim to Rome City at the very ends of the earth, that was it. I felt like a black cloud hung over me, as I couldn't see any use in anything without Sammy. My brother Hal and his new wife Sarah, who I lived with, father and mother having died years back, tried their

13

best to give me comfort. 'It's time we saw you smile,' Sarah said when I still had a long face weeks later. 'Yes, come on, Tom,' said Hal. 'After all he was only a cat.' Only a cat? I felt it so strong I could hardly speak. 'He was a friendlier, cleverer and more trustable God's creature than any human I ever met,' I told them.

I couldn't stop thinking of how he used to curl up by my feet when I went to bed, or patted me with his paw to wake me in the morning, or brought me a dead mouse, which, though it wasn't anything I much wanted, was kindly meant and given with love. Most of all I remembered when he'd jumped on the ledge of the well. If only I'd been quicker to stretch out to catch him. That thought gnawed at me every hour, like death worms eating you from the inside. I'd often babbled to him when he was alive and I still did now he was gone, telling him little things in my day like, this is a hard rain falling on us today, isn't it, Sammy? Or, I swear this fire will never take, my old beast, which was another name I called him by. I didn't care if others heard me and laughed. Don't take any notice of them, Sammo, I'd say, as they're just churlish grubs.

Then a month or two after he was taken he started coming to me in my dreams. I'd wake with a start, shaking and sweating, and it was always the same. There he was among flames and din and screams, looking up at me with his frightened eyes. I'd try to shout out, don't you worry, I'll get you out of there, Sammo, but it was like I couldn't open my mouth. Hal and Sarah said it was nothing to get troubled about. 'Cats don't go to purgatory,' Hal said, shaking his head. 'Just because he was in your dreams doesn't mean anything.' 'But then why does he come back to me again and again?' I answered. Because I knew my Sammy and from the way he looked at me I saw he was in torment, the poor little mite. What I couldn't understand was why he was down in purgatory. At least I hoped it was purgatory and not hell, because the two looked much the same so I heard, and if it was hell there'd be no helping him as nobody gets out of there. It was true that he'd slain bagfuls of mice, and he had a temper and would get into fights with other toms, while he'd done his share of swiving so there were plenty of little tigers round the village that were the very spit of him. But how could he be blamed for any of that when he didn't even know it was a sin? It wasn't as if he could've got wed and done his fornicating godly.

My Auntie Eva was the one who said I should go and see Father Will. Though she could be crabby she always watched out for me. Then she had no choice, so she told me herself and often. Because when my poor mother lay dying in her bed she'd made Auntie Eva promise out loud in front of witnesses to look after me. 'That's a lesson for you,' Auntie Eva would say. 'Be careful who you visit when they're breathing their last, as you never know what troubles you'll get.'

Her thought was that Father Will would make me see sense and snap me out of misery. Some in the village didn't much like the man and preferred Father Dan who we'd had before, and who'd been happiest perched on the bridge fishing, or gulping down an ale at Jenny's. Father Will, who'd learned all his lore at Eynsham Abbey before he came to us, was just the contrary and he loved nothing better than sticking his nose in a book. If he could get the Eynsham cloisterers to lend him one, that was. He was always going over there, though it was a good step from Minster, to beg another from their library. Some in the village said he was demoniac and that the abbot had sent him to us to be rid of him and it was true that his eyes had a wild, popping sort of look. But if you needed to know something about the world there was no better man to ask than him. And he had a cat himself, who he loved dearly, a comely little black and white creature called Prince.

So I told him about poor Sammy coming into my dreams and instead of laughing at me and telling me it was just foolishness, like Auntie Eva had said he would, he thought my dreams were so strange and uncustomable that they must have some meaning. He was no scholar when it came to animals in purgatory, he said, but he could find out and that was what he'd do, not just for Sammy and me but for his own lore too. Soon afterwards he took himself off to Eynsham to talk to his cloisterers and to read their books, and when he came back he'd scholared himself all about creatures going to heaven and purgatory.

The wise men of the world were in two minds, so he told me. Some said there were no beasts in heaven but only folk, who had no flesh on them and floated about lighted up like little candles. But other wise men of the world said this couldn't be right, because when the saints of ancient times had got a look at heaven in their visions, they'd seen all kinds of beasts up there. They all lived together mildly, the saints of old said, never eating each other, so wolves and lions would chew down grass like sheep, and at night they'd all be tucked up together in their straw side by side as dear friends. Father Will said that if there were animals in heaven then it stood to reason they must be in purgatory too, and some wise men of the world said they were there to bite and scratch all the wicked sinners. I couldn't imagine my Sammy doing that seeing as he was just a little cat. But then I didn't much care what he got up to. I just wanted him out of there.

Father Will said I should go to Saint Frideswide in Oxford, who was famed across the land for curing every kind of mischief, from warts and bad eyes to mislaying your horse, so she shouldn't have any trouble getting my Sammy up to heaven. He got Sir Toby's accord for my going, which I needed, being bound. And then he wrote me a script for the road, which I needed too, so people would know I was a pilgrim and not a thief or a vagrant to be hanged. I loved watching him write his letters so fine and handsome. The month being January when the fields were bare and there was next to no labouring to do, I didn't wait but went soon afterwards. My brother Hal wanted to come with me, which was kindly, but he'd promised to help our neighbour mend his outhouse door that wouldn't shut, and though his Sarah wanted to come too, she had to comfort her sad friend. So in the end the only one who came was Auntie Eva. As we walked out of Minster, feeling the ground hard like stone under our feet, as it was bright and cold with a frost, she told me time and again that she couldn't believe she was going all the way to Oxford to pray for a cat. Then she said that Hal and Sarah were a pair of lazy slugs for not coming, which wasn't right, as like I said they would've come if they could've.

It was a long mile to Oxford and it was close to sunset when we finally got there. I'd never been before and it was a comely place. It had a high wall and big strong towers so it made Burford, where we went to market when we went, which wasn't often, and Witney, which I'd also been to, look like a pair of dirty pimples. When we walked in through the West Gate Eva said we must be careful of getting caught in wars, which they had sometimes in Oxford between the scholars and the town folk, but thanks be to God they didn't have one that day, though I saw lots of scholars, as I guessed they must be, through the doors of the alehouses, drinking and talking loudly.

The other thing Auntie Eva said we had to be careful of was Jews, as there was a good crowd of them in Oxford and to reach Saint Frideswide's we had to go right through their nest, which was called the Jewry. We must walk fast and not look at them let alone talk to them, Auntie Eva said, as they might put a curse on us, or magic us with a spell, as they were famous magicians. Or they might take us off and crucify us like they had Jesus, which was another thing they loved to do to godly Christian folk, to scorn God's true faith. So I walked fast and with one hand I held tightly onto my cross and with the other I held tightly onto Auntie Eva. Though, being curious, I did throw a few glances at them as they stood in their shops and leaned in doorways talking to each other. I'd thought they'd have red faces and horns like the devils in the paintings in our church but they didn't have either. Another thing I expected was that they'd have gold hanging off them by the pound, being so rich from stealing good Christians' money, as Auntie Eva said they were. I thought they'd have gold necklaces and brooches and even gold hats, but they had nothing much. The men Jews had funny little round caps that sat on their heads but otherwise they looked much the same as all the other Oxford

folk and some had almost as many patches on their clothes
as me.

Saint Frideswide's was as fair as any church could be,
painted lovely colours inside and with pictures in the windows
that were lit up by the last sun. Dear Saint Frideswide's tomb
was covered with jewels and little hanging silver hands and
feet, which were thanks from those she'd cured, so I heard
the monks telling some other folk. There were four more
already there begging for her to help them, which made me
worry I should've got there sooner, as Saint Frideswide might
be so busy with them that she wouldn't have time for Sammy
and me. One was an old man with a canker in his neck that
was half the size of his head, and that he kept rubbing on her
tomb as he moaned. Another was a wild man who laughed
and twitched till he'd manage to stop himself and pray to stay
tranquil. There was a woman who prayed and dabbed blessed
water on her eye that was all red and swelled up. And there
was a younger one who kept very quiet, and who'd cut her
wrists and tried to die, so I heard the monks say to someone
else. They didn't say much to me. I suppose they didn't like
the look of my rags and when I told them about Sammy they
just sort of snorted, as if I should have had a more rightful
cause like the canker man and the rest.

Auntie Eva, being tired from the walk, lay down on a
bench nearby and was soon snoring away. I started to pray,
'Dear Saint Frideswide, I beg you please, ask God to get my
poor Sammy out of purgatory and up into heaven, which is
where he belongs, as I swear you never met a finer, friendlier
cat than him.' I'd heard the monks say Saint Frideswide
was more likely to help if you prayed all night so I decided

that's what I'd do, though it was hard to just keep praying and praying. Sometimes I'd stop for a moment and ask the canker man, 'Is your wound getting better?' and he'd answer, 'I think so,' which was good to hear, though it didn't look different to me. Or I asked the woman about her eye and the wild man if he was less demoniac and the younger woman if she still wanted to cut her wrists. Till finally the monks made me stop, telling me that wasn't how Saint Frideswide did her curing.

In the end I managed to stay awake, praying right through till first light, which was when a lot of noise started up. The monks gathered round the canker man and made him and his kin pray louder and then louder again, till one of them called out to him, 'Does it still hurt, Ben?' and he answered, 'Not so much, I'd say,' and they all cheered and said it was Saint Frideswide's miracle. After that they did the same with the wild man, who shouted out that he wasn't demoniac any more, and the woman with the eye said she was better too. The only one Saint Frideswide didn't cure was the one who'd tried to murder herself, and who didn't pray with them but just looked at the ground making little whimpering noises. I hoped they'd come and pray with me and Auntie Eva, who'd been woken up by then from all the shouting, but they didn't. I suppose they didn't like the thought of praying for a cat. And then they were busy with their book, where they wrote down how Saint Frideswide had cured the canker man and the eye woman and the demoniac, and how she was better at curing mischiefs than Tom Becket or any other saint.

I gave them my farthing, which was all Hal had said we could spare, and afterwards, walking back to Minster, and having had no sleep, I felt light and dreamy. You'll be all right now, Sammy, I thought. Saint Frideswide remedied three out of the four of them while the fourth was a sinner past hope, so I don't doubt she'll look after you, Sammy, especially seeing as I kept awake and prayed all through the night. Come into my dreams soon, my little beast, I thought, and show me how things are in heaven, as I'd dearly love to see what it looks like up there.

But then as we got near to Minster Auntie Eva grouched that Hal had been scarce only giving me a farthing to give to the monks. 'I saw their crabby faces,' she said. 'Mark my words, Saint Frideswide won't be content with one little farthing.' The canker man had given her tuppence ha'penny, she said, and even the demoniac gave tuppence. 'And you know how saints get if they think themselves slighted.' Which I did, as everyone had heard tales of folk who'd been cured but then hadn't given the saint what they'd promised, and who found their misfortune came back a hundred times worse than before. That was when I felt my joy dribbling away. And then that very same night I woke with a start, gasping for breath, as I'd just seen Sammy mewling worse than ever, poor little beast, surrounded by fire and smoke and screams.

After that I truly was lost in darkness, as the thought of Sammy being stuck down there for years and years tormented me worse than I can tell. But then, just when I'd almost given up all hope, an answer came and from one I'd never have guessed, which was Hal's Sarah. 'I know what you should do,' she said one morning when we were breaking our fast, dipping our bread in milk from the neighbours' cow. 'You should go as a pilgrim to Rome. Never mind Saint Frideswide as Saint Peter's the one you need. He has the keys to heaven and can whisper in God's ear and have him forgive anybody's sins, however bad. If he can get murderers and fornicators out of purgatory then he'll have no trouble with your little cat. I heard there's a pair over in Asthall who are going. You could go along with them.'

My Auntie Eva said it was the giddiest, most brainless idea she'd ever heard in all her life. 'Sarah and Hal just want you out of the house,' she said. 'They want you out of their bed. Sarah'll be after your end of it so there's room for her baby.' Because she was with child by then. Besides, I'd never get to Rome, Eva said, not a witless dotard like me. Of course I knew it wouldn't be easy. I asked Father Will about the way and he said I'd have to go across the sea, which I'd never set eyes on and couldn't imagine except that it must be like our pond but going on forever. Then I'd have to go through foreign lands where nobody spoke a word I'd understand. And I'd have to climb mountains that were so high they reached halfway to God's kingdom. All the while with every mile I might be set upon by robbers and murderers. But God would help me, Father Will said, as he loved pilgrims.

The more I thought about it the more I thought perhaps I should go. True it was far. Oxford had seemed a long way and that had only been one day's walking, while Rome would be dozens and dozens of days. Yet folk went and most came back home again. As Sarah said, if anyone could save my poor Sammy it was good Saint Pete. For all of its fighting scholars and magician Jews I'd liked seeing Oxford, while going as a pilgrim to Rome would be something to talk about, no mistaking. A few in the village had been to Canterbury or Norwich or Lincoln, and Sir Toby's father had gone all the way to Saint James in Spain once, but none of them had ever got to Saint Pete in Rome. If I managed that I wouldn't be just Simple Tom any more. I'd be Simple Tom who'd gone to Rome.

And I could ask Saint Peter to have God forgive my own sins. I'm not saying I'd done much, not compared to what most of them in the village had got up to, but I wasn't spotless white either, and you never knew how things might go on Judgment Day. There'd been the time at Meg and Stephen's wedding when Hare Lip Joe kept singing, 'Ragged Tom, Ragged Tom, he's a slutty witless grub,' till I got a stick and whacked him so he fell in the river and his mother screamed I was a murderer. And though he was all right in the end, just wet with a bloody ear, that was anger, clear as day. There were times when I'd sneaked a scrap from the pork that was being smoked above the fire, even though I knew it was a fast day, which was gluttony. And there was the summer's day when Pale Liz had been thrown over by her sweetheart Rob, and I saw her sitting in the meadow all by herself and she waved me over saying, 'Even you'll do today, Simple Tom.' And though she sobbed through it all she kissed me and had me touch her and then played me off with her fingers very sweet. Which was lust of course, and fornication, and spilling my seed, while it was worse again for being done on a Wednesday, which was sinful even if you were married. Not that it stopped me from walking down to the meadows and hoping I might find her weeping there again, though I never did.

So, although I still hadn't yet made up my mind if I wanted to go, one morning that was so foggy I could hardly see my own feet, I went over to Asthall and paid a visit to the two who

Sarah had said were going, Hugh and Margaret. They were a funny pair, though. He was a little stick of a fellow with eyes that were so narrow and squinting it was a wonder he could see out at all, while she was a big marrow of a thing, bursting out of her gown. Yet they seem kindly enough, Sammy, I thought. Hugh gave a hard look at my rags and asked me, 'Are there any real clothes under there?' which was right, though as they were so patched I could hardly remember what they'd been in the first place. But he gave me hospitality, inviting me inside his house, where his three sons were crouching by the fire, and he told his thrall to get me a cup of water. Then he told me how he was going to Rome to have good Saint Pete get his poor dear mother and father out of purgatory, and then Margaret told me she was doing the same for her mother and father, and when I said I was going for my cat they laughed like everyone always did.

But the strangest thing was how short of silver they were, which I'd never have guessed in a hundred years. They were delvers, not bonded like me but free, and their house was quite a palace, with an upstairs, which I didn't get to see, and a storeroom, which I saw through the door and which had a plough and a cart. Through the fog I could hear hogs snorting and cows lowing and cocks crowing, which Hugh said were his and were in an outhouse. Yet he hardly had a penny to his name, so he told me, which was because his neighbours were cheating thieves who never paid him what they owed. 'Don't listen to what anyone says,' he said, leaning close to me and looking at me with his little squinty eyes. 'The truth is you've probably got more than I do.' So I told him, 'A penny and three farthings, that's what we've got in our box in the house,' and he clapped his hands. 'There you are, see, Tom. I've only got two farthings.' Now he gave me a smile like he was telling me a secret and said, 'So I hope you've got a begging bowl as you'll need it. Because if you run short, though there's nothing I'd like better than to help you out, I won't be able to, see?' 'Don't you worry,' I said. 'If I go, and I still haven't fixed myself on it, then I'll take a begging bowl, no mistaking. I'll carve it myself.' Then Hugh slapped me on the back and said, 'I can see we'll get along nicely.'

After that he started telling me how he didn't want to go till after the harvest was brought in, as he didn't trust his three boys, who he called his idiots, which they didn't seem troubled by, being accustomed to it as I supposed. But he never quite finished because then something strange happened. I'd been looking towards the front door and I saw the boards below it went dark from a shadow. But instead of someone shouting hello cousins and stepping inside like I expected, the door clattered on its hinges and sort of shivered for a moment and the shadow was gone. Then one of the sons jumped up calling out, 'Not again,' and they were all running outside. I stayed crouching by the fire where it was warm, and then the little thrall female came over to take my cup. She was a sportful one, though. 'Don't you believe a word they say,' she told me, 'as it's all lies. Margaret's not going for her parents' souls. She just wants to have more pilgrim badges to sew on her hat when she goes to church on Sundays. She and the miller's wife are in a war over them, see, and they've both been to Canterbury and Lincoln and Walsingham and goodness knows where else. Last year the miller's wife went all the way to Saint James in Spain, so of course Margaret has to vanquish her now by going to Rome. As for Hugh, he's not going for his mother and father but for his own soul, which is. . .'

I'd have liked to hear the rest but that was when Hugh and Margaret came back. 'I almost forgot about you, Tom,' Hugh said, slapping me on the back again. 'Like I said, we'll set off after harvest, as I'm not going till that's safely in.' It seemed like we'd reached the end of our talk so up I got. And there was another strange thing, because when we walked outside I smelt a strongest stink of shit, and I saw one of the sons was rubbing away at the door with an old rag. 'What's all this?' I asked Hugh and he laughed like it was the gamest thing. 'They love a bit of play here in Asthall.' And how right he was, as just then something flew right out of the fog – from the shape of him he looked like a big fat turd – that hit the wall and then bounced off onto the ground.

Another odd thing was that though I still hadn't made up my mind to go to Rome, it turned out I had after all, without even deciding, just because everyone supposed it. All of a sudden people started knocking on our door to give me little cloth pretties or crosses or dolls that they wanted blessed by Saint Peter, and then Jenny of the alehouse said I wasn't to worry about money as she was making a collection and everyone in the village had said they'd give something. With them being so kindly and needing me to get their cloth pretties and such blessed I couldn't very well say no, so that was that. When I told Auntie Eva she gave me one of her crabby looks. 'That's all I need,' she said. 'But then I've got no choice, have I? I promised your mother. I'll have to come with you.' If truth be told I wasn't sure I wanted her grumbling all the way to Rome so I told her, 'Don't you worry about me, auntie, as I'll be all right.' But she shook her head and said, 'You're a witless fool, Tom. Everyone knows it and you know it yourself. You wouldn't last a day.'

It was as well Hugh wasn't going till after the harvest, as there was plenty to do. Auntie Eva got Uncle Bill to give his accord to her going, which wasn't hard as he did whatever she told him, and then she set about getting us our clothes and such. With her own hand she made both our pilgrim cloaks, which she sewed from an old piece of cloth she found in the house, and then she made our hats, which had a red cross on the front and a long scarf hanging off the back, like all pilgrims had. After that she had Uncle Bill, who worked leather when he wasn't delving his fields, put two new soles on our boots, which made them so high I felt like I was walking on stilts, though I'd need them if they were going to see me all the way to Rome and back everyone said. He made our scrips, too, and as he was busy with his fields by then, the sewing was done by Auntie Eva's girl, my cousin Mabel, who was a goggle-eyed squinter but kindly. I needed a pack, too, for all the cloth pretties and dolls and wooden crosses, and though Hal's Sarah said she'd make me one, she couldn't find her cloth nor her thread so in the end Mabel did that as well.

Father Will wrote us our testimonials so we wouldn't get hanged as robbers. Rightfully all pilgrims had to write a will too, he said, but I was lucky and had no need, seeing as I had nothing to my name, aside from what I'd be wearing or carrying in my scrip. Being bound, I went up the manor house to ask Sir Toby for leave to go, which he gave readily enough, all the more so as he had some favours he wanted me to do for him in Rome, as he told me. Father Will blessed my scrip and my staff, which was a stick I'd found in the wood and smoothed down, and he blessed my begging bowl, which I carved myself from a log. And a good piece of news was that Father Will had told his churchmen friends about us going and they found some others who were going at the same time as us, and who'd join us. We'd meet some at Witney, he said, and then some more at Oxford, and the churchmen would spread the word so we might have more after then, too. That way we'd be a proper party and would be less likely to be stabbed or robbed or cudgelled to death along the road.

Then one afternoon, when we were in the middle of the harvest and it was getting close to the day when we were to go, I was scything the crop in our strip by the river with Hal and Sarah, who was so swelled she looked ready to pop her baby that very day, when Uncle Bill came running over and called out to me, 'It's your auntie, Tom. You'd better come right away.' The three of us followed him to their house and there was Auntie Eva sat on the ground with a black scowl on her face. It turned out she'd been up on a ladder roping sacks of grain from the rafters so the rats couldn't get them and she'd missed her balance and come crashing down. 'My leg's broke, that's all,' she said, almost like it was my doing. 'There it is. You'll just have to wait till next year going to Rome.' As if I could leave my poor little beastie burning for another twelve months. 'I'm not waiting, I'm going now,' I told her, and Hal and Sarah were with me, saying, 'So you must, Tom, for your Sammy.' 'Don't you worry about me, auntie,' I told her. 'I'm doing God's pleasure and he'll watch after me. Father Will said it so I know he will.' Not that she believed me. 'Go then if you must, you great jobbard, as I can't stop you,' she said. 'But it'll go badly for you, that I promise.' And of course it wouldn't be long before I'd think back to her words.

Just a few days later I set out. How proud I felt when I went down to the green at first light and found every single body in the village had gathered to see me off. Father Will was there with his cat Prince running along beside him. Sir Toby and Dame Emma had come too and Sir Toby gave me six shillings, one to help me with my journey and five for the favour he wanted from me, which was to buy him a silver cross and a vernicle, which he said was a likeness of Jesus from a famous one they had in Rome. Dame Emma gave me a little cloth with a picture of the Virgin holding baby Jesus, which she'd sewn herself very prettily, and which she wanted me to take into every church in Rome and rub against the saints' tombs, or as near as I could reach. What with all the cloth pretties and crosses and dolls I could hardly close my pack.

Then Jenny from the alehouse had me open up my scrip and she poured in all the money that she'd collected, which, along with Sir Toby's six shillings, looked a handsome little heap. My brother Hal gave me three farthings and Auntie Eva, who Uncle Bill wheeled over in their barrow, gave me four. 'Quite a crowd you've got here,' she said and then, being the kind who loved to point out the one dirty cloud in a sunny sky, she told me, 'Of course most of them have come from curiosity as they don't expect to see you ever again.'

As for Hugh and Margaret, the only folk who turned up to say farewell to them were their three boys, the idiots, and a fourth, who wasn't such an idiot, as Hugh had had him taught his letters and who was bailiff at Asthall, which was another reason he had only two farthings to his name, so he'd told me, as it had cost him a pretty sum. And his tiny crowd said their farewells on Minster green and then turned back home while I had half of Minster walking with me on the road, all the way to the big oak tree on the Witney fork. When I bade them farewell Hal shook me strong by the hand and they all cheered so loud and hearty that I hardly knew where to look I felt so warmed.

We're started now, I said to Sammy when we passed over a rise in the land and they were all lost from sight behind us. I took my steps carefully, as it would be just like the devil to make me stumble and twist my ankle, so I'd never get to Rome and get my Sammy into paradise after all. After the crowd we'd been it felt quiet walking with just Hugh and Margaret. Worries gnawed at me. I hope we have God's blessing, Sammo, I thought, as we'll not get far on this long, hard road without it. I couldn't feel it, though. Hugh and Margaret were brawling as she grouched that her boots hurt, which she said was his fault for going to the cheapest cobbler in Burford, though he said that wasn't right at all and it was only that her feet were too big. After a while we stopped so she could take them off and give her feet a rest.

'You've got a lot of friends, haven't you?' said Hugh as we sat there, shaking his head like I should know better than to have so many. 'Don't mind him,' said Margaret. 'He just likes riling people.' I won't let him rile me, my old beastie, I thought. Though he tried. He started with my pilgrim gear that Auntie Eva had made. 'That's a strange-looking cloak,' he said. 'I hope it'll keep the rain off you. And your hat's all lopsided while that pack's bulging fit to burst. What've you got in there?' 'I'll be all right, don't you worry,' I answered.

Then he wanted to see how much the others in the village had given me. 'They gave me plenty,' I said proudly, remembering all the coins that had been poured into my scrip. He said I should count them, which I was happy enough to do being curious myself, and I poured them into my shirt, but I didn't find God's blessing like I'd thought, more was the pity. Aside from Sir Toby's five shillings for the silver cross and the vernicle, which weren't mine to spend, and his shilling, which was, all the rest were farthings, and though there were plenty of them altogether they only came to a shilling and sevenpence ha'penny. That made Hugh laugh. 'This won't get you very far, Tom,' he said. 'I heard the sea crossing to France alone is sixpence.' 'I'll manage, don't you worry,' I told him, though the truth was I didn't rightly know how. So I suppose he'd riled me after all.

But I felt God's loving eye on me when we got to Saint Mary's church in Witney, which was where we were to meet two of the others who Father Will's churchmen friends had found for us to go journeying with. They must've been peeking out of the door and watching for us, as when we walked in I heard bagpipes playing, not handsome at all and sounding much like the groaning of an afflicted beast, but very loud, which was their greeting to us as it turned out. The piper, whose name was Oswald, was a little smirking fellow with a long curly beard, though what you noticed most about him was his hat, which had so many saints' badges sewn onto it that there was hardly space for one more. Hugh's Margaret couldn't keep her eyes off them.

As we all set out onto the road to Oxford Oswald told us he hadn't gone to all those saints for himself but for other folk, most of them dead. He was going to Rome for Damian, a tailor from Banbury freshly buried. Years back this Damian had made a vow to go as a pilgrim to Saint Pete, Oswald said, but he never had and so, being fearful he'd have God's ire on him, he'd left money in his will for somebody to go in his place. Oswald had a trade as a carpenter, he said, but he hardly picked up a block of wood these days as pilgrimaging was like a livelihood for him now. It had taken him to almost every spot you could think of, from Lincoln and Durham to Norwich and Walsingham, and to the three kings in Cologne and to Saint James in Spain. He'd even been to Saint Patrick's Purgatory in Ireland where he'd been walled up in the cave all night, like all pilgrims were there, so he hadn't been able to see even his fingers for the dark and could hear nothing but the sound of his own breath.

Rome, and Jerusalem too, were about the only places he hadn't been to and he couldn't wait to get to Saint Peter's city. He'd heard a lot about the road, from others he'd met who'd been there, and his main care was the mountains that we had to cross, which were called the Alps. Because we'd left it late in the year to set out, he said, which meant we might well strike snow and blizzards. We should rightly have gone in August, as that was when most Rompetae – which is what Rome pilgrims call themselves – set off. He'd wanted to go then but Damian the tailor had been slow breathing his last breath, and when he finally had and his will was read his kin had grouched and made trouble, so several weeks had passed before Oswald finally got his shillings for the journey. That was often the way, he said, and many a time he'd been cursed and spat on by kin who said he was stealing pennies from their portion. Still he didn't mind, as there was nothing he loved better than to go journeying as a pilgrim, striding across some piece of land he'd never set eyes on before, or walking into a town playing his pipes. And of course he found joy praying for the poor dead unfortunates who'd sent him, begging the saints to let them out of purgatory and up to heaven, which was a rightful deed. Here's God's blessing, I thought. He'll look sweetly on us for having a good man like this in our party. And Oswald will guide us rightly on the road and help us stay clear of trouble, seeing as he'd been to almost every spot in God's Christendom.

I felt God had given us his blessing with the other newcomer, too, for all his sad looks. He was an advocate from Northampton named Jocelyn and it was no surprise he seemed doleful, as his reason for going as a pilgrim to Rome, which he told us as we plodded along, was as sorry as could be. Two years back the fiend had seized him, he told us, and held him tight between his finger and thumb like a little helpless grub. Though Jocelyn had a new young wife who was a sweet poppet of a thing, and was with child too, all that Jocelyn could think of was sin, and he'd couple with any pert female who was willing. 'My eyes were blinded to godliness,' he told us, sorrowfully. He'd swived other men's wives and he'd swived brewster women and bondswomen and women delving the fields, and if he couldn't find any who'd let him have his way he'd reach into his purse and give out to a bordel woman. He'd entice females with fine gowns or hats or pretty brooches and to pay for these he did every kind of unright in his advocating, lying and having his clients lie, taking bribes from his clients' enemies, and getting judges to tarry over a case so he could squeeze out a few more pennies. He didn't even care when his wife guessed it all and begged him to stop. Worst of all he didn't shrive one word of it to his priest. 'When I went to church,' he told us with a doleful shake of his head, 'and I heard what waited sinners who didn't confess, I took no heed but laughed to myself, as if such talk was meant only for other men and not me.'

Then one winter's day his wife said she felt strange in her womb and she asked him to go and fetch the physician. Jocelyn rode out to do as she'd asked, but then he came to a road that led out of the town to the house of a brewster woman he knew, who was a proper weasel to the eye and who he'd couched a good few times before, and as he looked down that road the devil filled him with wicked hunger. 'I'll just go and see how she is,' he said to himself. 'I won't be long.' So he went and he lay with her and had his delight that day and all that night too.

When he set out the next morning for a moment he glimpsed something by the road, pale like a shadow hanging in the air. Then it was gone and he thought no more of it. But as he rode up to his house and heard the wailing of his neighbours he knew that had been no shadow but one of Satan's fiends come to gloat. It turned out his poor wife's pain had been a warning and she'd gone into labour within the hour of his leaving her. There being no sign of Jocelyn, her mother had gone to call the physician and the midwife but the baby was caught and wouldn't come, and when the physician tried to free it, Jocelyn's young wife started bleeding and wouldn't stop. She cried out for her husband and the whole of Northampton went searching for him but of course he couldn't be found as he was away couching with the brewster woman. His dear, innocent wife had gone to God not an hour before he arrived home.

'After that I was like an outlaw,' Jocelyn told us, 'scorned by kin and friends alike. Nobody would greet me in the street and nobody would take me as an advocate to fight his cause. And strange to say, I welcomed it.' Because, too late though it was, he saw the wickedness of his ways and all he wanted was to be punished. He shunned all his women and shrived his sins in church, not once but every Sunday for a month. When the priest told him to walk to Brixham and back barefoot he walked there not once but three times and he cast his shoes aside and walked everywhere barefoot. When the priest told him to give four shillings to All Hallows' for the roof he gave eight. When he was told to fast every Tuesday he fasted for three days every week and even on the other days he touched no meat. Yet he still felt his sin weighing heavy on him. So he asked his priest what else he might do to show he was sorry and win God's forgiveness and the priest answered that he should go as a pilgrim to Rome. If he repented and prayed to Saint Peter and all the other saints there, then Saint Peter might look kindly on him and ask God to let him off his time in purgatory, or at least some of it. 'And so I'm here,' he said sadly, 'walking for my forgiveness. If I ever can be forgiven, that is.'

We all fell quiet then, as there's nothing to stir the spirits like a story of wickedness regretted. Till Hugh, being the kind who couldn't hear anyone's tale without saying the wrong thing, told him, 'That's a good strong pair of boots you've got. So you weren't tempted to walk barefoot all the way to

Rome?' But Jocelyn just gave him another sorry smile and said he would have, certainly, but his feet were in such a poor way after all his walking around the town barefoot that the priest forbade it. All the while I was thinking, God's with us today all right, Sammy. Because Jocelyn was a sinner who'd strayed from the path and then found it again, which God loved dearly, as everyone always said, so we'd have his smile on us for our journey no doubting.

By then I could see the walls and towers of Oxford City, where we were to meet some more pilgrims the priests had found to journey with to Rome. I wonder who these will be, Sammo? I thought. A great lord, perhaps? Or a holy man who's all starved skin and bones from his saintliness? The sun was shining and I swear I felt God's blessing on us as we walked through the gate, even despite Oswald playing a great blast on his bagpipes and getting us dirty looks. And then God showed his smile with my pie, because by then we were all hungry and Oswald, having been everywhere in Christendom, knew of a place nearby the gate where I got a pork one that only cost me a farthing and very tasty it was too.

But God's blessing didn't last long. As I chewed down my pie I saw the sky had suddenly turned dark though we were still far off from dusk, and as we stepped out from the shop, and I still had that sweet pork taste in my mouth, I saw a flash of lightning and a moment later there came a crash of thunder that made us all jump. 'It's not that far to the pilgrim hospital,' Oswald said, 'we can get there all right,' but just then down came the rain in a rush, being the kind that soaks a fellow through in half a moment and never mind what gear he has on his back. The only shelter nearby was the eaves of a little house, though it wasn't much and was less again for having a pair already standing beneath it, both of them in pilgrim clothes. They were a mother and daughter by the looks of them. The daughter was one to snag the eye, being very comely, with a sad, brooding countenance as she peered down at the ground from under her long black hair. They tried to make room for us but it was all we could do to stand back so the wet couldn't drench our boots.

If there's one thing I can't abide it's a tempest. Then who loves them? I swear you can feel the devil right beside you, conniving to catch you with a strike of his lightning, or leave you half deaf from a roar of his thunder. Hugh and Margaret, Oswald and Jocelyn all looked feared and I was wishing I was under a proper roof or, better still, crouched under a good sturdy table. To make things worse the mother and daughter pilgrims seemed set on provoking the fiend to do his worst. They were hardly troubled by the storm and were gabbling away, or rather squabbling away, and not in God's English but in some foreign tongue that I couldn't understand one word of. Mostly it was the mother, who was as loud and talkative as the daughter was angry and hushed. This'll catch Satan's eye, no question, Sammo, I thought. Why can't they just be quiet? And what are they doing here anyway? They should be going as pilgrims in their own foreign land, wherever that is, rather than making trouble here in ours. All in all I was more than happy when the storm finally died down and we left them there, bickering still.

But it wasn't for long as things turned out. The five of us took ourselves over to the East Gate Pilgrim Hospital as quickly as we might, before another storm could start up, and though the beds in the dormitory had a stench to them Oswald said we mustn't mind as that was often the way at pilgrim hospitals, while the blessing was that they wouldn't cost us a farthing, which was a true blessing so I thought. We'd hardly had time to claim a bed each when the hospital clerk, who was a smirking sort of fellow with a long grey beard, came up and told us he had two more that the priests had found to join in our party journeying to Rome. A moment later I heard footsteps on the stairs behind him. But instead of a great lord or a holy starveling like I'd thought we might get, it was the bickering mother and daughter. They looked as surprised as we did. The real wonder, though, was when they opened their mouths, because this time it wasn't foreignness that came out but English, and so ordinary and natural that you'd never have thought they knew a word of anything else.

It must be French, I guessed. I knew gentle folk spoke it, including even our Sir Toby and Dame Emma though I'd never heard them talk it out loud. And now I found out Jocelyn the advocate could talk it too, so they had a little gabble in it together, though the mother, whose name was Mary, was much smoother in it than him. And if I'd been a little anguished at her strangeness before, I saw she was a blessing now because I swear I never met anyone holier. She hardly said a thing without following it with a 'please be to God' or a 'thanks be to Jesus', or a 'praise be to our loving Lord', and the dear Virgin was never far from her lips. God will smile on us for that, Sammo, I thought.

As for the reason for their going as pilgrims to Rome, this was so they might pray for the soul of Mary's husband

Edmund, though he sounded like he didn't need much praying for. He'd died a few months back and had been as godly and virtuous a man as any you could meet, so Mary said, till the mournful day when he'd come down with fever and God had taken him from this earth. But though he'd been righteous, even the best stumbled from the true path once or twice, Mary said, while she and Helena, her daughter, both loved him so dearly that they couldn't bear the thought of him spending even an hour burning in the fiend's fires. So they were going to Rome to have Saint Peter spring him straight up to paradise.

She said her Edmund had had a butcher's shop which was the finest in all Gloucester City. That caught Jocelyn's ear. 'You're from Gloucester?' he said. 'I've a cousin living there. He's a shopman too, a cobbler. Dave is his name. A big tall fellow with a bad eye. You'll know him, I'm sure.' This Mary was a strange soul, though. Now she looked all miscomforted, though I couldn't think why, as what was it to her if Jocelyn's cobbler cousin with a bad eye was her neighbour? 'I can't say I do,' she said, stumbling over the words. 'Then we don't know a lot of folk. We keep ourselves quiet, you see.' Trust Hugh to make things worse. 'Your Helena doesn't look like a butcher's daughter with those pretty little hands,' he said. Now Helena, who hadn't said one word all this while but had been looking down at the ground like she did, surprised us by speaking up. 'I'm not,' she said, quite sharply. Which had Mary confounded and tripping on her words all over again. 'Helena's father was my first husband, you see, who died when she was young,' she said. 'He wasn't a butcher but a silversmith. But that was all long ago.'

Then she started telling us how she'd worked as a gown maker before she met Edmund, and she'd had her own shop, and she owned a fine big house in Gloucester, too. She got no further, though, as then there were footsteps on the stairs and shouting. 'I'm no cousin of yours, I'll have you know,' said an angry voice. 'To you I'm Sir John of Baydon.' Then up walked the clerk, looking none too cheery, and behind him came a big break-chest of a fellow followed by a little beaky-looking woman, who I guessed was his wife, and a tall leek of a boy, who'd be their son. I know his kind all right, Sammo, I thought, who gets into a fury if he thinks he's snubbed in the tiniest way. Back in Minster Rob William's son was the same, and he once broke Symon Neil's boy's nose just because he'd said Rob had an ugly pig. The clerk had an answer for this fellow, though. Rather than show himself crabbed or scared he told him, 'So you are, my good lord,' saying it so polite and respectful that somehow it wasn't respectful after all, and he gave a bow that wasn't just low but was much too low. Sir John twitched like he'd have gladly whacked the man if he'd only had a rightful cause.

I'd have found it all good sport and nothing more but then the clerk turned towards us, and I was just wondering if there was some law of the hospital he'd tell us about, but instead, with a little smirk on his face, he said, 'May I introduce Sir John of Baydon, who'll be journeying with you to Rome, and his wife Dame Alice and their son Gawayne.' This is bad, Sammy, I thought, as God won't smile on us if we have a troubler like this fellow in our party. But this was only the start of him, so we found. When Jocelyn asked him what took him to Rome he answered, and sourly, that he was going as a penitent, though it hadn't been his choosing. 'I was ordered to go by the archdeacon,' he said. He'd got into a squabble with the abbey that held the manor next to his, over a piece of land that everyone knew was rightfully his, so he told us, but which the abbot had found an old deed for, which said it belonged to his monks. 'Of course it was a forgery, as any fool could see,' said Sir John, 'got up by his cloisterers.'

Not that that was what had brought Sir John into mischief. One morning he'd met the abbot by chance on the road, they'd fallen into discord and Sir John had punched him right on the nose. 'None of it was my doing,' Sir John told us, scowling at his remembrance. 'It was all contrived. The abbot provoked me, of that I have not an ounce of doubt.' As if I'd know either way? Though I could see it wouldn't take much provoking to get this one into a fight. If it had been conspired by the abbot it had served him well, that was certain. Sir John had been called to the archdeacon's court where he'd not only lost the piece of land they'd been squabbling over but had been ordered to go to Rome in penitence for smiting a churchman, and to come back with a script from the clerks of Saint Peter's to show that he'd been. 'That'll have been the abbot's notion,' said Sir John darkly. 'He'll be hoping I never come home so he can steal some more of my land.' 'But you're sorry, too,' his little wife Dame Alice cut in, to remind he was penitent, seeing as he had to be. Though all she got from him was a grumpy, 'Of course.'

I'd have thought Hugh would have more sense than to rile a cur like Sir John but it seemed he couldn't stop himself. 'So how much land was it, my lord?' he asked, and when Sir John growled, 'A quarter of an acre of meadow,' Hugh, though his Margaret nudged him hard with her elbow, raised his eyebrows. 'Is that so, my lord? A quarter of an acre of meadow doesn't seem much to go clouting an abbot over, let alone to journey all the way to Rome for. Why, I bought two acres myself just last winter and that wasn't meadow but good growing land.' Sir John gave him a scowl and looked like he'd gladly have given him something more. 'It wasn't about the land,' he said. 'It was about the rightfulness of the thing. Like I said, the deed was a forgery, clear as day.' None of it would have happened, he said, if the case had come before a county judge rather than a church court. 'It's a disgrace,' he said. 'And to one who rode for his king against the Welsh, too.'

So he'd been a soldier. Our lord in Asthall, Sir Toby, had taken a few from Minster to Wales and one of them, Rob son of Bob, never came back, though that wasn't from fighting. He'd been kicked by his own horse. If Hugh was a riler I was the contrary. I always had been and I didn't care if some folk called me soft. Knowing that I'd be walking alongside this break-chest of a fellow for many weeks I thought I might as well try to set him friendlier towards us. 'So you fought in battles, Sir John?' I asked. But there really was no pleasing the man. 'I would have if I could have,' he said, looking down his nose at my rags. Then he told us all about his family, which had been as noble as any in the land, he said. They'd come over with William the Bastard, and Sir John's great-great-grandfather had fought with good King Richard to smite the Saracens and win Jerusalem back for God, but over the years they'd been robbed of their fortune, by Jew money lenders stealing with their cunning, by wicked fellows who'd lured his grandfather to play dice for gold, and by the extorcious cost these days of fighting gear. It had been two generations since any of his name had ridden as a knight and now they had only one manor. When he'd gone to Wales he'd hoped to catch the eye of his captain, or even of the king himself, with his bravery, so he might turn round the fortune of his family and set it to greatness once again, but there'd been no chance of that. 'I spent the whole war on guard duty,' he said sourly, 'whacking the arses of a crowd of lazy stonemasons repairing a castle that our enemies had broken down.' All he'd seen of his Welsh foes was the odd arrow that came whistling out of the trees, which were sent from too far away for them to prick any of his workmen. 'More was the pity,' Sir John said.

God will like him even less for clouting one of his own abbots on the nose, I thought. And yet there was blessing here too, I saw, as for all the wrongs he'd done Sir John would keep us safe on the road. Though he'd never drawn his sword in battle he must know something of fighting, having ridden for the king. God's watching for us, Sammo, I thought that night as I lay my tired head down to sleep. And how many we were now. I saw that the next morning when we walked out of the hospital, all scratching and itching ourselves, as the beds had had a good few biters. Ten of us we were now, I counted. We'd be a fine little crowd on the way. And Father Will had said we might have some more joining us later too.

Before we could set off from Oxford we found a cobbler to stretch Margaret's boots so they wouldn't pinch her toes, and we stopped at the market to get some bread and cheese for the road. Then Oswald threw his bagpipes over his shoulder and let out a blast, and I hardly even cared how it sounded, I felt so joyed by the moment. Here I am, I thought, Tom son of Tom, of Minster village, stepping down the road, a pilgrim journeying to Rome City, for God and Jesus, for the Holy Ghost and sweet Mary, and for Sammy my cat.

But it was Oswald's pipes that got us into mischief. We were walking down the High Street back towards the East Gate when I noticed, crouching by the roadside, a big slutterbug with a tangle of dirty black hair hanging off his head, all in strings, and a bad arm dangling by his side. Don't ask me how, but I knew he'd start on us and so he did. 'That's a sweet bit of music,' he said, and then laughed too much like a wild man will. 'Pilgrims, pilgrims,' he said next, more singing than saying it, and giving us a smile that I didn't like. 'Who are you then?' he called out. 'And what dirty sins are you off to have pardoned?'

Now I worried about having Sir John in our little fellowship, as I knew he'd not let this rest. Sure enough, he called out to the slutterbug, 'Friend,' in a voice that wasn't friendly at all, 'I urge you to watch your tongue.' I don't know if he'd ever come across wild men before, but I doubt it, as then he'd have known better. I'd seen one or two over the years, who'd come through the village begging for scraps, and if there was one thing I'd noticed about them it was that menacing only made them worse. Another thing was that they loved to tell you all about yourself, and sometimes their notions had a kind of demoniac truth to them. One had come through Minster and followed Bill Goddard round the green shouting out that he was a drunkard, which Bill was, and then telling Nicholas son of Roger that he was a soft scaredy cat who'd jump at a mouse, which was right too.

Sure enough instead of being afeared of Sir John, the slutterbug got up and started following us, and as he went he told us all about our sins. 'You,' he called out, pointing at Oswald, 'Badge Hat. You're going for your sloth.' Next, cackling away at his own demoniac cleverness, he pointed at Jocelyn. 'And you, Cousin Wriggler, you're going for lust.' Which was right, of course. By then we were all looking round and wondering what we'd be, and not just us, as we had a little crowd of Oxford folk following after us and laughing. Hugh was Cousin Getgold and was avaricious, while his Margaret, who was Cousin Giveme, was greedy. Which I could see was true too, as by then even I knew that all his talk of having no money was a lot of truffle. But Mary and Helena made no sense at all. For all her righteousness Mary got godlessness and was Cousin Saracen while Helena was Saracen Princess. Though it was just a wild man babbling it got Mary troubled and she gave him an anguished look. I got off lightly as I thought, my sin being filth, which was no sin I'd ever heard of and certainly wasn't one of the seven deadlies, while my name was Cousin Rags, which was right enough, no denying. As for the three Sir Johns, Dame Alice got highness, which I'd not heard of as a sin any more than filth, and was Lady Snorty Nose, while their boy Gawayne got sloth and was Prince Stink Fart, and Sir John himself got anger and was King Stink Fart.

Now we'll have a proper war, Sammo, I thought. Sure enough when the wild man called Dame Alice Lady Snorty Nose, Sir John turned and gave him a glare, calling out, 'How dare you insult our ladies?' But then Dame Alice tugged his arm. 'Leave him be, John,' she said. 'There's no honour here.'

Which was true enough, as if Sir John fought and won over a wild man with a bad arm he'd look a fool and mean too, while if he lost it would be worse again. Even Sir John saw it, and he told the slutterbug to fry in his own dirt and then turned and walked on. But I soon wished he hadn't even said that, as this was what got us cursed. 'The devil take you all,' the wild man shouted now, grinning at us with his wide, popping eyes. 'May the stones in the road swallow you up and drag you down to burn.'

Nobody likes to be cursed, especially when they're setting off on a journey to the ends of the earth, and we all fell quiet as we walked out through the East Gate and started up the steep hill beyond. All except Hugh. I swear he would rile the devil himself. 'What a mad, crazed fellow he was,' he said to Sir John, full of cheer. 'Tell me now, as I can't for the life of me remember, what was that foul thing he called your good, brave lad Gawayne? Stink breath, wasn't it?' Sir John, knowing he was being goaded but not seeing how he could counter it, answered with a growl. 'No. It was Prince Stink Fart.' 'Terrible,' said Hugh, frowning and shaking his head. 'And your dear, noble wife? She was Lady Big Nose?' 'Lady Snorty Nose,' said Sir John, looking like he might burst. 'Wicked, wicked,' said Hugh, squinting up his little eyes. 'And you yourself were King Fart?' 'King Stink Fart,' answered Sir John, bellowing the words. 'Well, at least you were a king,' said Hugh thoughtfully. 'That's something, I dare say.'

After we reached the top of the hill the way kept level for a good distance till we reached Tetsworth. This was halfway to Wycombe where we'd stay the night, so said Oswald, who knew the road, and we stopped there for our lunch, sitting on the wall by the church. After that the road climbed and climbed into hills that were called the Chilterns, Oswald said, and when we finally reached the top, hungry for breath, we all sat down for a rest. It was a fine view all right and I swear it seemed like half of England was there beneath us. And that was the moment when all of a sudden I was in a sweat, my heart was racing and I was fumbling with my fingers, because my scrip wasn't hanging down heavy like it should have been but was dangling light as pure nothing. Sure enough, when I loosened the string it was empty aside from one little farthing that had lodged itself in a corner. It was no mystery. The purse was made of a single piece of leather, sewed up one side, and the stitching had come away at the bottom. I suppose I should've known. Auntie Eva's girl, goggle-eyed Mabel, who'd made it, wasn't much of a stitcher.

I let out a kind of howl and then the others all hurried round me to see what was up. And though I asked them all if they'd noticed any coins on the road and picked them up, none had. The last thing I wanted was to go down that hill again but I had no choice. 'I'll have to go back and look,' I said. Some offered to come with me, though I could see they didn't much mean it, being tired, all except Oswald, while even he wasn't eager. 'You can't go off alone,' he said grumpily. 'You don't know where you are. Come on, I'll keep you company.' So the two of us started back down and all the way it was like I had a little scream inside me that wouldn't stop. I kept my eyes on the path, telling myself, who knows, perhaps they all fell out together and you'll find them in a little heap, though I knew in my heart it wouldn't be so. Every time I saw someone coming the other way I asked them, 'Have you seen any coins dropped, farthings mostly?' but they all answered no. All the way Oswald tried to keep friendly but I could see he was annoyed. Once he stumbled and cursed and then said to me, 'If you're going on a pilgrimage to Rome you need proper gear,' only to stop himself and give me a kindlier look. 'Never mind, Tom. That was just my foot talking.' Finally we got to Tetsworth, which I'd been dreading, as I remembered sitting on the wall when we'd had our bread and cheese and looking down at my purse and it had been full.

'That's that,' I said. 'It's lost.' So we started back. My feet ached and my shoulders ached where the straps of the pack dug into them and I kept thinking, how could I have been such a fool? I remembered Auntie Eva telling me I mustn't go. Or I remembered the wild man's curse, 'May the stones in the road swallow you up and drag you down to burn.' But mostly I thought about the five shillings Sir Toby had given me to buy his vernicle and the silver cross.

When we finally reached the inn at Wycombe it was almost dark. We found the others in the hall having their supper and I was so tired I could hardly even speak and just slumped into a chair. Oswald told them I hadn't found anything and only had a farthing left and they all looked at me, sorry but also a little irked, I suppose at my being such a dotard and making myself so needy. 'Have an ale,' said Sir John. 'You'll need one.' 'I can't,' I told him. 'I've nothing to pay for it with.' 'I'll get you an ale,' said Oswald, looking like he'd rather not. 'And I'll get your dinner,' said Jocelyn, looking the same. 'Of course you'll have to go back to Minster,' said Hugh, shaking his head. 'You can't go all the way to Rome on a farthing.'

So we ordered a round of ales and Sir John was right as I

swear in all my days I'd never needed one more. 'But he can't go back to his village,' Jocelyn said now. 'If there's one thing I know in this world, it's the law. Just think of how it'll look. If Tom's Sir Toby thinks he stole those shillings then he'll be hanged for sure.' It's all I deserve, I thought, as it was my doing that they were lost. But then, as we gulped down our ales, everyone grew a little cheerier. 'Don't you worry, you'll get to Rome,' said Oswald. 'I'll see to it myself. I'll teach you how to beg. It's not so hard.' He was quite a master at it, he said, because though he was given shillings by the dead folk who sent him pilgrimaging, they were never enough so he always had to crave more along the way. He even gave me a little of his lore there and then. He said I mustn't be too happy nor too sad, and that I should look folk right in the eye and tell them that giving alms would get them God's blessing, which blunted the prick of parting with their silver. 'Those rags of yours will help,' he said. 'But take care you don't get so slutty that nobody wants to go near you.'

Seeing all their faces, looking at me friendly now, gave me hope. Perhaps God hadn't turned his back on me after all. Of course there were still Sir Toby's five shillings, as I couldn't see how I'd ever beg them back, not in a hundred years. But one thing at a time. What matters now, I told my Sammy that evening as I lay on the straw in the barn next to the inn, is that we keep going. London next, my old beastie.

CHAPTER THREE

Constance

I was woken by voices and then an awful drone of bagpipes and just for a moment the thought that came into my foolish head was, what in heaven's going on in my orchard? Then I opened my eyes and knew I wasn't in my snug bed back in Thetford but in the pilgrim dormitory of the Southwark hospital. Was that din the ones we'd been waiting for? I dearly hoped so. They were supposed to have been here yesterday and I'd spent half the night fretting, wondering what could have become of them, and if they'd ever show themselves.

There was my little lad Paul and there was my sister Joan, both still fast asleep. Just seeing my Paul made me smile. How tranquil and handsome he was lying there beside me in the bed lost in his dreams. What an angel. It was a wonder he could sleep so sound with all that noise coming in through the window. If he was asleep, that was? Now my pulse was racing. But no, it was all right. When I leaned over I saw his chest was rising and falling just like it should.

A moment later the clerk of the hospital came up and told us that, just as I'd hoped, our fellow pilgrims had arrived. I woke Joan and Paul and as Joan pulled on her clothes she was wondering what her three were getting up to back in Thetford. 'I hope Dave and Emma are looking after them,' she said, which was her in-laws, who'd taken them in. 'I hope they're both behaving themselves. And I hope they're not too sour at their mother for going away and leaving them behind.' I knew she didn't mean for me to feel sorry but I did, and though I'd already said it dozens of times before now, I said it again. 'It's so good of you to come with us, Joan, really it is. I don't know how I can ever thank you.' She gave me a smile. 'Don't you even think about it, Constance. Anything for my little sister and her poor boy.'

From under my pillow I took my pouch. Before I tied it beneath my gown, where it would be safe from thieving Londoners, I opened up the buttons and looked inside just to be sure, as I was always anguished that something might be amiss. Lose this and we'd truly be stranded. No, there was my testimonial and the money scripts, there was my purse, where I kept most of my coins, aside from a few that I put in my scrip, and which was as full with silver as it should be. And there was the other little purse with my jewels. I would've left those back in Thetford if it hadn't been for Joan. 'It's best to be safe,' she'd said, 'and to have something spare just in case, as you never know what might happen.' So I'd brought every one of them, all of my Hubert's loving gift. 'I'm sorry,' I murmured to him. 'If you're already up in heaven, which I do believe you are, as you had no wickedness to you, then I beg you, forgive me. Don't go whispering foul slanders in God's ear. Tell him how sorry I am. We need all his help just now.'

We found the others in the hall, sitting round the table with their staffs and hats, and when I told them who we were they all got up to greet us. There were ten altogether, so thirteen with us three. Not a godly number. But then more might join us later, and at least we'd be crowd enough to keep safe on the road. They were a proper mix from fine clothes to rags. One who had dozens of pilgrim badges in his hat, and whose name was Oswald, had seen I was aggrieved at their being late and he said how sorry they were. 'We were all right till yesterday,' he said, but then, as they came up to a village called Ealing, it seemed like Satan had sent a mob of his fiends to slow them. The last two days had been all rain, so they were coughing and sneezing from getting so soaked, and just outside Ealing the way was worse than stew so if you stepped wrong you'd find your leg stuck right up to the knee. One of them, named Margaret, who looked like a rich delver, had had a cobbler stretch her boots, which he'd done too much so they kept coming off and she had to reach into the slobber a dozen times to pull them out.

Then they had to search for the ragged boy, Tom, who'd gone off by himself to beg pennies at Ealing market as he had none left. And after that they were slowed again when the manor lord among them, Sir John, accused a stranger of winking at his wife, though the fellow said it was just his trembling eye. It came to fists, which brought half the village out, and in the end Sir John only got away by paying the man a ha'penny. After that they'd all walked as fast as they were able but still they missed the London gates. They'd stayed the night at a Westminster inn, Oswald said, and then, knowing they were late, they'd risen at first light, hurried through the city and over the bridge to Southwark. It's all very well, I thought, but you'd better not be slow all the way. The last thing my poor Paul needs is to be walking to Rome with a crowd of snails.

If I'd had my way we'd have set off for Rochester right away as why tarry, but Oswald said he wanted to spend an hour or two on West Cheap begging, as that was the finest begging spot in all England, so he said, and the ragged boy Tom was eager too, while the rest, including even my Paul and Joan, wanted to look round the city. So we were to have another day here, another day squandered, which was all that I needed, but what could I do? Nothing, was the answer.

Walking out into the street I thought, not for the first time, how could these Southwark folk stand it? It seemed that every step we took there was somebody begging or trying to sell us trinkets or shouting that we were blocking their road. Or we had to squeeze past a crowd watching a juggler throwing balls in the air, or a big pig that scampered by and almost knocked us down, or we were nearly murdered by a cart racing past, driven by a boy no older than my Paul. And London, where we were going to, was worse again. What I'd have given to be back in dear, quiet Thetford. But there was no use thinking on that now, not till I'd done my penance and set my poor boy on the right road with God.

The three of us hadn't broken our fast and nor had any of the rest, and Joan, who hated being late with her meals, said we should go to the same pie shop where we'd gone the day before. The pies were tasty enough, though I'd thought them a little dear. Oswald with all the badges said he knew of another place that he liked and I was happy to give it a go, but then the others wanted to show themselves friendly to us newcomers so they all said no, let's try Joan's. Right as we got there the baker was putting out his first batch, hot from the oven. I felt a little shamed as I could see some of them were troubled by the prices, though in the end they all had one, except for the ragged boy Tom, who said he just wanted a bit of bread from a bakery next door. That was enough to get my Paul started. It didn't surprise me as I'd seen trouble on his face. 'I'll go with Tom,' he said. 'All I want is a little bread.' 'Have a pie, go on,' Joan told him. 'Only the best for our Paul. You need to keep up your strength for the journey.' 'Joan's right, Paul,' I told him and strongly too, as it didn't seem right for him to go elsewhere when we'd made all the rest have pies. 'You can't just have bread.'

So he took one in the end but he only ate half and then he held out the rest to Joan who'd already finished hers. 'Here,' he said. 'I've had enough.' I didn't like the way he watched her as she ate it down and, sure enough, the moment she'd finished he started up. 'Have another,' he said. 'Have two. Have three. Go on, only the best for Auntie Joan.' The others were all looking at us and if it hadn't been for how he was, I'd have given him a good slap. 'Paul,' I told him, 'show respect to your aunt who's coming all the way to Rome just for you.' Even then he just shrugged. I said to her, 'I'm so sorry, Joan,' but like always she couldn't have been sweeter. 'Don't you worry, Constance,' she said. 'I don't care what goes on so long as I can help my little sister and her poor tormented boy.'

I paid for Paul's and Joan's and mine and then on we went. With each step he took, the ragged boy Tom rattled his begging bowl, which he'd filled with pebbles to make it louder, shaking it at everyone we passed and shouting out, 'Alms for a poor pilgrim going to Rome. Alms for God's blessing,' till it gave me quite a headache. When we reached the gate to London Bridge I said, 'What do you say we take a ferry over,' which was because Paul and Joan and me had crossed over the bridge once already when we first arrived, two days back, and I wasn't eager to do it again. It was so piled with shops and houses that I'd feared it might come crashing down and drop us into the river to drown. And there were the heads stuck on their poles above us, too, which I tried not to look at but I couldn't stop myself, while the road was so narrow that it was hard to fight your way through the throng. But the ragged boy Tom looked anxious at the thought of paying out a ferry fare and none of the others was keen either, so the bridge it had to be. When we were halfway across, the manor lord Sir John almost got into a fight with someone he said had shoved him, though I'm sure it was only accident. I gripped my Paul's hand tight as I could and when he moaned, 'Mother, you're hurting me,' I answered, 'Better than losing you, any day.'

On the other side we went to see the Tower. As we stood by the moat looking across, Oswald said if we listened carefully we might hear roaring, as the king kept wild animals there including a lion, though we couldn't hear anything except Londoners gabbling at each other. Then we had a little disputation, as Sir John said it had been put up by William the Bastard while Oswald said no, it was Julius Caesar the Roman. Then Hugh the rich delver said, 'No it wasn't. It was built by King Arthur the Unready.' Here we go, I thought. Because on every pilgrimage I'd done there'd always been one like him, who thought there was nothing finer to do than say witless things and vex everybody.

After that we walked all the way across to West Cheap to the Conduit. That was a thing to see I dare say, as it was like half a river was pouring out from it and there were Londoners by the score lined up with buckets to take their fill, but if it had been crowded in Southwark it was three times worse here. The din filled my ears, the stink filled my nostrils and it seemed like every breathing Londoner was shoving past me or calling out over my head to someone they knew.

This was where Oswald and Tom and Hugh wanted to go begging. Seeing as I was here I thought I might have a try, as why not if it could get us a penny or two. I could see Paul was keen as well but then Joan said we mustn't, as it would be too wearying for him. 'He'll get tired out,' she said. So we sat on a church wall. Margaret came over to keep us company, which got her a dirty look from her husband, who was scarce with his money, I could see from the very look of him, and who'd have wanted to set her begging too. But I was glad of it as she gave us news of all the rest in our party. She told us how the ragged boy Tom had lost all his money on the very first day when he hadn't noticed that his scrip had split open. Then she told me something that made me laugh out loud, which was that he wasn't walking to Rome for his own soul or the souls of his kin but for his cat. Sir John was doing penance for punching an abbot, which was no surprise when he had a temper that snapped like a dry twig. 'That's a fellow with no money I'll bet,' Margaret said, because what got him angriest, she said, was if someone didn't bow and scrape to him. Oswald was one of those who do pilgrimages for other folk and was going for a dead tailor from Banbury. Jocelyn the advocate was a fornicator going for his blackened soul, and Mary, the mother with the fair daughter, was going for her dead butcher husband.

I could see where this was taking us and I tried to put us on a different road, asking Margaret about herself and her family, though it did no good. 'So how about you, Constance?' she asked at last. 'What's taking you to Rome?' My Paul, who till then had been sitting beside me, chucking a pebble in the air and catching it with one hand, didn't want to hear it told, of course, and he got up, saying he wanted to take another look at the Conduit. 'That's a long story,' I said, hoping to put Margaret off, but then my sister Joan broke in, as I knew she would. She was always telling me that confession was part of my penitence and that I must do it as often as I could, the more the better, if I hoped to stand with good Saint Peter and be washed clean. 'Go on, Constance,' she said. 'You must tell Margaret everything, every little bit.'

So I did, starting at the start, as there was nowhere better, and saying how blessed of God I'd been, wooed by Hubert, the wealthiest man in all Thetford. A widower with grey hair and no brood of his own, as God hadn't blessed him with children, he owned two taverns, two shops and four houses in the town, including the fine big one that he lived in. And he was a good, kindly man, humble in his attire and his tastes, though some folk in Thetford said he was too friendly with the Jews. That had Joan cutting in again, 'Which he was, too.' Because he'd done business buying and selling hides with one in Norwich named Isaac, and they grew so warm that Isaac asked Hubert to his daughter's wedding and Hubert would've gone, too, except that somebody told the bishop, who said he'd excommunicate him if he did.

Hubert asked for my hand, I answered yes, 'and that should've been the end of my tale,' I told Margaret, 'and a happy end it would've been, too.' But then the devil came tempting me with my cousin Mark, whom I'd been friendly with ever since I was young. Though Mark was married with two little boys, the fiend sent him calling on me just days before my wedding, when my poor mother was upstairs sick in bed, which of course the fiend would've known. Mark took me into the storeroom and told me he loved me to his very heart root and he said it wasn't right that a comely young female like me should spend all her nights with a dried-up old prune like Hubert. At the very least, he said, once in my life I should feel the touch of one who was as young and fresh as I was. 'Seeing him so sad and so handsome confounded me,' I told Margaret, 'and so, sorry to tell, the devil got his way and I did what I shouldn't have.'

I half expected Margaret to turn haughty on me now, as folk often did when I told them my trespasses, but she gave me a tender look. Then she could hardly expect saintliness from her fellow pilgrims. If we'd all been angels we wouldn't be going to Saint Peter to be washed clean. And Joan tried to make me look a little better. 'It wasn't that my sister was wicked,' she said. 'It was Satan, tempting her. No, my sister was just foolish and weak like so much dough in his hands.'

'So I married Hubert,' I went on, 'and straight away I found I was with child.' And though I prayed every day for it to be my husband's, I knew my prayers hadn't been answered that same morning when my little Paul was born and I saw my cousin's eyes looking up at me. When I told Mark he said I mustn't tell anybody, not even the priest, as then we'd both be undone, and he told me not to worry as he was sure Hubert wouldn't guess. And though I feared for my soul, I kept quiet just like he'd said, and he was right, as Hubert was so joyed at having a child at last, to dote on and fuss over, that he never questioned if it was his. But what did that matter when God knew? Day after day I begged his forgiveness and I prayed to him, 'Please God, I beseech you, don't punish me.'

Of course I'd soon wish I'd never prayed that prayer. Because God heard my words and, being so displeased with my wickedness, he decided to chastise me with something that was a thousand times worse than what I'd feared. He let me be and had the devil torment all those that I loved most dear. First he struck my cousin Mark. Just a year after my little Paul was born Mark was riding into the town when a dog barked at his horse, which reared up and he was thrown on his head and died that same day. But that was only the start of God's wrath. One year later he took my poor, goodly husband Hubert. He was skinning a rabbit and cut his hand on the knife, and badly too, then the devil put poison in the wound so it wouldn't heal but grew worse, till it turned green, the green spread up his arm, and within two months he was dead. Which some folk in Thetford said it was only his due for being such a friend of a murderer of Jesus like Isaac. 'And so it was,' said Joan.

But then came the very worst of all. On the day poor Hubert was buried, at his wake, which was very fine as I wanted to honour my poor husband as best I could, I saw my poor boy had turned pale and he was holding his belly like it ached and he told me, 'I don't feel very good.' He pulled off his tunic as he couldn't bear to have it against him and I saw that the skin on his back had turned red and would give him no peace, so he scratched and scratched at it. Then he started spewing and his eyes swelled up so he couldn't open them at all. I had him lie down on a bed upstairs where he was fighting for each breath. He's dying, I thought. My dear boy, who's everything I love most dearly in this world, is dying and it's all of it my own fault. I prayed to God, 'Please, I beg you, let my poor boy alone and punish me instead, as this wasn't his sin but mine.' But God didn't listen. I stayed well and my poor boy suffered, and though his misery eased slowly as the hours passed, he was weak and broken for days.

I know I'd promised my cousin not to tell a soul about our fornicating but that didn't matter now that he was gone, while I had to speak to somebody or I'd turn lunatic. 'So she told me,' said Joan, joining in. 'By then I was a widow too, as I'd lost my Robert just a few months before. Of course my Robert wasn't rich like Constance's Hubert, being a poor, simple, godly Christian man.' Joan had told me I couldn't keep secrets from God, nor from his churchmen or from my fellow men. Even though my husband had been a friend of Jews, still my sin against him was wicked and I must confess it all.

I had tears in my eyes now. 'So I did what Joan told me,' I said. I shrived my dreadful sin to Father Henry, who gave me two days' fasting a week for four months and made me pay three marks for a new altar cross. But Joan said that wasn't enough, not if I was to have a clean heart. I must tell everyone in Thetford. Which I did too, and I didn't mind the whispers and sniggering I got, or being called a strumpet and spat on by Mark's widow, as what did any of that matter so long as my Paul was saved. But it turned out God wasn't satisfied even then, and it wasn't long before my boy was struck again, and worse even than the first time.

After that Joan said I should take him on pilgrimage as penitence, which I did. She came with us and as my Paul had done nothing wrong, the transgression being all mine, she said he must have only the best, staying in good inns and eating tasty food. So we went to Norwich to see Little William whom the Jews killed to show their spite of our faith, and then to Lincoln to see Little Hugh whom the Jews killed as well, as those two holy boys were the most likely to help my Paul, Joan said, both being young lads like him. 'I had such high hopes,' I told Margaret. 'But then after we got back to Thetford he grew sick again, worse even than before. After that Joan said the only answer was to come to Rome and pray to Saint Peter, who could have God forgive anything. It would cost a good bit, of course, while Joan said we must travel commodiously for the sake of my poor boy, so I sold one of my houses in Thetford and one of the shops, and I gave a trader who was an old friend of Hubert's money to take to Winchester Fair to get me a script from one of the foreigners there that I could change for silver on the road. Then I went to the priest, Father. . .'

I stopped because Paul had come back and was rattling his drinking cup. 'Look,' he said. 'I begged two farthings.' 'We told you not to,' I said, and Joan was shaking her head, but when I looked at his angel face so thin and drawn, I couldn't feel annoyed for long. By then the others were all drifting back and saying they wanted to see more of London. So we set off for Saint Paul's but somehow we took the wrong road and found ourselves in quieter streets. I was glad of it after the crush we'd been in before. Oswald, being the one who knew London best, asked somebody in a shop, who put us right, and then a strange thing happened. I'd noticed that the mother and daughter Mary and Helena had drifted a little behind the rest of us and were having a hushed sort of chat, just the two of them, and then the next thing I knew I heard a cry. It was Helena and she was crouching over her mother, who was lying flat in the dirt. Everyone hurried back to them and when I saw Mary's face was white as snow I worried something awful had happened to her, but then she opened her eyes. Helena said she'd got into a swoon. Mary kept saying how sorry she was, though it wasn't as if she'd done anything wrong. 'I saw something that gave me a scare,' she said. 'It looked like a big grey rat.' Though that was strange too, as I hadn't seen any rat or anything else like it and nor had anyone else. Mary thanked God and Jesus and Mother Mary ten times over that she hadn't hurt herself falling and then she said she felt better and on we went.

Londoners always boasted about how noble Saint Paul's was but I couldn't see what the fuss was about. It had a tall spire, I'll own, and it was long inside with a big round window, but I swear that Lincoln Cathedral, which I'd seen with Joan, was bigger, while Norwich was comelier. After that Margaret wanted to go to Westminster Abbey, so we went through Ludgate to Westminster, which I'd hoped would be quieter than London, though it was hardly less busy at all. In the abbey we prayed to Edward the Confessor at his tomb, which was fine enough in its showy London way, covered with gold and pretty gems, though I'd have preferred our Saint Mary the Less in Thetford any day. I hadn't meant to stay for long but once I started begging Saint Edward to ask God to forgive me my transgression and to release my poor Paul from his torment it was hard to stop, and I kept thinking, if I pray just a little bit more then who's to say if he won't hear me at last?

Finally Margaret said she wanted to buy a badge for her hat, so I went with her, and she and Hugh got into a big noise, as she wanted the best they had, which was a pretty thing of Saint Edward riding a horse, but which Hugh said was too dear. 'If you want one like that then you should go out begging for it,' he said. She gave as good as she got and told him, 'You can pay for it out of the pennies you saved getting my boots so cheap,' which she'd told me about when we had our gabble. So she got her badge in the end. Joan said I should get one each for her and me and Paul, as they'd look handsome on our pilgrim hats, which only had Will of Norwich and Hugh of Lincoln, but Paul said it was a waste and in the end I just got one for her.

All the while, Satan was secretly watching and making up his cruel intents. There I'd been, praying from my very heart root, begging good Saint Edward to forgive me my sins and free my Paul from torment, and then, as we stepped out of the abbey, he looked up at me with scared eyes and said, 'Ma, I don't feel well. I've got a bad ache in my stomach.' In an instant I was on my knees hugging and kissing him and crying out, 'Please God, I beg you, spare my boy. Punish me instead.' Now Joan and Paul were praying, and when they saw what was happening the others in our party all did too. Mary was crying out, 'Sweet Jesus, help our little Paul,' and even strangers joined in.

All I could think of was, we have to get home to the inn right away so he can lie down before he gets worse. Back we started, past the grand houses and through the gate into the city, going as fast as we could. If I hadn't much liked Londoners before, now I hated each and every last one of them, as they pushed and barged and slowed us. The others in our pilgrim group did their best to help, especially Sir John, whose riotous nature was my best friend now, as he bellowed and waved his staff in the air to clear the way. All the while I was gabbling everything that flew into my poor dizzy head, telling the rest of them that the blame was all mine for the wicked sin I'd done, and saying that we probably wouldn't be walking with them to Rome after all, as if Paul had his sickness bad again then he'd have to lie quiet in bed for a few days. Joan said no, we must go anyway, for Paul, as otherwise I'd never be washed clean of my sins and he'd never be cured. We should buy a cart, she said, with a good strong horse. For that matter we could all ride in it. So we should, I thought, but then Paul said he wasn't going on any bumpy cart when he was sick, as he'd never last the journey, so I didn't know what to think after all.

And then, just when I felt all hope was slipping away, a most wondrous thing happened. 'You know I don't feel very good either,' said Oswald. 'Nor me,' said Dame Alice, and right then I felt a queasiness in my own gut. The joy, the joy. I could've sung. 'It must've been those pies,' said Hugh. 'And after all we paid for them, too.' He was right, though, as the rag boy Tom, who hadn't had one, was fine as could be, and so were Mary and Helena, who hadn't had pork like the rest of us, but fish. Which had Mary repenting to us. 'We love pork usually,' she said. 'We're always chopping it in the butcher's shop. We just felt like fish today.'

As if I cared about who'd had what pie? All that mattered was that my boy wasn't in one of his torments after all. We hurried off to the nearest latrine, which was on poles above the river, we took it in turns, and it wasn't so bad in the end. The only one who spewed was Joan, I suppose because she'd had half of Paul's too, while it was only once, and the rest of us just had squirts. Thank you, God, I thought as I squatted there. Thank you, dear Jesus. Tomorrow we'll be on the road to Rome and the sooner we get started the happier I'll be.

CHAPTER FOUR

Warin

Then just when I feared that God had turned his back on us all, he came to me once again, and out of the mouth of my own daughter Beatrix.

Who'd be a tailor in Margate? Though I worked hard I had few thanks and less regard, especially from the ones who had gold not love in their hearts. If Abbot Nicholas of the Augustines wanted new vestments, or Sir Timothy's wife wanted a handsome new gown, or if Samuel Harrison the clerk wanted one for his daughter who was getting married, they'd call on me quick enough, but if any of them passed me in the street I wouldn't even get a 'Good morning to you, Warin, and how do you do today?' They'd just give me a little nod that said, 'I know you, Warin the tailor, and I know you made me some thrifty cloth but you're low kindred and well beneath my dignity.' Let's see how you fare at the end of days, Abbot Nick and Sir Timothy and clerk Sam, I'd think. Then you'll have no fine robes or pomp or rank but will be as naked as the rest of us. There'll be no boltholes for false priests and rich leeches then.

In the meantime, though, I wished God could've made them better payers. I'd wait weeks, sometimes months, while I didn't dare chide them for fear they'd take offence and I'd never get another task out of them again or from their high friends. Nor was it better with the poorer ones who were most of my trade. They were friendly enough on the street but then it was always, 'Can you wait another week, cousin?' or, 'I'll have it next month for certain, when the porker's fattened and ready to sell.' All the while in our house we had hungry bellies, supper was porridge and cabbage again and my Ida was grouching at me, 'How are we going to pay for five dowries, answer me that?' Which was another reason I felt God had turned his back on me. Because what love was that, giving me no sons but five daughters living and two to mourn?

But then he hadn't forsaken us after all so it turned out. He'd just been biding his time. If I'd had to guess which of my poppets he'd choose as his voice I'd never have picked Beatrix. I'd have guessed Reynilda who was the oldest and the most earnest, always shouting out commands to the rest as she helped out my Ida, so she was almost like a second mother. Or Clarice who was the seemly one with her pretty blue eyes. Or Avice who was merry, always smiling and making us laugh. Or Edith who was the baby loved by all. Beatrix was so quiet that I didn't notice her half the time and I hardly knew if she was inside the house or out. Except when she had to clean the hens of course. They all had their chores that Ida gave them, from scrubbing the floors to fetching water from the well, and I'm not saying any of the others would have loved to wash down the chicken coop, which was dirty work no denying, but no God's creature in all Christendom could have hated it as much as Beatrix. It came once a month and each time she'd fill the house with her noise, right up to the rafters.

'I won't do it,' she'd howl. 'Why is it always me? Why can't it be Reynilda, or Avice or Clarice for once?' Which I wondered of too, as it would've made my days quieter, but like I said Ida had her ways in the house and I wasn't one to meddle. Beatrix would go in the end, though that didn't quiet her and we'd hear her screeching at the poor hens, 'I hate you and your stink and your muck. I wish the fox would take every one of you.' All the while her sisters would be smirking and giving each other looks and though I told them to stop it did no good. Females can be cruel.

It was on one of the hen-cleaning days that God first came to us. I was working on a cloak for Guy the dyer when Beatrix started wailing like usual, saying she didn't want to go, then the door slammed shut and I heard her scolding the hens. Finally I heard the bucket clanking, which meant she was cleaning herself off with water from the stream, which always took her a while. Chicken shit is strong and however much you work at it, it'll leave a whiff on you for a day or two. Then all fell quiet and I was listening for the door to slam a second time so I knew she was back in the house but there was nothing. After a spell passed I called out to Ida, 'Is Beatrix back?' and when she told me no I went out to see.

There was Beatrix, sat on her haunches on the ground. It was her eyes that caught me. She was looking straight ahead of her, staring fixed. Another thing was her humming, which was loud but wasn't a tune, just one note over and over. 'What's going on?' I asked, but she didn't move or look up and it was as if she couldn't even hear me. Fearing that she was sick or that the fiend had taken her, I shook her by the shoulders, calling out, 'Beatrix, stop this,' but there was no fight in her and it was like shaking a doll. By now the others had heard me shouting and they all stepped out of the house to see what was what, and I was just wondering if I should have Reynilda run and fetch Father Adam when Beatrix turned her head towards me, slow and strange, and out of her little mouth came a voice that wasn't hers, nor was it like any voice I'd ever heard in all my days, but was low and croaking like a frog. 'I am the father of him who gave his life to save you,' it said. 'I've come this day to warn you all. The fiend walks among you in Margate. Beware, time is short. Beware, the last days are coming.'

I didn't know what to think. A part of me thought, she's just playing at this. It's just because she's angry at doing the hens. But another part of me thought, that's not like her, though. What if it's true? As for the rest of them they were in two tribes. My Ida, who always got into fright over things, had turned pale as death and our littlest one Edith was covering her eyes with her hands, but the other three were looking at each other and smirking. Clarice said, 'Let's test her,' and then they were like cats playing with a beetle. Clarice put her hands over Beatrix's staring eyes, Reynilda pinched her cheeks and Avice tickled her. I thought Beatrix would squeal or laugh but no, it was as if she couldn't feel or hear them. And then, just as they were starting to lose heart, Beatrix let out a howl, so sudden and loud that it gave us all a start. Her eyes fixed on Clarice. 'Don't you see him? There's a devil right there in your blue eyes. The fiend has you.' 'She's just pretending,' said Reynilda, 'don't be fooled,' though she didn't seem so sure any more, while Clarice looked downright scared. It was like her fear was catching and I could feel my heart jump. 'And you,' said the voice next, as Beatrix turned her eyes on Avice, 'the devil's there in your laugh.' Edith had a devil in her smile, so the voice said, and Reynilda had one in her throat. But worst was my Ida. 'You have twenty devils in you,' the voice said. 'You're full of them. They make their home of you.' Poor Ida let out a little mewl.

Now Beatrix turned to me. I didn't like to think what devils I might have, but no, her face broke into a strange, staring smile. 'From this day you, Warin, will be my torchbearer,' the voice said. 'And your daughter Beatrix I will make my mouth, just as she is now. Listen well, as this is my command. Tomorrow morning you must all go and stand in front of Saint John's church where you, my torchbearer, must give the folk of Margate my warning. Tell them that the last days are coming and if they don't change their ways and repent their wicked sins then the fiend will have them all, every last one.' I wanted to know when the last days would be on us, and I tried to speak up but I got no further than 'Dear Lord,' when Beatrix let out another great howl and then tumbled onto the ground in a dead swoon.

We carried her into the house where she came round, though when I asked her what had happened she looked at me all confounded. 'How did I get here?' she said. 'I was washing myself down after the hens and then I can't remember a thing.' When I told her that God had spoken through her mouth she was shocked to her bones. 'Me?' she said, all humble. 'God's mouth?' Then she shivered. 'I feel so tired. Can I go to bed?' So I carried her to the bedroom and when I came back the rest of us got talking. Reynilda still thought she was feigning it all but she was the only one. Ida moaned that she wished none of this had happened as she had no doubt it would go badly for us, while the others looked scared as could be.

As for me, I had no doubts. I'd heard him loud and clear telling us, 'I am the father of him who gave his life to save you all.' What could be plainer than that? It was a miracle, nothing less. God had come and out of all the folk in Margate, of all the folk in Thanet, of all the folk in all Christendom, he'd picked me Warin the tailor as his torchbearer. But then why not? I might not be a thieving lord or abbot or alderman but I was a Christian and no sinner, or no worse than most of them. Warin the tailor, God's torchbearer? I felt a cheer in my belly that I hadn't felt in many a year. It was as if all those days of injury and insult just melted away, like salt in boiling water. 'That was God's voice no mistaking,' I told them. 'He's chosen our family for his mysterious ways and we won't let him down.' We shouldn't worry, I told Ida, but should be joyous. The end of days were coming, multitudes would perish and never mind if they were Satanist Jews or grasping rich or fat churchmen stealing farthings from the poor. Best of all, God had blessed us by picking our own dear daughter to warn the world. Which stood to reason seeing as we were good, poor, meek folk who didn't go stealing from our neighbours. I said they must all gather round me, and though Reynilda rolled her eyes, she did as she was told, and then I prayed, 'Great Lord, I've heard your words and I'll do everything you ask of me, and I'll do it with joy. As your torchbearer I'll go tomorrow to the church and tell them to repent before it's too late.'

Not that it was easy warning them. I had to threaten Reynilda with a slap to get her out of the door. Then there was the weather, as though it was July the day was cool with a rain falling so there weren't many folk about. Not being accustomed to preaching, I found it hard to shout loud and some of those who went by thought I was just saying hello or making a little friendly gabble. 'Who did you say came to Margate?' asked Simon the fisherman. 'Bob?' 'No, God,' I told him and though I'd been filled with strong intent at first it was hard not to feel a little foolish. 'Did he now?' said Simon, smiling and not understanding at all. 'He came to us just last week. I must've told you. Because I was sure that our poor Troy was breathing his last and three days later God cured him and he was off catching rats again.'

Nor was it much better when they did see. Wallace the carpenter smiled like it was the funniest thing he'd heard in a long while. 'Your Beatrix? Well, that's a surprise. I've hardly heard her say a word all these days and now God's talking out of her mouth.' A few were curious but most just laughed while it didn't help that more kept drifting by, so I had to go back to the start of explaining it all when I still hadn't got to the finish. And then, if things weren't wrong enough already, who should walk by but Father Adam? He'd never liked me, not since I'd made a fuss about my tithes. Though I hadn't owed him that ha'penny, that was God's truth, and why should I have to pay out anything anyway, just to make a fat cleric fatter, because Father Adam was no starveling. 'What d'you think you're doing, Warin?' he asked. I started telling him what had happened but it was all coming out wrong and getting tied in knots and then it didn't matter as God answered himself. Beatrix started humming and staring straight ahead of her so I knew what was coming. Sure enough here was her scream, which made Father Adam jump, and then out came God's croaky voice, telling us he was the father of him who'd given his life for us. If the folk going by hadn't listened to me, they listened up now.

'Be warned, my children,' the voice said. 'The last days are coming. Stop your sinning and repent before it's too late.' I thought Father Adam would be pleased to hear the voice of his master, but no. 'Stop this at once,' he said, wagging his little fat finger at us. 'This isn't our Lord speaking. This is Satan.' The fiend in my girl? I could have slapped him, priest or not. As for God, he didn't take kindly to be told to quiet his mouth. 'Satan's here in Margate,' he said in his croaky way. 'He walks among you every hour.' Now Beatrix's pointing finger started slowly moving back and forth from one spot to another, like it wasn't sure where to settle, aiming first at Kate's alehouse and then at Ben the blacksmith, and I could see the folks' eyes watching. It finally stopped on Father Adam. 'Here are devils,' said God and then out came a shriek so loud that everyone started. That gave me warning and when Beatrix swooned I was there ready to catch her. Father Adam gave me a glare and I gave him one back. As we helped poor Beatrix homewards he called out after us, 'Abbot Nicholas will hear of this.' 'So he should,' I answered. 'It's not every day that God comes to Margate.'

Ida fretted of course. 'This'll be our ruin,' she said, and it was no surprise that Reynilda was in accord with her, saying I'd been a fool for taking any notice of Beatrix and that we should never have gone. As if we could have done anything else? 'Remember Jonah hiding in his fish,' I said. 'When God calls you, you can't shut your eyes and plug your

73

ears. You have to do as he tells you.' Nor was it only me as it turned out. Our neighbours, or some of them, saw the truth too. Later that same afternoon Old Sybil came tapping at our door. She'd brought her cow, which was sick, and she wanted Beatrix to put her hand to the poor beast and cure her. Over the next days a number of others came by and not just from Margate either. One sad female came across the water from Richborough, hobbling as she had a warty foot that she wanted Beatrix to put her hand to. Some called me Lord, which made me laugh. But then why not, I thought, seeing as God himself had given me his blessing? And the ones who knew our tale well called me Torchbearer.

As for Beatrix, being such a quiet little thing usually, I wondered if she'd baulk at having strangers come to her, but no, she didn't seem troubled at all. When the weather was fine she'd take them behind our house where she made a special place for herself, sitting on our best stool with Clarice and Avice and Edith standing beside her. Because though Reynilda was still sour about the whole business, the other three were sweet about it now and I swear they were like Beatrix's servitors. If one of them was very bad, like the warty foot woman, Beatrix would take them down to the stream where she'd rinse their sores and then sprinkle their heads like it was holy water.

I knew it wouldn't be long before we had the abbot troubling us, and sure enough, four days after I'd preached outside Saint John's, a snorty-looking monk came to our house and told Beatrix and me that we must come to the abbey first thing the next morning. I wasn't much troubled. What we'd done was God's own bidding, after all, which was no sin but the finest and holiest righteousness. 'We'll be there,' I told the cloisterer, holding my head high. But then that same afternoon Beatrix broke into more humming and staring and for the third time that week we were blessed with God's words. This time he'd come to warn us. 'There's no use trying to fight fair with the fiend,' he told us in his croaky voice. 'You must answer his slyness with slyness of your own.' Because, God said, if a poor soldier found out that his own captain was a traitor and was secretly serving the enemy, it stood to reason that the lowly soldier couldn't fight the wicked captain all alone as he'd be destroyed. The soldier's only hope was to feign obedience so he wouldn't be suspected, and then to go to the highest in his host, being the king himself, as only he had the power to crush the captain and end his treachery. And so it was with us, God said. Father Adam was full of devils and so was his superior, Abbot Nicholas, so we must go above him, far, far above.

But where, I thought? To a cardinal, or the Archbishop of Canterbury? Yet it was neither. God's next command made me gasp. 'I want you to journey to the city of Rome,' he said, 'and you must see the pope.' When we did, God would speak through his mouthpiece and warn him that the last days were coming. And he'd tell him that Abbot Nicholas and Father Adam were Satan's creatures and must be cut out from his church like the cankers they were. He'd tell the pope of our own good service to him as his voice and his torchbearer, and he'd have the pope honour us both as we deserved. In the meantime, though, we must be careful or the devil would thwart us from righteously doing his work. With Abbot Nick and Father Adam we must be like players putting on a play, he said. We must tell them that our doings in front of the church had just been a foolish game that we were sorry for.

My head quite spun. Rome? I'd been to London once and Canterbury a good few times but never any further. 'But dear Lord,' I asked, 'how will we get ourselves there?' 'You must find your way,' God answered, 'that is my command,' and before I could ask him anything more Beatrix shrieked and swooned and he was gone. I tried to think through what he'd said. It wouldn't be easy, I knew. We'd have to beg our way there. But there was no gainsaying God. And it might be joyous too. I liked the thought of stepping into the pope's palace and meeting the man who was prince of all Christendom. How amazed he'd be hearing God's own voice and learning about the coming of the last days, and Abbot Nick and Father Adam being Satan's chicks. For that matter, seeing as God had chosen me as his very own torchbearer, there were a few other things I could warn him about while I was there. As I saw it, it was my rightful duty to tell him all about those fat, idle clerics who fed themselves off the labour of honest Christians. And I should tell him about the rich lords and merchants and aldermen who were no better, stealing bread from others' mouths. He should excommunicate every last one of them and cast them off from sucking at the sweet paps of the church.

In the meantime we did just as God had told us. The next morning all seven of us set out for the abbey and I made Reynilda, our troublemaker, promise to sit quiet through it all and never say a word, which she did. Abbot Nicholas looked stern and said it was wicked to make a game of God's voice but all he gave us in the end was fifty Hail Marys each and tuppence for the abbey roof, which by God's blessing I had, as Dame Celia had finally paid for her gown just two days before. After that I set to work getting us ready. I borrowed six shillings from my cousin Daniel, who'd been lucky with his fishing lately, though he wasn't eager to give it over. Then I got Ben the blacksmith to lend me his horse so I could ride over to Canterbury and get some good cloth for our cloaks and such.

I would have bought enough for seven of us, as I supposed we'd all be going, but it so happened that early on the very morning when I was to set out, Beatrix hummed and stared and God spoke to us once again, and he told us that, our journey being long and hard, it was his wish that only his voice and his torchbearer should go and the rest should stay in Margate. That troubled my wife and my other four daughters. Clarice and Avice and little Edith all sobbed and said they wanted to come to Rome too and Reynilda kicked up a real noise, saying it wasn't right at all. As for my Ida, she moaned that we might never come back, and even if we did, how would she live for months and months on nothing? I was sorry for her, of course I was, but what could I do? As I told her myself, there was no gainsaying God. Besides, as he'd told us to go it stood to reason he'd take care of them all in his mysterious ways. So I got just enough cloth to make cloaks for Beatrix and me, along with something heavier for our hats, and then I had Tom the tanner make us some good boots and scrips.

Of course most folk hadn't heard about our visit to the abbot, especially those who were far away, and all the while they'd still come tapping at our door. And though I knew that would make new trouble for us if the abbot heard, I couldn't bring myself to turn them away seeing as they'd come to honour God. What's more I was soon very glad that I'd let them come. Though most were poor folk who wanted Beatrix to cure their sores and warts and such, one was a merchant and a rich one, who had a big bald head like a shiny egg and who'd come all the way from Sandwich. He'd heard about our wrangling with Father Adam and Abbot Nicholas and he told us how he too had been tormented by false clerics possessed by the devil. His foe had been the prioress of a convent next to his storehouse, Lady Clara, with whom he'd got into a quarrel after she said the storehouse was on their land, which was a barefaced lie, he said. He took his satchel from his shoulder, which I'd seen was heavy from the way he'd carried it, and he took out four purses. Each had two and a half marks, he said, and he'd give them all to us and gladly, if we'd only tell the pope that Lady Clara was in the devil's palm and must be flung from the church like she deserved.

Ten marks. Here was joy. With that we wouldn't have to beg our way after all. Ida was full of gladness, saying we must leave half of it with her, and I would've given her some of it, but then God came to us once again and he said that those ten marks were his own gift that he had contrived for us to have and we must use them all for the great task we had of going to Rome. Though he said Ida could have the four shillings and thruppence that were left over from what I'd borrowed from my cousin Dan. Another command God gave us was that we must get a donkey for his voice to ride, and a good strong one, too, seeing as she was so dear to him and he didn't want her too fatigued on the way. That was because, as she was like his daughter now, he wanted her to ride into Rome just as his dear son Jesus had ridden into Jerusalem. Here's honour, I thought. Our little Beatrix is like God's own daughter. It so happened that Ben the blacksmith's wife, who'd died not a month earlier, had had a donkey that she'd ridden everywhere because of her bad feet, and who was a healthy, good-natured beast, so I bought him off Sam and for a good price, too. His name was Fawn, this being his colour, but we called him Porker instead, which was because he was a greedy beast who'd sneak any food that was left nearby, and he snorted when he ate just like a porker.

Then, just when it seemed as if all was ready, trouble struck. I'd told Father Adam that we were going to Rome, saying we wanted to repent our pretencing of God's voice, and he'd given his accord, but now when I asked him to bless our scrips and staffs and to write out our testimonials, which we needed for the road, he gave me a crabby look and said he'd heard that folk were still coming to see Beatrix with their warts and sores and such, which broke our promise to Abbot Nicholas, and he said he wouldn't write a word for us till we'd stood in front of his church and told all Margate that Beatrix's voice wasn't God's but Satan's. That was a bitter laugh, to have one of the fiend's own ordering us to confess that we were his creatures.

I thought we should do as he asked as otherwise we'd never get started, but Beatrix said that would be a betrayal of God. Besides, she said, what if news of it followed us to Rome? We'd never get the pope to listen to God's words if he knew that we'd told all Margate that they were the devil's. I don't know what we would have done if God hadn't shown us a way. A couple of days after we had our words with Father Adam a little cloisterer with a big thick beard came knocking on our door. I wasn't eager to let him in the house, having no great fondness for clerics as you'll imagine, and especially one who smelt ripe, like this one did. So I stood there, blocking the doorway, and though it was raining he didn't seem to mind and stood in the wet and told me his story. Dennis was his name, he said, and he'd lived for years as a hermit in the woods, eating berries and roasting acorns and feeling God in his heart every hour, till finally he'd joined some cloisterers out beyond Canterbury who had a friary in the woods that I'd never heard of. Just a couple of days back word had reached them that God was speaking his truths through the mouth of a little maid in Margate called Beatrix. Dennis hadn't waited even a moment, he said, but had filled his pockets with bread and turnips – he offered me some though they looked very well journeyed – and he'd set off down the road. All he asked of me, he said, was to let him kiss the hem of the gown of God's voice on earth.

So I let him in, as it seemed unkindly not to when he'd come so far. Being one of those changeable days when nothing stays for long, the rain was soon gone, the sun came out and Beatrix received him by the stream, sitting on the stool with her sisters to either side. Dennis dropped to the ground and kissed the hem of her gown and he couldn't have looked happier when she sprinkled water on him and gave him her blessing. It was only when we went back into the house that he saw our pilgrim hats and asked where we were going. I told him how God had told us we must go to Rome and as he seemed friendly I said that Father Adam wouldn't give us testimonials. From the way Brother Dennis's eyes glittered I knew he'd had a thought. Sure enough he started railing about false priests who slept on soft beds and who drank wine and ate meat for their dinner, calling them Satan's poppets. 'Come with me to my friary,' he said. 'Come right away. My abbot will write testimonials for you both.'

So, in the blink of an eye, what had seemed just an ordinary day became the day of our leaving. It was just as well we had our cloaks and scrips and hats and staffs ready. I gave Ida the four shillings and thruppence that God said she could have and, having spent sixpence on nuts and such for the road, I put the other nine marks, twenty-nine shillings and sixpence in my scrip, which hung heavy round my neck from the weight. Ida begged us to come home soon and save them from hunger and want. I promised I would, and then, with tears in our eyes, Beatrix climbed onto Porker, we all said our farewells, and I made sure to take the little path that led round the village so we wouldn't run into Father Adam.

That was an anguished journey. With my every step I feared we might be stopped by a constable or a priest who'd ask us for our testimonials. We didn't go through Canterbury but round and I kept slapping Porker's rump to hurry him up, as if you left that beast be even for a moment he'd stop and chew at some grass. The more I saw of Brother Dennis the more I warmed to him, as I swear we could hardly have been more in accord, especially about the folk whom we passed on the way. If we met a poor fellow in drab clothes who was carrying a heavy load on his back, we'd both call out to him, 'Good day to you, cousin,' but if we passed a well-fed cleric, or a gentleman riding on a high horse, we'd glance at each other and Brother Dennis would growl under his breath, 'Another of Satan's own.'

It was a long day's walk to Brother Dennis's monastery and when we finally got there my poor feet ached so that I could hardly take another step. By then it was almost dark but there was light enough for me to see that this was like no other house of God I'd cast my eyes on, being small and built all from logs so it could've been a charcoal burner's hut. As we stepped inside I saw there was no danger these clerics would live too softly as it was just one room, full of smoke from the fire, and was more like an outhouse for beasts than a monastery. There was a table, stools and some dirty-looking straw by the walls for sleeping and that was all. As for the brothers, there were only six of them including the prior, and they were each as beardy and ripe to the nose as Brother Dennis. But they gave us a warm welcome and some dinner, and though it was as simple as everything else, being bread and parsnips, Beatrix and I, who'd had nothing since Margate, ate it down hungrily enough. Beatrix got into a fuss to me about the dirt, as it wasn't the cleanest spot and there was a host of little biters in the straw so we both scratched away as we tried to sleep, and she whispered to me, 'It's not right, not for God's own voice.' I told her, 'It's just for a night. Tomorrow we'll get our testimonials and we'll be off.'

But it wasn't so easy as that so it turned out. The next morning I asked the prior a dozen times, can you write them out for us now then, and his answer was always to smile and tell me, 'I will, I will, don't you worry, I'm a little busy just now,' though I couldn't see what he was doing besides praying or sifting acorns and taking out the bad ones. Finally, when half the morning was gone, I understood what was what. I'd seen how the prior and the other monks would follow Beatrix around, not step by step but keeping close. Of course, I thought. They're all hoping to hear God's voice and they don't want us to leave till they have. So I asked Beatrix, very quiet so the others couldn't hear, can't you pretend that he's speaking, just to please them? She got quite angry, saying that it was nothing to feign, being holiness itself. But God must've been listening as he spoke up soon after. When Beatrix started humming, which I'd told the monks what it meant, they flew round the place like so many birds, fetching one who was outside chopping wood and another who was picking berries, and when God's words came out they were like statues, staring in wonder. As usual he told them the last days were coming and that they must mend their ways and repent their sins, and then he said that they must help his voice and his torchbearer get to Rome as fast as they could, so he could warn the pope and all Christendom would know. Lastly he said they should give us nourishing food for the journey.

After that things couldn't have been easier. The prior wrote our testimonials there and then, and they gave each of us a sack of parsnips, berries, nuts and bread, and the prior gave me a piece of cheese that he said they'd been keeping for a special day and which he held out to me like it was a gold chalice. We said our farewells and set out down the hill, though the cheese, which was black all over, gave off such a stink that in the end we chucked it into a hedge.

By dusk we were in Canterbury and full of joy, at least till the monks at the pilgrim hospital gave us some sorry news. It turned out a party of pilgrims on their way to Rome had passed through just a couple of days before. Being late in the season there wouldn't be many others on the road, so we might be journeying alone. That was a shame, as I'd hoped we'd find other pilgrims to go with, both for companionship and also our safety, especially with close to four marks in my scrip. The next day we had a doleful walk. Autumn had arrived, no mistaking. A cool wind blew in our faces and several times we got a soaking from the rain, while, this being our third day on the road, we were both aching, me on my feet and Beatrix, who was on the donkey, on her arse. All the while my eyes were on the hedges by the roadside, as I feared a gang of brigands might jump out at any moment.

But none did and then when we walked down into Dover town, God showed us he'd not forgotten his voice and his torchbearer. There beside the road I saw a young fellow in pilgrim gear, if you could call it that. As one who knows how to sew a seam it was all I could do not to laugh out loud. His hat was crooked and the cross on the front was all askew, his cloak sat so badly on his shoulders that I swear it might have been tailored by apes, while beneath it all he wore a set of rags as poor as any you might see. But the strangest thing about him was that, even though he could see that Beatrix and I were wearing pilgrim clothes just like him, he shook his begging bowl at us with all his might, which made a proper din as he'd filled it with pebbles to make it rattle louder. 'Please, kindly lordlings,' he said, 'can you spare a penny for a poor pilgrim on his way to see Saint Pete in Rome? It's just another penny I need to get me across the sea to France.'

'Rome?' I asked, full of hope. And so it was we learned that the group we'd heard of in Canterbury was still here. They'd been stuck in Dover for two days thanks to the wind, which was blowing from the south and had snared every ship in the harbour. The ragged boy, whose name was Tom, told us that the rest of his party were at the town's pilgrim hospital, the Maison Dieu. He wasn't one to give up, and as we turned to go, though we'd be his fellow pilgrims for weeks to come, that didn't stop him rattling his bowl at us again, saying, 'Can you spare a penny for a poor pilgrim on his way to see Saint Pete in Rome, lordlings?' So I gave him a ha'penny, as it seemed unkindly not to.

At the Maison Dieu we left Porker in the stables and then in we went to meet the party we'd be walking with, and though they weren't as poor and meek as the rag boy, Tom, they seemed righteous enough, mostly. The widow from Thetford, Constance, was especially joyed when I told them our tale. It turned out her boy was afflicted with torments thanks to her own sins, and she had Beatrix put her hand to his belly, which was where his torments first struck him, she said, and she had Beatrix pray to God that the devil would leave him be. One I didn't like the look of was the manor lord, John. Here's trouble, I thought, and haughtiness too. But when he heard of our travails with Father Adam and Abbot Nicholas he slapped me on the back like we were old friends. It happened he'd had a squabble with an abbot who was his neighbour, whom he'd punched in the nose. So I liked him well enough in the end.

There were a mother and daughter, Mary and Helena, whom I noticed on account of their gear, which was very tidily done. 'Who made those?' I asked, wondering if they'd cheated some poor tailor, but it turned out they'd made them themselves. 'I was a gown maker before I met my dear husband the butcher,' Mary told me. 'And so, thanks be to Jesus, I learned stitching then.' She'd learned well, too. Too well for my Beatrix, who was quite sour at me afterwards. 'Why couldn't you have made me something handsome like they have?' she asked. 'It's not right that a butcher's daughter should have finer clothes than God's own voice. With all the silver you've got you could make me a dozen pretty gowns.' As if I could start sewing gowns on the road to Rome? 'That'll have to wait,' I told her.

The one I didn't take to at all was the rich planter with little eyes, Hugh, as the man had no respect for sacred holiness. 'So you're God's throat,' he said to Beatrix, which I was sure he'd got wrong on purpose as he'd heard me say clear as a bell that she was his voice. 'Can I beg a favour?' he asked then, all false innocence. 'Could you have God tell us how next year's harvest will go? Or if we'll have another war with the Welshmen? Or if we'll have rain or sunshine tomorrow? Or, if those are too troublesome, perhaps you could have God tell us what number I'll get from a throw of a dice?' He started digging in his pack. 'I've got one right here.' I saw Beatrix looking crabbed, as well she might. 'That's not how it is,' I told him sharply. 'God doesn't speak through her to tell throws of a dice. He speaks through her to warn his children that the end of days are coming.' Not that that took the rotten smirk from his face.

Soon after that the ragged boy Tom came in looking joyed and told us he'd begged his last ha'penny for the boat and even had a farthing spare for some bread for his dinner. 'That's thanks to Beatrix,' said Constance. 'She'd brought us God's smile.' Which was right and proper, I thought. What's more, we then brought his smile again. First thing the next morning I was woken by a shout of, 'If you want to get to France then you'd best come down to the harbour right now,' and it was a shipman from one of the boats, come to tell us that the wind had swung round and we were good to set sail. As we hurried to pack up our things I couldn't resist saying to Hugh, 'Two days you've been stuck here waiting for the wind to turn, and the moment we turn up God brings it round.' Not that it changed him. 'A shame God didn't tell us that last night,' he said, 'as then we could've been packed and ready.'

There's no troubling over fools, I thought. I fetched Porker from the stables and off we went, and though the one who had pilgrimaged everywhere, Oswald, made a nasty racket with his bagpipes, that didn't spoil the sweetness of the moment. It was still only first light, the streets were quiet, seagulls were cawing in the sky above us, making me think of Margate, and the day had that tender feeling about it, like a newborn. Beatrix looked cheerier than she had since we'd first set out and I felt my face break into a smile. Here we were on our way to the city of Rome, off to see the pope in his great palace and to set him right about the world. The tide was in and the ships were riding on their anchors and as we waited for the little fellow who'd brought us to find a boat to row us over, I heard humming and I knew what was coming next. This'll put a stop in you, Hugh delver, I thought, now you hear God himself speak. Then here he was. 'My children, I bless you all,' he said in his croaky voice, as the rest of them looked on with wide eyes. He told them to honour his voice and his torchbearer as they were dear to him, and why not, I thought, giving Hugh a smile. Then he gave us sweet news.

'Go on in strong heart,' he said, 'as great good fortune will come to you soon.' Constance piped up then, begging, or shrieking, for him to cure her boy, but I saw Beatrix's eyes were closing and I only just had time to reach out to catch her when she swooned.

I laughed at them all when we got aboard. You can't grow up in a place like Margate without getting your feet wet and I'd been out on the water many a time, helping my uncle and my cousin, who were fishermen, and even Beatrix knew her way about a deck, but the rest of them were like babes in a treasure house, looking at everything and wondering what it was. 'How strange it feels, rocking under our feet,' Constance said. Not half so strange as it'll feel when we get out of the harbour, I thought. It wasn't a bad boat and the shipmen knew their work. They had us wait on the deck while they rigged up a stall below decks for Porker, and when that was done the ship's master told us to go down and he handed us each a jute sack. Mary smiled like she'd been given a lovely present. 'What's this for?' she asked. 'You'll soon know,' said the master with a half smile. 'Just try not to make a mess on the hides.' Oswald, who'd been a passenger before, knew, and he looked at his glumly. I won't need mine, I thought. Which was pride, I suppose.

It was dim down below, with just a little light coming down from the hatch. Poor Porker was rigged up with ropes in his stall, tight as a fly in a web, and he gave me a mournful look. 'You'll be glad of it, no mistaking,' I told him. The hides were sheep and there were so many that they filled half the space down there and they reeked. We all crammed ourselves into what was left to us. I showed the others the rings in the ship's side to hold on to and they rattled them about as if it was all a great sport. Finally the hatch was slammed shut, putting us in darkness, and then the ship moved free a little. 'We're off,' said the rag boy Tom like it was Christmas Day. 'I'd hold on tight if I were you,' I said, but of course they'd forgotten by the time we passed out of the harbour and struck real sea, and then they were all shouting and falling onto one another. Soon she was bucking like a mare, rising up and coming down with a crash. 'It's going to break,' Hugh's wife Margaret wailed. 'We're all going to drown.' 'I wouldn't worry,' I told her. 'It's just a bit of weather.' Soon afterwards I heard one of them spewing, then a second, and soon we had another stink to fight that of the hides. Then they were all praying and bickering about who helped best at sea. Some said it was Saint Clement and others said it was Saint Elmo. 'Saint Nicholas is as good as any,' I told them, as one who knew, so they all prayed to him.

Just weather and waves, I said to myself. But as time passed it grew worse and then worse again, till I knew this was a storm, and badder than any I'd known on Uncle's boat. Even I had to use my sack, shameful to say, though it wasn't easy, as I couldn't hold it right without letting go of the ring in the side, which I wasn't going to do. There was mess all over. 'This is the end for certain,' Jocelyn the advocate, who was next to me, kept moaning, and from the way the prow juddered and crashed I thought he mightn't be wrong. Surely God wouldn't let his own voice and torchbearer drown before they'd had a chance to do his work, I thought. Unless Father Adam had been right after all, and it had been the fiend speaking through Beatrix's mouth? She kept praying she was sorry, though I didn't know what for, unless it was her screaming over the hens. I started praying too: 'Please, good Saint Nick, see us safely through this, I beg you.' Trust that slimy fellow Hugh to make things even worse. Just then, when everyone was frightened as could be, I heard a kind of idiot cackle in the dark and he called out, 'What I want to know is, where's that great good fortune that was coming to us?'

Finally I felt the ship grow a little calmer so it was easier to hold my place and I knew we were past the worst of it. Then I must have fallen asleep as I woke to find one of the shipmen was shaking me by the shoulders. 'Up you get, cousin,' he said. 'We're here.' The hatch was open and, my legs feeling weak, I climbed up and found that it was first light again and we were riding at anchor in a little harbour. But it wasn't Calais. The shipmen said the storm had blown us to Boulogne.

We all went down to the water to try and clean ourselves off and then, feeling hungry from our empty stomachs, we found a market. It was strange hearing them all gabbling in words that made no sense, and were more like geese honking than real talk. The rag boy Tom rattled his bowl at anyone who came near, saying his beggar's chant, and even though they couldn't have understood a word he said he got a couple of coins. I suppose they were for his rags. I'd guessed Oswald would know a word or two of French from all his pilgrimaging, which he did, while Sir John knew a little too, and Jocelyn the advocate spoke it nicely enough, but the one who could say it smooth like butter, strange to say, was the woman from Gloucester, Mary. Whoever heard of a butcher's widow speaking fine French? She was the one who helped us buy our wares, some of which I'd never seen anything like till then. There were some that looked like parsnips but were no colour any decent parsnip ever was, being yellowy red. Oswald, who'd been everywhere under the sun, knew. 'They're called carrots,' he said. You could boil them or eat them raw and they were crunchy and a little sweet. 'Have one,' he said, but I said no. Why should I try something that I didn't know what it was? Another foreign thing they had looked like soft cabbages and were the size of hedgehogs. 'That's lettuce,' Oswald told us. 'They eat it raw and call it salad.' 'Good for them if they like it,' I said. 'I'll keep to my stew and sops, thank you very much, if they have such a thing here.'

The comely widow Constance wanted us to set out on the road straight away. They'd been a whole day in London, she said, and then two more waiting for the wind to change in Dover and if we stayed another day here we'd never get to Rome, so she feared, and her boy would never be cured. But all the others of us wanted some rest after that bad night on the boat. So we found an inn and had a sleep, though it was daytime, all aside from the rag boy Tom, who went out begging again. Then early the next morning we started out for Taruenna, which Oswald said was where we'd catch the main pilgrim road from Calais. It was a nasty day, the sky was wide and grey and mean little drops of rain blew into our faces. All the while Hugh did his best to make it worse. With every mile we walked he'd say, with that idiot smile of his, 'I'm still waiting for that great good fortune.'

I didn't trouble to answer him and neither did my Beatrix, though I did murmur a prayer under my breath: 'Dear God, your loyal torchbearer begs you, have him trip on a stone and break his shins.' Finally, just as my feet were getting tired, I saw a crossroads up ahead which would be the road from Calais, and coming down it I saw a party approaching us, all on horses, and with a cart too. It was a good-sized group of half a dozen, two of them riding chargers, and we slowed our pace a little, wondering who they could be and if they'd do us ill. When they grew nearer, though, I breathed more easily as I saw the ones on chargers were a man and a woman, and both were wearing pilgrim clothes. She was small and dark and very comely looking, while he had long blonde hair that he kept sweeping out of his eyes.

'Gentle folk by the look of them,' said the advocate, Jocelyn. Which was right, as even from this distance off I could see their clothes were too well cut for normal pilgrim gear, and the woman's cloak was very seemly around her shape. Three others, who were riding little rounseys, would be their servitors, and there was another who looked like a priest. Beside the cart driver sat a little lad who must be their boy. Of course the others in our party were looking at them with wide eyes like they were God's gift to us all. Then there's nothing your Englishman loves like a great lord, and even my Beatrix, who should've known better, was lost in smiles. 'I wonder who they are?' said Sir John like he couldn't wait to learn. 'They don't look like French or Flemings.' 'Germans would be better attired,' said Oswald, 'as they like to travel looking well. And they wouldn't be coming down the road from Calais.' I knew they were all praying to God to make these fine noble folk be English. Of course none of you stop to wonder, I thought to myself, how hard they've squeezed their tenants and their bondsmen to get those fine horses.

You never ask, have they paid the tailor who stitched those handsome cloaks?

But they had their wish. One of the gentle folk's party, the priest, cantered over to us and called out in English, 'Lady Lucy de Bourne gives you her greetings.' 'And John of Baydon gives our greetings to Lady de Bourne, and most heartily, too,' answered Sir John, and then they were both smiling and smirking at finding that none of us were foreign. The priest asked where we were on pilgrimage to and when Sir John told him Rome they both smiled and smirked all over again, as it turned out that was where Lady de Bourne was going as well.

It wasn't that I wanted to put an end to their merriness but I had been wondering why their party had been introduced in the name of the lady. As the priest was about to ride back to his party I asked him, 'Tell me, Father, is that gentleman with the fair hair Lord de Bourne?' My supposing was right as it happened, and the priest looked awkward now. 'No, that's Lord Lionel,' he said, 'Lady Lucy's travelling companion.' I'd thought as much from the way he'd hung back as they rode, so he was always a little behind her. If he'd been lord he'd have been ahead of her or at least beside. He looked younger than her, too. A travelling companion, and what was that? I wondered. Had these fine, gentle folk been fornicating together? Were they going to Rome to ask forgiveness of their wicked sin? For that matter, were they sinning still? As the priest rode away I saw the rest of our party looking a little sorry. What did you expect? I thought. Did you think that your fine folk would be pilgrimaging to Rome white as snow?

But there was a blessing here, I saw. There was no doubt about it, God was looking out for his voice and his torchbearer. If we ended up travelling with this crowd to Rome, as we might, then my marks would be safer for sure. One of the thralls was a big, strong-looking fellow who'd be handy in a skirmish. I saw their cart was piled up with sacks and barrels that looked like food and drink, so we wouldn't starve with them alongside us. For that matter the cart could come in useful for Beatrix if Porker went lame. I stepped over to the rich delver. 'Now you have your answer, Hugh,' I said, giving him a hard slap on his back that made him miss his step. 'Here's the great good fortune God promised us.'

CHAPTER FIVE

Lucy de Bourne

Sometimes in my darkest moments when my life seemed cursed I'd tell myself, don't feel neglected, Lucy. It's no surprise that God doesn't always hear you. Think how often you see folk praying to him, at home or in church or as they're taking a rest from tilling their fields. Think how many voices beseech him every hour. Think how deafened he must be by all that clamour and how hard it must be for him to hear one entreaty from another. If I woke in the depths of the night and couldn't sleep I'd tell myself, this tossing and turning may seem like torment, Lucy, but it's also a blessing. It's a chance to be seized. Now that everybody else is asleep God will hear your prayers more easily. So I'd pray and pray. But then my doubts would creep back. I'd wonder, what if many others are also being kept awake by their troubles and are praying just as I am, as then he may not hear me after all? Or what if God himself is asleep? Once, when I was especially anguished and I prayed every waking hour, begging God to show me a little kindliness and take my husband Walter from this earth and throw him down to hell to burn, I asked a priest, 'Father, tell me, does God sleep in the night like we do?' I'd have been wiser to ask a scholar. He squinted his eyes and said that the ways of God were a mystery not known by men, which seemed no answer at all.

When I was younger, only twelve or thirteen or fourteen years old, and nobody in the world thought that one day I might be heiress to a great fortune, let alone two fortunes, of course I loved God, as every good Christian must, but the one who was oftenest in my thoughts was brave Lancelot. That was all thanks to Eleanor, my little brother Hugo's betrothed. It was she who said to me one day, 'Lucy, wouldn't you like to learn reading and writing like your brothers and the wards?' I wasn't eager if truth be told, as my notion of joy wasn't to sit staring at letters but to go riding Pomley over the Wolds, as fast as he'd take me. But Eleanor was my best friend, being the only gentle female in the castle who was close to my own age, and I could see she was keen. So, thinking she'd soon lose curiosity, I gave my accord. We went to Father Tim as he taught the boys and he agreed readily enough. Then he'd always been a little soft for me, and he would be more so again later, when I was grown. He found us both wax tablets and each day except Sunday we'd go to him in the hall around noontime, when the boys were out riding or practising swordsmanship. And strange to say, though it had all been Eleanor's notion, I was the one who took to it quickest and liked it best.

Once we could both mumble out our words our next thought was what we should read. Father Tim gave us our catechism, which was no use as we knew it already, and then he gave me Saint Catherine's life, but I can't say I loved that either. So I went to Father, who had several books. They were all tales of King Arthur and his knights, Father said, these being his favourites. All were in French but Eleanor and I both understood that well enough as Mother spoke to us in it when she remembered, like gentle mothers will. So we took one and mouthed it in turns, and after that I'm sorry to say that poor Pomley was quite neglected as all I cared about was those stories. I adored every one of them, whether they were about Tristan and Iseult, or Percival and Blanchefleur, or Merlin and his wicked enchantress Viviane. My favourites, though, were Lancelot and Guinevere.

Poor Lancelot, I felt sorry for him. He was so lost in his passion that he was like a man in a trance, forgetting everything, even his knightly vows, so he betrayed his own lord, Arthur. Guinevere could be cruel, making him into her slave, but then she had to be sure he was worthy of her love. Eleanor liked those tales as much as I did and sometimes we'd go up the east tower where hardly anybody went and act them out together in play. Eleanor was no good at Lancelot as when she tried to make her voice deep it sounded foolish, while she'd get scared of her quests, even though I only gave her easy ones. So she was always Guinevere and would sit on her throne, which was an old chair that we'd found up there, and tell me I must show my valour by sneaking into the pantry to get her a wafer, or I must bring her a beetle in a goblet, or a frog from the moat.

I never failed once but still there was no telling how she'd be. Sometimes she'd smile and tell me I'd proved my love very well but other times she'd look annoyed and say I hadn't done it right, so I must beg her forgiveness and do another. I never gainsaid her, as how could I when I was a poor knight lost in passion? So I'd kneel down, beg her forgiveness and then go off to fetch another frog or whatever it was. Once, when she'd made me get her a flask of mead from the pantry that we both drank, she said I'd proved my love so well that I might kiss her. And so I did, there and then, right on her lips and for the longest time too, with my arms round her neck so it was like we really were Lancelot and Guinevere. What a funny thing that was. I often wondered if she'd tell me I might kiss her again, especially when I'd done well with a quest, but she never did.

When I was almost seventeen and was to marry Geoffrey I prayed to God, please Lord, make him my own Lancelot, though I didn't think it was very likely. I'd met Geoffrey several times and he was two years younger than me and short, so I could look down at the curly hair on the top of his head. And though he tried to be courtly with me, asking me if I was hungry or thirsty or if he should have something fetched for me, his voice was so high and chirpy and his aspect was so timorous that I swear I'd been courtlier myself when I was Lancelot to Eleanor's Guinevere. My father, who was always kindly to me, as I was his favourite of the three of us, said I mustn't worry, as my wedding was only the beginning. With time Geoffrey would grow taller, most likely, and we'd become accustomed to each other.

My mother told me I must obey him and I mustn't fuss if he beat me, as that was what husbands did to keep their wives on the right path. Then she told me what I must do on my wedding night, which seemed so foul and strange that I could hardly bear to think about it, but she said it was God's will so I must welcome it as my joy. Finally she gave me a gift of a little paring knife with a sharp pointed end and she told me how to counterfeit that we'd done it, in case it didn't go right, because Geoffrey's mother might look for signs afterwards.

And it was as well she did as, despite all the mead we drank on our wedding night, Geoffrey was more anguished even than I was and in the end his ugly mushroom squirted out its grease before I'd touched it, let alone had it go anywhere. I used Mother's paring knife to spill a little blood from my finger onto the sheets and Geoffrey was so thankful he cried.

It was hard living among his kin. The only familiar face there was Brigit, our cook's daughter, who was made my foot maid and who was always trying to cheer me up. 'Look on the bright side, ma'am,' she'd say. 'With time he'll learn how to get his load into port before it spills.' And if he was a milksop and no Lancelot, at least I could rule a milksop with ease. 'In time you'll get used to being among his folk,' she said, though I wasn't so sure. Geoffrey's mother, who was also his guardian, his father being dead, was a stony woman and even when she tried to be friendly I felt a little scared of her. She was always telling me how lucky I was to have married her boy, what a good marriage gift I'd got, and what a fortune he'd have when he came of age. But then my father had said Geoffrey, whose family had been bailiffs and not gentle folk at all, should think himself lucky to marry a de Bourne, whose great-grandfather had sailed with King Richard to fight the Saracens.

And then in the end I didn't need to grow accustomed to them after all. My mother once told me, 'Death has always been your best friend, Lucy de Bourne,' which was a hateful thing to say but it was true. I'd been trying my best and every morning and night I prayed, please Lord, give Geoffrey's mushroom more patience, as each week his mother would look at my flat belly and ask, 'No news for us yet, Lucy?'

Geoffrey did seem to be getting better, though he still hadn't made it all the way to harbour. Finally at Christmas his mother had a feast for all her tenants. I was seated next to Geoffrey and, seeing a sweet-looking piece of meat on the platter in front of me, I thought I'd show myself the goodly wife. I took his knife, I stuck the piece and popped it into his mouth. He smiled at first and started swallowing but then I saw his eyes open wider, his hand went to his throat and though I screamed and everyone jumped up to help, knocking over the chairs and plates, it was no good. He'd choked.

I'll always owe Brigit for that time. She heard all the news from her gabbling with the other servitors. I'd seen the foul looks Geoffrey's mother gave me but it was Brigit who told me what she was telling everyone, which was that I'd choked him not by mistake but purposely so I could get my dower. That was a wicked lie. He hadn't been much but I'd done my best by him. I was sorry he'd gone and my wailing and tears were heartfelt enough, mostly, while it wasn't my fault that he hadn't troubled to chew. 'You must get away from here right away,' Brigit warned me, 'or something bad will happen to you, mark my words.' I'd find myself pushed down the stairs, she said, or I'd taste ground glass in my stew. So we made up a tale that she had to visit a sick cousin in Lincoln and instead she went to my father. He'd have come to Geoffrey's burying anyhow but he took care to bring most of the thralls and a cart for my marriage gifts. I left with him.

As we rode homewards he surprised me with his laughter. 'I shouldn't, I know,' he said, 'and I'm sorry for poor little Geoffrey, of course I am, but still I can't help but smile.' Though he'd thought it a good match, he said, which would serve me well and give me a commodious life, he'd never liked Geoffrey's mother, whom he'd found a hard, greedy sort of woman. But now, instead of giving her grandchildren de Bourne ancestors, so they had proper, worthy kin, she'd yielded up half her fortune. Which was quite true, because when you added together my marriage gift and my dower, which I'd have when I came of age, and was a full third of Geoffrey's kin's estate, it came to nearly half. 'You're an heiress,' Father said.

And soon I'd be one twice over, sorry to say. I was happy to be back at Bourne Castle, at home among my family and the wards and Eleanor. She was pleased to see me but also a little anguished, as my brother Hugo was fourteen so they'd soon be wedded rightfully and she'd join him in his bedchamber. I tried to soothe her by telling her about Geoffrey. Though I felt troubled too, wondering what kind of husband I'd have next. My father was already searching. 'With half Geoffrey's lands due to you when you come of age, you'll have your pick,' he said. 'I'll find you a fine fellow, don't you worry.' I told him, and firmly too, what manner of man I wanted. He must be a little older than me and taller. He must be seemly but lovesome and mannerly. And he must be gallant and manly too. Father gave me a look like he knew what was in my thoughts. Then he knew me well enough. 'A Lancelot, eh?' he said.

But he never did find me a husband, Lancelot or otherwise. One day at the start of spring our steward Ralph, who'd been to Lincoln to get spices for the cook, came back with news that there was more trouble in Wales, and after then it seemed that all I heard about was Wales and war, Wales and war. The Welsh were cheating, treacherous devils, so everyone said, and there was no treating with them now except by the sword. Whenever we had visitors in the hall there'd be songs and toasts with everyone jeering that the Welshmen, being savage woodsmen, would be crushed to dust in a week. But my father, who'd fought them in the last war, wasn't so sure. Welshmen had a way of making themselves look just like trees, he told me, so you couldn't see them till it was too late. 'We'd be marching past a forest and there might be a hundred of them in there, or a thousand, and we'd never know till they rushed out at us with their long spears.' Another thing he told me about was the damp. 'I swear it rains like no rain you've ever seen. There's fog too and sometimes it rains through the fog.' If his squire forgot to polish his sword and his mail, he said, within days it would be black with rust and there'd be mould on his clothes. 'Everybody grows sick. I swear you could lose a whole army to Welsh fungus.'

It wasn't long before King Edward sent out writs for a levy of the host. Father wasn't eager. 'I've done my warring,' he said, and Mother was with him so he'd have paid his fee instead if it hadn't been for my little brother Hugo. He was fervent to go and said he'd be shamed if he didn't. In the end Father agreed and said he could ride as squire to one of his vassals, Arnold de Thurlby, whom Father had fought alongside in the last war and who'd been assured enough then, Father said. But then Father, and my mother too, didn't like the thought of Hugo going with no kin to watch over him, and Father decided to go after all. So we said our farewells to them both as they rode away with Father's little party of warriors.

They'd hardly gone when the most worrisome news came to us. A horde of Welsh devils had trapped the Earl of Gloucester and his army in an ambush and many a good Englishman had perished. After that I prayed every morning, noon and night, please dear God, I beg you, keep my father and my brother safe from Welshmen pretending themselves trees. Bring them both home safe. It was quiet for us who were left behind with nothing to do but wait and hope. With Eleanor's betrothed gone and my father and many of the young men, too, there'd be no weddings for us till they got back home. I rode over the Wolds when I could, though Mother was steadfast that I must always go with Ralph the steward and three of the thralls, as she feared that, as an heiress, I might be seized by some malefactor and forced as his bride.

But it wasn't me whom Mother should've feared for. One December afternoon I'd been out riding like usual and as we came back into the castle yard I heard a wailing that I knew at once as my mother's voice. So it was I learned that God had taken my littlest brother, Edward. He'd been as hungry as Hugo to go off to war but was too young. That day he'd been playing battles with one of the wards and to make it more real he'd put on some old, half-rusted armour he'd found, though it was far too big for him. They'd been chasing each other about, stabbing and clouting one another with their wooden swords, till Edward ventured too near the moat, over by the postern where it was slippery, and in he'd gone. The ward had done his best, jumping in after him, but it was deep there and the weight of Edward's armour gave him no chance. My mother was beyond all comforting and shrieked blame at anyone she could: the ward, of course, and also me for going off riding with Ralph and the thralls, who might've saved him if they'd been about. That cut me deep and it wasn't right, either, I thought. If anyone was at fault it was the Welshmen, as if it hadn't been for their treachery that forced war on us then Edward would never have been playing at battles in the first place.

So we put poor Edward in the ground and, instead of being full of cheer that Christmas, our home was a place of silence and mourning. Afterwards we wondered every day if Father and Hugo had heard our terrible news and if they'd come home, which we dearly hoped they would because it was hard to bear our sorrow alone. They had the right, their forty days being long finished, and that's what they chose so it turned out. The first I knew of it was when I heard a clatter of hooves in the bailey and, looking down from my chamber window, I saw it was the men Father and Hugo had ridden out with. There was quite a little crowd of them and my eyes roved back and forth but I couldn't see either Father or my brother. I watched as my mother walked out to greet them and I swear it was as if I knew what would happen before it did. She talked to Arnold de Thurlby just for a moment, then she took a step back and started toppling over so two of the thralls jumped forward to catch her. I ran down the stairs too shocked for tears, and the same thought went through my head over and again like the fiend's rhyming. It's Father, I thought. It's Father, it's Father. And it was done by those devil Welshmen pretending themselves trees.

But I was wrong both times. It was the two of them and not from fighting but from lunch. It hadn't even been in Wales but at a Chester inn. They'd gone there to meet a cousin of ours who lived in the city, and while the rest of the party, being tired from the ride, had gone up to rest in their rooms, my poor father, feeling he deserved something tasty after all the muck he'd eaten while soldiering, had ordered a big platter of fish with sauce. They'd thought it very fine, so we were told by father's old war friend Arnold de Thurlby, and ate down every morsel, but soon the three of them were spewing and squirting in the latrine. At first everybody laughed at their being caught out by their greed for fish but then their sickness wouldn't stop, they couldn't keep even a drop of water down, till they were shivering and feverish and their skin turned wrinkled. My little brother Hugo was the first to go, then the cousin and finally my father. 'I beat the cook black and blue with my own hands,' Arnold de Thurlby told us, 'and the landlord, too.' As if that was any comfort.

So one bad fish changed our lives forever. With tears on my cheeks I found I was heiress for a second time. As if I hadn't lost enough dear ones already, now I lost Eleanor too, as, her betrothed being dead, she had to go back to her family. She wept as she said her farewells, telling me how she hated to leave me at such a moment as this. In a strange way the one thing that helped me during those black days was that my mother was worse even than me. She was like one who's so bruised that any slight touch is agony, and she'd get into wrangles with the thralls or with me over the tiniest thing, and especially anything that was spoiled or gone. She'd find a spot of grease on her shoe, or a chip in a chair leg that had probably been there for years, or she'd lose a cheap ribbon or a favourite plate, and she'd be railing and demanding to know whose fault it was. And then, as quick as it had come, her rage would leave her and she'd start sobbing. Seeing her so broken let me keep my own grief at arm's length. I wished I could have stayed with her longer but, being still only nineteen years of age, I was made a ward of Earl Henry, to whom Father had been in fealty. He'd been warring in Wales like all the rest of them but when he came home I was sent to him in London, with my maidservant Brigit at my side. London was a place I'd always dreamed of seeing but now, in my sorrow, I hardly cared for its noise and crowds. Not that I was there for long. After only a few weeks Earl Henry offered my marriage rights to sell.

'Dear God,' I prayed, 'I know I haven't been as righteous as I should have. I know I choked Geoffrey to his death, though it was only by accident. I beg you please give me a good and lovesome new husband.' But there must have been too much clamour from other prayers that day, as God didn't hear. The one who won the bid was Walter de Kingerby. He was from Lincolnshire like me but from the north and I'd never met him nor heard much about him. Earl Henry did his best to make him seem worthy. 'He's a handsome fellow, no question,' he told me. 'And brave.' He'd ridden against the Welsh with all the rest, Henry said. But the moment I set eyes on Walter as we knelt side by side, praying at mass, I guessed the truth. Though he showed me every courtesy, praising my fine manners and my seemliness and telling me how joyed he was that we were to be wed, his eyes had a way of flicking aside and never quite looking at me. Brigit, who loved to make up nicknames for people, called him the Twitcher.

I soon learned why he wanted me and it wasn't for my fair face or my good name or my fine manners. He wanted my fortune, which he had the moment we were wed. He needed it, having only three manors of his own, and he'd borrowed from his cousins to win the bid for me, so Brigit heard from his thralls. He couldn't wait to move into Bourne Castle, as his own manor house, where we only stayed a few days while he had his scant movables packed up, was a poor sort of place, poky and damp, with rot on the west side by the moat. I'd looked forward to going home to Bourne but when we got there I wished we'd stayed at his place, for all its funguses. My dear Eleanor was gone, my mother was gone, moved to a manor that was part of her dower, taking Father Tim and all our servitors, and Earl Henry had sold off the wards, so the only familiar face left there was my Brigit. It felt sad seeing rooms and views that I knew so well but feeling like I was a stranger. Nor was it helped by Walter. Though he'd been hungry as could be to live in Bourne Castle he was forever belittling it, complaining that the moat was too shallow or the hall fireplace didn't draw properly, or wondering what fool had added another floor to the west tower, though he knew full well it had been my father. I could see what was really in his mind. He couldn't bear the fact that my kin were nobler than his and wanted to beat me down till I felt I was beneath him.

And of course he wanted an heir and without delay. He had no trouble managing what Geoffrey never had, and from our wedding night onwards he'd visit my bedchamber morning, noon and night, but he did it with so little sweetness that I soon dreaded the sound of his tread on the stairs, and I quite wished I'd had Geoffrey back. He soon knew my time and when he saw from the moon that it was come he'd ask me, 'So, Lucy? D'you have any news for me?' But I never did, more was the pity, and that was what brought out the brute in him like nothing else. The second time I had my bleed he cried out, 'What's wrong with you?' like I'd done it purposefully. The third time he put his hand to my face and when Brigit shrieked he looked like he might give her a turn, too.

'There's nothing to be done,' Brigit said afterwards when we sat sobbing together. Which was true, or so I thought then. So I made do with prayer. 'Please God,' I'd beg, 'make me with child so my grub of a husband will leave me be.' Or I'd pray, 'Please, dear God, please start a new war and send Walter, and have him struck through with arrows by the Saracens or Welshmen or Mongols or whoever it is that he's fighting, and be sure you give him a slow and painful end.'

But the clamour of other prayers must have been too loud as, like before, God didn't hear. How I stood that life for so long seems a mystery to me now, but for almost two years I stomached his curses and his swiving and his slaps. I might have put up with it all for another two years if it hadn't been for my Pepin. He was a little terrier who'd belonged to Walter's bailiff who'd died of fever not long before, and he belonged to nobody and everybody till I began feeding him and he became mine. He hated Walter to his bones and would growl whenever he came near, and Walter hated him. One day when I'd had my bleed again and Walter started slapping me, Pepin, being a loyal, fearless creature, jumped up and sank his teeth into Walter's leg. Walter let out a howl and pulled him off, though he took a biteful of calf with him, and then he dashed his head against the wall so hard that that was the end of the poor little animal.

After that I knew what I must do and I didn't care how much sin or shame to my family name it brought. Good

Brigit was in accord with me. 'If he could do that to your poor whelp,' she said, 'then who knows what he might do to you?' There was not much I could do all alone, I knew, and the only one I could think of who might give help was my Uncle Marmaduke who'd always been friendly to me when I was growing up. He lived not far away so Brigit feigned a story of needing to go to Lincoln to see a sick brother and paid him a visit. His first answer, which Brigit told me on her return, was that I should bide my time as God might bless us with a child yet, and that would make Walter kindlier towards me, but I was long past waiting. Then I remembered Marmaduke had a softness for dogs and how, when I'd been young, he was always telling me about his pack of hunters and which of them had just pupped or liked to have his belly stroked. So I sent Brigit back to tell him about poor Pepin. That was the right road, it turned out, and Brigit said that Marmaduke was so furious that he could hardly speak.

In a few days it was arranged. Late one evening, when Walter was away visiting one of his manors and the household was fast asleep, Brigit and I took all the goods that I held dearest and, load after load, we sneaked them out through the postern gate to a nearby barn. Marmaduke was true to his word and at first light the next morning he was waiting there with horses for us, and half a dozen thralls who were already loading up a cart. So I kept my rings and my jewels, my best cups and napkins, a new hood and all my best gowns and sheets, and though I had to leave behind my bed and two chairs that I was fond of, they seemed cheap payment.

I knew leaving Walter would be like punching the devil in the nose, and I expected him to come at us with every man he had. Marmaduke set his serfs watching day and night like they were his own little army, but that wasn't Walter's way so I found out. No, his answer was slower and colder. He liked to squeeze your last breath from you with laws. Worse, he started not with me but with Marmaduke and Aunt Juliana. As well as charging them with abduction and seizing my goods – which he wanted back of course, having so few himself – he sued them both with a writ of ravishment. Seizing was one thing but if they were found guilty of ravishment then that would be jail or hanging. When Marmaduke heard, he said he'd challenge Walter to a combat, which was wild folly as he was far too old, and happily Aunt Juliana talked him out of it. She'd hardly look at me and I can't say I blamed her. How wrong I felt for bringing danger to the very ones who'd saved me.

All in all it was as well I had somewhere else to go. Because only a few weeks after I fled Walter my twenty-first birthday came, so I was finally of age and could sue Geoffrey's mother for my dower. She fought me, as I'd known she would, but the case was clear enough and before long I was a lady of fortune. Together with my marriage gift I had fourteen manors to my name, which was more even than Walter had robbed from my family heritage. The best manor house was at Ropsley and, though it was no castle, it had strong stone walls and a moat. It had last been lived in by Geoffrey's grandmother, who'd died only a few years earlier, and was in good repair. I wasted no time and moved from Uncle Marmaduke's and made it my home. I had my goods brought and I purchased kitchen gear and hangings and carpets for the floors. My mother, who lived not far away at Ancaster, gave me two of our old thralls whom she said she could spare. One was Alwyn, who'd been Father's footman and whom I made my steward, and the other was Jack, who'd done small work about the house, including in the kitchen, so I tried him as cook and not a bad cook he made.

Mother said I also might have Father Tim if he was willing, which he was, saying he'd be joyed to his heart. I was joyed to my heart to have him, in part because he was a dear old friend and in part because I'd far rather shrive my sins quietly to one whom I knew and trusted than say them aloud in church for every reeking delver behind the screen to hear. As the manor house had no chapel I had one made from the storeroom next to the hall, and though it was small it had an altar and benches and a pretty statue of Jesus on the cross, while it was all rightfully blessed. With two more thralls from my manors I had a full household. I started attending my lordly duties, visiting my tenants and making sure they paid their dues, and getting the bondsmen on my manors to pay their rents and debts and fines, which I found I had a talent for. I saw through their guiles so well that I made my land pay better than Geoffrey's mother ever had, so I heard.

All the while I was at war with Walter, and our battlefields were the courts of Lincoln City, church and royal. I launched my first foray by going to the dean and chapter of Lincoln and suing for divorce on grounds of consanguinity. I had a case as Walter and I were cousins, so I'd been told by Earl Henry when he sold me to him, and which was no great surprise seeing as most of the gentle folk of Lincolnshire were cousins to some degree. Nobody was sure if we were close enough to make it incest, which must be four times removed or less, but if I could win round the court then my marriage would be annulled clean, and I'd get back all my lands without any more squabbling. For good measure I also sued that I shouldn't be forced to return to Walter's bed because of his violence. But he was cunning. When I next went to Lincoln, bringing my uncle as a witness to my incest, we both had to flee as Walter had set the sheriff to arrest us. So I had another cause on my hands, petitioning the king to rescind his order to the sheriff, which I did on the grounds that it was delaying my suit and it was putting my soul in danger, as I might die in sin. Though I won, that set me back a few months. Then, though, I had good fortune. Walter lost his suit against my uncle and aunt, which made me laugh, because he might have won if he had only been more temperate. The justices ruled against him because he'd accused my aunt as well as my uncle and they said no female could ravish another female.

After that I made my peace with Aunt Juliana, which was a joy to me. And I had a triumph of my own, as the church court ruled that because of Walter's violence I needn't return to him, which was a great respite. Then I heard Walter had appealed over the church court in Lincoln to stop me getting my divorce, and he'd sent a plea direct to Rome. I answered with a new suit of my own, for money for my living, which he should have been giving me, and when he didn't pay I sued for him to be excommunicated, which the court agreed. After that I hungered each day for news to come that he'd drowned in a river or been kicked dead by his horse and, being cast out of the church, he was gone straight to hell, but it never came, and it wasn't long before he wriggled his way back into the church's communion.

Law wasn't the only way he assailed me. Once when I was riding back from Lincoln and yet another day in court, I'd just reached the way that led up to the manor house when I noticed something white hanging from a tree. It was a sheep tied by its back legs, its throat freshly cut and dripping red onto the ground below. The bailiff said it was from our little flock that we kept on the hill above the house. I had the steward Alwyn ask every delver in the village if they'd seen strangers but none had. After that I brought two more thralls into my household, not because they were needed but so I felt safer. When I went to court at Lincoln I'd always take Alwyn along with me, and Jack the cook, who was a big strong fellow, and three others, and I never went out alone even for a stroll round the moat.

I'm not asking for pity as it might've been a good deal worse for me, as I soon learned myself. One day I was riding over Gate Bridge at Lincoln, on my way to court once again, when I saw a woman walking the other way whose face I knew, and it was dear Eleanor, with whom I'd played Lancelot and Guinevere all those years ago. What with Walter and everything else that had happened I hadn't seen her since she'd left us, and I hardly recognized her as, though she was younger than me, I swear she looked seven years older. She told me her tale, which wasn't a happy one. Like me she'd been an heiress and though her heritage wasn't very much, being only two manors, still it had been enough to bruise her life. After she left us and went back to her family she was walking in an orchard close by the house when four men jumped out from behind the wall and seized her. So she fell into the hands of one of the worst malefactors in the county, Albin of Snarford, who took poor Eleanor to a pond and dunked her head under the water so she thought she'd drown, till she finally spoke up and agreed to wed his son, which was done before witnesses. Eleanor's father went to the king's court and with time he won her back but by then she was already with child, a little boy who was frisking about beside her on the bridge. It was no wonder she looked older. 'My father's looking for a new husband for me,' she said. 'I just hope he finds a good man.'

Her story made me more anguished than before and that was what sent my days on their next turn. My uncle and aunt, being warmer towards me again, now that they weren't feared of finding themselves in jail, bid me come to their oldest boy's wedding, and that was where I met Everard de Lessingstone. I knew him, as his father had been a tenant of my father's and Everard had been Father's ward for a time, just before my father died, though he'd changed since then and was now grown into a tall, strong, handsome fellow. He'd heard all about my leaving Walter but didn't cast blame onto me, like some did, but was very tender, and said he'd always thought Walter a foul brute. When I told him about poor Pepin and the dead sheep, and that I was anguished even to leave the manor house, he gave me a look that was full of care. 'Let me come and guard you,' he said. 'It would be an honour to watch over such a seemly and noble lady.' He'd ask for nothing but bed and board, he said. 'I'll be your very own mercenary, paid with lunch and dinner,' he said, which made me laugh. So I gave my assent.

Uncle Marmaduke said I was being very foolish. Everard was a second son with no fortune to his name, he said, so all he was thinking of was getting mine, while the last thing I should do now, when I was battling Walter in every courtroom of Lincoln City, was to become sinfully and adulterously entangled with another. 'Everard knows he can't have my fortune,' I answered him, 'as I'm still married to Walter.' As for the rest, Everard was to guard me and nothing else. Or so I thought. But then when Everard was in my home, strutting about with his sword, looking grave as he hurried to keep watch from the battlements, or marched off to tour the grounds, it was hard not to wonder. One evening we stayed up late, just the two of us, drinking ale and then mead and then a bottle of malmsey wine that I'd been keeping, and Everard grew very hot about Walter, saying he was a wicked man who deserved to die. He'd go himself, he said, carefully so nobody saw, and he'd slay him. 'I'll be doing a favour to all Lincolnshire,' he said, 'as he's loathed by all. It'll be like killing a wolf.' If Walter was gone there was no denying that my life would be a good deal sweeter. Not that I said Everard should do such a thing but I didn't say he mustn't. His fervour made me warm, which he saw, and when the last of the malmsey wine was drunk, without so much as a word, but just with looks, we'd reached an accord and we went up together to my bedchamber. We were there till dawn. Everard wasn't a brute like Walter, nor too sudden like Geoffrey, and we had a very merry night of it, as busy as a pair of ferrets.

Everyone in the household knew, of course. Brigit, who was never one to reproach me, just gave me a look and asked, 'Are you tired this morning, my lady?' while I could see the other thralls smirking at each other. Father Tim was sour, which was no surprise, as I'd seen the looks he'd give me when he thought I wasn't watching. He had a good mind to tell the archdeacon, he said, but he never did, and though I had to say a hundred and twenty Hail Marys he gave me absolution. I knew what I'd done wasn't righteous but I couldn't think God would look on it so very harshly. After all, he was the one who'd made us and had given us the power to love and had made it so very sweet. Everybody said Walter was one of the devil's chicks so how could God be angry with me for finding a brave protector? Once Everard had settled Walter I'd be free and the two of us could marry so I wouldn't be adulterous any more. In the meantime, though I knew our being bedfellows wasn't exactly right, at least it would make him more earnest to keep me safe.

Except that it didn't, so I found out. The freer he was to visit my chamber in the night, the less troubled he seemed about guarding me. Now we were lovers he hardly ever went up to the battlements to keep watch, or toured the grounds, and when I asked him when he'd do so, he'd tell me, 'In a little while, my Kitten,' which was his endearment for me. 'See how it's raining? I'm sure Walter won't come in this.' Soon the only walking he did, aside from up to my bedchamber, was from his chair by the fireplace to the dinner table, where he helped himself so freely that he was already growing quite corpulent. If Walter does come, I thought to myself, I'm not sure Everard will still fit in his leather coat.

It was my next visit to the king's court in Lincoln that parted us. When I told him, 'You'll come with me, of course,' he screwed up his eyes like he had a headache. 'I don't feel well,' he said. 'I'll come with you next time, that I promise, Kitten.' Being in no mood for honey I told him if he didn't come then I'd throw him out of my house, and when he answered with more coaxing and excuses, that's what I did. It was only after he took himself away, looking surly and hardly giving me a goodbye, that I discovered what he'd taken and what he'd left. A gold ring of mine was gone as well as a pretty necklace and two silver goblets. As for what he'd left, another thing that I missed was my bleed that month.

'Look on the bright side,' Brigit told me, trying to cheer me up like usual. 'There's nothing that will vex Walter more. Now the whole county will know that it wasn't your womb that God made dry and barren but his sorry little member.' Looking back, I suppose I shouldn't be too angry with Everard. True, he was a liar, a thief, a coward and a glutton who gave me yet another cause to fight in the king's court, which was to get my goods back, though I never did see the two silver goblets again. But he gave me my beautiful boy, Peter, which was the best gift I had in all my days.

And for that matter it was thanks to him that I met Fulke, who was the one I loved most dearly of all my husbands and paramours, at least for a time. It happened that Walter must have heard about Everard and me, and though Everard was gone from my house by then that didn't stop the church court from accusing me of adultery. The archdeacon said I must walk barefoot to Humby church and back, I must pay sixty marks to the canons of Lincoln Minster for the roof, and I must stand all night in Little Hugh's chapel in Lincoln Minster praying for forgiveness, holding a lighted candle and wearing only my underclothes. Though I wasted no time paying the canons and walking to Humby and back, I put off the night vigil till after little Peter was born. When I did finally go I brought Father Tim and all my thralls, from Alwyn my steward to Jack the cook, to awe any troublers, as the sight of a noble sinner shamed will always summon up a foul-minded crowd. It went well enough too, and though some jeered they kept to their places behind the screen and as curfew hour drew near they drifted back to their homes.

It was only when they'd gone that I took proper heed of the other one who was doing penitence in the chapel. I'd seen him before, which was no surprise, the gentle folk of Lincoln county being a small world. And though I couldn't recall his name I liked the sight of him, as he was a strong fellow, no denying, and looked very comely standing there in his unders. Seeing as I was supposed to be praying all night I could hardly start gabbling with the fellow, especially with Father Tim frowning at me, but after a while, as I grew weary of repenting my unrights, which I'd done forty times over, it came to me that I might make a little chatter with him, not straightly, but through my prayers. So I said in a clear, loud voice, 'Please, dear God, forgive me my wickedness and tell me, I beg you, who is this good fellow doing his penitence just beside me?' God heard, or at least my neighbour did and he prayed back, 'Dearest God, please forgive your poor sinner Fulke de Barnetby, and I beg you, tell me the name of the lovely dame confessing her sins here this night.'

So, though it was all done by way of our Lord, we had a good long chatter. I learned he was a widower with no heirs, as his wife and baby had both died in childbirth, poor creatures. He'd just come back from the Welsh war where he'd fought several skirmishes and had been given a shilling by his captain for cleaving a Welshman's head in two with one blow of his sword. Fighting was certainly his way and his penitence was for battling three churls who'd reviled him in an alehouse and whom he'd wounded, all three of them, though he'd fought them alone. He may not be rich, I thought, which was true, as he told me himself that he was a second son, with no land to his name and not even a thrall to ride at his side, but he's a true Lancelot. Better still, when I told God I was seeking a divorce from Walter de Kingerby and why, Fulke let out a jeer. Then he prayed to God to say that he was a near neighbour of Walter's and that they'd got into a bad dispute over a horse and that he hated the man with all his heart. Nor did he like Everard. At dawn, when I felt light-hearted from praying all night, the two of us walked out together and down to the river where, very suddenly, so it seemed like it was something willed by God himself, we kissed. Fulke vowed to avenge me for all the ills I'd suffered at Walter's hands. Then we kissed once again and he was gone.

After my dealings with that worthless dastard Everard I was doubtful anything much would come of Fulke's words, but how wrong I was. A week later he came to visit me at Ropsley and, full of gladness, he told me his news. He'd found Walter in a hostel in Lincoln, he said, where he was staying as he plotted to make more trouble for me in the king's court. Fulke had challenged him to a combat for insulting the honour of my name and they'd fought. Walter, soon seeing himself beaten, had turned and run and Fulke had cut him right in his buttock. 'He won't sit down easily for a good long while,' he told me, laughing. For good measure he'd then found Everard who, as chance would have it, was also in Lincoln, staying in a cheap tavern, where Fulke had beaten him black and blue with his fists. That night, in spite of Father Tim's sour looks, it seemed only right to show Fulke all my thanks, seeing as I'd given them freely to Everard, who'd done nothing.

But I didn't have to put up with Father Tim's scowls for long. Walter wasted no time setting the courts at us. In the king's court he sued Fulke for wounding him in the arse, which was false, as Fulke had challenged him rightfully and Walter had accepted his challenge. Then he set the church court on me. The archdeacon ordered me to go as a sister to Stixwould nunnery to repent my adultery with Fulke. As if I'd give myself to life with a lot of crabbed sisters? The two of us fled Ropsley and became outlaws. Uncle Marmaduke and Aunt Juliana kept us for a time and so did other kin and friends, and every week or two we'd move to a new hiding place. I well remember our night-time journeys, riding by the light of the moon, just the four of us – Fulke, me, my dear little baby boy Peter, and another in my womb, who was Fulke's.

Strange to say, it was when my flight came to an end that my troubles truly began. Uncle Marmaduke knew one of the clerks at the church court and with the help of a few shillings a new judgment was given. If I walked barefoot again to Humby and back and gave another sixty marks to Lincoln Minster, I'd not have to go to the nuns after all. I was joyed at that news. But poor Fulke wasn't so lucky and had to stay in hiding. There were plenty of lurking places in Ropsley manor house so I said he should stay there and that was where sorrow struck us. First God took my baby, who came too soon. She was a girl, poor little lamb. God nearly took me too, as I bled and bled, and afterwards it seemed like everything in the world was grey and sorry. I looked to Fulke for comfort, which he gave for a few days but then it was like his compassion leaked away. I suppose he wasn't the kind to be penned. Instead of showing me love he'd get vexed over small things, and would fall into a great rage if he didn't like the hay his horse was fed, or how his clothes had been washed. I brought a minstrel to stay for a week and play for us, thinking that would cheer him up, but it made things worse. Fulke said I'd couched with the fellow secretly and though I told him that was false, as all I'd done was talk with him, and that only because the minstrel showed me more pity than my paramour had, it did no good, as by then jealousy had got into Fulke's heart and wouldn't leave him be. He said the minstrel had stolen his boots and he beat him half to death, though of course the boots were found later. Then, the very next evening, Fulke got drunk on ale and put his hand to my face.

I knew what I had to do. Having been married first to a rabbit and then to a wolf, and then taking a thieving idler into my bed, I'd found love – despite of all he'd done I loved Fulke still – and I wasn't going to let it be ruined by the devil. It must be undone so it could be kept alive forever, if only in my own remembrance. It so happened that Brigit had a cousin in Ryhall who knew the lore that I needed, so Brigit paid her a visit and the next morning the two of us went together for a long walk in the woods, and then to Lincoln, to collect all that we needed. Late one night when the others in the household were fast asleep, we went down to the kitchen and boiled it all into a potion that came out like Brigit's cousin said it should, being thick and dark like black gravy. After that I told Fulke I'd heard word that the sheriff's men would come looking for him so he must stay in the cellar. I brought him his stew and sops myself, adding just a few drops of the potion, like Brigit's cousin had said. Sure enough before long he was spewing and squirting like he had dysentery, or a canker in his bowels, and though it pained me to see him so, I was joyous too, because as he grew weaker his rage eased away and my love could flow once more. I'd kiss his cheek and stroke his fevered head and tell him I'd made a special medicine to cure him, and of course I'd always add a few more drops of the black gravy. Being the dear he was, he drank it all down without complaint, answering my smile with one of his own.

One rainy April afternoon, after the physician had come for the seventh time and had left as confounded as ever, I knew it was almost done. I had the thralls carry Fulke up to my bedchamber, I sent Brigit away so we were alone and it couldn't have gone more sweetly. By then Fulke was so weak that he could hardly murmur a word. I slid into the bed and when I climbed on top of him, feeling how frail he was as he struggled to breathe beneath me, it was a curious thing, because the touch of him, all bones and no flesh, made me think of my dear little Pepin. 'See,' I whispered, giving him a smile, 'now our love will live forever. Now nothing can ever spoil it.' I saw his eyes open wider as he finally understood, but I was quick and before he could ruin things I reached out with my fingers and squeezed his nostrils closed, and then I gave him my kiss. And though he tried to bite me, poor dear, he was so gone by then that his teeth just trembled around my tongue.

Afterwards I had to confess it. Seeing as what it was, I imagined Father Tim would tell his bishop, which would mean a nunnery for me, or even hanging. He might have, being a veritable man, except that he'd always hated Fulke. He said my sin was grave indeed but was lessened because Fulke had been so wild of nature, which meant I'd done it not from malice but to preserve my own life. Then he gave me fasting twice a week for six months and praying all night in our chapel four times. After that Fulke's older brother came knocking on the gate, which I feared would be the end of me, but he hardly asked about Fulke. All he wanted was his horse and the rest of his things.

After that came sorry days. Though I had no regrets as to what had been done and I'd certainly have done it again, the house seemed sad and empty with him gone. And I had fears. At night I'd dream that Walter and an army of men were climbing the walls of the house on ladders, or that he was already inside and was creeping his way towards my chamber. Most of all I was scared for my little boy, Peter. Though he was always kicking up a noise asking to be allowed to play in the wood I wouldn't let him outside the manor house wall. I dreaded paying my visits to the courts and Lincoln and I'd take every thrall I could. Though this gave me another fear, that Walter would come to Ropsley while I was away, and I'd return home to find it burned to the ground.

Brigit tried to give me comfort. 'You have your boy, you have a fine house and everyone in your household would do anything for you. It could all be a good deal worse.' Which was true, as I saw twice over a few weeks later when a visitor came knocking at the gate. It was Eleanor, though it took a moment or two to know her, as she was changed even more than the last time. She'd always had a pretty plumpness to her but now her face was drawn, while her clothes, though not rags, were worn and threadbare. 'Dame Lucy,' she greeted me with a sorry smile. 'I stand here shamed before you. I've come to ask if you might lend me two shillings.'

So she told me her news, which was worse even than before. Life had treated her well at first. Her father had found her a husband, George, who'd been a good man just as she'd hoped, kindly and lovesome, and she soon gave him three healthy, noisy babies. When her father died it turned out she wasn't an heiress after all, as he'd gambled away his little fortune, but Eleanor wasn't too troubled, being happy with George, who made enough as a trader to keep them. Then one day a writ came from the church court. A brewster woman from Grantham named Susan said she'd lain with George before he'd married Eleanor and that she'd had his child. None of this was a surprise to Eleanor as George, being honest and goodly, had told her all about it when they'd first met. It had all been drunken foolishness, he said, and he and Susan had only couched a few times. He knew it had been wrong and he'd shrived it all to the priest and done his penance.

Now, though, Susan claimed that George had promised her marriage before he swived her, and in front of witnesses too, which was enough to make her and George lawfully wedded in the church's eyes. George tried his best and he told the church court Susan was telling lies but it was no use and the archdeacon took her word against his. So Eleanor's marriage was nulled and, though she and her husband were sobbing, the court ordered her from his house and told George he must take the brewster woman into his bed. As for his three children, who were to go with their mother Eleanor, they were all named bastards. 'George and I were both in tears,' Eleanor told me. 'Even Susan the brewster was sobbing and she told us none of it had been her wish, but that the church had demanded it be done so righteousness could prevail. As if this is righteous?' The only one who'd take Eleanor in was a seamstress cousin of hers, though her home was very small and it wasn't easy for her and the children. They all helped out with the stitching and mending but it hardly brought in a farthing. 'I didn't want to come,' Eleanor said, trying to keep herself proud, though I could see she was close to tears. 'But if I don't do something my children will go hungry next week, and I'd rather be shamed than endure that.' I gave her six shillings and I was glad to.

Poor Eleanor's tale helped me decide what road I'd take next. That evening I knelt down in our little chapel and prayed: 'Dear God, I know I've not always been as righteous as I should have. I choked my first husband to death, though that was only an accident, and I left my second, creeping out at dawn. I was adulterous with Everard and had his child, and I urged Fulke to do harm to both men, and then I took Fulke's life with the black gravy and my kiss. But it was all done only from love, which is a goodly thing that you yourself put in my heart. So I beg you please, kindly God, let me live quietly now with my dear boy. And give me my divorce so I can get my lands back and throw Walter out of Bourne Castle, as I can't abide the thought of him strutting about my home.'

But the clamour must've been too loud again. True, I was left in peace. I did my lordly duties and when there was new trouble in Wales from another traitor, Lord Merrydud, I raised a troop to send and I made sure all who didn't go paid their dues. I cared for my wards and had them schooled by Father Tim and I found wives for the older two of them. That was work I much loved and I did well by those two lads. Though they each had only one manor due to them, I scoured the land and didn't settle till I'd found them brides who'd please them, which they seemed to. But all the while instead of growing nearer, my divorce drew ever further away. The archdeacon of the church court at Lincoln died and his place was taken by one of Walter's kin, distant kin but kin still, which would set everything further against me. It seemed like I'd never be free of Walter. And so it was that I, who'd hardly once been outside Lincolnshire, found myself pondering a great journey. The advocate who'd spoken for me in my causes had only one idea remaining. 'You must make a plea to the pope,' he said. 'But not by letter this time,' which I'd tried before, just as I'd tried everything else. 'No, you should go to Rome and plead yourself.' He'd heard that if one went there and made one's plea and paid fees in one's own person it could help a good deal.

Go all the way to Rome? I'd never contemplated such a thing. But I thought on his words for a few days and the more I pondered them the more they seemed to make sense. If there was one lesson I'd learned over the past years it was that there was little use taking a case to the courts of Lincoln unless you went yourself. It would be a hard journey and long, and perhaps dangerous, too, but it would be worth it if I'd finally see Walter thrown out of Bourne Castle, like he should have been years back. For that matter it could serve me well in another way, too. Alongside going for my cause I could also go as a pilgrim. I'd always hoped God would show me forgiveness for my little transgressions with my husbands and Everard and Fulke, seeing as I'd done them all only for love, but there'd be no harm in asking good Saint Peter to put a word in his ear for me. And it could be a joyous thing. I'd take Peter, of course, as I wasn't leaving him behind, and though he was still only four I felt sure he'd like to see all of those fine places. For that matter I'd like to see them myself as, what with all the wrangling I'd had in courts swallowing up my days, the only time I'd stepped outside Lincolnshire was when I'd gone to London to see Earl Henry.

So I made up my mind and started getting prepared. First I chose who should come with me. I'd need Brigit, of course, and Alwyn the steward, who could arrange our wants and drive the cart, which I'd need for my gowns and for food, as who knew what there'd be along the way. Father Tim would be useful for his Latin, which would be understood wherever we went, and he'd be useful again when I made my plea at the papal court. Finally there was Jack our cook, who'd be most helpful if we met trouble. With Peter that made six of us altogether. I had Father Tim write out our testimonials and then I rode to Lincoln and had cloaks and hats and scrips and a stout pair of boots made for us all. And I thought of what foods I might buy to carry in the cart, in case we strayed into a land struck by famine. Grain, certainly, and nuts, and some jam, too, as that would keep.

I was still in the midst of making everything ready when, one August morning, I heard shouting and the watch said there were two fellows outside calling for help. Fearing it might be a trick by Walter I didn't let them in but sent out all my thralls to see, yet Alwyn said they seemed true enough and so I had them brought into the hall. One was a young gentleman named Lionel. He was only just of age by the look of him and was very seemly with a great mane of blonde hair, though he was in a poor way, with a cut to his head and mud on his clothes. The other was his manservant, Dobbe, a big hulking fellow with slow eyes. Lionel was most courteous, repenting that he'd troubled me and for bringing dirt into my fine home. He was from Nottinghamshire, he said, and was a second son, younger brother to Gilbert of Barnby, a name that meant little to me. He'd been on his way to Norwich to visit some kin when a bolt of lightning struck a tree close by the road. 'Our horses reared and we were both thrown,' he told us. Though his leg wasn't broken it was too bruised for him to walk. Nor could he ride, as, though Alwyn and Jack the cook went out searching for their horses, they were nowhere to be found. So I told Lionel he must stay at Ropsley till he was healed, for which he gave all of his thanks. His manservant Dobbe I had put in the barn behind the house and, to show rightful concern, I had Lionel put in the chamber next to mine.

Peter didn't like him, but then he wouldn't, as he always wanted to keep me only to himself. As for the others, I saw them rolling their eyes, especially Father Tim, though he had no right to. I told him myself, 'You're wrong to look so stern, Father Tim, as I know what you're thinking and it isn't so. There's not a thing I need to confess as you won't find a godlier and more righteous man in all Lincolnshire than this poor, injured fellow.' Which I'd found out myself, because I'd thought it only hospitable to pay him a visit or two in his chamber to make sure he was comfortable, and somehow it happened one evening, when I brought him some mead to ease his pain, that we got to talking, and he listened most sorrowfully as I told him about my struggles to win my divorce from Walter, and how I'd soon be leaving to plead my case before the pope's court in Rome. Then I offered him my sympathy for his mishap and somehow our comforts to each other became holding hands, and then our holding hands became embracing, and then our embracing became kisses, and I could feel through the bedclothes that his fellow was up and eager. All at once he let out a little cry, making me fear I'd leaned on his bad leg, but it wasn't that at all. 'Lucy dear, we can't,' he said. Then he confessed to me like a sinner to his priestess, and told me he'd been much taken with me from the moment he'd first set eyes on me, and that he now desired me as much as any man with hot blood in his veins could do, 'but it's not right,' he said. 'What will God think if I couch with another man's wife, even though she's pleading in the courts for a divorce?' There was no moving him. When, just from merriment, I took his hand and pressed it to my belle chose, I heard his breath come quick but then he pulled it back. 'We mustn't, Lucy,' he said. 'It's sinful.'

It felt strange, though, as in all my days I'd never had one who'd said no. Even Geoffrey, my poor rabbit, who'd had no craft for it, would wake me in the night sometimes and have me touch his mushroom and make it squirt. I was used to being the doe and now I was the hunter. Lying in my bed, knowing he was there next door, warm and comely but not to be had, I could hardly sleep, and over the next days the more he said no, the more I wanted him. His leg was mending well and I dreaded the moment when he'd go. But it wasn't only me, as it turned out. After a week Lionel was strong enough to get down to the hall by himself and I saw tears in his eyes. 'I can't bear to leave you, Lucy,' he said, looking at me so sorry and handsome. 'I'd marry you here and now if only you were free.' So we kissed and wept and then I saw he was wondering. 'Here's a mad, wild thought,' he said. 'I have no duties to bind me. I have no kin who need me. What if I journey down to Rome with you? I'd like to go as a pilgrim, which I've never done till now, and to confess my sins before Peter and the other great saints there. I could watch over you on the road, which would be a great joy to me, as there's no work I'd love better. And who knows, if you still feel warm for me when you've won your divorce, as I dearly hope you will, then we can be married rightfully and lawfully in the eyes of God, and in Rome, too, that noble, holy city.'

Of course I said yes and so we made our accord and sealed it there and then with a long, sweet kiss. How modest he was. As Alwyn never had found his or Dobbe's horses, Lionel said he'd walk to Rome, as humble pilgrims did. 'That way I'll be more virtuous and I'll better show my love of God,' he said. But I told him no, I'd buy two horses for him and Dobbe, and likewise, as Lionel's clothes, though they were handsome enough, were not the kind of gear he'd need for a great journey like this, and as he clearly had little silver about him, I got them both new attire, too, and their pilgrim cloaks and scrips. And when he protested that as an honourable man he could not accept such gifts from a lady who was married to another, however much he adored her, I laughed and told him, 'They're not my gifts, then. I'll lend them to you. And when we're married they'll be a part of my wedding gift to you.'

I'd have liked to take him to meet Uncle Marmaduke and other kin of mine but he had to go and tell his brother of his new plans, while it was already almost harvest time, which was late in the season to leave. I'd feared we'd be slowed even more, as I was sure that Walter would've heard word of my journey and would put in a plea to the king's court to stop me going, on the grounds that I was still his wife and needed his accord, but no, for once he left me be. One late September morning, a week after he'd gone, Lionel came back to Ropsley and the very next morning we all set out. What a strange feeling it was to be with a man who wasn't hated by all of my household. Brigit, who'd loathed every fellow I'd been with, seemed quite tranquil about Lionel, while Father Tim, though he didn't much like him, was still in wonder that he hadn't had to confess me a score of times. Even my Peter didn't scowl at him much. When we rode out of Ropsley and I turned to give the manor house one last look, I vowed to myself, when I next see this view I'll be riding beside my handsome new husband, and all the afflictions I've endured over the years will be remedied once and for all.

South we went, along Ermine Street. Father Tim was most knowledgeable and wherever we stopped he'd tell us, in his voice that sounded like bees humming, all about the town we'd reached, how many towers and gates and churches it had and what crafts it was known for. I'll confess I hardly heard a word, as I'd be watching Lionel, and my remembrances of each spot were all of him. Alconbury was Lionel on his horse as we rode into the town, the evening sun catching his comely blue eyes. London was Lionel puffing out his chest on the ferry over the Thames, which we had to take as Alwyn the steward said London Bridge was too crowded and narrow for our cart. Canterbury was Lionel springing off his horse and giving his seemly arse a slap to get the dust off his hose. As for the Channel crossing, which wasn't so bad as I'd feared, as we left Dover at first light and were in Calais well before dark, while the only one who was seasick was Father Tim, that was Lionel standing in the rowboat as we were taken across Calais harbour from our ship, and his flicking his long fair hair out of his face as the wind blew it this way and that.

So we'd reached France. How strange it was to find French, which I'd only ever heard from the mouths of gentle folk or churchmen or advocates in Lincoln courts, spoken by every soul, low and high. 'Here we are at our first French inn,' I said to Lionel that evening. Then a notion came to me. Because it happened that, rather than having dormitories, like most of them did, this inn had little rooms. What was more now that we were gone from England it struck me that all those court rulings didn't matter so very much. How could they, seeing as we were in a different land? So, after we drank down our sixth ale and I toasted our arriving in France once again, I said to Lionel, 'Here's a thought, my dear love. We have two little rooms. Why don't we put Brigit and your man Dobbe in yours, my Peter can go with them, and we can take mine, not to do anything wicked but just to lie together side by side and perhaps have a kiss or two.' Which got me a scowl from Brigit, who didn't want to be with that big glob of a fellow, Lionel's manservant. But she needn't have worried, as then Lionel smiled sorrowfully and shook his head. 'Lucy, you know that's not right,' he said. 'When we lie together it must be as man and wife, with God's smile shining on us both. Nothing else will do.'

How righteous he is, I thought as we rode on the next day, my head sore from all the ale I'd drunk, and as thin drizzle stung my face. How very noble and godly and pure. The country here was so dreary. Though it seemed like we'd already been travelling for an age since Ropsley, I knew we'd hardly begun and I found it hard to imagine how I'd endure journeying all the way to Rome. Brigit, riding her little rounsey beside me, kept singing a foolish song that made my head ache worse, and then Father Tim droned in his bee voice, telling us all about our next stopping place, which was called Taruenna, and which had a fine cathedral, he said, along with several churches and which was home to a good number of cloth makers. As if I cared a worm what wretched trade was done there? All I wanted was that it should hurry up and show itself. Mile after mile of flat we rode through and there was no sign of anything but rain, till finally we came in sight of a crossroads. 'It won't be far now,' said Father Tim, looking anxious, as I'd scolded him for being wrong before. 'Remember the fellow with the pig? He said it was soon after a crossroads.'

'Look,' said Alwyn the steward. 'Another party of pilgrims.' Following the point of his finger I saw a group of walkers were making their way towards the crossroads from one of the side roads and though they were still a way off I could make out their cloaks and hats. They were a good-sized fellowship, all on foot except one little maid who was riding an ass. 'They're sure to be dreary,' said Lionel. 'Let's hurry on.' But what did he know about these folk? 'D'you know,' I said, 'I'd like to meet them. It would make a change to see some new faces.' And though Lionel rolled his blue eyes I paid him no heed and sent Father Tim over. A few moments later he came back with the news that they were all English. None were gentle folk aside from one fellow who had only one manor, they were bound for Rome like us, they hadn't come from Calais, as we had, because their ship had been blown off course, and they were most eager to meet me. 'I think we heard about them,' I said, because I remembered that at Canterbury and Dover there'd been talk of another Rome party that had gone by just before us. 'At the very least we should travel with them to Taruenna, seeing as we're almost there,' I said to Lionel, and though he gave me a sorry look to say, must we really, that was what we did.

Just as Father Tim had said, none were of high parage and the one gentleman among them, John of Baydon, could have been one of my tenants, swaggering about and looking like he'd fight anyone who so much as brushed against his elbow. Yet I rather liked this fellowship, even though they were little folk of no rank. As we rode the short distance to Taruenna a rich delver named Margaret trotted along beside my horse, eager to make herself my friend, and she was very jolly as she told me about all the others in her party. 'Whatever you do, take no notice of him,' she said, pointing at a weaselly fellow with tiny eyes, 'as he's an idiot. I should know as he's my husband,' which made me laugh. She was right, though, as he was most anoyful, asking me three times over if I wasn't fearful that all the fine things in my cart might be stolen by robbers. Another one I didn't much like was the Margate tailor, Warin, whose daughter rode the ass, and whom God had chosen to make her his voice, as Margaret told me. My father always said that tailors were trouble. 'Just because they know how to sew a seam they think they should rule the whole world,' he'd tell me. Though Warin's daughter seemed amicable enough and she complimented me on my gown, saying how very seemly it was.

I laughed out loud when Margaret told me the boy Tom was going all the way to Rome for his dead cat. Yet if you looked past his rags and the dirt on his face he was quite comely in a way. The one who was handsomest was the sorrowful advocate, Jocelyn, who'd been a famous fornicator, Margaret said, which I could well believe. What really caught my notice, though, was when she told me about the amour that was going on in her little fellowship. 'Just look at them,' she said, casting a glance behind her. 'We'll have wedding bells soon, mark my words.' Sure enough there they were, walking side by side, Sir John's son Gawayne and the butcher's daughter Helena. 'Their parents are most eager,' said Margaret, which I could see was right, as I saw Helena's mother Mary was gabbling away with Gawayne's olders.

Margaret had the weather of those two all right. 'Sir John'll be after Mary's silver,' she said, 'as he looks like he has little enough himself.' She told me he was going as a pilgrim to Rome as penance for punching an abbot, and all over a quarter of an acre of meadow. I had tenants like him, abiding in their little dark manor houses with rain coming through the roof and mould on their hangings. And Mary was rich, Margaret said. Her dead husband's butcher's shop was the best in Gloucester and she lived in one of the finest houses in the city. 'She's strange, though,' said Margaret. 'There's something not right about her. I can't quite put my finger on it but it's like she's not natural.' There was an anguish about her, certainly. It was there in her smile that never seemed to leave her face. I couldn't stop myself from looking back and taking another glance at the two sweethearts. How attentive Gawayne was, chattering to her and casting her little glances as they walked. As for her, she was all modesty, not saying a word and keeping her comely eyes down on the ground.

What I liked best about this party, though, was little Paul, the adulteress Constance's boy. Though Margaret told me he was very sick he seemed well enough to me and, finding there was another boy in the party, he hurried over to Peter, riding in our cart. That Peter was just four and Paul was twice his age didn't seem to matter, they got to talking and before long my Peter asked, shyly being the younger one, if Paul wanted to join him on the cart, which Paul did, and in a moment they were laughing and making foolish sport like they'd been best friends for years. Paul and Peter. Peter and Paul. The very thought made me catch my breath. It could hardly be chance that they had the very same names as Rome's great saints, whom we were journeying to visit.

We reached Taruenna, where we were greeted by a low fellow who was so offended by the pilgrimager Oswald's pipe playing – and I'm not saying it was good – that he pulled down his breeches and showed us his arse. Otherwise, though, it was a fine enough place. That evening in the hospital where we all stayed I sat watching as Peter and Paul scampered about, laughing and shrieking as they played chase. 'I like this party,' I said to Lionel. 'I think we should keep with them.' He frowned.

'But my dear, sweet love, just think how they'll slow us down,' he said. 'We're on horseback and they're on foot.' Which wasn't rightly true, as with our cart we'd travel hardly faster than they could. 'We'll be safer with them,' I told him, 'and the journey will pass more quickly if we have some company.' Then I told him how it could be no accident that the two boys had the same names as Rome's saints. 'That's a sign if ever there was one,' I said. 'It's God telling us we should journey with them all.' Which he had no answer for as there's no gainsaying God.

The next morning when we broke our fast I asked the others if we might journey with them and, aside from sour Warin, they were all most eager. 'It'll be a great honour,' said Sir John, and his little wife Alice gave an excited nod of her head. So our two fellowships became one. We followed the road to a town named Brouay, and along the way Margaret's husband Hugh, the anoyful one, went to piss in a field and was butted by a ram so his arse was bruised black and blue, which I shouldn't have laughed at but I did. Then we went on to another town named Arras, where Lionel's glob of a manservant Dobbe lost his boot down the latrine, which I laughed at too. All the while I gave thought to Gawayne and Helena. If they were going to be wed soon, as Margaret thought, then why not do it in Rome? If I could win my divorce speedily, as I dearly hoped I would, then they could have a double wedding with Lionel and me. When I told Lionel he made a joke of it, of course, saying that one wedding was enough for him, but the more I thought about the notion the more it pleased me.

Unless God wanted more weddings even than this? I'd had such joy finding brides for my wards back at Ropsley and I'd done it very well, as I thought. So my mind turned to whom else God might want married alongside us. Father Tim was no use of course and I had no wish to lose my Brigit, while there was no woman I'd want to torment with Lionel's idiot lump Dobbe. Among our new travelling friends, though, there were a number who might be wed to one another. The pairing that struck me right away was Jocelyn the advocate and Constance, the mother of poor, sickly Paul. They had much in common after all. Jocelyn was a widower and Constance was a widow, each had a decent fortune, both were seemly looking and each had a sorriness of spirit to them, which was no surprise considering their sad tales. For that matter they were united also in their sin, both being fornicators. All in all I found it surprising that a bond hadn't already formed between them.

After that it was more difficult and yet, I thought, not beyond hope. Oswald was a bachelor and was well ripe for marriage, if not overripe. In truth I couldn't see why he wasn't already wed as he looked well past thirty. Margaret said he'd had a wife once who'd died but that had been many years back and was little excuse now. He had no money to his name nor any real work. Margaret said he had a trade as a carpenter but he hardly attended to it as he was always going as a pilgrim for dead folk. He was a funny-looking fellow with so little flesh on him that he seemed almost like a skeleton with skin, and of course there was his foul pipe playing, yet he was godly as well, seeing as he'd visited almost every saint in Christendom. Beatrix was too young for marriage and had that hateful father, Warin the tailor, but I might pair Oswald with Constance's sister Joan. Though she was richer than him she wasn't so very rich, and nor was she comely like Constance. Or I could wed Oswald to fair Helena's mother, Mary. True, Mary was far wealthier than Oswald was, which would likely set her against him, and yet the anguished look I'd seen on her face told me she might find comfort in a husband, however poor and starved-looking he was. Of course then Joan would be left all alone, poor creature. What a shame it was that Warin wasn't a widower too, as then, however irksome he was, he might be put to use. As things stood I saw no hope of coupling up Mary and Joan both at once.

Or was there? On the morning we left the town of Arras Father Tim led us round the city, showing us the minster and the abbey and droning to us in his bee voice about how the town was well known for its tapestry makers. A boy was following us about begging and I opened my scrip to give him a small coin so he'd let us be, but then Lionel, who couldn't abide beggars, told me I shouldn't. 'Don't,' he said. 'It's throwing good money away, as no good will ever come of a misborn grub like that.' Why Father Tim grew so warm about it all I can't say. I suppose he thought Lionel had been uncourteous to interrupt his droning talk, while he'd never liked him. He stopped telling us about the tapestry makers and gainsaid Lionel instead. 'That's not true,' he said. 'Poor though he is, this little lad may find his way. If he follows God and keeps to the path of righteousness, he'll find paradise before many an earl or king.'

I slipped the boy a little coin but that didn't stop their squabble, which took us right around Arras and which was about the moulding of man. Lionel said men were forged by their elders and it was God's will that a child born of noble parents would be noble in spirit, while one born of rude, churl parents would grow up churlish and rude. Which was true enough, I thought. Father Tim, being riled, answered quite wildly and said that even the highest-born lord, if he followed a road of wickedness and sin, was lower than a beetle in the eyes of God. Though I didn't want to provoke him worse I couldn't help but laugh at that. 'God will always love a lord above a beetle,' I said, giving him a little look to remind him who gave him his supper and ale each night.

I'd hoped that would be the finish of it but no, now all the rest joined in. Sir John, being a sensible fellow, for all his rough ways, favoured Lionel, while of course Warin the tailor spoke with Father Tim, and then Hugh the planter added his usual idiot trespasses. 'Would you say a bailiff has a noble sort of labour?' he asked. Lionel shrugged. 'I wouldn't say it's ignoble.' 'And what of a poor bondsman?' Hugh asked next. 'There's nothing lower than that,' Lionel answered scornfully. Which was true, no denying, though I felt a little sorry he'd said it in front of the rag boy Tom, who was a bondsman himself, and who looked like he'd been stung on the nose by a wasp. 'Well, here's a thing,' said Hugh with a little goading laugh. 'You see, my grandfather was a poor bondsman while my eldest son is a bailiff who can read and write as well as any man. And for all that we know his son or grandson may become lord of his own manor.'

As if that proved anything at all? But Father Tim clapped his hands like he'd won a great victory. 'You see,' he said. And so our war moved to a new battlefield, which was learning. Father Tim said that anyone, however poor and low he was, could become a great philosopher if he was taught well enough, which Lionel said was pure folly. 'I tell you now,' he said, 'a bondsman in rags who spends his days digging up parsnips and shitting in his own strips can never be a philosopher. He'd never even be able to learn his letters, because God, who knows the rightful order of all things, wouldn't permit it.' And that was how we came to a wager. 'I'll show you you're wrong,' said Father Tim, his eyes burning, 'and I'll take your silver doing it, too, unless you're scared to risk your money. I bet you thruppence that by the time we reach Rome I'll have taught this little fellow to read and to write.' With that he pointed at the ragged boy Tom, who looked confounded like he didn't know what to think. Lionel was so handsome when he was angry. He had to accept the wager, of course, after being taunted like that. 'I accept your bet,' he said. 'And though I'll be sorry to take thruppence from a poor clerk who has hardly a penny in his scrip, I'll have it.'

So it was agreed. Father Tim would try and teach the rag boy Tom his letters by the time we reached Rome. Though my heart was with Lionel I'll own that a part of me rather hoped Father Tim might win the wager, if only because it could be very useful for my pairing plans. As I saw it, if Tom could be schooled to read and write then even he might find a bride. Joan, being ten years older, not rich and the most unlovely in our party, might take him. Of course being a bondsman he couldn't wed without his master giving his accord, but a way might be found. I counted them out on my fingers. Lionel and me, Gawayne and Helena, Oswald and Mary, and then Tom and Joan. That would make four weddings in Rome. Lionel and mine would be the finest, of course, and the rest would be quite simple, but having so many would be a most merry thing.

That very same morning when Father Tim and Lionel made their wager I saw a way I might help advance matters and which, at the same time, would answer a little conundrum that I'd been having with myself, which was how Tom would look if he was cleaned up. We were about to leave Arras when we came to a clothes market and, feigning that I couldn't bear to think of Tom freezing to death in his rags when we crossed the great mountains that lay ahead, I said I wanted to buy him some new attire, and though Lionel scowled, I suppose because he felt I was favouring Father Tim's side of the bet, and Tom said no seven times over, I insisted, saying he must take them or he'd be gainsaying a lady. So I got him a simple shirt and a tunic and a new pair of hose. I made him wash in the river, which he did most anxiously, as he probably hadn't bathed properly since he'd first come into this world. Being so used to his familiar rags, he seemed scared of his new gear, putting it all on slowly and suspectingly like it might take a bite out of him. Even then he still didn't seem finished. When my eye fell on a barber's stall close by, I knew what must be done and, though by then the rest of them were impatient to be on their way, I was steadfast that Tom must have his hair cut as well, as it was now out of step with his clothes. I swear that changed him more than his new gear. Before then he'd had a delver haircut that looked like a hat made of mud, but now his hair sprang up like grass. For a moment we all stood staring, amazed. As I'd thought he might, Ragged Tom looked handsome and, if not a gentleman, he seemed at least like a gracious, honest fellow.

Now it'll be easy, I thought. All I needed to do was praise them to one another. Gawayne and Helena I didn't trouble with, as by Margaret's account they were as good as betrothed already, but over the next days, as we journeyed on, sometimes dry and sometimes soaked by the rain, passing through more dreary, flat country then through cheerier, hilly land, and as they all moaned about their sore feet and the sneezes they'd got from being so wetted, all the way I told Constance how handsome Jocelyn was, and how full of grief, and that what he most needed was a good woman to bring joy back to his life. To Jocelyn I said how fair Constance was and how she wanted for a husband who'd help her and her son. To Mary I said what a fine, godly man Oswald was and how helpful he'd be around the house, making a chair or a table or mending things that were broken. To Oswald I said how warm-hearted Mary was, and how lucky any man would be to live in her big home in Gloucester, and to eat any tasty pieces of meat that found no buyers at her butcher's shop. Finally to plain Joan I said how handsome Tom looked in his new clothes, and how young and healthy he was, and how he'd bring warmth to any woman's marriage bed. And to Tom I said how lucky any man would be to have as much ale as he pleased from Joan's brewing. I swear, though, it was like herding a flock of sheep that all scampered away the moment your back was turned. Though they all listened to me patiently enough, I didn't see them talk to each other, let alone gaze into each other's eyes.

What was needed, I decided, was to take all my paramours away from the rest of the party so they'd be more alone. Constance wouldn't look at anybody if her boy Paul was nearby, nor would Mary if she was with her daughter Helena. The problem was how it might be done. Then, at the pilgrim hostel at Lauon, which was a dirty place like they usually were, we met three Frenchwomen, and when I asked if they were going to Rome like us they laughed and said no, they were only going to Saint Joseph's church, which was very close by, so they'd be there and back tomorrow. All three were widows, they told us, and as Saint Joseph was the saint of husbands and families they were going to pray to him for their dead spouses. That very moment I saw it clear. This was what we all had in common. The two sisters, Constance and Joan, were both widows, I was a widow, and Mary was a widow twice over, while Jocelyn was a widower and so was Oswald, if from years back. Tom wasn't, of course, but I was sure there'd be a way I could sneak one more aboard.

That night I lay awake in my bed in the dormitory, fighting off biters and thinking. The only way I could see it might be done was with a little lie, which wouldn't be sin seeing as it would be told out of goodness. The next morning, as I heard them all stirring awake, I called out, 'My dear friends, I've just had a most wondrous dream.' Then I said that God had come to me and told me that all the widows and widowers in our party must go to Saint Joseph's church and pray for their poor dead spouses. After that I went through everyone who was a widow or a widower, pretencing surprise that there were so many. Finally I gave them something to make it a little sweeter for them. 'We'll need food for lunch,' I said, and then I told them I'd get some tasty things from the market, which would be carried on Brigit's rounsey. She could walk to Rains, our next halting place, with the others. 'I'll get some bread and cheese and ham, and we can have some of the apples from the cart.'

Even then it wasn't easy. The way to Rains was long and Oswald worried that we wouldn't get there before curfew. I calmed him down by telling him the three Frenchwomen had said Saint Joseph's church wasn't far at all and was very close to the Rains road. Next, as I'd guessed would happen, Constance wanted to bring her boy Paul, and she wasn't happy when I said no, God had told me it must only be widows and widowers. 'I'm not bringing my boy, either,' I told her, and she softened when Sir John and Dame Alice said they'd watch over them both. And in the end I managed to sneak in Tom, too. Just when we were all set to go I squinted a little like I'd had a grave thought. 'Now I think of it, there was one other whom God said should come,' which was Tom of course. I said it was for his cat, as though he was only an animal Tom mourned him almost like a spouse. And though some of them didn't seem convinced they didn't fuss, as by then we were almost on our way.

CHAPTER SIX

Tom son of Tom

I knew what nobody else knew about Dame Lucy. She wasn't just a dear and seemly gentlewoman. Dame Lucy was God's angel sent secretly to earth. I swear once I saw a sort of shimmering behind her back that looked like a pair of wings. Most of all she was God's own lovesomeness. Thanks to her I was like a worm who weaves himself into his nest and then creeps out a butterfly. When I'd worn rags I was hardly seen by people passing on the road but with my new clothes and my hair they'd look me right in the eye and give me a smile and perhaps a 'bon jour', which is French for 'and good day to you, cousin'.

And she gave me learning my letters. Because if she hadn't joined us then Lionel and Father Tim would never have had their wager. In all my days I'd never dreamed that such a thing might come to be. It's a wonder, Sammy, I thought, Tom son of Tom getting schooled in his letters. I wished I could've told Auntie Eva and Hal and Sarah and all the rest. Who knew, one day I might be able to read clever books like Father Will. Hugh was quite sour about it. 'Aren't you the lucky one,' he said. 'I had to pay out a small fortune to have my eldest schooled.' But the rest of them couldn't have been kindlier and Constance said, 'Just think, Tom, one day you might be able to buy your freedom.' It was like wonders were coming so fast I couldn't catch them all.

I suppose I should have known. As folk say, when fortune's with you take care, as the fiend's not far away, and I swear I could feel him sniffing about, conspiring to do me ill. First he tried to set my letters against me. I'd be looking at Father Tim's wax tablet and it was like they'd all go dancing about, so a B would shape himself like a D, or a P made himself a Q, or an M and an N pretenced themselves a U or a W, till words were just squiggles. Father Tim grew quite crabbed. 'You're just not trying,' he said, which wasn't right, as I couldn't have strived harder.

Then the fiend tried to spoil my new clothes. A good few times I caught him out just in time, as he coaxed me to trip on a stone in the road or snag my hose on a nail. In truth, much though I liked having such handsome gear I sometimes wished I could keep it safe in my pack and wear my old rags, which I'd washed in the river and kept, though they made my pack so full and swelled it was like a ball with straps. For one thing my rags were better for begging. In the days since I'd had my new clothes I'd seen how folk looked at me when I rattled my bowl, like they were thinking this one doesn't look so needy. And though I craved alms every hour that I could, as we walked the road and wherever we stopped for the night, I got less than I had before, and it was hard to fill my stomach. Another thing was that in my pack my new gear would be kept perfect. Because I did wonder if Dame Lucy mightn't mind if, when we got to Rome, I sold the new clothes, as that was the only way I could think that I might buy Sir Toby's trinkets and so not be hanged after all.

Then Dame Lucy had showed herself an angel all over again, as God came into her dreams and told her anyone who'd lost kin should go and pray to Saint Joseph to help get them into heaven. And though Sammy wasn't rightfully my kin, being not of humankind but a little cat, Dame Lucy said he was as good as being my kin because I was so very mournful for him. Who knows, my beastie, I thought, we might get you out of purgatory early, even this very day. I'd still have to go to Rome, seeing as I'd promised everyone back home, while I wanted to go having started. But how I'd love to see my little Sammy in my dreams, sunning his belly in paradise.

After the big party we'd been till then, we were just a little clump of folk now, with Dame Lucy looking like an angel princess on her high horse and the rest of us walking. She asked me to lead Brigit's rounsey who was carrying our food and drink and you never saw a beast led more carefully. 'This way, Dobbin,' I'd tell him, steering him away from any holes in the road where he might catch his hoof. Dame Constance looked anxious, being fearful for her little boy, and Dame Lucy, angel that she was, tried to give her comfort. 'Don't you worry about Paul,' she told her. 'Sir John and Dame Alice will look after him, and he has my Peter to play with.' Not that Constance seemed much cheered. Then Dame Lucy's little Peter wasn't easy, as I'd seen myself. He wanted to play with Constance's Paul every moment and when Paul had had enough and needed time to himself, Peter, knowing he was the high, noble one, would cry and wail and say he must play with him. Their mothers, being friendly with one another, would grow abashed and would each tell their boy to do as the other asked, but Constance would say it stronger and in the end Paul would play with Peter, but sulkily.

Now Dame Lucy, wanting to raise Constance's spirits, called out to Jocelyn, 'Poor Constance is fretting about her boy. Come and cheer her up?' which Jocelyn happily did, gabbling away and telling her sportful tales till she laughed and showed her pretty smile. Oswald was side by side with Mary while I was happy enough with Dobbin. Until, after we'd walked a mile or two, Dame Lucy rode over and asked if I'd mind keeping Joan company, as it was a shame to see her all by herself. Anything for my angel. 'Come along now, Dobboes,' I said and I put some pace in my legs to catch up with her. Though I soon wished Dame Lucy had let me be. When I asked Joan, 'How now, cousin?' she answered with a little snort like she wasn't any cousin of a low grub like me. When I tried again and asked her, 'Are you looking forward to praying for your poor husband?' she answered, 'More than I would be praying for a cat.' Which seemed an unneedful and unkindly thing to say, I thought.

By good fortune I was spared having to try any more. I heard a cry of, 'Wait, wait, I beg you,' and looking round I saw, coming along the road behind us, and red in the face from hurrying in the cold, was Mary's daughter Helena. Mary looked scared as could be and called out, 'What's happened, my love? Are you all right?' but Helena answered, 'Nothing's wrong, Mother, don't you worry. I just wanted to join you and pray for Father.' Gawayne won't be pleased she's got away from him, I thought, because he was always hanging about her, smirking and chattering. 'Please, Dame Lucy, I beg you,' Helena said, 'don't be angry and send me away.' As if she would? Though in truth she didn't look happy to see her. I supposed it was because she wasn't a proper widow or widower, and had no cat to mourn like I did.

So on we went, eight of us now. Mary and Helena walked together, murmuring to each other in low voices like they always did. And I was happy to find that I didn't have to keep Joan company any more as she'd found her own. She was now walking with Constance and Jocelyn, who had one sister on each side of him, though he didn't look too joyed about it and nor did Constance. As for me, I walked with Oswald and we had a merry game of looking at faraway trees and guessing what kind they were, which I won after getting two oaks, an elm and a chestnut one after the other.

Then poor Dame Lucy had another thing to irk her, which was our road. Because the three Frenchwomen had told her it wasn't far to Saint Joseph, but it turned out that what they'd meant was that it wasn't far for them. I thought we all walked at a good pace but we were snails compared to those little widows. For a time they kept with us, though they were always getting ahead and having to stop themselves, till finally they tired of being slowed and away they went like hares, and all I could see of them was a smear of dust on the way far ahead. On we walked and on we walked. After what seemed like an age we met a fellow coming the other way with two donkeys, so loaded up with straw that they looked like great hedgehogs, and when Mary asked him in French how far it was to Saint Joseph, he shook his head and said it was miles off still.

By then we were all wondering if we'd get to Rains before the gates were locked. When Dame Lucy asked us if we'd like to stop and have some lunch by the road, with ale and mead, which was only kindly of her, everyone said no, thank you very much, even though we were all getting hungry, as we needed to keep going. After that we met the three Frenchwomen again, as they'd finished praying for their dead husbands and were on their way home, and though they said we were almost there that was no truer than what they'd told us before, and by the time we finally got there most of the day was gone. I wanted a good long pray to Saint Joseph for my Sammy, seeing as that was what I'd come all this way for, but the rest hurried me on and I'd barely started, so I couldn't believe Saint Joe would have heard my beseeching, when we were back on the road again, taking the fork for Rains.

After we'd walked a mile or so the afternoon was losing its light. Oswald was the one who stopped. Till then I'd only ever seen him tranquil but now he looked quite annoyed. 'We'll not get to Rains today, Dame Lucy,' he said. 'That's another day lost and we've had a good few now, what with looking round London and then resting after the sea crossing. I worry about getting over the Alps so late in the season.' Constance was troubled too. 'What about my little boy?' she said. 'I didn't think I'd be leaving him alone all night.' Jocelyn did his best to comfort her. 'I'm sure he'll be all right,' he said. 'Try not to worry.'

As if it was Dame Lucy's fault that the three little widows had set us so wrong. I knew our angel wouldn't let us down and nor did she. 'Here's a thought,' she said, smiling at the notion she'd come up with. 'I'll ride to Rains now. Passenlande's fast so I'll easily get there before curfew. I'll make sure your Paul is being looked after, Constance. And you can all go over to that farm.' She pointed to a stone building that was half a mile or so from the road. 'They're sure to have a barn. I'll come back first thing in the morning with all the horses. We have eight, which is enough for every one of us. That way you'll be in Rains early and will have time to reach our next halting place tomorrow night, so we won't have missed a day after all.' I didn't much like the thought of her riding off by herself. 'I'll come with you,' I said, 'I can ride Brigit's rounsey,' but she wouldn't hear of it. 'He's too slow,' she said. 'Now don't you worry about me as I'll be all right. Just go and enjoy yourselves. There's plenty of food in those packs, and lots of ale and mead, which is all for you, so I don't want to see a drop of it left over in the morning, d'you hear?'

That was that. Away she rode and we started down a path towards the stone building, just like she'd said we should. But that was a sorry surprise. I swear I'd never thought the folk I'd been pilgrimaging with all this time might be so currish and unthankful. Poor Dame Lucy, who'd showed us only kindness, ordaining that we should go and pray for our dead dear ones, and even giving us dainty victuals to eat, was hardly gone from our sight when they started. Joan was the worst. 'I don't know why she made us all come out here anyway,' she said. 'God told her, remember,' Constance answered, 'though I wish he'd said how far it was,' which was unkindly, too. Now Joan scoffed, 'Of course. God talks to her in her dreams.' It was said in such a foul, unbelieving voice that I had to speak up. 'If Dame Lucy said it was in her dream then it was in her dream,' I said, 'and that's the end of it, d'you hear?' But rather than shaming them, my speaking up just brought their meanness onto me. 'Is that you talking, Tom,' Joan asked, 'or is it your new clothes?' I tried to answer but I've never been good at quick, clever chatter and I was still confounded when I saw a wicked look come into Joan's eyes. 'You'll never guess what Hugh said. Last night he had some ales with Dame Lucy's cook, Jack, who told him his mistress is quite the wild woman. She's couched with half the gentle folk of Lincolnshire, so Jack said.'

'Stop it now,' I said. 'You're doing Satan's bidding, can't you see?' But I swear it was like trying to stem a river with a stick, as now that Joan had given them some poison they were all hungry to hear more, while Joan was only too happy to oblige. According to Jack the cook, she said, Dame Lucy had slain her first husband by throttling him as he ate his dinner and then, though she still wasn't divorced from her second husband, she'd lived sinfully with two dozen lovers, one being the father of her boy Peter, and another that she'd murdered with spells. 'That'll be why she wanted you on this venture today,' said Joan, looking at Jocelyn, Oswald and me. 'So she can start on you three.' Jocelyn and Oswald, who should have known better, both laughed and even Mary and Helena were smirking.

That's enough, Sammy, I thought. No more devil talk for us. I stuck my fingers in my ears, humming loud, and I walked on just as fast as I was able. They're dead to me now, every one of them, my old beastie, and they'll not hear one more word from Tom son of Tom till we reach Rome City, that I vow. But vows aren't always easy to keep. As to what came next, I'd have noticed it sooner except that, having my fingers in my ears, my elbows were sticking out forwards, so I was blinkered like a horse. Finally, even through my blocked ears and my hums I heard a little shriek and, looking round to see where it had come from, I saw there was a tree with a ladder against it. Up in the branches was a female picking apples and down below were two more holding a net to catch them. Though they weren't troubling with apples now, but were all staring at me. I dare say I made a strange sight, what with my elbows and my humming. But the thing I noticed most about them wasn't their apples or even their shrieking, but their gear, as they weren't wearing ordinary delvers' clothes but nuns' wimples. It seemed this wasn't a farm after all.

So much for my never speaking another word till we reached Rome City. I stopped, the others caught up with me and we all watched as the nun in the tree flung herself down the ladder as fast as she could and then all three of them flew back to the stone building, which must be their convent. After that we were all wondering what we should do, not that there was much to choose from. 'We have to stay there, if they'll take us,' Jocelyn said. Which was true enough, because this was the place where Dame Lucy was coming to fetch us in the morning, while by the looks of it there was nowhere else nearby. I couldn't see another roof in any direction.

On we went. The three sisters must've warned the whole convent against us and we had to knock at the door half a dozen times while Mary and Jocelyn shouted and begged in French, saying, 'Pelegrans, pelegrans,' which even I knew meant pilgrims. When they finally opened up, the prioress peered out from behind a little crowd of nuns and looked at us like we were a set of dirty grubs. Though she softened a bit when Mary opened the packs on Brigit's rounsey and showed her we had our own food and drink. Even then she wouldn't let us inside till we'd heard her rules, which

Mary made into English for the ones of us who didn't know French, though there were only two. Firstly for dinner we must eat along with all the sisters and secondly the females among us could sleep in the convent but us males must stay in an outhouse nearby.

We agreed and after that a pair of sisters took Oswald, Jocelyn and me to our sleeping place. Those two were as different as sky and cabbage. One was sour like her prioress and hardly spoke while the other was a smiler and wouldn't stop gabbling, chatting away in French to Jocelyn, who knew it. Though I couldn't understand a word, when we got to the outhouse I guessed from the sound of her voice that she was being sorry about it, which was only right as it was cold and damp and had nothing for bedding but a few pieces of straw that wouldn't soften the floor for a whelp. Standing there, getting goose pocks from the chill, for once in my life I felt a little envious of Sammy. We'll wish we had a few of your flames in here tonight, my old beastie, I thought.

The smiling sister said we could go back to the hall, which we were glad to, crouching as close to the fire as we could. As I'd had nothing to eat since I'd broken my fast at first light, my stomach was rumbling and I couldn't stop thinking about all the tasty-looking bread and ham and cheese that I'd watched Dame Lucy get at market that morning, and how fine it would be to feel warmed by the mead and ale she'd got too. All in all I was more than ready when we were called into the hall to eat. So you'll well imagine my feelings when, after the prioress led everyone in prayers, all that was brought to the table was a pot of cabbage stew and another of barley paste and not very much of either. We all looked at it and then looked at each other. Not that anyone spoke up, as complaining to that prioress would be like poking a lion in his eye.

When we'd finished our sorry repast the three of us slunk back to our quarters. I lay down and wrapped myself tight in my cloak, though it did little good, as it was one of those spots where the damp gets into your very bones. And whenever I began to drop off, Jocelyn started up again, as he couldn't let go of the dinner we'd had. 'It's just not right,' he'd say. 'That was our food. We'd have shared it with them, of course we would, but for her to take it all and just give us cabbage stew and barley paste, that's plain wrong.' Finally, just when I was nodded off for the seventh time, he said, 'D'you know what? We should go and get our redress. We should find their pantry and take back our food and drink.' 'What if we run into the prioress?' said Oswald, which was my thought exactly. 'We won't,' said Jocelyn. 'They'll all be fast asleep by now and won't stir till nocturnes, which is hours away. It's not like we'll be doing anything wrong, seeing as it's our own meat. And what can she do? She can't put us in a worse place than this.' Which was true enough. And there was no denying that a little mead would be warming, and might help me get to sleep in that cold hole of a spot.

So up we got and we crept back towards the convent. Wish me well, Sammy, I thought. It seemed like God was with us as the sky was clear and there was enough moon to light our way. Though the main door was locked from the inside there was another at the back where the bolt hadn't been pulled true and with a shove it opened nicely. It didn't take us long to find the pantry, which was right by the kitchen. But then we struck trouble. There was a lock on the pantry door. 'Looks like there'll be no mead for us after all,' I said, but Jocelyn wasn't giving up. 'One of the sisters must have a key,' he said. 'I'll go and see.' Oswald said that was lunatic. 'You'll wake them all,' he said, which I thought too, but Jocelyn was already going off towards their quarters. I expected to hear the prioress's voice screaming out next but instead after just a few moments there were footsteps and here came Jocelyn, with not one but three sisters. There were the two who'd taken us to the outhouse, the smiler and the snarler, and another who I'd sat opposite at dinner and who'd kept very quiet as she maunged down all the cabbage stew and barley paste she could get. 'I woke Rosalind here,' Jocelyn told us in a low voice, pointing at the smiler. 'But she didn't have the key, which took us to Lisa,' who was the snarler. 'And by then we'd woken Georgette,' which was the third one, 'who said she wanted to come along too.'

I was surprised Lisa the snarler had come at all, but when Jocelyn got the pantry door open she was inside quicker than any of us. Dame Lucy had done us proud all right, and as well as plenty of ham and cheese and bread and apples there were two skins of ale and a whole cask of mead, no less. It was too dark and cramped to stay in the pantry so we took it out to the cloister nearby, where we sat side by side on a bench like six little rabbits all in a row. For a time nobody said a thing and we just chewed it down. 'I suppose we should leave some for the others,' said Oswald, though he didn't sound keen while it was so tasty and we were so hungry that it was hard to stop, and before we knew it we'd finished every crumb. 'Now for something to wash it all down,' said Jocelyn. He pulled the stopper from the mead, filled a big goblet he'd got from the pantry and passed it round. It was lovely and sweet and I could feel my head grow light.

Then Jocelyn started gabbling away to the three sisters in French. The only word I understood, and which he said a dozen times at least, was Ongliter, which I'd heard before and meant England. Whatever he was saying was strong, though, as Rosalind squealed and giggled, so did Georgette while Lisa looked sour and said, 'No, no.' Then Rosalind and Georgette were whispering to Lisa both together and they kept saying Ongliter too. Whatever they said won the day as Lisa gave a shrug like she wasn't happy but she wasn't saying no.

I could see Jocelyn was fighting not to laugh. 'What's going on?' I asked him. 'I told them that in England we have a custom,' he said, 'that no woman can have a swallow of mead unless she's kissed afterwards.' 'Kissing nuns?' I said. It didn't seem godly. 'Why not,' he answered, 'if they're all right with it? It's just a little kissing.' So the flask started going round. Lisa got it first and she giggled and took a good taste. Jocelyn, who was beside her, gave her a quick kiss on her cheek but then he caught her out by giving her another right on the lips, which made her squeal again. Next was Georgette, and though Oswald seemed like he wasn't sure what to do, he gave her a peck on her cheek and then she gave him one back on his lips. Finally it was Lisa and me. I looked at her, and even though she didn't have her wimple on, still it didn't seem righteous to kiss God's wife. But the rest were all watching so I felt I had to do something. I supposed there was no great harm in just a little kiss. And it wasn't much of one in the end, as Lisa gave a quick turn of her head so all I got was hair.

The mead went round a second time and then a third and a fourth. By the fifth time Jocelyn and Rosalind didn't take any, as they were locked together by the lips, tight as could be. Georgette and Oswald were hardly different, though with them it was her who was doing most of the work and she had him pushed back against the wall. Lisa, though, just showed me her hair to give a peck to each time. It's probably all for the best, Sammo, I thought, as it wouldn't be right. Though what with the mead warming me, and having her right beside me, so warm and soft, it was hard not to want to pull her a little closer.

Jocelyn left off his kissing for a moment. 'We need to split these three up,' he said in a low voice. Oswald looked quite feared. 'But it's not right,' he said. 'They're nuns.' Jocelyn shook his head. 'I knew you'd be no use,' he said. 'At the very least can't you take yours somewhere else? There's the pantry. Give her some of the ale.' Still I wasn't sure and as Oswald and Georgette went off I said to Jocelyn, 'It does seem wrong, though. What'll God think?' He gave a little laugh. 'Tom,' he said, 'you just don't understand God. I know exactly what he'd say if he were here. He'd say good luck to you, Tom, that's what.' Because, so Jocelyn told me, though everyone said he was a god of love and a jealous god and the rest, which was all true enough, that was only half the story. 'The real honest truth,' Jocelyn said, 'is that God's an advocate. I should know, being one myself. Just look at all the laws he has. He can't be anything else.' And one of God's laws was that if we went as pilgrims to Rome and prayed to Saint Peter and said mass at the shrines and repented our sins, then our punishment in purgatory would be undone. 'Which means,' Jocelyn said, 'that God's telling us, go, my good friends, go and have some joy along the road as it's what you deserve and it'll all be forgiven anyway. It stands to reason he must mean that, or why would he have set his laws that way?'

Then he took Rosalind by the hand and they both went round the corner of the cloisters. That left Lisa and me sitting on the bench. Though it seemed quiet being left with the snarler, I thought, don't be sorry, Tom. Because even though Jocelyn was schooled and clever this still didn't feel righteous, while the last thing I wanted was to get into trouble with God when I was trying to get my poor beastie up to heaven. But then it didn't go like I'd supposed. We sat for a little while side by side, looking out at the cloisters, but then Lisa let out a sigh, picked up the cask of mead and took a great swig. Next she murmured something in French that sounded almost like a curse and she turned to me, put her hands round my neck and gave me such a kiss I swear I feared my eyes might pop. I tried not to answer it but if anything that made her more eager. She got my hand and put it through her gear, so I could feel the softness of her beneath, which had me trembling, and then she was pulling at my hose. Till I thought, perhaps Jocelyn's right. Perhaps God does think it's rightful. If he didn't then why would he make it so very sweet? So I kissed her back and before I knew it we were on the ground just in our unders, lying on her habit and my clothes to keep us off the cold stone, though I hardly noticed the chill, what with her fingers on my thing and mine on hers.

I suppose God was testing me. If he was I hadn't done very well. And now I had my reward. All of a sudden the quiet was broken and a voice cried out, 'I won't do it, d'you hear.' Lisa and me both stopped still. Now the voice came again. 'Get your hands off me,' and then there was a kind of howl. As it was spoken in English I knew it was one of our party and it sounded like Helena, though I found it hard to believe it could be, seeing as I'd hardly heard her speak let alone howl. I wondered who she didn't want touching her? Was there some monk hidden away in this place? She'll have woken the whole convent, I thought, which cooled me right down. I tried to roll away from Lisa, though she wasn't troubled and wouldn't let go of my fellow. Then I heard a sort of clapping noise, of bare feet running. I looked up and it seemed like I'd been right about the voice after all, as there was Helena, flitting along the far end of the cloisters. Her long black hair was wild around her face and I know it's foolish but all I could think was, what a dear seemly creature she is.

She stopped and stood shivering, holding her arms round herself against the cold. Don't look round, I thought. Please, sweet Helena, don't look round. I heard her mumbling to herself, as if she was going on with her disputation with whoever it had been. Now she seemed like she was wondering if she should go back to where she'd come from and she took a couple of steps. That's right, I thought, hardly daring to breathe, back you go, as I felt Lisa give my fellow a little squeeze. It might've gone well after all except that just then there was a low moan from round the corner, which must've been Jocelyn's Rosalind. Helena stopped and looked over. Don't ask me why but I tried to smile. For a moment she squinted, trying to see what was what through the gloom, next she stared and then she let out a scream.

That'll have them all out here, I thought. Lisa and me got into quite a dance. I jumped up, hiding my fellow with my hands, and then I was on one leg, pulling up my hose, while Lisa was trying to get her habit, which she couldn't because it was caught under my foot, till she tugged it so hard that I was back on the ground again. From round the corner I heard cursing and then breaking glass, which would be the goblet going over. And then there were more footsteps. Here came Mary who had a gleaming face like she'd been crying. At first she only saw Helena but then she followed her stare and her eyes opened wide. By then I'd got my hose on though not my tunic. Lisa scampered off with her habit wrapped round her middle just as Constance and Joan showed themselves. Joan smirked and Constance gave us a black look, especially Jocelyn, who was coming round the corner of the cloisters that very moment, just about dressed though his bare feet told his story. He raised his hands like he was giving up in a fight, and with a funny little laugh he said, 'It's not like you think.' As if that would help? It didn't persuade the four nuns who turned up next. One wailed and the others laughed. And then, last of all, here came the prioress.

So I found there were worse places than our outhouse after all, as the seven of us tried to find shelter from the drizzle under a hedgerow by the road. Of course Joan made all the foul jokes she could. Constance said not a word but just looked at us like we were a set of filthy dirts. The only ones who didn't seem disgusted were Mary and Helena, as they were too busy with their own squabbling. Most of it I couldn't catch as it was French and murmured too, but Mary grew so warm once that she said out loud in English, 'I beg you, you'll be safe,' and Helena answered, 'I won't do it, d'you hear?' Safe from what? I thought. Though mostly I was thinking, I'm sorry, Sammy. I just hope I haven't ruined your chances of getting to paradise. Or I was thinking, what will my dear angel Dame Lucy think of me now?

CHAPTER SEVEN

Matilda Froome

Once I was foolish and proud and all I thought of was to be the best. If I was playing a game of tables with my brother I had to win, which I usually did, and if I lost I'd be crabbed all day. If I was dancing or singing I had to dance or sing better than any of the other girls. For gowns I had to have the finest, so when I walked through the town I'd turn every head, while I never cared if folk said I was vain and sluttish or showing off my shape. And when I married I had to marry the ablest, handsomest man in all Bishop's Lynn, which was Roger, or so I thought.

Of course all the while God was shaking his head and getting ready to pull me back down, as was only right. My father lent Roger money to get started as a trader in sheep hides but he soon showed himself an idle fool with no talent for the craft. He thought he was clever buying the cheapest hides to send overseas but he wasn't clever when they arrived rotten and full of fleas, and his name grew so blemished that hardly a German or Fleming would buy from him again. Nor was he clever at picking ships. He lost a whole bulksworth of pitch and fish when the *Holy Ghost* went down on her way back from Hamburg. Which Lynn folk laughed at, saying what fool would risk his goods in a leaky old bucket like the *Holy*

Ghost? Even his seemliness didn't last and within months of our wedding he was eating and drinking himself old.

Never mind, I thought, in my haughty foolishness. Just because you've married a dotard doesn't mean your whole life is spoiled. So I started a business of my own as a brewster. Just you watch, folk of Lynn, I thought. One sip of Matilda Froome's ale and you'll know it's the tastiest in all Norfolk. But God tutted his tongue and pulled me down again. However much I tried, my ale always came out sour. After a few months I gave up brewing and I had to watch as my neighbours smirked at my misfortune.

But the worst way my pride threw me into the dirt was with my own children. When I first fell pregnant I was full of joy. It'll be a boy, I thought, and he'll grow up handsome and wise. He'll be the richest trader in Lynn and everyone will look at me with wonder for being his mother. As things turned out he was a boy and he would grow up handsome enough, and rich too, but I never cared. A few months after he was born the strangest thing befell me. Now it happened that one morning many years before my lifetime, as I heard, the moon passed in front of the sun, hiding its dazzle completely, and for a short while day became night, you could see the stars, and foolish people were filled of fear and wondered if the last days had come. And so it was with me. I swear it was as if the fiend set himself between my mind's eye and the face of God, so I couldn't see his wise, loving visage any more. All of a moment everything in the world seemed hateful to me. I slandered my father and mother and brother, I slandered Roger and I even slandered God. As to my baby, he was like nothing to me and seemed only a doll that would give me no peace. Wildness took me and I'd shout and gibber for hours. Finally I had a fancy to murder myself and, having no knife to do it, I ripped at my skin with my fingernails close by my heart so it bled and bled, and I bit my hand so hard that the mark is still there to this day.

But out of this lowest of times came my sweetest joy. After I scratched and bit myself Roger and his servitors bound me with rope, tight so I could hardly move even a finger, and they put me in the warehouse where I couldn't trouble them with my noise. I'd been there for a few days when one morning, as I waited for Roger and the thralls to come and loosen my ropes, and let me go to the latrine and break my fast like usual, I felt a great peace settle upon me. I heard a beautiful melody and smelt a smell that was sweet like a fine scent, and I saw little white things flying about that I didn't know what they were. Then a man came in and sat down beside me, young and handsome, and he looked at me with such love that I knew it was You. 'Don't fret,' You said. 'You've done well, Matilda, my poor dear creature. I'm proud of you. You've denied my foe, the fiend, who tried to coax you to his side. You've shown your righteousness. Now you'll feel my love, that I promise.' Then You quietly slipped away.

From that day, in my mind's eye I've been your poor dear creature. Now I see my road, your poor dear creature thought, and I swear your creature laughed out loud at all the foolish pride she'd had till then. When Roger came with the thralls she prevailed on him to unbind her, telling him she was at peace now and wouldn't gibber or bite herself. Though he almost bound her up again a few days later when she started giving away her fine gowns. Yet that wasn't because she was demoniac but because she wanted to live plainly, just like You'd told her she should. She'd made a vow, which she spoke out loud many times, 'From this day onwards all I seek is to show You honour.'

Not that it was easy. As well as being a poor trader, another thing about Roger was that he had no forbearance. When your creature had just been with child and was still stretched and sore from her labour and drained like an empty cup, she'd see him looking at her with his little famished eyes, like he was numbering in his head how much longer he'd have to wait. Sure enough, on the very first night after she'd been churched, and when she finally felt clean in God's eyes, he'd close the curtains round the bed and creep over so he could dirty her again. Worse, it always seemed to take straight away. Some females waited for years, or never got barnished in their whole lives, but not your poor dear creature. From the birth of her first hardly a month passed without her feeling sick and waddling about with a full belly or getting sudden hungers for things she never wanted usually, like a bowlful of parsley or to chew on a mutton bone. Then there'd be another pair of greedy little lips sucking at her paps, and another set of lungs to fill our small house with noise so it seemed more like a tavern than a home.

And yet, even with all these troubles reining her back, your poor dear creature kept to her vow. She honoured You by wearing a hair shirt, even if it gave the babies rashy legs when they suckled. And when You came to her in her bodily eye as she prayed, and You told her what to do, she did it right away. If You commanded her, 'My dear creature, come to see me at the church of my beloved Saint Margaret,' then up she'd get that very moment and go. And if Roger shouted to her, 'Where d'you think you're going now, Matilda? What about the children?' she'd answer in a merry voice, 'Ostrid can look after them,' as Ostrid was your creature's foot maid, whom she paid from her own purse. Or she'd tell him to call his mother to help. And of course the bigger ones could watch over the little ones. And if there was a suckling among them, as there almost always was, your creature would tell him to send for Agnes, or whoever was hiring herself as wet nurse at the time.

Then off your dear creature would go to Saint Margaret's as she felt like that dear church was her true home. Each Friday she'd wake up in the dark womb of the night like a nun, and she'd go there and kneel at the altar from matins right through to noon, praying to You. And every day she'd go there not once but three times to seek out Friar Alan and make her confession. Even though Friar Alan said she didn't rightly need to go more than once a week, seeing as she had no new sins to tell him. Because, he said, it was no offence to God if Roger had planted his seed again seeing as we were lawfully married. Nor, Friar Alan said, did your creature need to tell him where Roger had put his hasty little hands, or where he'd kissed her, or about his mouth, which he didn't keep well so it smelt like pond water. But she told it all to him anyway out of love for You. And she knew it was right because afterwards she'd see You in her bodily eye, smiling at her and giving her your blessing.

After a time your creature realized that it wasn't enough to please You by living proudlessly and cleansing her own soul. All the world must be made clean for You. So on market days she'd stand beside the town hall and warn people that they must live with You in their hearts. And when Friar Alan said Saint Paul had written that it was against God's laws for women to preach, she told him that she wasn't preaching but was only recounting the bliss of your visits to her soul, which he had no answer to. Never mind if it was cold or raining or if a gale was blowing, your creature would go about the town to drive the lost sheep in Bishop's Lynn back onto the path of righteousness. If she spied a young couple hiding in an alleyway, kissing and touching each other, your creature would call out to them in a gentle voice, 'Cousins, stop your lustfulness. Not in sweet Jesus' town.' If she saw two drunks fighting she'd tell them, 'Friends, stop your anger, which is displeasing to God's eyes.' And if she saw one who had a fat belly and a double chin, she'd tell her, 'Leticia' – because one like that was Leticia Stiles, who used to be so sharp at your creature back when your creature was foolish and proud, and which sharpness your creature was glad of now for having set her on the right path, so she longed to help her in return – 'Leticia, my dear cousin, can't you see that you'll be far more lovesome in God's eyes if you stop your gluttony?'

Some saw the holiness that dwelt in your creature. Old Betty, who lived in a shed near the churchyard, and who some folk said was lunatic though she was wiser in her soul than they were, would smile and curtsey whenever your creature walked by. But most of them, sorry to say, were blinder than moles and they'd tell her, 'Who do you think you are? The Archbishop of Canterbury?' They'd call her foul names and jeer when she went by, which was hard to bear. But then You would come to your poor dear creature in her prayers and tell her, 'Don't listen to them, Matilda. The devil has covered their eyes so they see not. Remember, my poor dear creature, that the more you're forsaken the more I feel love for you.' And your creature's spirits soared with joy once again.

Now it happened that another thing that drew your creature to Saint Margaret's was to listen when Friar Alan read out a saint's life for the day, as she found them beautiful to hear and most of all she loved the female saints of recent times. There was one from Sweden named Truda who, when she was first married, entreated her husband that they should live chastely like a brother and sister, and she got him to give his accord. So she remained pure and undirtied and she spent her days righteously, kissing lepers and going on pilgrimages all across Christendom, and when her husband died, which he did young, poor sweet man, she founded a new order of sisters whom she went to live with, far away from all men. Another from Flanders, whose name was Sipper, had a vision of You on the cross on that terrible day, and afterwards felt your suffering so sharply that she'd often weep and sob at her remembrance.

Imagine your creature's amazement when, one Friday morning as she knelt at the altar of Saint Margaret's, doing her vigil, she saw You in a vision, just like Saint Sipper had done. You'd been taken from the cross and were pale and lifeless on the ground as a mob of hateful Jews bayed at you in their strange tongue. Then your creature heard your sweet voice call to her, 'Don't be sad, sweet Matilda. Be full of joy. You are so dear to me that I have given you this vision as clear as if you were there yourself, and clearer and nearer even than I gave it to any other saint.' And your poor dear creature knew it was so.

But these wonders weren't finished even still. Later that same day when your creature was walking back to Saint Margaret's to make her second confession of the day to Friar Alan, she recollected the vision she'd had of You, and a sorrow filled her that was so strong that there in the street she broke into loud weeping, just like Saint Sipper did. Thomas Wilson the fishmonger, hearing her, shouted out, 'What's wrong, Matilda? Has something happened to one of your poor little babes?' and she told him, 'No, far worse. I'm remembering our saviour's day of torment,' and, being blind like the rest of them, he didn't understand and gave her a sour look. From that day on she'd often break into weeping, sometimes once in a week and sometimes many times in a single day, and she might weep for five hours without stopping, which was more than even Saint Sipper had. If she saw a suffering soul, like a dog with a hurt leg or a horse being whipped, her tears would start. And with time her sorrow came to seize her in another way, too, and without any warning a mighty roar would rise up through her and spring out from her mouth, so loud that it made people jump or shriek, especially if they'd never heard her do it before.

Yet the greatest honour was still to come. One day You came to her ghostly eye like usual and You said, 'Dear Matilda, you are so pleasing to me that from this day in my sight you will be my virgin of godliness. You must have no fear ever again, as I tell you now that you won't spend even one year in purgatory, nor one day, nor one hour, but you'll come directly to sit by my side in heaven. And as my virgin of godliness I want you to clothe yourself always in white.' So your creature had a beautiful white dress made, such as a novice nun might have, and she wore it each and every day. And even though she wasn't a virgin she felt clean and pure almost like she was.

Of course like always there were some whom the devil kept blind and when your creature went by they'd call out, 'Look at Matilda Froome in her white dress, trying to catch everyone's eye.' But your poor dear creature paid them no heed, not even if they sang songs that made unkind rhymes from her name, or if small boys threw pebbles at her, or pieces of dung, like they sometimes did. As though ire welled up in her at the dishonour that they showed, not to your creature of course but to You, then You'd tell her, 'Don't feel hurt for me, dear Matilda, as I've been wounded a thousand times worse than this, as you very well know.' So your creature would clean her dress till every mark was gone and she was your virgin of godliness once more.

And often they didn't get the chance to insult her as she wasn't there. You would send her to pray to Little William in Norwich, whom the wicked Jews killed, or Little Hugh in Lincoln, or Frideswide in Oxford or some other saint. And then one day, after your creature had given birth to her eighteenth, of whom only four died and fourteen lived, which everyone said was a great blessing, You sent her much, much further. As your creature prayed one night You came to her ghostly eye and gave her two most sweet commands. 'Dearest Matilda,' You said, 'from this day, as my virgin of godliness, I ask that you and your husband live chastely like a brother and sister.' Nor was that all. Next You commanded your creature to go on a great pilgrimage that would take her far away from the blind sinners of Bishop's Lynn, all the way to your holy city of Rome, to visit the famous saints and the sacred places, and become known to your servants there. 'Because, sweet Matilda,' You said, 'I have plans for you. When you reach my city of Rome I will give you a great gift.'

The very next day after she heard this, your creature started making herself ready. Friar Alan was eager and ready to help, as he always was when your creature went on a pilgrimage, sweet clerk that he was, and that very same morning when she told him of your command, he wasted not a moment but wrote out her testimonial, and he blessed her scrip and her staff the instant she had them. Roger was more difficult, of course. He grew quite sour when your creature told him You'd commanded him never to dirty her secret thing again. 'I'm your husband,' he said. 'It's my right.' And he moaned about her going away. 'To Rome? How many months will you be gone this time?' But your creature was helped by his poorness at trading, which had become her best friend. By then he had so many debts that it was a wonder he hadn't been thrown into jail, while your creature, her father having died some years earlier, now had her heritance, which was no small one. When she'd gone on her pilgrimages to Norwich and Lincoln and the rest, she'd got Roger to give his accord by giving him a shilling or two and now she did the same but much more. 'If you give your agreement to these two things,' she told him, 'then I'll pay off your debts right down to the last penny.' She saw a hunger come into his eyes and sure enough a few days later, and before witnesses, as she didn't want him going back on his word, he promised he'd never trouble her private thing ever again and he gave his assent to her journeying to Rome.

And just after then and with more joy in her heart than she'd felt for many a year, your poor dear creature said her farewells and set out for London. It would have been easier to take ship from Yarmouth, which is how any trader would've gone, but by the king's law all pilgrims had to leave his realm by way of Dover. Walking at your creature's side was her foot maid Ostrid as, the pilgrimage being so very long, your creature wanted her for company and to carry her things. Ostrid was a strange one, though. She'd been with your creature since before her first was born and yet your creature sometimes felt like she hardly knew her well. Often her eyes had a strange, still look to them, as if she wouldn't blink even if the fiend himself jumped out at her. As we walked down to London and then to Canterbury and on to Dover, your creature, being so full of joy, said to her many times, 'Isn't this wondrous, Ostrid? Here we are on our way to the city of Rome,' but all she ever got back was, 'So we are, ma'am.' Your creature laughed at the time, thinking it most sportful, but of course she knew better later, when she saw Ostrid's rightful nature.

Most of the others aboard our ship to Calais were pilgrims from Yorkshire on their way to the three kings at Cologne, and though your creature was only friendly to them, the devil soon blinded their eyes and turned them against her, just like he had the folk in Bishop's Lynn, and they smirked at your creature's weeping and howling and her white dress. But if they were proud at first they lost their smiles when a great storm blew up, which got them repenting and praying and groaning that their lives were over. Your creature had no fear because You'd promised her she'd go to Rome to get your great gift, so she told them, 'Stop your moaning as you won't drown,' and nor did they, though we were blown halfway to Denmark, so the shipmen told us, and it was all they could do to claw their way back south-westwards. By then we were so low on water and food that they didn't put in at Calais like they should have, but at Antwerp in Holland.

Never mind, your creature said to herself. The more miles I have to journey, the more I'll honour You and the happier I'll be. On the evening she landed she walked around Antwerp City, her legs feeling drunken as if she were still aboard ship, and knowing that she was in a foreign land and that her journey was truly begun, she became filled with great joy so it seemed like she was floating and that every fleck of light was golden with your smile. Then, passing near the harbour she saw a poor beggar woman who had a sweet, sorry face, and at that instant a great feeling of love rose up through your poor dear creature and she knew straight away what she must do to show You honour. From her belt she took her heavy scrip and, keeping back a few pennies, she gave all the rest to the old woman, who looked up at her in wonder.

But how meanly your creature was thanked for her kindness, and by the very one who should have kept loyal to her. That evening at the inn where we were all staying, when she told Ostrid about the loving thing that she'd done, instead of being full of joy Ostrid gave her a foul look and, not calling her ma'am like she should have, she said, 'I'm not coming with you to Rome now.' Then she went and talked to the Yorkshires and, as if she hadn't been currish enough already, she said that they all thought your creature was demoniac, and as they felt sorry for her they said she could go with them to Cologne, and that they'd pay her to wash their clothes and make them their dinner as they journeyed. After all these years of giving her a livelihood your poor creature could hardly believe Ostrid had said such words. But the cruellest blow came when your creature asked her, 'What about when you get back to Bishop's Lynn? Because I tell you, I won't take you back,' and she answered, 'I'm glad of it as I wouldn't work for you again, Matilda Froome, and look after your foul rabble of children, not if you paid me a hundred pounds.'

Never mind, your creature said to herself. Let her go, as she's nothing to me. And early the next morning your poor dear creature set off alone towards Brussels, which the shipmen had said was the right way to get myself back onto the road from Calais to Rome where other English would be journeying. Not that the going was easy. Your poor creature's pack was heavy on her shoulder now that she had to carry all her own things. And though there were a good number of pilgrims on the road she met not one Englishman or Englishwoman. She dearly wished she'd learned French, which she would have if her mother had known it, or if her father hadn't been so scarce, because he'd had her brothers taught it but not her. Or Latin. Most folk on the road were Dutch, she guessed by the sound of their talk, and were going to Spain, as they'd tell her in that throaty way of theirs, 'Santiago.' They weren't unfriendly but, being in parties, they kept to themselves and they'd look at your creature strangely so it grieved her that she couldn't tell them all about herself. When she saw them staring at her white dress she'd say, 'God's son said I was to wear it as I'm his virgin of godliness,' but they'd just look confounded. When she remembered her vision of You and burst into sobbing they'd look sorry and perhaps put an arm round her to give her comfort. And when she roared they'd grow angry and scold her and one tried to push her into a ditch.

Another thing that was hard was keeping fed. With her last penny your creature bought a begging bowl that she'd rattle at anyone going by but there weren't many who'd stop and drop in a coin. Even then your creature didn't lose heart. She said to herself, don't you see, Matilda Froome, this may seem like hardship but in truth it's a blessing? After all the fine living you had when you were young, growing up in your father's house, which was one of the grandest in all Bishop's Lynn, it's only right that you should live without comforts, in righteous poverty. But she was often hungry. And when she stayed the night in barns, which were all she could afford, she hardly slept as she would start at every little noise, thinking, some wicked felon has come to ravage me, though in the end it would just be a mouse or other tiny beast.

For a time she walked in the company of some poor Frisians, and though your creature couldn't understand a word they said, she found them much more lovesome than Ostrid or the Yorkshires had been. But they were very dirty. Before they reached a town they'd stop to pick fleas and lice off one another, though these were so plentiful that their labouring did little good. By the time your creature reached Cambrai she had fleas and lice too and she was glad that the Frisians were going to pray to the saints in Paris so their way parted from hers. It was hard for your creature to get pure again, though she bathed in cold rivers and she washed her clothes many times, and dried them over smoky fires, and as there was no getting them out of her hair she ended up cutting it all off with her dining knife. Sometimes You would come to your creature in her ghostly eye and tell her, 'I know this is hard for you, my sweet Matilda, but I love you all the more for it.' Yet even this dear comfort seemed sorrier than before. It was the strangest thing but your sweet voice, which had always been so clear, sounded fainter now and smaller, almost as if You were speaking from inside a wooden chest.

What joy your creature felt when, with tired, aching feet, she finally reached the town of Saint Quentin, which lay on the pilgrim way from Calais to Rome. Now I'll meet some English, she thought, as by then she felt a great hunger to talk again in her own language. But when she hobbled into the pilgrim hospital she found there were only the usual Dutchmen and Germans, most of them bound for Spain, while there weren't many even of these. One of the monks spoke a few words of English and when she asked him why there were no Englishmen he said it was because she was walking so late of season. It was true that it was getting cold now, so your creature wished she'd brought warmer clothes, as she had only a shawl and her cloak, which she didn't like to wear as they covered up the lovesome whiteness of her dress.

Never mind, she told herself. I'm sure I'll meet some of my own people soon. But when she walked on to Lauon, which was the next town on the way, the strangest thing happened. It was a bright, fine autumn day but to her it seemed as if all the colours were faded away to grey. Another strange thing was that her sweet sobbing and roaring left her. She'd see a lame dog or a man beating his mule and she'd be ready for her tears to flow, but nothing would come. Your poor dear creature found this very troubling, as it felt almost like she'd been robbed of her godliness.

From Lauon to Rains was a long day's walking and when she finally reached Rains, just before sunset, her feet were so tired that she could hardly stand. And then, the next morning, and barely an hour out of Rains on the road to Chalons, where she was to spend her next night, your creature was walking so hastily, seeing as she knew she had another long day's journey, that she didn't notice a hole in the path and she twisted her foot, and when she tried to stand she fell back to the ground. I won't be able to go another yard this morning, she thought, nor for several days most probably. Then she sat and waited by the empty road till finally a merchant with a cartload of skins came by and offered her a ride. And though she was full of fear that he would ravage her, he never did. Instead he helped her hobble into the pilgrim hospital in Chalons, where she took to her bed.

But all of the troubles she'd had till then were like nothing compared to what came next. Because it happened that your poor creature had another eclipse, which she hadn't for years, and this one was worse than any she'd had since after she first gave birth. All through the night she was troubled by a foul, coaxing voice. 'What a fool you've been, Matilda Froome,' it told her. 'All these years you thought it was God's son coming to your ghostly eye, and instead it was me.' Your creature shouted back, 'That's a lie, fiend,' even though her noise made the Germans and Dutch and French in the dormitory wail that she was keeping them awake. Worse, folk in Lynn used to say the very same dirty slander, that it wasn't You who made your creature weep and howl, but the devil. Ten and twenty times your poor lost creature called out to You, 'Speak to me, I beg you. Come to my side. Silence this fiend,' but you said not a word.

Rather than taking pity on your creature in her need, the monks grew sour at her and over the next few days one kept coming over to her bed and pointing at her foot, by which she knew he meant, it's surely better by now? When he brought her bread he'd scowl and shake his head like he was saying, we can't keep feeding you forever, you know. And when she railed at the fiend and begged You to come to her aid, he'd tell her shhh and point at the other beds. Yet how could she keep quiet when Satan provoked her so? 'You thought he was guiding you to Rome where he'd give you his great gift,' he'd say, 'when all along it was me guiding you, and not to Rome but to this dirty place, and not for any gift but to meet your own death. This is where you'll die, Matilda, and then you'll come down to dwell in my fiery realm.' 'It's not true,' your creature cried out to him. 'Jesus promised me I wouldn't spend even an hour in purgatory, let alone go to hell, and that I'd be taken straight up to his side in heaven.' But the fiend just cackled. 'That wasn't his promise but mine. And sorry to say you can't set much store by any promises I make.'

By the third day your poor dear lost creature felt a weakness come upon her, as if life was seeping from her soul. Worst of all, she felt her very faith was become fragile, like a glass goblet with a crack through it, so one tiny knock might shatter it into pieces. But then, at her very lowest moment, help finally came. As your creature lay moaning and trembling in her bed she heard noises down in the courtyard. There was a clatter of horses' hooves and a drone of bagpipes, played not well, and voices chattering, and though they were too faint for her to hear their meaning, the very sound of them was wondrously familiar. Sure enough the unkindly monk came into the dormitory and told her, 'Anglais, Anglais,' so your creature knew that, just as she'd hoped, the arrivals were from her own land. And that same moment she saw You in her ghostly eye, come at long last, and You told her, 'You see, Matilda, I didn't desert you. You have passed my test. Now all will be well.' And though your creature was still angry she murmured, 'I forgive You. I knew You'd come in the end. Though I wish it might have been a little sooner.'

Now the monk brought them crowding into the dormitory, a whole lovely throng, and your creature was weeping, not for You for once, but from pure joy. How sweet it was to talk and to be understood. So your creature told them all in a rush that she was from Bishop's Lynn from a good trading family, and how You'd come to her in her mind's eye many times till You told her she must go to Rome. And she told them she'd given her money away to the beggar woman in Antwerp, and how ungrateful Ostrid had left her to journey on alone, till she'd sprained her ankle and had to stop here, where the fiend had driven her almost to lose her wits, and how You had gone from her till You'd returned just now. She saw them looking at her like she was a strange thing. Of course they would. 'I know I must seem a little wild,' your creature told them, with a laugh to calm them, 'but my journey's been hard and I had to cut off my hair to get rid of lice I got from some dirty folk I walked with.' All at once a great fear came over her. 'You won't leave me here, will you?' she asked. 'You'll let me come with you?'

One of them, a delver by the look of his sunbrowned skin, squinted at your creature with his little eyes. 'If your foot's bad then perhaps you should stay on here till it's fully right,' he said, but then a gentle lady whose face was all sweetness gave your creature a kindly look. 'Of course you must come with us,' she said. 'You can ride in my cart.' And though the one with the little eyes said, 'But where will your boy go?' she answered him, 'He can ride with Lionel,' pointing at her husband, or so your creature thought he was then, and though Lionel looked none too pleased he said nothing and so, joy of joys, your poor dear creature was saved.

The gentle lady, whose name was Lucy, said it was a wonder that You came to speak to your creature, because it happened there was another in their party who'd also been chosen, though not by You but by your father, who had chosen her as his voice and spoke through her. 'How blessed we are,' Dame Lucy said, 'having one pilgrim who's visited by God and another by Jesus.' This other's name was Beatrix and your creature couldn't help but smile because she was just a little foolish child of a thing. 'How often has he come to you?' your creature asked, and when she said he'd come half a dozen times your creature smiled and told her that You had been coming to her for many long years before Beatrix was even born, and that your creature couldn't count how often You'd spoken to her, as it was many score times.

That evening your creature scrubbed and scrubbed at her dress, which had become quite dirtied during her bad days, till it was whiter than it had been for a good while, and the rest of them were amazed when they saw her walk down in it to the dining hall. And what gladness your creature felt when she put it on the next morning, hobbled down the stairs and took her place beside the driver, Jack, in Dame Lucy's cart and watched the fields creep by. The colours seemed not grey any more but bright again, the sun still had a little warmth to it – more than it would have in Lynn in this season – and your creature felt You in it, healing her. Dame Lucy gave her some bread and apples and cheese, which were all in the cart behind her, so your creature had only to lean back and she could take more when she felt like it, till she had a fuller stomach than she had had for many a day. She had a fuller scrip, too, thanks to lovesome Dame Lucy, who gave her fourpence and then asked any who had a penny to spare to give it as well, which got her a shilling and thruppence altogether. I could ride like this forever, your creature thought. There's nothing I need, not food, not drink, not even a word of chatter.

We were in chalk country and the road was pale under our feet, stretching out ahead of us as straight as an arrow's flight, rising and falling over the land like a ship on the swell; there was forest to either side so it wasn't an exciting stretch of way, with little to console the eye. The miles passed quite slowly and after a time your creature thought it was only right to show herself friendly and to learn about her fellow pilgrims, and so she began a little chatter with the cart driver, Jack. He wasn't the easiest fellow to gabble with and most of his answers were a 'nope', or a 'I s'pose', or a 'I couldn't say', but your creature kept up with her merry asking till he couldn't help but speak. What a surprise that was, though. Your creature had supposed that, like she herself, these pilgrims were all journeying to Rome only to show You honour, but no. This was only so of the little doll Beatrix, who sought to warn your father's servants there that the end of days were coming. Which your creature found hard to believe, because if that were true then you'd have warned her, wouldn't You, my good, sweet Lord? A few wanted to fetch their dear ones out of purgatory, including one idiot boy who was going for his popelot of a cat of all things, but most were journeying to try and get your forgiveness for their sins, which needed forgiving all right, as the truth was their souls were black as soot.

Aside from the manor lord, John of Baydon, who'd punched an abbot, most of them were fornicators. The kindly widow Constance had cast her boy into sickness by whoring with her own cousin and, seeing how blessed your creature was, she had her pray for them both. The advocate Jocelyn had killed his wife with his lust, which one would think would be enough for any man, but no, even then he'd not learned wisdom. Your creature had noticed how he kept himself apart from the rest and looked most sad. Oswald, who went as a pilgrim for folk for silver and the cat boy in rags Tom were much the same, though they kept far from Jocelyn. 'Those three all shamed themselves,' Jack said with a laugh. So your creature was scandalled to learn that, even though they were on a holy journey to please God and You, a couple of days back these three had spent the night at a convent where they'd been caught with their gear round their knees, swiving away at three poor sisters. Dame Lucy had been wild at them, Jack said. Not long before she'd bought the cat boy new clothes to tidy him up, but after what he'd done she'd taken them from him, so he was back in his old rags, which were so bad they looked hardly clothes at all, your creature saw. And she'd barred Father Tim from teaching him his letters, which was another kindness he'd been given.

That all spoke well of Dame Lucy, so your creature thought, but then it turned out she was hardly more righteous herself. Jack, being her cook, was loath to speak about his mistress but after your creature gently wrung him he told her that his mistress was going to Rome to get a divorce, and this not from her first husband but her second. Then, when your creature wondered why her boy Peter wasn't back with his father like you'd expect, being her only son and so his charge, Jack said Peter hadn't been born of either husband but by another man. Which made the poor lad a bastard and his mother a sinner to her very bones. As for young Lionel, who your creature had supposed was her husband, he was her latest wooer, whom she wanted to marry once she'd divorced her last. But why, dear Dame Lucy? your creature thought. Now that you've finally found peace and cleanness, why throw it all away and let him foul you every night and fill your home with bleating, pewking little bairns?

Never mind, your creature told herself. It's not for you to judge others, as that's God's work. Just be glad of the joys you now have. And there were so many joys. As well as the company and the cart and the cheese and apples, your creature found that she could confess once again. Her last true shriving had been weeks ago back in Dover, and though she'd tried churches she found along the way, that hadn't seemed properly righteous, seeing as the priests hadn't understood a word she said nor she a word of theirs. She called Father Tim over and as he rode beside the cart she made a longer confession than she had in many a month. She told him how she'd been guilty of anger towards Ostrid for leaving her, at the Yorkshires for taking her, at the Frisians for giving her the lice and fleas that had been so hard to be rid of, and then at the monks at the hospital in Chalons who'd been so crabbed. After that she repented her anger at the delver with the little eyes, Hugh, for saying she should stay behind at the hospital, and for his unkindly mean jokes at her, which she said loud enough for him to hear, for his own good so he might know to be godlier. Father Tim absolved and blessed your creature. But what amazement was on his face when, scarcely half an hour later, she called him back and told him, 'Father, I want to confess.' 'But you just did,' he said. So your creature smiled and explained that it was her custom to shrive her sins at least three times each day and she began once again, and though Father Tim said she'd already confessed all of these unrights to him, she answered that it was godlier if she did it more than once, as You yourself had told her, which he had no answer for.

The next morning it was hard to confess, what with the weather. The sky was dark and the very moment we stepped out of the hospital where we'd stayed the night the rain started, being the kind that falls so heavy that it gets through every stitch of your attire, chilling you to your blood. We were on the same straight, chalky road that we'd been following the day before and the wet made it slippery, so the riders kept having to dismount and lead their horses, and twice your creature feared the cart might slide into the ditch. Then the rich delver Margaret stepped in a hole and hurt her foot, which was her own fault for not looking where she was going, so she rode on the cart too, squeezing your creature to the middle, so she had to make her change places as otherwise she couldn't call Father Tim over and do her shriving. Though he kept making scuses so your creature had to ask him four times before he finally let her start, and then it was all spoiled by the stranger.

Your creature was opening her sorry heart, telling Father Tim how, as a young girl growing up in Lynn, she'd been proud and vain, and as she talked she couldn't help but notice that there was a little fellow ahead of us on the road. He was slower than our party so it was like he was on our fish line and we were slowly pulling him in. What made your creature smile was that, even when he was only a few stone's throws ahead of us, he still hadn't noticed that we were just behind him. We were making a fair din, what with the horses' hooves and the cart, but the rain falling on the trees and the claps of thunder must've been louder again. Nor was it only your creature who'd seen him, as the others in the party smirked and smiled at each other as the fellow's back strayed ever closer, till one of us might soon be able to reach out and give him a prod. Trust that useless fellow Hugh to spoil it. When the man was just a dozen or so paces away he called out, 'And a good morning to you, cousin.'

That was strange, though. The man turned round, much startled to see the great fellowship just behind him, so we all burst into laughter, and your creature saw he had a thick black beard that covered his face almost up to his eyes, so it looked like he was wearing a woolly helmet. But instead of joining our laughter or giving us a hello back or some foreign greeting of his own, like you'd expect, he looked quite riled. Then he hurried away just as fast as he could, more running than walking, and though some of the party called out to him, 'What's your hurry, cousin?' he paid them no heed and kept going till he was far away.

But he spoiled your creature's shriving even then. Though it took a good while she finally got Father Tim back so she could finish her confession, and she was telling him how when she was young she'd been guilty of anger when her brother dropped a beetle down her dress and she scelped him on the head with a stick so his ear bled, when Alwyn called out to Dame Lucy, 'We could stop there if you want, ma'am?' and he pointed to a grassy clearing beneath the trees up ahead beside the road. That would be for lunch, and though it would be a wet sort of stop, still your creature was glad, as by now she was ready for a little more of Dame Lucy's bread and cheese and apples, and perhaps a swig or two of ale to wash it all down. But then everyone was shouting in surprise as right then up from that same grassy spot sprang the little bearded stranger, like a startled hare. He must have been sitting there hidden by the trees. Off he went just as fast as he could go, and though the rest all called out to him to stop and Sir John said he must come back and be punished as he'd insulted our ladies, he was soon gone from sight again.

In the end your poor creature never was absolved from her childhood sins, as after that everyone was gabbling about the stranger, wondering who he could be and why he'd spurned us, and saying how he merited a good scolding, if not more, for his rudeness. The rest of them all hoped we'd catch up with him wherever we stayed that night, though your creature hoped we wouldn't as he'd looked like a ravager to her. 'Didn't you see his lustful eyes?' she told the others. 'I'll be glad if we never see a hair of him ever again.' Happily, when we reached our halting place that evening, which was a village with a small inn, there was no sign of him. I'll have a peaceful night here, your creature thought to herself, but how mistaken she was.

The inn being so small, there were beds enough only for Dame Lucy and her company and all the others of us had to make do with straw in the barn, and though your creature did wonder if Dame Lucy might find a bed for her, too, seeing as she'd ridden in her cart, which made her one of her party in a way, as your creature saw it, she didn't and so your creature was humbly on straw with the rest. She chose her corner and then she went down to the stream to give her white dress a scrub, as there was nothing she loved better than to keep it clean and pure, and when that was done she went back to the inn to look for Father Tim, so she might do her second confession of the day, if it even was that, seeing as she'd never finished nor been absolved for the first.

Your creature knew something was amiss when she saw Mary and Helena coming towards her on their way to the stream. They had no clothes with them to wash and it seemed a strange moment for a walk, as it was raining again and supper would soon be ready. So your creature asked them, 'Where are you two going?' but Mary, who your creature could see from her red eyes had been crying, answered only with a sob. Helena, who seemed a little cheerier, said, not to your creature but to her mother, 'You had to,' which made Mary sob all the louder. Being curious, as any loving soul would be, your creature asked what was wrong but Mary just cast a glance back towards the inn. 'Go and ask them. They'll tell you what a wicked fool I am.'

Your creature did as she'd been bidden. The others were in the little hall, which had a hush to it, as everyone seemed anguished, aside from the three Sir Johns who looked only angry. By then your creature had guessed what had happened, as she'd seen how Gawayne had been wooing Helena every hour that he was able, and sure enough when your creature asked Constance, she answered, 'It's a sorry thing, Matilda. Gawayne and his father asked Mary for Helena's hand and Mary told them no. She gave no reason. Then she and Helena just fled out from the inn.' The one who seemed most upset was Dame Lucy, which was strange, your creature thought, seeing as she was journeying to Rome to be divorced and so should know as well as anyone that living as a wife was no paradise.

'There must be something we can do to change their minds,' she said, though Sir John, being pricked by the affront done to him, told her she shouldn't trouble herself. 'My offer is taken back,' he said. 'If a butcher's daughter feels herself too good for my son then she is not welcome in my family.' By then the innkeeper was bringing in bread and a big pot of stew and as it didn't seem right that Mary and Helena should miss their dinner your creature went out to fetch them, and though Mary said she couldn't bear to go back, your creature told her, 'You've done nothing wrong. Why shouldn't Helena keep herself clean and pure, if not for herself then for God, as it's well known that virgins are the ones he holds dearest of all?' Then Helena said she was too hungry to miss supper and so back they went, though they'd hardly sat down when Dame Lucy hurried over and tried to talk them round. 'This is a fine proposal,' she said, never caring that Sir John had just said it was nulled. 'I beg you, Helena, think again. Do you want to spend all your days in a nunnery?'

What a thing to say, your creature thought. Now You came to her in her mind's eye, saying, 'Leave it be, my sweet. Don't gainsay Dame Lucy who's been so kindly to you. She's been wed twice and hungers for it again so she won't take kindly if you start casting marriage down.' But how can I do otherwise? your creature thought. As your very own virgin of godliness I must speak the truth. For that matter as her loving friend it's my duty to help Dame Lucy, as she needs warning off from Lionel. And so your creature did just that. 'There's nothing wrong with a life spent in a priory,' she said, and though You murmured to her, 'That's enough now, say no more,' it needed saying forthrightly, so your creature added, 'The early saints told us clear as day is day that there's no state of womanhood dearer to God than virginity, and if marriage is honourable in its way, it's an unholy, noisome, dirty business, and though it may seem sweet at first, too often it turns sour.'

It was wise advice well meant but Dame Lucy had no ears to hear, sorry to say, and she gave your creature a look like daggers. 'We weren't asking for your wisdom, Matilda,' she said, and Lionel gave her a scowl too. There's my reward for telling what's righteously true, your poor dear creature thought sorrowfully. Though she didn't know the full truth of it till the next morning. Your creature would never have imagined Dame Lucy might be meanly or spiteful, but when your creature was about to take her place in the front of the cart like usual, she called out to her, 'Your foot seems much better now, Matilda. Peter and Paul will ride in the cart today,' and inside half a moment the two of them had darted past your creature and jumped up next to Jack. And though your creature hobbled a little, not so much from pain but from the wrongness done to her, Dame Lucy pretenced not to see. Nor was that all. A mile or so down the road your creature happened to be walking beside the cart and, feeling suddenly a little famished, she reached towards the sack to take an apple but she'd hardly got her hand inside when Dame Lucy called out to her, 'I'd rather you didn't, Matilda, or there'll be none for the rest of us.' Which wasn't right as there were plenty left. Finally, when your creature thought to make her first confession of the day to Father Tim, which was a righteous and holy thing after all, and pleasing to You, Dame Lucy said she couldn't as Father Tim was very busy, and she said that from now onwards your poor creature could only shrive to him once a week on Sundays like everyone else.

Rise above it, my poor dear angel, You told her. Leave it be. And so I will, your creature vowed. What a mood there was in the party now, though, which was cleaved in two. Sir John and his brood were at the front, where he thumped his boots like the very road itself had done insult to him, while Mary and Helena hid themselves away right at the back. All the rest were in between, though where they kept themselves gave away their fealties. Poor Mary and Helena didn't have many friends it turned out. Your creature kept with them and so did Constance, at least some of the time, and Oswald would hang back to talk to them on occasion. So did the boy Tom, who seemed cheered that Gawayne had been spurned, which was no surprise, as your creature had seen him blinking and looking awkward whenever Helena was near. As if he'd have any hope with her, who was a beauty and rich while he was a penniless bound delver? Another who seemed pleased was the foolish little maid who thought she was God's mouthpiece, Beatrix. Which was for the same reason in opposite, as your creature had seen her on her ass, casting sly glances at

Gawayne when he wasn't looking, though she had no more chance than Tom with Helena, the idiot child. As for the Sir Johns at the head of our party, they had quite a crowd walking with them. As well as Beatrix there was Margaret, Jocelyn and all of the Dame Lucys, as well as Joan, while her seemly sister Constance would walk with them sometimes. The only one who showed no fealty at all was Beatrix's father, Warin, who kept to himself in the middle of the group, looking sour like he had no wish to join either party.

How drear this is, your creature thought. The road was drear, as we were still on the same straight, chalk-white way with walls of trees to either side that we'd been on for three days now. And our fellowship was grown drear, too, everyone plodding or riding along and hardly saying a word. Your poor dear creature couldn't even confess her sins, being banned. So she tried to bring a little life to the party by telling the others about her own fights with Satan, and how she'd battled to do your bidding by bringing righteousness to Lynn. But sorry to say, none of them paid her much heed, while some were nothing less than uncourteous. Your creature wasn't surprised that Hugh the delver was rude, nor Warin and Beatrix, nor Joan, nor even Sir John, as none of them had been loving from the moment she joined this fellowship, but she was sad when Lionel told her, and most rudely too, couldn't she lower her voice as he was trying to talk to Dame Lucy. And though your creature hoped Dame Lucy would tell him off and call out, no, no, dear Matilda, finish your tale I beg you, she didn't say a word but just sat on her horse looking straight ahead.

Never mind, your dear creature thought. What does it matter so long as I have your sweet love, which I have more than any of these poor sinners. And then recalling her days back in Lynn, she thought of something that she might do. What this party needs most of all, your creature thought, is to be raised up to pure white godliness. The kindest thing I can do this day is to pray for them all and guide them to better ways, just as I used to do for my neighbours in Lynn. And so, in good strong voice that all might hear, she prayed to You that Sir John might fight the fiend and not give in to his worst vice, of anger, that had caused him to strike a poor servant of God. Next she prayed that Hugh should strive not to be sour minded and grasping, that Margaret should try not to be so vain and eager for baubles, that Mary and Helena shouldn't be so strange and secretive, that Oswald should overcome his hunger for dead men's silver, that Lionel should staunch his greed for great fortune, and that Beatrix and Warin should guard themselves against being lulled by the fiend into false prophesies. Finally your creature prayed that any in the party who were fornicators should find the strength to overcome their foul and abominable lusts, though she didn't trouble to say who they were as there seemed no need, seeing as half the company was guilty.

But though it was all done from kindness, to help them find their way to your heart, they weren't grateful at all. None of them said much and some rolled their eyes and others scowled. The only one who seemed understanding was Constance, who had tears in her eyes. And how unfriendly they were. When your creature walked beside Beatrix and showed her loving nature by asking how her ass Porker was today, as he'd been a little lame the day before, she wouldn't even answer but turned her face away. And when your creature asked Oswald about his neck, which had been marked by pustules and pocks ever since he'd been nipped by biters in a dirty barn a few days before, he slung his pipes over his shoulder and let out a horrid blast. Finally when your creature went up to Dame Lucy and said, 'How now, ma'am?' which was only friendly, she didn't even look down at her from her horse but just said, 'I think you've said enough for today, Matilda.'

But your creature knew she'd done right, and that it had been your own wish because soon after that You showed her your sweet blessing. We were passing by a little woodsman's cottage when your creature's eyes chanced upon a dog beside the road that had a sore on his side and all of a sudden she recalled her vision of You lying on the ground on your day of torment, then she felt a shudder rise through her, from her eyes poured wet tears and she fell into a great weeping. When Constance asked if she was all right your creature laughed through her sobs and told her, 'Don't worry, dear friend, as I'm not sad,' and she explained how a great wonder had come to her, as You'd given back her passion. Better again, the very next morning she was blessed with her roar, which was so loud that Lionel's horse, which your creature happened to be walking beside, reared up and Lionel was nearly thrown into the dirt. Thank You, my dear friend, your creature thought, smiling to the heavens.

But the fiend was closer than your poor dear creature knew. Our party walked on for several more days, which weren't easy, as the rest of them were no warmer than before, even though, filled with joy by her weeping and roaring, she did her best to bring them cheer. We stayed the night in the pilgrim hospital in a little town named Champlitte and in the morning your poor creature came awake and, like she always did, she reached out for her white dress from the floor beside her bed. She knew right away from the weight of it that something was awry. Sure enough when she held it up she was aghast to see that half of it was gone. It had been scissored and she could see the cut marks. Getting up from her bed, she held it against her and saw that it hardly reached to her knees, so it looked like a bordel woman's gear. Hearing her cry out, the others sat up in their beds and sorry to say some of them, including Dame Lucy's cook Jack and Lionel's manservant Dobbe, laughed most cruelly, like they'd never seen anything so game, and though Dame Lucy and Lionel didn't join in, being gentle folk and so more courteous, even they smiled. Peter and Paul smirked and looked at each other and seeing them your creature, who'd had a house full of brutish boys herself, guessed the truth right away. Who else would do such a wicked thing but those two?

Your creature, hoping she might yet find the missing part and sew it back, which wouldn't look handsome but would be better than nothing, put on the remnant and hurried through every room in the hospital. In the hall her eye was caught by a glimmer of white in the fireplace, which she found was a tiny shred of cloth, burned at the edges. That brought tears to her eyes. The fire was almost cold so it must've been done hours ago. When she went back the only one who showed her any care was Constance, while even she didn't show very much. So your creature knew she had only one true friend in this world, which was You.

Your creature did what she could. She went to the market and bought a blanket for tuppence, which she cut in two parts, one that she'd use as a scarf and the other that she sewed to the bottom of her dress so she didn't look scandalous, and though it seemed a little strange she didn't mind. After all, what did it matter to You if your creature wore fine clothes? All You wanted was that her soul was clean as clean could be. Perhaps there's blessing even in this horrid affront, your creature thought, because after Champlitte the road climbed steadily and she could feel the cold closing in around her, so she was glad to be warmed by the blanket sewed from her skirt, and the part that she used as a scarf.

Your creature thought that would be the finish of it all, but no, sorry to say there was no end to the foulness the devil would put into her fellow creatures' hearts. After two days' walking we reached a place called Besantion, which lay in a curve on a river and was a fair-looking city, though it would be only monstrous in your poor creature's remembrance. It was All Hallows' Eve so everyone went to mass and then Dame Lucy said we should have a game of apple bobbing, like was done by the young folk back home, when they'd give an apple a name and if they caught it that would be their sweetheart for the evening. But your creature said it wasn't righteous seeing as there'd been more than enough dallying in this fellowship already, and on God's holy road, too. So we had a quiet evening, as they usually were now, what with the sundering of the party between the Sir Johns and Mary and Helena and nobody speaking to your creature any more.

Your creature slept well and when she woke in the morning in the dormitory of the hospital, this being All Souls' Day, she could hear the others praying for their lost ones, whether it was parents or children or husbands whom they'd cuckolded with their whoring. Your creature prayed for her father and mother then her uncles and aunts and grandparents and the four mites she'd lost, too. She told them she was sorry she couldn't go to any of their graves but she knew they'd understand seeing as she was on God's adventure. All this while she'd noticed a nasty reek in the air but she thought little of it as it was a dirty place like they mostly were. She pulled on her dress, got up from the bed and then slipped her feet into her boots, only to find that they didn't seem to fit her right any more. Pushing harder, she felt her toes press into something smooth and soft. That was when your creature guessed what this was and let out a screech.

Constance called out, 'What's wrong?' but your poor dear creature couldn't even answer. Your creature took off her shoes and sure enough it was just what she'd thought. Peter was looking at her laughing to his lungs and so was Paul, as were most of them. Carrying her shoes she went through that place, paying no heed to them all, and going at a run, barefoot, she took herself all the way to the river. There she did her best to wash her feet and then her boots in the water, though she doubted they'd ever be clean again, not properly, not in her mind. I know who did this, your creature thought. It was the same ones who cut my lovely white dress into two and burned it in the fire.

Stay quiet, sweet Matilda, You told your creature. You don't know for sure that it was them. That's all very well for You to say, your creature answered, but You aren't here by the river washing it out of your boots and getting it all over You. So your creature, having cleaned herself as best as she was able, walked back to the hospital, her feet squelching in her boots as she went. By now they were all down in the hall, breaking their fast, and though she could see some of them had been laughing they fell silent when they saw her. Your creature looked at Dame Lucy and then at Constance. 'I know who did this,' she said. 'It was your two boys. I want them given a lashing, and a good one too. I'll do it myself. And after that I want Father Tim to excommunicate them both.' Father Tim held up his arms like he had some clever holy reason why he couldn't do the thing your creature had asked, but he never had the chance to speak up as his mistress cut in. 'Did you do this?' she asked the boys. 'No,' wailed Peter, pretencing himself scared, the little shit. As if he'd say anything else? 'There you are,' said Dame Lucy. 'It wasn't them.' My sweet Matilda, You urged, don't do anything rash now. Think of your own good grace. But I must, your creature answered, for the sake of truth, which is your own friend. Then she said it, loud and clear so all would hear. 'It's no surprise they're sinners seeing as they're both bastards born from the foulest adultery.'

There, have that with your bread and milk, your creature thought. They were all staring. Warin and Beatrix had the strangest little smiles on their faces. Mary and Helena were looking down at the table, Constance was blinking like she might cry and Dame Lucy gave your poor dear creature a face that was harder than white stone. 'That's enough,' she said. 'You'll not walk another step with this party.' 'I'm glad of it,' your creature answered. Then she looked round to see if anyone would take her side and when nobody did she said to them all, 'Better and better. I'll walk alone.' Up to the dormitory she went to fetch her things and when she went back through the dining hall they were all busy with their food, or so they pretenced, and they didn't pay her much heed. So she said again, 'I'm glad of it, very glad,' and she put on her dripping, stinking boots and out of the hospital she strode.

It's a blessing and I thank you for it, your creature told You as she climbed the steep hill out of the town. Not only will I be purer, I'll be faster too without those transgressors slowing me down. As she walked through fields and then into forest, your creature counted her coins and found she had eightpence left from what they'd given her. That's more than enough, she told herself. I'll beg better than ever without those sinners putting folk off. Still it felt strange being alone again. She could have sworn the birds were singing louder and more harshly now, the wind was blowing harder through the trees, and her boots were noisier as they squelched on the ground. The way was narrow and winding and the tree trunks seemed very close around her, squeezing her in.

Around noon your creature ate one of the pieces of bread that she'd snatched from the dining hall as she walked out. Her feet felt tired so she sat down to rest for a moment in a little clearing in the wood. She hadn't meant to but she must have dozed off for a moment as she came awake to the sound of footsteps coming up the path behind her. It's them, she thought. They've repented their hatefulness towards me, I'll bet, and they'll all beg me to join them once again. Will I forgive them? I suppose I must, seeing as it's your way. Though the footsteps didn't seem very many. Perhaps one of them has got ahead of the rest, your creature thought. She peered through the trees but they were so thick and tangled that all she could see was a glimpse or two of garments between the trunks. She didn't remember any in the party wearing those colours. And then, just as she started to grow uneasy, she saw, walking out onto the path just a few yards back along the way, and looking at her, surprised and not pleased at all, was the bearded ravager.

CHAPTER EIGHT

Iorwerth

I don't know what you're fussing about, Iorwerth, you'll all say. What could ever be wrong with a gift? A gift is kindness and love. A gift warms the heart. So it can be, I'll answer, but a gift can also be a chain that binds a man and drags him down. Accept that gift, feel it in your hand, and straight away you're a debtor with a new shadow cast over you, of your own bad conscience. Who knows where that gift may lead you?

Of course I'm not saying all gifts are trouble. The first I took that mattered was given sweetly enough and wanted little back from me, though it set me on the way to all the rest. It was given to me by Uncle Rhodri. My father was a blacksmith and not a rich one, but Uncle Rhodri had married well and owned a herring salting yard in our town, Llan Ffagan Fach. Uncle Rhodri always had a soft spot for me, perhaps because he had no sons himself, only daughters, and he'd often tell my father, 'Your boy Iorwerth has a quick head on his shoulders. That shouldn't be wasted.' Till one day he made sure it wasn't, and put in a word with the Bishop of Bangor, who was a cousin of his wife's. So I said my tearful farewells to my family, I took the ferry to the mainland and walked along the shore to Aberconwy Priory to begin my schooling. Uncle Rhodri was right as it turned out. I learned my letters and numbers and catechism so well that I was given another gift. Prior Hywel kept me on to study scripture and to learn Latin and French and Saxon. When I'd finished I was made a lector at the priory. Next I'd be taking orders and then who knew, one day Iorwerth ap Rhys, son of a poor blacksmith from Llan Ffagan Fach, might be a bishop or a prior. Or so I thought.

One bright spring morning when I'd just finished reading in the chapel, Prior Hywel called me over and I could see from the sly look on his face that something was up. 'I have great news for you, Iorwerth,' he said. 'Dafydd ap Gruffudd just sent word to me. His scribe died of fever a few days back and he's looking for somebody to take his place. I thought of you. You're well schooled and able and you have a fine, clear hand. What d'you say, Iorwerth? Here's honour for you.'

There was no doubting it was honour, at least of a kind. Who didn't know about Dafydd ap Gruffudd? Dafydd ap Gruffudd the great man, lord of two cantreds and younger brother to the Prince of Gwynedd, Llewelyn. Dafydd ap Gruffudd the traitor, who'd plotted to murder his brother and had turned against his own people. One winter's night at Prince Llewelyn's court, so the story went, Dafydd had kept watch through the dark hours, waiting to open the gate and let in his brother's enemy, Owain and his followers, who were to murder Llewelyn in his bed. After that Dafydd would become Prince of Gwynedd and Owain would marry his young daughter. It would have happened too, no doubting, except that Owain never showed his face. God saw the wickedness that was purposed and sent a snowstorm that was so strong and blinding that it forced Owain and his men to turn round and go back the way they'd come. Dafydd waited through the night in vain to do his evil.

When the plot was discovered Dafydd fled to England where King Edward gave him his protection, and gladly, as there's nothing Saxons love better than to set my poor countrymen at each other's throats. And when war came Dafydd thought nothing of fighting with the Saxons against his own people. The strange thing was that, given time and a little good fortune, Dafydd would likely have become Prince of Gwynedd anyway, seeing as his brother Llewelyn had no wife or heir. Many put blame on Dafydd's Saxon wife, Elizabeth, saying she was the one who'd pushed him on, but knowing Dafydd as I do – and there's no man still alive who knows him better than I do – I'm not so sure. The man had no patience, you see, not a hair of it. And there was his pride.

But I'm getting ahead of myself. Back on that bright spring morning it wasn't for me to judge Dafydd or what he'd done. Prior Hywel gave me a careful look. 'The priory often has dealings with Lord Dafydd,' he said. 'You won't forget where you were schooled, will you now, Iorwerth?' That was clear enough. This wasn't a choice for me to make but a command to obey. Like I said, beware of gifts. I owed Prior Hywel for the learning he'd given me and now I must pay my debt and go to Dafydd and, if the chance came, I must use my place to serve the priory.

So I gathered up my few possessions, I said my farewells to the other brothers and set off on the road to Denbigh, which was a sorry little place, with a castle that was always being repaired and a hall that leaned to one side like a lame man. As I walked through the gate it was only natural that I should worry what might befall me here. From what I knew of him, I guessed Dafydd would prove a mean master. I'd probably be mocked and scorned and perhaps beaten. What I never expected, of course, was that I'd be given another gift that I wouldn't seek or ask for, and that would take me down a road that I couldn't begin to imagine – a gift of confidences. Looking back I suppose I shouldn't have been so surprised. I swear there was something about my face, so it was as if letters were scrawled across it that read, 'Here's one who'll sit quiet and listen as you moan about your woes.' I might be sitting in Aberconwy cloisters mouthing my reading for the day, so I'd say it better, when a stranger would stop and ask what I was doing, and though I never urged him, in two moments he'd be sitting beside me telling me how he missed his wife who'd fallen in a river and drowned. Or I'd hear all about some fellow's neighbours, and which one of them he suspected had cursed his cow and made her sick.

Not that anything happened right away. In my first days at Denbigh I was a servant and no more. I'd write letters for Dafydd and make a note of each pig and cow and sheep and sack of grain that was paid to him by his people. He wasn't a brutal master like I'd feared. He'd sit back in his big wide chair in the hall, speaking to me sometimes in Cymraeg and sometimes in Saxon, which he spoke well, having lived there as a boy, as a hostage to the Saxon king of those days, and when he spoke Saxon he'd have a slight smile, as if he were saying, you understand, Iorwerth the scribe, but nobody else round here does. Which was true enough. Some of his followers spoke a little, which they'd learned when they were all in England with King Edward, but it wasn't much. When

Dafydd and I spoke it I'd see their looks, like they feared we were keeping them in the dark.

It was Saxon that first gave me confidences, and these came not from Dafydd but from his wife, Lady Elizabeth. A month or two after I arrived at Denbigh she had him give me another task besides writing, which was to work as a tutor for her two boys. Which they needed as till then they'd been taught by one of Dafydd's followers, a rough old brute whose notion of learning was swordsmanship – though he wasn't very able even there – and telling them a lot of lies and truffle about his great bravery in battle. I was made his helper so he wouldn't feel dishonoured and I started teaching them letters and numbers and giving them Latin and French and Saxon, and though they weren't the quickest they learned well enough. Lady Elizabeth would ask me how they were doing and with time she began to tell me her woes, too. 'I only wish there were more people I could speak to here,' she'd say. 'I've tried learning Cymraeg. I know everyone says it's quite like French or Latin but however hard I try to know them, the words just won't stay.' She gave a little laugh. 'Then to me it hardly sounds like a language at all but more like someone coughing and spitting.'

That was always how she was with me. Because I talked to her in Saxon it was as if she'd forget where I was from and think of me as one of her own. She'd moan and complain about my country and my people, I'd bite my tongue and then she'd look at me with a smile, sure that I agreed with her every word. 'As if I care that some fellow's great-great-great-grandfather was cousin to Prince somebody ap somebody,' she'd tell me. 'And I can't abide the food. I swear Dafydd's cook makes one peppercorn last a whole month.' Then she'd tell me about some shop in Derby where you could buy twenty different spices. She had four manors in England from her dower, she said, as well as a fine house in Leicestershire. 'I've told Dafydd time and again,' she said, 'why don't we go and live there, where it's peaceful and isn't so damp that if you leave your coat in the wardrobe for a week you find it covered with mould? But of course he won't hear of it.'

There was proof if I needed any. It wasn't her who'd set Dafydd against his brother and his people as he wouldn't have listened to her. No, sorry to say Dafydd had done it all of his own accord. If I had any doubts, they were ended when, soon after his wife had, he began giving me confidences of his own. These were a little different from hers, being more careful and knowing, and they began one morning when he asked me to write down a letter in French to the Bishop of Worcester. 'One of my good Saxon friends,' Dafydd said, giving me a watchful sort of look. 'Some will say I have too many of those. You probably think so yourself, Iorwerth.' Now he was looking at me, waiting. And you lied to him, Iorwerth, you'll all say. So I did. Then how could I have done anything else? He was my master and it wasn't for me to throw dirt in his face. And it was those gifts again. He'd given me my place as scribe, which was an honour, just as Prior Hywel had said, and now he'd let me teach his boys, which was an honour again. So I told him, 'Not at all, Lord Dafydd.'

And d'you know, that was all it took. A sad, trusting look came into his eyes, the kind of look that I'd seen on others who chose me for their confidences, and then out came his woes. 'I had no choice, Iorwerth,' he said. Then he told me of a banquet where, in front of all of Dafydd's followers, his brother Llewelyn had laughed and called him fumble fingers because he'd knocked over a goblet of ale. And how Llewelyn never showed him the respect he should have but treated him like an idiot boy, 'though by then I was more than thirty years old and was married with children, which was more than he was.' Another thing was that Llewelyn didn't know how to answer King Edward, so Dafydd said. 'I know just how to deal with the man, which is with care, as he's a sly brute, but my brother always has to throw his weight about and start squabbles. It'll end badly for him, no mistaking.' It was strange, though, because there was an anguish to him. Though he was royal born and lord of two cantreds and I was nobody at all, a tanner's son from Llan Ffagan Fach with not one great ancestor to boast of, I swear he looked like he feared to see disapproval in my eyes.

Beware of gifts, and soon I had another in Myfanwy. She'd caught my eye, as how could she not? With her grace and her bright, knowing smile, she seemed to glow in that sorry place, at least to me. She saw my glances and glanced right back until, with fear in my heart that I'd misread her looks, or that she was mocking and playing with me, I plucked up courage and asked her if she might come with me for a walk around the castle and to my joy she said yes. Before long, walks led to kisses. Her father, who'd been Dafydd's bard, was dead so she was his ward. One sunny morning I asked for her hand, she filled my heart with joy with her answer, and I was about to ask Dafydd for his blessing but then I didn't need to. That same afternoon I was just finishing a letter for him when he said to me, 'Oh and by the way, my answer is yes.' For a moment I wondered if that was another part of his letter but then he laughed. 'I'm not blind, Iorwerth. I see the smile on your face. And I've seen you going off for your walks.'

We were wed soon afterwards and very happily too, and that same summer Myfanwy was with child. How blessed you were, Iorwerth, you'll all say. What honeyed hours you had. And so I did, though that time wasn't all sweet. Looking at Myfanwy with her swelling belly I'd feel joy and pride, but fear too. That was a strange season, though, which felt like a close summer's day, when the sun's warm on your shoulders but you can see dark clouds rising in the sky, telling of thunder to come. Like it usually did, the trouble sprang from a Saxon, Reginald de Grey, whom King Edward had lately made justiciar of Chester. Why King Edward picked him I couldn't say. Perhaps he owed his kin a favour. Perhaps, as many said later, he was hungry to make trouble with his Cymry neighbours. Whatever his reason, trouble was what he got.

De Grey was one of those Saxons who thinks it's his duty to smear a little shit on his savage neighbours, so they know their place, and I swear Dafydd's face was like a mirror, reflecting his every provocation. First came confoundment that Saxons, whom Dafydd had thought his friends, could treat him so. That was when de Grey seized dowry land that was rightfully Dafydd's, as every man and dog knew. Next came anguish at his own weakness. This was when de Grey cut down Dafydd's woods of Lleweni saying they hid marauders, though it wasn't for him to say, while de Grey will have made a good few shillings from the timber. Finally came plain, burning anger. That was when Dafydd was summoned to court like a half-acre nobody over his lands in Hope and

Estyn. What made that worse, if it could have been worse, was that these lands had been given to him by King Edward himself as thanks for his having turned traitor and warred against his own countrymen. Dafydd had already fought in the courts for them once against another Saxon, William de Venables, and he'd won. Now Reginald de Grey said the case should be tried all over again and he summoned him to Chester to make his case.

I didn't think he'd go but he did. He took me with him and I watched him glower at every tree we rode by. He told the court that he hadn't come to fight the case but only to show respect for King Edward, as the dispute, being about Cymru lands, shouldn't be tried in Chester by Saxon law but in Cymru under Cymraeg law. Afterwards, when we got back to Denbigh, he had me write a letter – and it wasn't the first – to King Edward asking for his help. That was the iron that really burned him. Edward's answer, when it finally came, was all sly evasions and offered no help at all. So my master learned a hard truth. Even though Dafydd had turned against his own people, Edward would never take his side against one of his Saxon lords. So Dafydd finally saw how he'd been gulled. I knew what Dafydd was and what he'd done but still I swear that any man with a heart would've felt a little sorry for him then, betrayer or not.

From the day he got that letter Dafydd was changed. He wouldn't speak a word of Saxon with me any more, only Cymraeg. With his wife, who could speak nothing else, he had to, but he'd spit out the words like they were poisoned. Gone were the times when he'd told me his hopes and his woes and now he was closed and careful. He'd still have me

write letters in Latin or French, but for anything in Cymraeg
he'd send for his cousin who was a clerk at Denbigh church,
even though his hand was far poorer than mine. When I
asked him once, 'Aren't you happy with my work, my lord?'
he didn't even answer. It was strange, but I could feel it wasn't
only secrecy. It was as if our having joked together in Saxon
had left a stain.

Though I didn't write his Cymraeg letters I could guess
what they said. Lords I'd never seen before would come to
visit, hurrying into Dafydd's hall, and though they kept their
names to themselves I knew from the few words they said
that they came from all across the land of the Cymry, some
from as far away as the Severn Sea. Dafydd went on journeys,
which he didn't ask me to join him on, and which took him
and his followers away for days at a time. Lady Elizabeth saw
it as clearly as I did and was full of anguish. 'He won't talk to
me any more,' she told me, tears in her eyes and, for all her
Saxon haughtiness, I felt for her. 'I can't bear to think what he
might do. Iorwerth, speak to him, please, I beg you.' So I did
as she asked and urged him to be careful, and to beware that
he might gain nothing and lose all he had, but as I'd known
it would, it did no good. His answer was a warning look. 'If
we're giving counsel, then I'll give a little to you. You know
I've always been fond of you, Iorwerth. My advice is, don't say
another word unless you want to make an enemy of an old
friend.' That was enough for Myfanwy. 'Just do as he says,'
she said, 'or you'll bring trouble to us all.' So I kept quiet and
watched as the whole world inched closer to ruin.

It was on Palm Sunday that Denbigh was filled with news.
Dafydd and his followers had seized Hawarden Castle and

raided Flint and Ruddlan. Nor was it just on our borders that there was fighting. Over the next few days word came that my countrymen had flung themselves at the Saxons and seized their castles right down to the Severn Sea. I'm not saying I didn't feel the wild joy of it, to strike back at our old enemies, who'd been insulting us and murdering us and stealing our lands for eight hundred years, but mostly I felt fear, knowing it was a demoniac thing to have done. Dafydd had gone to war alone without his brother. There didn't seem much likelihood that Llewelyn would join. Why should he help his little brother who'd plotted to murder him? Besides, Llewelyn had something to lose now, as he had his own English wife, who was pregnant with his heir.

Myfanwy and I tried to keep our fears to ourselves, as it was no moment for long faces. We were at war and Denbigh was filled with a kind of wild jubilation, as every man sharpened his sword or practised with his spear or his bow. The only one who stayed quiet in her quarters was Lady Elizabeth. Her two boys, young though they were, had no time for letters or arithmetic now, as all they wanted was to play at fighting. Even I, who was no kind of soldier, made a show of throwing a spear at a target. And in the midst of all this joy for war Myfanwy gave birth to a beautiful baby boy. So I had another gift to trouble my dreams.

As for Dafydd, when I saw him, hurrying through Denbigh with his followers on his way to some new skirmish, he was friendlier than he'd been for a good while. 'How now, Iorwerth?' he'd ask, not distant like before but needy again, blinking at me in that way of his, like a dog that knows he may have done wrong but wants to be loved. And before long he had something to crow about, at least as he saw it. Prince Llewelyn's poor wife died in childbirth and though the baby was saved it was a girl, which meant Llewelyn had no heir after all. Now that he had nothing to lose he joined the rest of his countrymen and brought the kingdom of Gwynedd into war. Dafydd wasted no time but hurried to see him at Aberconwy and he took me with him. 'There might be something I need to have written for me,' he said, though I knew that wasn't the true reason. Sure enough when he stood beside his brother and they made toasts to victory, he looked right at me, as if to say, see Iorwerth? I've done right after all. I've made peace with my brother and now all will go well. And what did you do, Iorwerth? you'll all ask. Did you shake your head? Did you scowl and berate him? No, I smiled back, though all the while I was thinking, that's the finish of it. Now that Llewelyn's joined there's nothing that will be saved. This is the end of the world.

Nor was I wrong. King Edward's Saxons came upon us in great swarms. First they marched along the coast to Ruddlan Castle and broke our siege. Next a fleet of their ships sailed to Ruddlan and carried their army to Anglesey, my own homeland. How are you faring, my dear brothers and sisters? I thought to myself. How are you faring, Uncle Rhodri? Though little news came to us from there, except that the Saxons had taken the harvest, which was why they'd come, to feed themselves and starve us. Then word came that they were building a bridge of boats across the strait, so they could menace us from behind. Next Edward marched his main army into Dafydd's cantreds, not hasty and foolish, which might've given us a chance, but slow and careful, creeping forward inch by inch and never letting down their guard, so our raids against them were like beating an anvil with nettles, and the only ones to suffer were ourselves. All the while we heard of the terrible things they did in the lands they'd seized, burning our churches, ravaging women and slaughtering any who came into their hands. By October the Saxons were nearing Denbigh. Dafydd sent his daughters to Aberconwy Priory, where I'd done my schooling, in the hope that they'd be safe there and Myfanwy and I and our little boy said farewell to the only home we'd known together, and we clambered up the slopes of Snowdon to Prince Llewelyn's lands.

For a moment the devil taunted us with hope. Soon after Myfanwy told me she was with child again, Llewelyn outwitted an army of Saxons sent to catch him, and that under a flag of truce, too, and he drove them into the sea, so even I let my heart soar and wonder if we might be saved after all. But no, within a month Llewelyn was dead, lured into a trap by the Saxons near Builth, and after that anyone with eyes to see knew the war was lost. Because there had been plenty who would gladly have laid down their lives for Llewelyn, but that wasn't so of Dafydd, which was no surprise after all the things that he'd done. I watched them slip away, promising, 'We'll be back at the end of the winter,' though I had my doubts. As for Dafydd, he was merrier than you'd ever guess. Then he'd finally got what he'd always wanted. He was Prince of Gwynedd and, strange to say, he didn't seem much troubled that his was a kingdom of sand, vanishing beneath the rising tide. 'Mark my words, Iorwerth,' he told me, with that look of his, worried I mightn't agree, 'King Edward won't keep this up for long. He's had his lords and soldiers here since June. They won't stomach much more.'

But Edward didn't give up and his lords and soldiers didn't turn against him. In March, when the weather was calmer and the days longer, Edward's men swarmed across the Conwy and up the slopes of Snowdon, and more marched over the bridge of boats and came up from the western side. By then we weren't an army any more but a little group of fellows who were like foxes running from the hounds, always on the move, travelling from one shepherd's hut or barn to another. Only Dafydd and his family and followers had horses and the rest of us walked, going at night, when the Saxons kept warm in their shelters and it was safer. How I feared for my poor Myfanwy, and the baby in her belly. We'd all curse and stumble as we struggled to see the way, as the rain blew into our faces and we slipped on the wet stones, yet I swear my brave Myfanwy hardly complained once. Lady Elizabeth was the sorriest in our party. On most days her eyes were red from crying and she'd have a dazed look to her, as if she couldn't rightly understand how such a thing had come. Dafydd tried to comfort her, telling her in Saxon, 'Cheer up, Liz. It'll all be well, don't you worry,' but even his two sons, who'd been so full of fight before, looked uneasy now.

Did I think of taking Myfanwy and our boy and slipping away? Of course I did. Other followers of his had done just that, creeping off when nobody was watching. But who was to say we'd be any safer out there, at the mercy of Edward's soldiers? And then the chance was gone. Myfanwy came down with a bad fever and was much too sick to flee anywhere. By then we were keeping ourselves in a hut hidden in trees close to Llanberis, on the north side of Snowdon. Lady Elizabeth was bad too, and one of her boys. It was no surprise as we'd all been hungry for weeks, eking out our stores, and getting cold and wet on our night walks. All I could think of was, I beg you, God, spare my dear wife and our little boy. Spare our unborn baby.

Yet even then, when the end was looking at us right in the face, hard to credence though it was, Dafydd was still full of plans. 'Here's what we'll do,' he told me with that anxious smile of his. 'You'll stay here and watch over Elizabeth and Myfanwy and the little ones. I'll go with the rest and ride to Bere Castle.' Bere Castle? That was fifty miles away, at the very edge of Gwynedd. 'I'll raise my standard,' he said, 'and I'll summon a great new army. I'll catch the Saxons by surprise, attack them from behind and then drive them from our land once and for all. Mark my words, Iorwerth, I'll be the new Arthur.' From his look you'd have thought he already was. As he and his last followers rode away I prayed quietly to myself, please God, let this be over with. Let the Saxons catch him. Please God, let my family escape alive from this place.

But God didn't listen. For a week we stayed there, eating scraps of barley, which was all that was left of our stores, and berries that we gathered from the woods, and every day Myfanwy grew worse, till her voice was so faint I could hardly hear her words. There were Saxons just across the valley, in Dolbadarn Castle, and twice Dafydd's two boys, who kept watch, saw some coming towards the wood so I had to get poor Myfanwy onto her feet and we hobbled into the trees to hide. Though we needn't have troubled as they didn't find our hut either time. Early one morning I heard hooves then footsteps and I thought, they have us now, but no, it was Dafydd returned with his followers or what remained of them, as I only counted seven. Even Dafydd had finally lost his smile now. He'd raised his standard, he told us, but instead of finding a great Cymry army rallying to his side, he found betrayal. Someone told the Saxons he was there and they were soon swarming up Cadair Idris just as they had Snowdon.

'What's your counsel, Iorwerth?' he asked me that same morning after he returned, watching at me with those anxious eyes. And what did you tell him, Iorwerth? you'll ask. Ride into the straits and drown yourself? Swallow a bowl of deadly nightshade. Hurl yourself from a high cliff. That's all you deserve for bringing ruin on your country. But you'll know by now, I've never been skilled at telling people truths they'd rather not hear. So, instead of poking at his misery I tried to cheer him up, telling him, 'If we can hide out for long enough here then, who knows, perhaps they'll give up and leave us be?' Then I sat quiet and listened as he told me, for the hundredth time, how he'd had no chance but to make all the witless, ruinous choices that he had. 'There was nothing else I could do,' he said, looking to be sure I agreed. 'They'd insulted my honour, you see.' Then he smiled at me like I was his last friend in all Christendom. Which I probably was. 'You're the only one who understands, Iorwerth.'

That same afternoon I went to Myfanwy and whispered into her ear and she looked at me with her feverish eyes. 'You must,' she murmured. 'Just do it, I beg you.' And now finally God gave me his help. Dafydd and his followers had found some mead at Bere Castle that they'd brought back with them and that evening they opened up the bottles. Being famished as they were, their words soon grew slurred and when the last drop was gone they fell fast asleep, including even the one who was supposed to be outside on guard. I had no trouble slipping away without being noticed.

It was a clear night, the moon was almost full and I reached Dolbadarn Castle easily enough. Five calls it took before a Saxon answered from the battlements. Having been marching back and forth through the wet and cold for weeks they were more than happy to agree the little I asked. They followed me back to the shepherd's hut, laughing and cursing themselves for not having thought to search that part of the wood. Then, just as I'd wanted, they let me creep back inside. The only eyes that saw me lie down were Myfanwy's, and even through her fever I saw her relief that I was back. I gave her a nod to say it was done. I couldn't sleep but lay there, praying again and again, please God, I beg you, spare us.

And this time God listened. At first light I heard the door creak open. I took Myfanwy and our boy and huddled us tight against the wall, staring at the timbers before me, and trying to think of nothing, nothing at all except, isn't that a strange little scratch in the wood that's shaped almost like a dog. And there's another that looks like a willow. I listened as, quietly as they could, they came in, their boots scraping over the floorboards. One of Dafydd's followers heard them and he let out a shout, Lady Elizabeth shrieked, so did some of the children and then the hut was filled with cries and clanging steel. It was all over in a moment. When I finally looked back from the wall, three of Dafydd's followers lay still on the ground and he was leaning against the doorway, his eyes closed, no sword in his hand and a gash to his arm. All I could think was, we're all safe. Myfanwy and me and our little boy, we're all safe. We were the only ones that the

Saxons let go, but even then Dafydd didn't guess. The Saxons trussed him up like a pig for market and threw him over the back of a horse and as they were about to set off he jerked his head up to give me a last look, calling out to me, 'Goodbye, Iorwerth. Goodbye, my dear, good friend.'

So I got everything I'd wanted. Once Myfanwy had some food in her belly she soon grew well and within a month she'd given birth to our daughter, both of them as healthy as could be. How lucky you were, Iorwerth, you'll be saying to yourselves. You saved yourself and your family, which was all you cared about. Which was true enough, and for a time I was filled of joy. There's no keeping secrets in Gwynedd, and once the Saxons had told their tales every man and dog knew what I'd done, and I got some sour looks and sharp words. It would have been far worse, no doubting, if Dafydd had been more liked. D'you know I didn't even much care, not at first.

No, my enemy was time. Each month seemed to bring something new. First there was Dafydd's trial by King Edward and his parliament in Shrewsbury. The only blessing was that I didn't have to go myself and see Dafydd's accusing stares. Nor did I have to see what was done to him. For treason he was dragged by a horse through the town. For murder he was taken up alive, if barely, and hanged by the neck. For having started his war in Holy Week his bowels were torn from him and burned. And for plotting to murder King Edward, which even Dafydd had never thought of doing, he was cut into quarters that were ridden to each corner of England. As for his head, that went to London, where it was put on a pole above the Tower, beside his brother Llewelyn's. His children were spared but only just. His young sons were locked up in

Bristol Castle to rot and his daughters, along with Llewelyn's little girl, were sent to nunneries, to make quite sure the royal house of Gwynedd died forever.

Then time brought me Reginald de Grey, Dafydd's goader who'd begun this whole ruin. King Edward gave him Dyffryn Clwyd, one of Dafydd's two cantreds, which de Grey ruled with the same greedy, provoking haughtiness that he'd shown as justiciar of Chester. He offered me work, not as a scribe of course, as that kind of office went only to Saxons now, but as a translator, and, as this wasn't a time when a man could pass by the chance of earning some bread, I said yes. So my little family moved to Ruthin Castle, where I kept quiet and bore de Grey's baiting sneers about Dafydd and Llewelyn, and I stayed silent when he joked about my poor, grieving countrymen, and laughed at how low and barbarous they were. Mostly I worked for his bailiffs, translating the words of those few farmers who'd managed to keep hold of their lands, instead of seeing them snatched away and given to Saxons. I'd listen as, looking at me with scared, rabbit eyes, they slipped in murmurs meant only for my ears. 'They've already had everything we have.' Or, 'We've nothing stored. We almost starved this spring.' I did what I could to help them, though it wasn't much.

And I travelled with de Grey, running to keep up with his horse, when he journeyed round Gwynedd, and needed me to translate his wants to the barbarians who lived there. I went with him to Caernarfon when King Edward and Queen Eleanor came to honour their new kingdom with a visit. Edward had come to see the castle that was being built for him there, with its walls that were to be high and sturdy enough to make sure no Cymro would ever see liberty again. All of King Edward's new lords and sheriffs and officers of Gwynedd were there, to show that Prince Llewelyn's old kingdom would now be ruled in the Saxon way, like any shire of England. Edward wore Llewelyn's crown and afterwards he and Eleanor, being fond of the stories of King Arthur, took their party on a pleasing little journey round their new realm, to see some of the places in Arthur's tales. And I'm sure neither of them troubled to remember that Arthur was a hero of the Britons, our own ancestors, who'd fought and beaten Edward's Saxon kin.

Finally Prior Hywel gave me a post at Conwy Priory and I escaped from de Grey's household. Being married I couldn't take orders so he made me a clerk, looking after the stores and reading at the lectern just like I had done years before. But even here time had done its work. By royal command the priory that I'd known and loved was no more, broken down and moved so Edward could build another of his fine new castles. Myfanwy and our children, three of them now, lived in a simple hut high up the valley, watching as a new priory was made.

All the while there was a thought that wouldn't let me be, and was like an accusing finger wagging at me. Of all the gifts I'd had and all the debts I'd owed for them, I'd forgotten the one that was very greatest of all. I'd forgotten the gifts given to me by my own country, of my language, of spirit, of liberty. Worst were the times when I woke in the night, having dreamed that I was back in Denbigh, none of it had happened, and Dafydd was talking some nonsense and looking at me with his anxious eyes, wanting to be liked.

Then my eyes would open and I'd remember, almost like it was something new, that the sun had fallen and my world had died. My land was no more. Worse, I was the one who'd given them our last prince.

Myfanwy fretted about the dark rings I had under my eyes, and how silent I'd become, hardly saying a word to anyone, and speaking so quietly that even when I read from the lectern nobody could hear. She was forever urging me to eat. 'Can't you see, you're starving yourself to death,' she'd say. I just found it hard to feel hungry. 'Just be glad we're all still here,' she'd tell me. 'If you hadn't done it then somebody else would have. I beg you, be kindly to yourself, Iorwerth.' Finally, when nothing she did seemed to help, she brought Prior Hywel to talk to me, and he was the one who said I should go to Rome. 'What you need is to repent and be forgiven,' he said, 'and there's nobody better to urge God to forgive you than Saint Peter. And while you're there you can do something for the abbey,' because some years back he'd appealed to the pope's court for recompense for the lands that the Saxons had taken to build their castle, as the lands they'd given had been smaller and poorer. I could see Myfanwy was troubled at the thought of my journeying so far but she gave her accord. 'I don't want you to go,' she said, 'but anything's better than seeing you stay and waste away.'

So it was decided. Prior Hywel gave me silver from the priory to keep me on the road, then he wrote a script to take to the pope's court, and my testimonial, in Cymraeg, Latin, French and Saxon. Then he blessed my scrip and my staff and early one September morning, with many tears, I bade farewell to my dear Myfanwy and our three little ones and

I set off. It was strange, though. I'd see the hills and fields and villages as I went along but it felt like they lay behind a kind of curtain and weren't quite there, not truly. Though it was hard to feel joy, I walked and did what I must. After a couple of days I left singing Cymraeg voices behind and heard only flat, Saxon talk. I'd been to England a few times of course, with Dafydd before the war and then with Prior Hywel, though I'd never gone further than Chester. What a wide land it was, and how rich, with green fields everywhere you looked. Gwynedd's best farming land was Anglesey while here were a thousand Angleseys and more. No mistaking, when the Saxons stole this island from us, they kept the best for themselves and left the worst to us, its rightful owners.

When I was still close to home nobody was bothered where I was from, as they'd have seen plenty of Cymry go by, but as I went further, past Nantwich, and my feet felt the miles, I was met with hard faces and jeering smiles. I soon grew tired of it and so, when people on the road heard my strange way of talking and asked where I was from, I'd pick another nation, any that came to mind. Scottish or Irish were no use, I found, as they made me hardly more welcome than I'd been as Cymraeg, or Welsh as they called me. Matters were better but not much better when I was French, Castilian, Italian or a Greek Roman from Byzantium. If I picked some faraway place whose name I'd heard, like Bohemia or Dalmatia, I'd get wary looks for not being clear and known. I was best liked as a German, a Dane, a Swede, a Fleming or a Dutchman, so usually I chose one of them.

I'd hoped I might miss London altogether but there was no avoiding the place as I had to cross the bridge. Walking through those crowded, noisy streets I felt that if hell had a cousin on earth this was surely it, and looking at the throng shoving by I was amazed anew at my countrymen's foolishness. How had Llewelyn and Dafydd ever hoped to win against these great hordes? And now they were both here, poor fellows. When I walked over London Bridge I tried not to look but I couldn't stop myself and there they were above the Tower, no mistaking, two little dots atop their poles.

It was a relief to me when I left the ship at Calais and found myself in France. Now at least I didn't need to pretend myself Flemish or Aragonese. The land was dreary, flat and more flat, with only the hope of a big river to divert the eye, but the people were friendly, most of them. When I told them I came from Cymru, or the land of the Gauls as they called it, they'd smile and make me welcome. Then the French had had their own troubles with the Saxons. I heard a good deal of talk about the Battle of Bouvines, when they'd fought them and Flemings together and given them both a good beating. 'Next time we'll come and help you,' they'd say to me. Which I thanked them for, though all the while I was thinking, it's too late now. You should have come seven years ago, as that would have been of some use.

After a week or so the land grew less dreary to the eye, becoming hillier with some fair-looking towns and fine churches, especially at Lauon and Rains, but my spirits were still low, and it didn't help that in a little village that I reached after the town of Chalons, I was taken sick with a fever and had to stop for several days. The villagers were kindly enough, bringing me food and potions to drink, but I was left much weakened. And that was when I met some unwelcome fellow pilgrims. It was raining hard and the road was chalky, so I had to be careful not to slip, and I was plodding along, none too fast after my sickness, and in my own sorry thoughts, when I heard a shout, in Saxon, of, 'And good morning to you, cousin,' and turning round I saw a great crowd was just a few yards behind me. How they'd crept up on me I couldn't say. Pilgrims or not, the last thing I wanted was to go walking with a throng of Saxons, sneering at my countrymen and crowing at their victories. So I hurried on with all the pace I could manage, and left them behind. And how right I'd been. An hour or two later I was having my lunch, sheltering from the wet among trees by the roadside, and there they were again, coming up the road behind me and snarling in Saxon, saying I'd insulted their ladies and demanding to know why I hadn't stopped. As if they had some God-given right to my company? I sped away almost at a run, chewing down my bread as I went.

That put some pace into my legs, I can tell you. All that day I kept glancing behind me to be sure they weren't sneaking up on me again but there was no sign of them. As I went on and days passed I hoped they'd peeled off onto another way, to Santiago in Spain perhaps? Or that they'd drowned themselves in some river. For a couple of days I walked with a group of French from a little town in the south, who were merry enough, till their road took them away from mine and we said our farewells. I must have slowed my walking because then, as I journeyed through jagged country, all gorges and chasms, towards a place called Besantion, I stopped for a rest, looked back and there were the Saxons again, far down the road behind me. They must be journeying to Rome as

I was. That was poor luck. I walked on as fast as I was able and as I heard no shouts I guessed they hadn't seen me this time, which was one blessing. That night I didn't stop at the pilgrim hostel in the town, where they were sure to stay, but I slept in a barn an hour or so beyond.

The next morning the farmer whose barn I'd slept in asked me to help him mend the broken wheel of his cart, which I couldn't say no to, and which took a while, so when it was done I kept glancing over my shoulder in case the Saxons were close behind me. The road soon led into forest, which wasn't my favourite kind of country as, being alone, I feared I might be set upon and robbed. The wood grew darker then lighter and then darker again, till I saw a little patch of white through the tree trunks. Someone was there. I gripped my staff tight, readying myself for a fight, only to hear a scream as a figure jumped up and I saw this wasn't any forest robbers after all but a female, not a young one, with wild hair and staring eyes who was wearing a dress like none you ever saw, half white cloth and half what looked like bedclothes. Stranger again she shouted out, in Saxon, 'The ravager, the ravager. Dear sweet Jesus, protect me.'

A madwoman. And not a sweet-smelling one either. As I stepped round her I caught a strong whiff of latrines. That was strange, though. Seeing as she'd screamed and called me a ravager I thought she'd be happy to see me gone but as I walked on I could hear her steps close behind me. After a while had passed I heard her call out, 'What's your name, friend?' It seemed the reeking Saxon madwoman wanted my company now. Having no wish for hers, I remembered the gaming I'd done in her country and told her, 'No English.

Me Hungary.' That'll get rid of her, I thought, walking on at a good speed, but it wasn't so easy as that. I'd hear a twig snap and when I looked back there'd she be, three or four paces behind me, giving me a demoniac smile. She was a fast old bird, no denying.

Perhaps she was scared of walking alone in the woods? But when the trees came to an end and the path reached open country there she was still, three paces behind, so it was like an invisible cord tied us together. Now she was gabbling and for a moment I supposed she was talking to me, till I realized it was me she was talking about. 'He's Hungarian, you see,' she recounted, to nobody, as there was nobody there except the two of us. 'I know, I know, but I don't think so now. It's just that he looks like one. Yes, it's so thick you can hardly see his face at all. And he ran away from us, not once but twice.'

So she'd been with that big party of Saxons. Had they chucked her out? I wouldn't blame them. Now she was telling her friend who wasn't there about someone who had insulted her and cut her dress – so that was why it looked so strange – and who'd done something horrible to her boots. They were a bad crowd by the sounds of them and I was gladder than ever I'd kept well away. Next she was griping about a monk who'd been cruel to her when she'd been in bed with a hurt foot. I hadn't noticed any monks' habits, but then I'd only seen them for an instant. And now she was moaning about some fellow who was forever plaguing her with his penis, and who I hoped wasn't the monk. Then we climbed over a ridge and I saw high mountains up ahead, some with snow. It was empty country here and we'd hardly passed through a village all day, but God was with me and as the light began to fade towards dusk we came to a place with a dozen or so houses and a tiny pilgrim hospital. That's for you, Saxon madwoman, I thought, taking her to the door, and she seemed content enough. Leaving her there I walked to a farm a little further on, where they were kind enough to give me bread and bean stew and some straw to sleep on in their barn.

I made sure to get up early the next morning and soon after first light I was all set to go. But when I walked out of the barn who should I find, sitting on a rock and giving me a demoniac smile, but the madwoman. How she'd found me I didn't know. I walked by her without a word, though I could hear her walking just behind me. A little later I heard her start weeping and wailing. I'm not heartless and, fearing I'd hurt her feelings, I stopped and turned but she wasn't looking at me but up at the sky. Later I heard a great roar that made me jump, thinking a bear was at me, but no, this was her too. That's enough, I thought. No more of this dame. I stopped and sat down on a tree stump, waiting for her to go on, but she found a big flat stone and waited too, merrily babbling to her friend who wasn't there, thanking him for showing her something that somebody called Supper or Sipper hadn't seen as clearly as she had. I'll outwait you, I thought. You'll have to go on in the end. But I'd forgotten about her Saxon friends. Hearing their voices behind us, I jumped and of course she followed just like before.

Perhaps she's part of my penance, I thought, given to me by God? She seemed like a penance, certainly. As there was no getting rid of her I decided I might as well let her walk with me for a day or two. At the village where we stopped that night I was too tired to find different places for us both to sleep so we both stayed in the same barn, and as we lay down I heard her gabbling again to her friend. 'D'you think Hungary will try to ravage me in the night? No, I don't think so either.' That made me chuckle. Don't you worry, you shit-stinking Saxon madwoman, I thought. You'll have no trouble from me.

Over the day or two somehow I grew almost used to her. Better a mad Saxon than a sane one, I thought. And she wasn't all bad. She had a talent for begging, no denying, and she'd give one look at a fellow on the road and know just how to squeeze him. If he seemed kindly she'd ask in a sweet gentle voice if he could spare something for a poor pilgrim on her way to Rome, and seeing the state of her, with her strange ruined dress and her wild hair, he'd often give her a French farthing or two. If they seemed harder she'd burst into demoniac sobbing to break their will. If they looked anxious she'd creep up and roar at them so they jumped, and they'd give her something to make her go away. When she did well she'd usually give me a coin or two, saying, 'Here you are, Hungary.'

And with time she reeked less. Her boots were the heart of the stink and whenever we came upon a stream or a pond she'd wash them out so they'd squelch on the road, which seemed to help. Madwoman or no, I decided I might as well see her over the Great Saint Bernard pass which we'd come to before long. For that matter it would do me no harm to have a little company up there as everyone said it was a perilous and desolate spot. I could see it would be, as with each mile we walked the mountains grew higher on the horizon, till they made Snowdon look like a little midget. Yet when I asked a priest along the way in Latin, he said that these were the Juras and that they were nothing compared to the Alps that were hid behind them, and were where we'd cross the Great Saint Bernard.

Then the Juras were right above us and we were climbing and climbing. At least the madwoman was too out of breath to gabble. By then I'd realized from her words that she wasn't talking to a friend but to Jesus. So she was a holy madwoman. There were more than a few of those in this world. It seemed like the climb would never end but when we finally reached the top I swear it felt like I could see half the world. To the left was a lake and straight ahead was another, larger one, which must be Geneva. Behind it were the Alps, looking sharp as dogs' teeth. They had plenty of snow. I just hoped there wouldn't be too much on the Great Saint Bernard.

By nightfall and with tired feet we were at Lake Geneva and the next morning we took a rowboat to the far shore, which saved us a good few miles of walking, so we were told. Just before dark we reached the small town of Villeneuve at the far end and then our work truly began. Up we clambered beside the River Rhone and my pack had never felt so heavy on my shoulders. We spent the night at a little place called Saint Morris and the next day each mile seemed steeper than the last. Worse was to come. After Martigny the path went not along the valley like before, but straight up the side, weaving back and forth, and it was a rough way, with sharp stones that dug into my boots and scree that slipped and slithered beneath my feet. How I wished I might have some soft Cymraeg grass under my toes. It was cold too and misty with a steady rain falling through the white, so drops dripped from my hands, and off my hat onto my face to run down my nose. All in all

I was more than happy when we reached the next town, of Orsieres. And we had good news there. In the hospital where we spent the night there were two merchants from Florence who told me, in Latin, that they'd come down from the Great Saint Bernard pass just that morning and that there was next to no snow up there. We were lucky, they said, as this was unusual so late in the year. They knew a little English so I left it to them to tell my madwoman.

From Orsieres most people took two days to climb up to the pass, the friars told us, though it could be done in one. I was all for getting it over with before any snow came down, and when I had the Florentines tell this to the madwoman she gave her accord most readily. So, first thing the next morning we set out through the mist. We soon left the last trees behind us and the slopes were bleak and empty. As for the path, this started well enough but after an hour or two it brought us to a couple of empty shepherds' huts and after then it seemed so narrow and slight that I couldn't see how anyone would get a cart up here, as even a mule would struggle. I tugged at the madwoman's arm to stop her but she just laughed.

'Don't you worry, Hungary,' she said. 'It's going up so it must be right,' and on she dashed. Now I wished I hadn't told her I spoke no English. My growling stomach told me that it was past noon when I finally saw the horizon falling lower before us, so I knew we were almost at the top. The madwoman had seen it too. 'Here we are, here's the pass,' she cried. Sure enough the land flattened out ahead but there was no pass and no great hospital. We'd reached a ridge with a small patch of grassland and all around were little pellets of goat shit. We must've been following their track. Clearly we'd taken the wrong way out from Orsieres. The madwoman saw it at the same moment I did. 'Why did you take us up here?' she said, which wasn't right at all seeing as it wasn't my doing but hers, then I saw she was looking up at the sky, so it wasn't me she was scolding but Jesus. It wasn't him, you demoniac old fool, I thought, it was you. I pointed back down the way we'd come and she gave a nod.

The trouble was that though the path had seemed clear enough on the way up, it was anything but clear going down. It didn't help that the mist was thicker than ever. We scrambled over rocks and I soon had no idea which way we were going except that it was down. The light was fading and the mist was so bad that I could hardly see my own feet. I took a step and felt a softness in the ground beneath my toes which made me stop still, and through a slight thinning of the white I glimpsed the slope falling away to nothing. I reached out to stop the madwoman from dropping over. She was as shocked as I was and so we both sat down. If only this cursed fog would lift, I thought, but if anything it seemed to be growing worse, if such a thing were possible. So we sat side by side. I was shivering and shivering, and that was when the thought came to me, is this little spot where I'm to spend my last hours on this earth? Is this God's reward for betraying my land and my lord? Is he going to take me this night and give me to Satan as my punishment? Will I never pray to good Saint Peter, or go to the pope's court like I promised? Most of all I thought, will I never see my dear Myfanwy again, or my three little ones?

The madwoman was shivering as bad as I was and she pushed up beside me for warmth. I got out the food that I had, she got out hers and it wasn't much, just a little bread and cheese and a couple of apples. I'd thought I wouldn't need much as that evening I'd be enjoying a good hot dinner at the hospital on the Saint Bernard. We ate it down and as darkness fell we lay side by side, using every scrap of cloth and even our packs to cover ourselves, though I was still shivering and quaking on the cold wet ground. That was when the anger that had been swelling inside me for hours finally found its way out. 'I knew we shouldn't have gone up that idiot track,' I said in Saxon, my voice quaking from the cold. 'But you wouldn't stop, would you? You had to go on.' I heard her gasp. 'You speak English? You spoke it all this time?' 'So I do,' I answered her, with no apology. 'I'm not Hungarian but Welsh. I didn't say so because it didn't please me to spend my hours talking to a demoniac old woman of a nation that's ruined my own. And if you're curious, I'll tell you now that, thanks to your own foolishness, I don't think either of us will live to see the dawn.'

She went silent. She'll be angry now, I thought. She'll start weeping and roaring. I quite wanted her to, to know she was anguished as she should be, but no, to my surprise she didn't seem troubled at all. 'We won't die here,' she said, like there was not one ounce of doubt in her mind. 'Jesus promised me he'd give me a wonderful gift in Rome, you see, which means he has to get me there, and he'll get you there too, I promise.' It was strange because even though she was a ragged madwoman who babbled to Jesus for hours, hearing her say it did make me feel better. Though in truth I couldn't see it. The fog was as bad as ever and I could feel the wet of it on my face. I was so tired. 'So why don't you like speaking

English?' she asked with chattering teeth. 'What do you care?' I answered. 'Let me sleep.' But she wouldn't let me be. 'Come on, tell me,' she said. And so, though I hadn't meant to, and it was all I could do to make my mouth speak the words, I started telling her my story, about how I'd worked as a scribe to Dafydd ap Gruffudd and had betrayed him to the Saxons. And that was strange too, because even though I knew I was about to die, somehow saying it all made me feel better than I had for a good while. I'd never actually told it all to anybody till then, not even to Myfanwy or Prior Hywel.

'What's that up there?' said the madwoman. 'It looks like the moon.' So it was, a little white smear in the mist. I'd felt a slight breeze, though I'd thought nothing of it except that it made me colder even than before. I watched in wonder as the fog began to lift around us, blown away by the wind. The moon was almost full and by its light I could soon make out snow-covered peaks on the far side of the valley, looking pale and ghostly. 'Come on,' said the madwoman. 'Let's go before it comes down again.' It was hard to find the strength to get up but I managed, and I saw the drop I'd almost fallen over was only a steeper part of the slope and not a cliff at all.

Even then it wasn't easy. The moonlight was too faint to light the land well and I'd often trip or scrape my shins and knees but there was hope now and walking warmed me a little. After an hour or so we found a track and followed it till we came upon a shepherd's hut, and though there was nobody there, it was dry and there was straw to lie on and even some sheepskins to use as blankets. The madwoman, whose name was Matilda she told me, reached into her pack and pulled out two sausages. 'I took them from the friars' larder when they weren't looking,' she said, with no shame. 'Jesus said I should.' And though she'd kept them hidden from me I didn't care but was just glad to have something to eat. So, shivering side by side, we lived to see the dawn, and a glorious dawn it was too, with the rising sun colouring the snowy peaks a beautiful pink.

Now I could see the Great Saint Bernard pass, high to the south of us, and the path we should have taken down below. We hadn't gone as wrong as I'd feared. We had to clamber across country for a couple of hours but then we found the road and up we went, slow as snails, as it wove back and forth, ever steeper. Till finally, as the day was turning to dusk, I felt the way growing gentler under my feet and the horizon fell lower before us so I knew we were almost at the top. Sure enough, a moment later I saw a good-sized building up ahead that had to be the hospital. We both let out a cry of joy and then trudged our aching feet over the last yards and hammered at the door. A friar ushered us into the hall, which had a fine, welcoming fire burning. And there, sitting at two long tables close by it, was the party of Saxons.

How glad I was that I'd kept clear of them before. We'd hardly got inside the hall when one of them jeered, 'Look who it is? The fellow who insulted our ladies. And with Matilda, too.' Now they all turned to see. I would have answered but Matilda was faster. 'He won't talk to you,' she said, quite spitting out the words. 'He's a proud Welshman who doesn't like to speak to Saxons and why should he?' I couldn't think that would help and nor did it. 'A dirty Welshman?' the same one answered, giving me a smirk. 'Watch out for your horses, Dame Lucy, as he'll have them all, mark my words. They're thieves, every last one of them.' I'd never thought I'd be glad to hear Matilda howl but I was then. Raising her arms in the air and looking like some wild-haired demon she silenced him with a scream. 'He's ten times more righteous than you are, Sir John, who goes round punching abbots. He's a good, brave, noble-hearted man and a clerk of the church, too.'

They went quiet then, having not a word to say. The two of us sat down on the other side of the hall, as far from them as we could. Then the friars brought us soup and bread and stew, and simple though it was I swear I've never known food to taste so good. Matilda told me I should take all my things into my bed that night, as there was no telling what foul things they might do. 'Take your boots,' she said. 'Especially your boots.' That was the moment when, remembering her howl at the Saxons, I made up my mind. 'I'll keep you company to Rome if you like, Matilda,' I said. She smiled. 'I'd like that, Iorwerth. I'm fearful of robbers and ravagers, you see.' And so we were agreed.

Though my bones still ached from the climb, we got up early the next morning so we could set out before the others. That was a strange thing, though. The first dawn light was just coming up, it was bitterly cold and I thought we were the only ones out there but then I heard angry shouting. It sounded like it was coming from behind the hospital, near the latrine. Curious now, we both went to look. Peering round the corner of the building I saw a woman, whom I knew as one of the Saxons, and who was disputing with two men. I'd seen them the evening before, sitting by themselves in the corner of the dining hall. The three of them were too lost in their squabbling to notice us. Though I couldn't hear well enough to understand clearly what they were saying, it seemed like the two men were accusing the woman of something. The strangest thing, though, was the language they were speaking. Mostly they spoke French but sometimes they broke into Saxon and then they'd throw in words that were in no tongue I knew.

'That's Mary,' Matilda whispered. 'D'you think we should say something?' I was in no mood to get myself caught up in their trouble. 'Let's leave them be and go on our way,' I said. Then, just as I was about to turn away, I glimpsed, only for a moment, something moving at the far end of the building. It looked like a face pulling back out of sight around the corner. It seemed we hadn't been the only ones watching.

CHAPTER NINE

Tom son of Tom

If an oak starts from an acorn and a chicken starts from an egg then all my new troubles hatched from that big blundering hulk. This was the same morning when Dame Matilda stormed off because somebody had laid turdies in her boots. Most of them were happy to be rid of her and her weeping and howling and preaching at us all, though I thought it a shame too, as she wasn't so bad for all her anoyful ways. I couldn't help but feel sorry for her when she marched out with her dripping, stinking boots and her snatched bread, trying not to cry. Warin said it wasn't any of us who'd done it but two Dutchmen he'd seen creeping about in the night and who'd left early. 'I'd have told her if she'd only given me the chance,' he said. Which might've been right, I supposed, though it did seem strange that such a foul thing would be done by strangers who she'd hardly howled at even once.

We all left the hospital and were walking through the town of Besantion and like usual I was rattling my bowl at everyone who walked by, as like usual I was down to my last few coins. Though I might have had even fewer, as if there was one good thing about being back in my rags it was that I did better begging. Anyway, we came to a narrow way and that was where we struck the hulk. He was loading a sack onto his donkey's back and being a big jobbard of a fellow he all but blocked the road. I tried to step round him but I swear it seemed like he shoved into me on purpose. Perhaps he did. Perhaps he didn't like pilgrims. Some folk didn't and said we were just living off them with our begging to be at ease and do no work. My bowl flew out from my hand and clattered onto the ground and when I picked it up, along with all the pebbles I kept in it to give it more noise, I saw it had a crack. It was small enough. Never mind, Sammo, I thought, as that won't do much harm. It'll still see me to Rome and probably all the way back home too.

But over the next days, as we went through empty country, where we'd hardly pass three villages in a whole day, which was hard on my begging, the crack grew a little longer and then a little longer still, till the bowl didn't feel solid any more but like two halves creaking together. The truth was I needed that bowl as much as I needed my own legs and arms, as if I couldn't beg I couldn't eat. Up ahead we saw the first of the mountains, which were called Juras and which were a hard climb, though there was worse to come, Oswald told us. After the Juras it was easier and I begged some French ha'pennies in Geneva but then I had to spend most of them on the boat we took across the lake. If I'd had a choice I'd have saved the ha'pennies and walked round even though it was longer, but the rest were all for the boat and I didn't want to be left behind. Then we were climbing and climbing for days and I felt light-headed from famishment. Alwyn would ask me to lend a hand pushing Dame Lucy's cart, which the horse couldn't manage alone, the way being so steep and stony, and it was a sufferance giving it my shoulder and finding my nose so close to her sacks of bread and grain and apples and cheese. I know they smell good, Sammo, I thought, but I can't ask my angel now. Not me, who shamed himself pawing at Lisa the nun. Being so starved I'd sometimes slip and fall and Oswald, who saw how I was, would give me some of his bread and cheese though he had little himself. Brigit sneaked me some apples from her mistress a couple of times, and others who helped me were Constance and also sweet Helena, who'd quietly hand me some bread and cheese, and when I tried to thank her she would slip away without a word.

Finally, though I'd thought I'd never see it, we reached Saint Bernard's Hospital, which was where we came across Matilda and the strange fellow who'd spurned us. The rest of them were all praising themselves and saying they must have God's blessing seeing as there'd been no snow but all I could think was, thanks be to this wonderful stew. The first taste made my head spin so that I feared I might swoon and knock over my bowl and spill the rest, so I held the edge of the table tight to steady myself. I swear it was like God himself was in there it was so fine and though I didn't like to seem greedy, I couldn't help myself and when my bowl was empty, which it soon was, I asked the monk for more, and I must've looked properly starved to him I dare say, as he filled it up right to the top.

After that I vowed that the very first chance I had I'd carve myself another begging bowl and a good one too, that I could rattle seven times louder than this poor, broken thing, so I wouldn't go hungry again. I'd need help, as I had no tools besides my dinner knife, which was too blunt to carve porridge, but God gave me his helping hand. A couple of days after the pass we reached a good-sized hospital and when I asked the monks, one said he did carpentry for the place. 'Go into the forest just behind here,' he said in French, which Father Tim turned into English for me, 'find a piece of wood you like and I'll carve it for you.'

So I went off to do as he'd bidden me. We'd stopped walking earlier than usual that day, being tired after Saint Bernard's pass, and it was still afternoon. Though it was cold from being up in the mountains, the sun was peering at us just above the peaks and still had a little warmth in him yet, and Lionel and his man Dobbe were lying back on a big stone with their faces in his glow, such as it was. Nearby on a patch of grass Sir John, who never tired of showing off his soldiering days, was teaching the two lads, Peter and Paul, how to fight with swords. Not that they had real ones of course but sticks with smaller sticks tied crossways with twine to make hilts. Sir John was showing them how to parry and the rest and they were both laughing and smiling like they'd never had such joy.

It wasn't easy finding the right piece of wood. The monks must've been through the forest not long before as the ground had been cleaned of every twig. I went higher and then higher again till finally I found a horse and cart track which, just like I'd hoped, led to a little shelter with a big pile of wood beneath, all chopped to dry for the fire. Those cloisterers won't miss one piece now will they, my old beastie? I thought. Let's make sure it's a handsome one that will last. After a time I found one that wasn't too big nor too small and that didn't have any crack or weakness that I could see. This'll do, Sammo, I thought, and back down I went.

I knew something was stirring even before I got out of the forest, from the shouts I heard, which sounded like the two boys. Sure enough, when I walked out into the open I saw Sir John was gone and the younger one, Dame Lucy's Peter, was squealing, 'I won't be the Welshman. You're the Welshman,' and though he was only a little mite he was thwacking away at Paul with his wooden sword with all the strength he had. As for Paul, knowing himself bigger, he wasn't striking out but just stopped Peter's blows, though even that was hard for him, Peter being so worked up. I wouldn't have thought anything of it except where they were. Don't ask me how but they'd fetched themselves away from the grass and were on the rocks right above the river. It flowed through a little kind of chasm there, like a worm in a hole, and if either of them lost his balance he'd be over, I could see, to drown in the cold water or bash his head in on a rock, like my poor Sammy had in the well. The surprise, though, was Lionel and Dobbe. The two of them were laying back on their stone in the glow just as before, like nothing was amiss, and I swear Lionel had a smile on his face like something had made him laugh. I could hardly believe that, as though they were facing a little away they must've heard.

'Stop that,' I shouted out to the boys, but they were too riled to notice. So I ran towards them as quick as I could, shouting again, 'Stop that fighting this moment.' Now they heard me, or Paul did, and he turned towards me. Little Peter, though, seeing him look away, grabbed his chance and whacked him with all his strength right on the knee. My heart was in my mouth as he'd struck out so hard that he looked like he might tip himself over the edge. That gave him a scare and after that they were both shamed and still.

It was only now that Lionel paid any heed. 'What's going on?' he asked like it had only just begun. I could hardly look at him, gentleman or no. Back in Minster there was nothing folk were more watchful of than little mites getting up to trouble near the river or the well, as everyone knew how that could end. Even being watchful we'd lost several, including my poor Sammy of course. So, though I was only Simple Tom, poor and bound and of no highness at all, and the boys were seven times gentler of birth than me, I cried out at them, 'You two, come inside right now.'

They both got an earful from their mothers. Paul had it worse and Constance quite shrieked at him, 'Can't you see I'm already worried to death about you, and now you do this.' Though in truth it hadn't been him at fault so much as the other. Then isn't that just the way? The worst churl gets off light if he has a fine name. The mothers both thanked me for stopping them and bringing them in, though they thanked Lionel more, seeing as he was the gentleman.

I dare say it shouldn't have, but that gnawed at me. It wasn't that I cared who got thanks. It was the thought of him sitting back on his stone and doing nothing when those two fellows were close to murdering themselves. I took my piece of wood to the cloisterer who carved it into a bowl, which he did nicely, but the thought of it all was still working away inside me. I had to tell someone and so, as we waited for our supper, I told Oswald, seeing as he was the one I was most amicable with in the party. He was as anguished as I was. 'You're sure they heard the boys?' he said. Of course they had, as those two had been squealing loud enough to wake a man from his grave. Oswald gave me a dark, knowing look. 'Perhaps Lionel wasn't troubled if one went over,' he said. 'Especially Dame Lucy's boy. She's his betrothed, after all. He could be happy to have the road clear for any progeny she bears him.' But then right away he gainsaid himself. 'That makes no sense, though,' he said now. 'Lucy's boy Peter was born out of wedlock so he's nothing to Lionel.' Which was true. If Dame Lucy bore Lionel's child then he'd be heir. 'Unless he just thinks Peter's in his way,' I said, 'and he's happy to be rid of him.'

The truth was that anyone with a beating heart would've shouted out. There was something awry here, no mistaking, and though I wasn't one to go poking into the doings of high ladies and lords it didn't seem right to do nothing either. Oswald was clear. 'You have to tell Dame Lucy, and Constance too,' he said. 'All the more so seeing as Lionel and Dame Lucy are to be wed. Who knows what he might do. Saying nothing is the devil's road, no mistaking.' It did seem the right way to go. And it would show me better in my angel's eyes and help make up for my having pawed at Sister Lisa.

Or so I thought. By then it was almost dinnertime and the rest of them were already gathering in the hall with their bowls, waiting for their bread and stew. Seeing Lucy and Constance were sat side by side, which seemed a blessing, I plucked up courage and started telling them about Lionel and Dobbe doing nothing, and though I tried to do it quietly somehow the place fell into a hush and everyone began listening. Dame Lucy and Constance were looking at me with wide eyes. Dame Lucy didn't let me finish but turned to Lionel. 'Is this true?' she asked.

Already I was beginning to wonder if I'd been a proper fool, and I thought of the old saying, rich folk's justice is a penny to pay, poor folk's justice is dangling from a rope. Lionel frowned like he was amazed. 'But we all ran to the boys together,' he said, giving a look that wasn't angry but more sad and puzzled. 'I've never done Tom any harm,' he said. 'I can't understand why he'd say such a thing about me.' It would have been better for me if he'd raged and shouted, as that would have made him seem guiltier. For a moment I had hope, when Constance asked her boy, 'What happened, Paul? Did they all run to you together?' but Paul just waved his arms. 'I didn't see,' he said. Nor would he have. He'd have been too caught up in their fighting.

'Well, Tom?' Dame Lucy asked, looking at me. Somehow everything had turned around and now I was the one with fingers pointing at me. 'Did you make all of this up?' Dame Lucy asked. I tried to answer her, truly I did, but somehow all that came out was stammering, and though I hadn't confessed one thing, I could see it looked like I had. What a fool I am, Sammo, I thought. As if Dame Lucy would take kindly to me slandering her beloved paramour. Now she gave me reasons for doing it. 'Is there something you have against poor Lionel?' she asked. 'Or did you hope that by reviling him like this you'd make yourself look better in my eyes, and that I'd forgive you for what you did in the convent and give you back your fine clothes?' That was worse for having a scratch of truth in it and I was stammering even more than before.

If there was one blessing, and it wasn't much, it was that there was nothing more I could lose seeing as I'd already lost it all after the sisters. But there was what I gained, which was shame. I swear as I sat at the table eating my stew and sops with the rest of them, I had my head bowed and felt like I really had told foul lies about Lionel. What if I'd been wrong about it all? What if the boys had only just gone close to the river a moment before I'd come out of the wood? Then it would be no wonder he hadn't paid them heed. He was cheery enough now, making a great fuss of Dame Lucy, whispering in her ear, wicked things as I guessed, as she shrieked with laughter and pretenced to look shocked. Trust Hugh to make me feel worse. 'Who did you think you were, King Edward?' he asked me with a smirk. 'A nobody, a poor planter, and bound too, pointing your finger at gentle folk.' Oswald murmured that he was sorry, blinking and looking down at the ground. As if that was much use.

That night I swear it was like I had a fever. I couldn't bear the thought of walking on, shamed though I'd said nothing but the truth. I lay awake till at some hour in the dark I knew my mind. If she wants to believe Lionel then she can believe it without me, I thought. I don't care how alone or in danger I'll be, as it's better than going on like this. I'd seen there was a fair moon shining so I took up my scrip and pack and staff, I went quietly from the dormitory and then I started down the road, and I never cared when clouds hid the moon's face and I stubbed my toes on stones I couldn't see.

I don't need any of them, Sammo, I thought. Though it was hard being alone. I'd never thought I might miss the sound of Oswald's bagpipes but when I reached the next town I did. Waiting to fall asleep in a barn that night I had a little fight with myself. Perhaps they'll all stop here, part of me thought, and they'll be sad that I went off, and will be friendly now. But the other part of me said no they won't. You've walked too far, having started so early, and they won't stop here but at the village you passed through three hours back. And even if they did come here they wouldn't be friendly. Dame Lucy will still think you a liar, Lionel will still give you sorry frowns, Hugh will still smirk at you and the ones who say they're your friends will do nothing, just like before.

At least begging was a little easier, as folk were sorrier for me now I was all alone. Not that I was rich but after a couple of days my scrip had a bit of weight to it, which was the first time in a good while. It wouldn't pay back Sir Toby's shillings nor anything like, but it was something. And in the end I wasn't alone for long. By the second afternoon after I'd set out by myself the mountains were well behind me and the hills were growing rounder and softer looking, while the air had lost its cold touch. I walked into a village beneath a great castle and a local fellow pointed me towards a barn to sleep in, where I found six pilgrims already there, and so I met my new fellow journeyers. They all had mops of hair that were pale as straw and where they'd come from I couldn't say as I couldn't understand one word they said, nor they me, yet it didn't seem to matter at all, as they were the friendliest folk you could meet. Instead of sidling away at the sight of my rags, like most folk did, they shook my hand and greeted me in that strange tongue of theirs, saying – so I imagined, as there was no way of knowing – 'Good day to you, cousin, and how are you?' They had a fire going and they made a place to warm myself and even gave me some bread and nuts and berries they had.

These are kindly fellows, Sammo, I thought. I can't see these coaxing me into wickedness with nuns or making me out a liar when I was telling God's own truth. So we all had a most merry evening in a way, sitting round the fire, sipping a little kind of wine they had, which was sweet and tasty as could be. When we all got ready to sleep I thought, these fellows love their gear all right, my old beast, because they lay down all in a row with their cloaks rolled up as pillows and their hats above their heads by the wall, where nobody could reach them without stepping over and waking them. Then again it was nice-looking gear, no denying. Their cloaks looked thick and warm and so did their hats. Mine wasn't up to much I knew, having been sewed by Auntie Eva, and Hugh had laughed at how it was all skewed, but, being taken with their ways, I followed them as far as I was able, making a nest for myself in the corner opposite.

Waking up the next morning I dearly hoped they might let me tag along with them, as I liked having company even if I couldn't understand what they said, but I needn't have worried. They shared their bread with me as if I'd been with them for weeks and then we all walked together. So we passed the next few days, going through land that was hilly and then flat as a table. We took a ferry over a wide river whose name was Po, as I guessed, as that was what they said when I pointed at it and shouted, 'What's that?' Though of course they mightn't have understood and Po could've meant water, or river, or even fishes. Everything was growing different by the day and the game I'd played with Oswald wouldn't have done now, as we passed trees I'd never seen before, let alone could name. The food was strange, too. In my stew I'd find little black fellows with pips in them, which were sharp and sour to the bite, and though I didn't like them at first I grew used to them with time, till I quite liked their foreign taste. 'Olivy,' they were called, so said a monk when I asked him. It was often foggy in those parts, especially in the early morning, not so thick that I couldn't see my way and would lose my step, but enough that you couldn't see far. This is good robber weather, I thought. Not that I had anything that anybody would much want. But, so you heard, if you had nothing some robbers would cut you just for thwarting them. So there was another reason I was glad to have company.

We reached a place called San Donen, where there was hardly a house that wasn't burned down so there must've been warring not long ago I guessed. It was no place to stay and we were just coming to the gate to leave, which was one of the few things that hadn't been wasted, when three fellows who looked like they were the town watch blocked our way. I thought nothing of it, as all they wanted was to see our scripts, which happened often enough, when we were going over a bridge or into a town, and was to be sure we were rightful pilgrims. The mops handed them theirs, I did the same, the fellow with little beady eyes looked through them and gave them all back, and that's that, so I thought. It nearly was, too, and who knows how the rest of my journey might've gone if it had been. But then I saw Beady Eyes was squinting up at one of the mopheads' hats. Next he was holding out his hand to be given it, which the mophead wasn't keen to do, but did. Beady Eyes started feeling the cloth with his fingers and then he had a wide smile on his face. Now he was shouting, the mopheads were protesting but they handed over their hats and their coats and so did I. Beady Eyes cut one of their cloaks with his knife and pulled out a big pebble of pretty yellow glass and then he started doing the others, too, till he had a whole bowlful of them. The mopheads went quiet then and we were all steered into the gatehouse and locked into a little room with one small barred window.

I just wished I could understand what was going on. The mops were shouting at each other and especially at the one whose hat Beady Eyes had picked out. Then I had a worrisome thought. Back in Minster Father Dan told us once of the wicked folk in long-past days who worshipped stones and other devilish things, while Father Will had warned me that when I was in these foreign lands I must be watchful for folk who said they were Christians but who were really Satan's whelps, having been lured by the fiend into devilish ways. Heretics and Cathars, they were called. Oswald had talked about them too, and had told us we must be careful who we talked to on the road. 'You don't want to end up being burned on a pyre,' he'd warned. Had I been walking with a crowd of them? I wondered. That might be why they'd been so very friendly. As they all argued with one another I crouched in the corner, trying to keep as far away as I could, though, being a very small room, it wasn't easy. I didn't sleep much that night. Have they got my soul now, Sammo? I wondered when I woke. Have they given it to Satan and am I one of his own creatures? That put fear in me. I didn't know how I'd even know.

Never in all my life was I so glad to hear my own tongue spoken as I was later that morning. First I heard a rattle of wheels in the distance, then the clop of horses' hooves and finally, just as I'd hoped, I heard voices that had a dear, familiar drone to them. The moment I saw them I called out through the little barred window with all the voice I had,

'Stop, my friends, I beg you. Come and help me. It's Simple Tom and I'm to be burned as a heretic.' I feared that, still angry I'd sneaked out in the night and left them behind, they'd pass me by but no, up they all came to the window. Even my angel Dame Lucy was friendly and, looking at me through the bars, she laughed and said, 'Oh Tom, what have you done now?'

Best of all it turned out I wasn't a heretic after all. Father Tim talked in Latin to Beady Eyes, who had me brought out of the cell and pick out my hat and my cloak, which Beady Eyes had scissored open like all the rest, and I was let go. 'Your friends are traders pretending themselves pilgrims so they don't have to pay customs dues,' Father Tim told me. He said the yellow stones weren't false gods but a jewel that was called amber. 'They shouldn't have kept you,' Father Tim said, 'seeing as you had no amber hidden in your clothes.' So I wouldn't have been burned after all but just hanged perhaps. That was a gladful moment. Though, looking back, and seeing the mopheads all peering out of the little barred window, I couldn't help but feel sorry for them, who were still in jail and in fear when I was free.

But what a joy it was to be back among my own fellows. I never even minded when Hugh made a sport of me, laughing at my scissored gear, which they all did, saying it looked like feathers and that I was like a chicken, and then telling me, 'I swear there's no end to your wickedness, Tom. First it's lust with nuns, then it's lying and now it's journeying with felons and cheating the customs.' I told Dame Lucy I was sorry I'd fled from them. 'Now you'll know not to do so again,' she answered, quite kindly. And so I did. Nor was she the only one who was welcoming. Oswald said he'd been worried for me. But the best was Brigit. As we walked out of San Donen she took me a little away from the rest and told me in a quiet voice that she'd never much liked Lionel, though she'd tried her best to, as she'd wanted her mistress to have a righteous paramour for once, and not a low cur like all the rest. Then she said that when Lionel and Dobbe had first come to Dame Lucy's manor, covered with mud and bruises, Lionel had said they'd both been chucked from their horses after a bolt of lightning struck a tree close by them. 'But I thought it strange,' she said, 'because I heard no thunder that morning.' And their horses were never found. Brigit said she'd half expected him to show a malign side like all Dame Lucy's other curs had, and be found groping a brewster or bordel woman, but he'd stayed always very clean, and wouldn't even lie with Dame Lucy, saying it wasn't righteous, not till they were wed, which kept her famished for him. 'But I saw him once in one of the inns,' she said. 'He'd caught a mouse from the straw and with one hand he was holding it by the tail and with the other he was pricking it with his dinner knife, making it squeal and squirm from the blade. I know it was only a mouse, but the way he smiled as he did it I didn't like at all.'

I hope Dame Lucy knows what she's doing with him, Sammo, I thought. Then all I could think of was the climb, because I'd reckoned we were finished with mountains but it turned out that we had to go over some more now, which were called Apennines, Oswald told me. These weren't so high as the Alps, which we'd got over easily enough, so I wasn't much troubled, at least not at first, but as the hours passed I wasn't so sure. It had been chilly down below in San

Donen and with each step we climbed it grew colder. Then
the sky turned dark, an icy breeze blew from behind us that I
felt all the sharper because my cloak and hat were scissored,
so it blew through three dozen holes, and I was shivering and
my teeth were chattering. Oswald said there was a hospital on
the pass, which couldn't be too much further, so he thought,
and I hoped he was right.

But I saw no sign of any pass nor any hospital. The way
grew so steep that the riders had to come off their horses and
walk and then we were struggling with Dame Lucy's cart just
like we had at Saint Bernard's pass, getting a second horse
tethered to the front to pull while a crowd of us pushed from
behind. And then it started to snow. D'you know, I think I
laughed. Isn't that just all we need, Sammy, I thought, which
I shouldn't have, I dare say, as it was just the sort of thing that
will goad the devil. Before long it was coming down quick and
thick, the horses were slipping and so were we. We stopped to
change one of the two pulling the cart for another who wasn't
so spent. And don't ask me how but nobody remembered to
hold the cart from behind, and next thing I knew the beast
who was still fettered was getting dragged backwards and
reared up, the shafts came off him and the cart started rolling
back down the road, slow at first but then faster till it was
making a great rattle. And though we all ran back to try and
stop him it was too late and he crashed clean into a tree.

'You know what,' said Dame Lucy, 'we'll just leave it. We'll
load everything onto the horses.' Which hardly needed saying
as the whole rear part was broke and both the back wheels
were smashed to splinters. So we set to work in the snow
getting everything onto the horses' saddles, which wasn't

easy. What a lot of stuff she has, Sammo, I thought. She can't ever have used half of it. Under the sacks of apples and such there were Jack's pots and pans and there were boxes of plates and pretty knives and forks and spoons, which we had to tie on the saddles as best we could. There were two heavy little chests, which were bowls and plates Alwyn said. Worst was a huge one full of her gowns, which would have sunk any horse, so we had to empty it and put them all in sacks, though Dame Lucy wasn't happy at all. 'They'd better not get spoiled in the wet,' she said.

Finally it was done and on we went. It was easier without the cart but not much, as by then the snow was coming down so bad that we could hardly see a thing and I had little notion if we were on the road or no. Then, though, the slope ahead grew lighter with more sky showing, giving me hope, and Jocelyn, who had the sharpest eyes of any of us, for nuns and anything else, shouted out, 'Look, over there.' Following the point of his finger through the snowflakes, which were flying about like mad things, I saw a straight line going crossways, and then another straight line at the end going down. It's the hospital, I thought. We'll be all right now, my old beastie. Let's hope they've got a good fire going and some stew hot and ready for our supper.

I soon saw I was wrong. It was a building all right but the nearer I got the smaller it looked, and then I noticed a kind of dark smudge in the roof. 'It's a shepherd's hut,' said Sir John crossly. It wasn't much of a hut either. The door was gone and the smudge in the roof was a hole, so when we got inside we had snow whirling down through it and there was quite a covering of it on the floor. If it had been left to me I'd have gone on, as all I could think of was that tasty stew I'd been dreaming of, while by then I was so cold that it was like I was wild and happy with it. But the moment Margaret got out of the wind she sat down in the corner. 'I'm not taking another step,' she said. Then Alwyn said we were probably so far off the road that we'd never find our way and might wander for hours and freeze to death in some hollow. His notion was to try and light a fire. He had a set of fire irons and a box and so did Oswald. There was some wood piled up in the corner and some kindling. We tethered the horses and Beatrix's donkey and then piled up Dame Lucy's things in the doorway to try and block it, though they didn't make much of a door being mostly sacks. Alwyn climbed onto the roof and put some sackcloth over the hole, with stones on it to hold it down, though it flapped so loud that I was sure it would soon blow off, while we still had snow coming round Dame Lucy's things and through the doorway.

Alwyn and Oswald started working away with their fire irons, trying to strike a spark. They wanted some scorch cloth to catch, and can you believe it, Hugh said they should use bits off my shirt. 'Just because it's rags doesn't mean I don't need it,' I said, through my chattering teeth. The one who had plenty of cloth to spare was Dame Lucy, of course, and though she wasn't keen, saying it was fine gear, in the end she gave us a couple of pairs of worn-out stockings, and Lionel, though he wasn't eager either, gave us a set of his toe rags, which Oswald cut up into pieces with his dinner knife. Still I couldn't see it going well. Whenever one of them struck a spark and it looked like the cloth had caught, the wind and snow would put it out.

Don't folk say if the devil's bit you once he'll bite again and then again? We'd lost the cart and lost our way, it was almost dark, the snow was coming down thicker than ever, so it was hard to think how things might grow worse but then they did. The first I knew of it was a shriek and then I saw Constance kneeling over her boy, who was lying very still and moaning, poor mite, and I saw he'd spewed on himself, his face was all swelled up so his eyes were closed and I could hear him struggling to breathe. 'I can't believe it,' Constance moaned. 'I was so sure he'd be all right till he got to Rome and could be saved.' She started praying, Joan joined her and then everybody was, and not only for little Paul but for ourselves, too. I was as loud as any of them. 'Please God,' I called out, 'make the poor lad better. Save our poor souls and don't let us freeze to our deaths. All we want is to get to Rome and to do it for you, seeing as it's your own holy spot. Please God, let me save my dear little beastie.' Father Tim was praying in Latin, which God would like, I thought, seeing as that was what he spoke to his angels.

And then, just when everything seemed so dark, something gave hope after all. I heard another sound beside moaning and praying, which was one note hummed again and again, and which I knew right away. It was Beatrix getting ready to be God's voice. God's help, that's what we needed now all right, and if anyone would bring it to us it was her. Everyone stopped praying to listen and, aside from her humming and the roar of the wind, the hut fell quiet, and even Father Tim, who'd always sneered at Beatrix before, looked at her with wide, hopeful eyes. And there it was, his lovesome, sweet, croaky voice. 'My dear children,' he said, 'I wish I could help you but I can't.' Everyone gasped and I could hardly believe it. Why have you come then? I thought. To scold us? But he wasn't finished. 'Because,' he went on, 'there are some here among you who pretend to love me but they lie. In their secret hearts they scorn me, and my dear son who gave his life for you all, and the sweet virgin too. Their curses have led you to this place and have made this poor boy sick. Until you cast them out from your fellowship I cannot help you.' I was looking round now, trying to think who could do such a thing, and Constance said it aloud. 'Who?' Then the strangest thing happened. Though the light was dim I saw Beatrix's finger point straight up at the ceiling and then come down again, moving this way and that ever so slowly, till it finally pointed at Mary and Helena. 'Here,' said God. 'These aren't my children. They're Jews.'

Jews? My thoughts were in a swirl like the snow. Mary let out a shriek. 'That's a lie,' she cried out, but then Beatrix's father shouted her down. 'No it's not. I saw you, Mary, early that morning on Saint Bernard's pass, over by the latrine, arguing in foreign words with those two travellers who knew you. And they were Jews just like you. The clerk said so.' Now Mary was spluttering. 'Yes, they were Jews and we knew them long ago, but we're not Jews, not any more. That's why they were angry with us. We converted. We're as Christian as any one of you. I can tell you my catechisms and prayers as I've learned them all, every one. And. . .' But she got no further as Sir John let out a roar. 'Jews! And you almost tricked us into letting my boy marry your godless daughter.'

Now God was speaking again. 'You must save yourselves and cast them out,' he croaked. 'And take their food and their cloaks. They won't need them, as Satan will keep them fed and warm.' That was enough for Sir John. 'Out you go,' he shouted, giving Mary a little shove, which made her shriek again. Jack the cook was at his side, Warin too, and I heard some others, I think it was Hugh and Margaret and Joan, add their voices to Sir John's. 'Out with you, out.' I didn't know, I just didn't. It didn't seem right but then God himself had said we must. Mary was wailing, 'Don't do this, I beg you,' but Helena was strangely calm. 'It'll do no good, Mother,' she said. Then, giving Beatrix a long, hard stare, she let her cloak drop from her shoulders and stepped round Dame Lucy's things and out of the door, and Mary followed her.

Down went Beatrix like a doll as she did when God had left her, and then in a confounded voice she was asking where she was and what had happened, so Warin told her. After that everyone sat there, very quiet. Alwyn scratched away with his fire irons to try to get a spark and the wind howled and moaned. Till somewhere in the din of it I realized that there was something else, a little whisper that might have been going on before, but had been too weak for me to hear. It was Constance's poor boy, Paul. 'It wasn't them,' he murmured. 'They're nice. They weren't with us when I was sick before so it can't have been them.' Constance tried to soothe him. 'Don't trouble yourself,' she told him. 'You'll be all right now. Just lay still and rest.' But he wouldn't stop. 'It's not right,' he said in a whisper. 'Fetch them back.'

And all of a sudden, don't ask me why, but even though God himself had said so, I knew that Paul was right. 'I'm going out to find them,' I said. 'No you're not,' said Sir John, but here was an odd thing, because his voice, which was usually strong as stone and had no doubt in it, didn't sound sure of itself any more. It was like a little door had opened and let something in. 'I'll come with you,' said Oswald. 'And so will I,' said Jocelyn. So it was the three nun treaders all together. Next it was Father Tim. 'And me,' he said. 'They're as Christian as us, whatever they used to be.' He might've said that before, Sammo, I thought. But then I might've too. It just hadn't come to me. It was like a kind of wave rushed in and swept you up. Then it was Brigit, as well. 'I'll come too,' she said. And though Lionel said to Dame Lucy, 'D'you think she should?' Dame Lucy didn't answer and Brigit went to the door with the rest of us.

Oswald took Helena and Mary's cloaks, which Beatrix had been using as blankets, and out we went. The wind hit me hard. The snow was still coming down fast and it was deep to step through, though the cloud had thinned so at least there was still a glimmer of light in the sky now. 'Here, take this,' said Oswald and he gave me Helena's cloak. That's a good warm bit of gear, Sammo, I thought, as it was better than anything I'd ever worn. But we could see no sign of them. We all called out, 'Mary, Helena, where are you?' as loud as we were able but the wind snatched the words right out of our mouths. This won't do, I thought. We'll never find them.

Then Oswald tapped my shoulder. 'Wait here,' he shouted above the wind. 'I won't be long.' You'd better not be, I thought, or we'll all be snowmen when you find us again. The three of us stood there, getting colder and colder and wondering why, but then I heard a faint noise through the howl, and I swear that though it sounded like a moaning donkey, I never loved any sound better. There he was, blowing on his pipes and on we went. And though it took a good few steps, after a time we saw them, stumbling through the dusky white towards us. Though they were half frozen, and Helena said she didn't even want to come, we gave them their cloaks and coaxed them back. And there was another miracle. You see, Sammo, I thought, that proves that God didn't want them cast out. Because when we stepped back into the hut I saw a lovely red glow. Alwyn had got a fire burning.

CHAPTER TEN

Constance

Of all the times God had punished me by striking my poor boy with sickness he'd never been so cruel as this. By dawn, as we made our way into the snow from that broken cottage, Paul seemed a little better, giving me hope. Dame Lucy put him on one of her horses, even though that meant her cook Jack had to carry some of the packs, which she said he must, God bless her sweet heart. But then after half a mile Paul was tearing at his back again with his fingernails because it was so burning, he could hardly swallow a crumb of the honey biscuits I gave him so he'd have some strength and when he started wheezing bad we had to take him down from the saddle again and set him down onto the snow. I could hardly bear to look at him as he sat there, spluttering and gasping for his very life. Till slowly he grew better and we could go on.

And at least God didn't let us get lost. By midmorning we'd reached the hospital on the top of the pass and the moment we were inside I put my boy to bed, where he seemed tranquil. But within the hour he was retching and trying to catch his breath for wheezing worse even than before. Mary and Helena came up to see how he was, so I supposed they'd heard how he'd spoken up for them both, and though he smiled at them, Joan told them, and not friendly at all, that he was weak and must be left alone, so away they went. Then she told me that it was their secret magic that was keeping him sick, and she said something that was hard for me to bear, which was that my boy's affliction was my fault, as if I'd only been sterner with Paul and done God's bidding, and the Jews had been kept outside like he'd asked, Paul would be well again by now.

When Paul got bad all over again that afternoon and his face started turning bluish I lost all temperance and, though I knew it was wrong, I couldn't stop myself and I raged at God himself. 'Why didn't you do this to me and not him?' I said, for the thousandth time. 'Why can't you show some kindness to a poor young lad who's never done anything wrong in his life?' Then I felt shamed so I begged forgiveness for being short with him and I prayed, 'Please God, show your mercy. Take pity on my boy.' And it seemed like he heard me this time, as Paul wasn't afflicted again after that.

I hoped more snow might fall so we'd be fixed in the hospital for another day or two and Paul would have time to recover, but there wasn't a flake and in the morning the others, though they were all full of sorrow for him, wanted to go on. 'Couldn't we stay just another day?' I said but my Paul said, 'Don't worry about me, Ma. I'll be all right,' and Joan was with him, saying that if we stayed and more snow came we might be caught there for weeks. Dame Lucy's steward Alwyn and some of the monks made up a sled with cloth stretched over a wooden frame that could be dragged behind one of the horses and Paul, being too weak to walk or even sit in the saddle, used that. I can hardly stand to think of that time. How Paul bore it I don't know and I swear there was no knight in battle braver. I hated to see how the sled jolted him whenever it went over a bump or a stone, scraping his back or his legs that were all torn from where he'd scratched them in his misery. When the road was bad he had to climb out and walk, though he could hardly stumble and was white as a sheet. Then he'd be back in the sled and I'd be beside him holding his hand. It seemed like the fiend had shaped those mountains purposefully just to vex us, as we went steep down then steep up and then steep down and up again, till it felt like they'd never end.

Finally after two days I was joyed to see plains below us and the sea in the far distance. By the time we got onto the flat Paul was stronger and more himself. Father Tim led us all in praying thanks and the two Jews joined in louder than anyone, though Joan said they were only feigning. Dame Lucy's Peter, who'd cried and cried when his playmate had been sick, was so happy to see him well once again that I had to warn him with a lovesome smile, 'I know you're pleased, Peter, but don't tire him out too much, not yet,' and he understood and was very good, just walking with Paul and making his gaming talk. All the while I couldn't stop praying, 'Thank you, God, from all my heart. I'm sorry I was short at you back at the hospital, really I am, but it was only because I was so worried for my boy and because I love him so dearly,' and I hoped he'd understand.

Soon after then we reached a town called Lucca where we stopped for a couple of days so he could recover himself fully. We went to the Saint Martin's Cathedral and prayed to the famous talking crucifix. I stayed there all morning and then went back in the afternoon, to pray my thanks for Paul's getting better and to beg to keep him well till we reached

Rome and he could be saved. By then I was growing short of silver so I took some from a merchant with my money script from Winchester Fair, and I made sure it was a good amount, too, as who knew what I might need? I'd have spent every penny on a cart and horse if it helped my boy but I had no need, as Dame Lucy bought one, and though it was a poor sort of thing compared to the cart she'd had before, it was sturdy enough to take her chests and sacks and she said if Paul was sick again he could lie on top, which would be seven times better than that cursed sled.

Then something hateful came to pass. The hospital in Lucca where we were keeping ourselves had a little garden and Joan said I should take a walk there, as it wasn't right that I spent my every moment by Paul's side watching him in case he grew sick again. 'Don't you worry, I'll keep an eye on him,' she said, and though it was hard to pull myself away, I did as she said. The garden was seemly enough if plain from the season, as by then it was almost December. I took a turn round and was thinking of going back and seeing how my boy was when I heard a little moan from behind one of the shrubs.

Fearing there might be a child there who'd hurt himself, I stepped over to look, and whom should I find but Jocelyn the advocate. He was sitting on a tree stump and kneeling before him was a woman with long black hair like a lot of them had in those parts. For a moment I thought she was mournful about something and he was giving her comfort, as he had his hands round her head, but then I saw through her hair that she had her fingers round his tail, which was up, and her tongue was licking the end. When I let out a cry she jumped up and ran off. As for Jocelyn, he wasn't sorry like he should've been but looked quite aggrieved. He put himself away in his hose and then told me it wasn't right that I'd walked in on them and shrieked, as he'd done nothing amiss. He'd just been honouring local ways, he said, as there was an old custom that Lucca women welcomed visiting strangers with a special lovesome kiss.

I didn't know. Perhaps there was, I thought. But then Father Tim, who'd been in the hall and had heard my cry, hurried out, and when I said what had happened he called Jocelyn a dirty, lecherous cur. But what really troubled me was what Joan said just afterwards. 'Going with a bordel woman,' she said. 'He'll bring God's wrath on all of us, including your poor boy.' That made me wild. As if we weren't cursed enough already, now this fellow had put my boy in more peril with his foul lusts. Dame Lucy was as strong about it as I, good woman that she was, and she told Jocelyn he must confess to Father Tim and show himself penitent before our whole party or he'd be outlawed, which was quite right I thought. But Jocelyn, who had no shame about him, said it was nothing to do with us or Father Tim but was between him and God's laws alone. And though Father Tim told him to think again for the good of his own soul, Jocelyn took himself away, slipping out of the hospital early the next morning before we woke. I was glad of it. Good riddance, I thought. You see, God, I prayed, he's nothing to do with me.

After that all I wanted was for us to reach Rome as fast as we could, before the devil could snare us with something else. He did everything he could to thwart us. Most of all he made the rest of them so slow. Joan blamed the two Jews and it was true they often trailed behind the rest, though Paul said that was only because they were anguished after what had happened in the mountains and wanted to keep apart. I was surprised they'd stayed with us at all, but then I suppose they were scared to walk alone. They'd often ask after Paul, saying, 'How's your boy doing today?' When we stopped for the night Helena would help Tom with his letters, which I suppose was her thanks for his going out in the snow to save her and Mary that night, and she never minded that Dame Lucy gave her looks, what with having banned him for pricking his nun. Not that he got very far with his learning, as I heard him trying to read from her wax tablet and growing anguished when he kept getting it wrong. I said to Joan, 'She seems kindly enough. And they often ask about my boy,' but she thought I was a fool right through. 'You're as bad as your husband was,' she told me. 'Can't you see they're just gulling you? They scorn and curse us in secret every hour.'

It did seem like somebody was cursing us. Soon after my boy was better, Satan put his touch on one of the axles of Dame Lucy's useless new cart and gave it a crack so it had to be changed, which wasted a whole day. Next, at a town called Saint Geminiano, which was full of tall towers, Sir John got into a discord with a tavern owner who he said had watered his wine, and Sir John punched him in the face so the watch were called and we had to stay there a whole day, till the Saint Geminians agreed to let Sir John go free if he paid tuppence in their money to the tavern owner, which he did, if sulkily. Then that same evening, when I thought we were finally set to go on once more, Lionel came down sick, or so he said. I felt his brow myself and I told Dame Lucy, 'He doesn't feel hot to me.' It was nothing after what my boy had suffered, that was certain, but Dame Lucy moaned and fussed and in the end we stayed there wasting our time for another four full days. The rest of them weren't much troubled. Margaret polished her badges, Oswald sewed a new pair of soles on his boots and Ragged Tom spent every hour begging till he'd got enough coins to take him almost to Rome, so he said. All the while I was stamping round the place, hating those towers and thinking, will we never be gone from here?

'Come along now, put your best foot forward,' I told the others when we finally got back onto the road. 'If we hurry we'll be in Rome for Christmas.' Because by Oswald's reckoning we still could be. How God would love that, to see his pilgrims in his holy city for his dear son's birthday. The days being short we needed to use every hour we had and if we reached a place in the afternoon where the rest wanted to stop I'd tell them, 'Let's keep going a little longer, lordlings, and stay at the next spot along.' And when they grew scared we might find ourselves walking in the dark and be set upon by brigands, I told them, 'Don't you worry as there's hardly a robber round here any more, that was years back,' which was true, Oswald said, as the pope had got rid of them all. Each evening my feet ached so badly that I could hardly take another step but I felt only joy that we'd gone so far as we had. We passed through a fair city named Siena and then went by a mountain that stood alone by himself and was called Amiata, till we reached a town called Bolsena, which was perched above a wide lake with little islands, and which I came to hate as much as I had those towers. Because that was where Lucy's steward Alwyn said her horses needed pasturing as they were tired out, and Beatrix said her donkey needed resting too. So we wasted three more days and every hour I was glancing at Paul to be sure he was still well.

After that, though, we kept up a good pace. I asked folk coming the other way how long they'd taken and, wonder of wonders, they said that, for all our tardiness, if nothing else slowed us we'd still reach Rome for Christmas and perhaps even a day or two sooner. Finally we got to a little place called Sutri where we stayed in the strangest kind of hospital, which was in a cave in a cliff, and the monks said that though folk usually took two days to reach Rome from there, some did it in just one. 'Let's do it in one,' I said to the others. 'Just think of it, we'll be in Rome tomorrow.' Some of them grouched and Hugh moaned there was no need. 'It's three days till Christmas,' he said. 'Where's the hurry?' 'But why wait?' I said. 'Just think, tomorrow night you'll rest your tired heads in the holy city of Rome.'

I hardly slept that night. I got up well before first light and lit a candle from the fire burning at the mouth of the cave and then I woke them all. Jack the cook grumbled that I was the devil's friend for spoiling his sleep, and Joan complained that she'd hit her toe because it was too dark to see, but I got them all on the road in the end. As we walked I kept telling them in a gaming voice, 'Hurry now, lordlings. All these months and now we're almost there.' We went by a lake, which was like the one where we'd had to wait while the horses were rested only smaller. After that I could see we were getting near as the road grew ever more crowded with walkers and riders and with carts loaded with sacks, or coming towards us empty. All the while we had to take care as the way was sprinkled with little turdlings. Those'll be from sheep driven to Rome to sell for Christmas feasts, I guessed. Then I caught a glimpse in the distance of high walls and fortress towers by the score rising up behind them, so many that they looked like the spines of a great hedgehog. 'There it is,' I shouted out, 'there's Rome,' and they all gave a cheer.

Not long after as the day began to wane I saw a river up ahead of us, the Tiber as it had to be. We crossed a bridge that Father Tim said was called Ponty Milvio, and was where Emperor Constantine had won a great battle over the Pagans that brought Jesus and God to all the Romans. There was the city wall, stretching away to right and left, and ahead of us was a mighty gateway that grew a little taller and broader with each step I took. Now Oswald slung his bagpipes over his shoulder and let out a great blast, and when someone threw a piece of dirt at him he didn't care but laughed out loud. And then, with joy in my heart, I was coming up to the gateway, I was passing through it and here I was, arrived, standing in a wide square that was in the city of Rome. I was weeping and I felt like singing. I hugged my boy even though he didn't like to be hugged, and I said to him, 'We've done it, Paul, we've done it,' and then I hugged Joan. 'Thank you, dear God,' I cried out. 'Thank you with all my heart.'

Already a little crowd of Romans had gathered round us, and one of them pulled at Brigit's arm till Alwyn and Jack the cook chased him away. 'They all want us to stay in their inns,' said Father Tim, and though he told them we were staying at the English Hospital it made no difference. Oswald was the one who managed to rid us of them, which he did by taking one as our guide. 'That's the only way,' he told us. 'Pick one monster to fight off the rest.' It was as well we had a guide, though, as we'd never have found our way without. He led us across the city, through lanes so narrow that Dame Lucy and her party had to come off their horses and walk, while it was all we could do to coax her cart between the buildings. 'Getting here is only the start, remember,' I told Paul and Joan as we went. 'Now we have to earn good Saint Peter's help to get us God's forgiveness for me, so Paul can be saved. We have to visit churches, pray to saints and say mass everywhere we can.' For all my aching feet I'd have gladly begun there and then, except that it was already coming on to dark.

I asked Father Tim, 'How many churches do we need to visit here to do things right?' because there was nothing I feared more than to get back home and find we'd not done enough. Not that he gave me an answer I was happy with. He said we should take communion in all the famous churches, where the pope said mass, and that he thought there were about a dozen altogether. 'Going to them will lessen your years in purgatory,' he said. 'You should go to all of those,' said Joan, looking sadly at me, 'what with all your sins.' Which was true I dare say, but what mattered was my boy. When I asked Father Tim, will that be enough, and are you truly sure, he said it was hard to know. Then when I asked how many churches there were in Rome he thought there were about three hundred but he wasn't sure. Should we go to all of them? I asked. But he didn't know that either, the useless fop. By now the rain was coming down, as it had half a dozen times that day, and I was soaked once again. Never mind, I told myself. I'll learn what we must see from somebody, somehow. I'll find a way.

It turned out the English Hospital was full, though the clerk said there'd be places the next morning as a big party was leaving Rome. In the meantime he pointed us all to an inn down the road. I'd meant to sit down with Joan and Paul and make a plan for us but in the end all I could do was buy straw and then I was too tired to talk, too tired even to eat, though I was famished, and all I could do was lie down and close my eyes. My last thought as sleep came upon me was, tomorrow we won't rest. Tomorrow we'll use every moment we have to make my boy safe.

But I swear the devil would give us no peace. If he'd been against us on the road down from the mountains, he was worse now we were arrived. First it was the others in our fellowship. Because we'd all agreed that on our first morning we'd go to Saint Peter's together, seeing as it was the most renowned church in all of Rome, but when I tried to wake them they were like a crowd of slugs, groaning and whining and saying they were tired and their feet were sore. I soon lost patience and just worked on Joan and Paul, though they were hardly better. When I finally had them both out of their beds I told the others, 'We'll go on ahead and we'll see the rest of you there.'

Next the devil put his touch on Joan, who started fussing about where we should get bread and milk to break our fast, because at one place the bread looked old and at another the milk didn't look clean. 'As if it matters,' I told her sharply, which hurried her up. But then Paul started, because he'd seen a big stretch of wall down a side alley, so tall that it made midgets of the houses all around. 'Let's go and see,' he said. 'Not now,' I told him, and if I was sour it was only because

I loved him so dearly. 'Can't you see that it's saints we need now, not old walls?'

But the devil was only just started. The next thing he put in our path was Rome itself, as I swear it made even London seem easy to pass through. We had to pick our way past porters and donkeys carrying loads and sellers who blocked half the road as they pushed badges of Peter and Paul into our faces, or hats or bales of straw, or offered to fix our boots or pull our teeth. Most of the streets weren't proper streets at all but narrow, winding lanes, sometimes arched over above us, which made them so dark that we could hardly see our way, and it was all I could do to save my boots from puddles or mud or worse. With every yard we walked I got a whiff of some new stink, while it was as noisy as it was too foul-smelling, with metalworkers hammering away at pots and bowls. Another thing was that these Romans didn't seem troubled where they went about their business. One would be cooking lunch on her little brazier, another was washing clothes in a bucket, another skinning a sheep or pulling offal from a goat's carcass, and another stretching out skins to dry. I even saw one Roman squat down to purge himself right beside us. I gave Joan a nudge then. 'You wouldn't see that back in Thetford,' I said, and she nodded. 'Not often, that's certain.'

Then, as the way widened a little and I guessed we must be getting close as we were among a crowd of pilgrims, all walking in the same direction, the devil slowed us over again and this time it was, of all things, with Matilda Froome. A shepherd was driving his flock of sheep down the road and the idiot beasts were pushing and shoving so the three of us had to squeeze ourselves back against the wall and I shouted out, 'Watch out for my boy, can't you?' as I tried to shield him with my arms, and that was when I heard a voice call out, 'Is that you, Constance?' and there she was, sitting crouched by the roadside, a begging bowl in her hand, and her white dress that was half blanket looking dirtier than ever. Next to her was the Welshman who'd spurned us. Now we'll have trouble, I thought, as she'll still be angry over what was done in her boots, but no, she was tranquil enough, just a little melancholy. They both were. 'We've been here ten days,' Matilda complained, which wasn't a surprise to me, seeing as they wouldn't have been held back waiting for the cart to be mended, or for Beatrix's donkey to pasture or for Lionel's sniffles to be cured. Ten days. What I would have given to have already been in Rome for ten days.

Not that the time had been of much use to them. 'We've both been waiting and waiting,' Matilda said glumly. The Welshman, whose name was Iorwerth, had been trying to make his plea at the pope's court for a cause his abbey was making, which was why he was here, Matilda said. As for her, she'd been waiting for Jesus' gift. 'I hoped it would come when I first got here,' she said, trying to keep a smile on her face. 'I'm sure it'll come soon, whatever it is.' Then she wanted to hear news of our party. As if I could spend all morning gabbling? I told her we'd be at the English Hospital that night and we'd see her there, but that started her all over again. 'We're not staying there,' she said, looking like I'd thrown muck at her good name. 'Iorwerth would never keep with Saxons.' As there was no Welsh Hospital in Rome they'd gone asking at all the rest and they'd ended up at the Hungarians'. 'They said they had room even for foreigners, and they're most kindly and friendly folk,' said Matilda, giving me a look, as if to say, which is more than I can say of your fellowship. Iorwerth, who had a gift for languages, so she said, had been learning Hungarian from them, and Roman too, to pass the time. 'We'll come and visit you,' I offered, not thinking I ever would, but just to get away.

Now the fiend slowed us with other pilgrims, as the closer to Saint Peter's we got the more there were, till it seemed like we were in a sea of cloaks and hats with crosses. We went over a bridge where I used my staff and my elbows like clubs to keep them from shoving my poor boy. On the far side we went into a street lined with sellers and that was so dark and narrow and thronged with pilgrims that I knew we must almost be there. Sure enough, out we popped like rabbits from a hole, into a wide square, and on the far side was a grand stairway covered with pilgrims pouring up like so many ants. Joan said we must stop at a big round fountain where pilgrims were stripping off and washing themselves, and though I said, 'Do we have to?' she told me of course we must, as I had to clean my body before I asked Saint Peter to have God clean my dirty, sinful soul. The water was cold and it was as well there was a good flow going as you never saw any so black. Then up the great stairs we went, squeezing our way past a crowd of sellers through an archway and into a courtyard with cloisters and a grand fountain in the middle, and which was filled with yet more sellers. Joan was telling me, 'This is where we should've got our straw. I can see from the fingers he's holding up that it's half what you paid on the street last night.' Then she wanted to look at a belt, and at candles and rosaries and little phials of oil, till I told her, 'Not now, Joan, not now,' and I didn't care that she sulked.

But now we were slowed again, not by the fiend this time, but by good Saint Peter himself. I suppose he was just making sure we did our penance right. First we had to join the throng to get through the great doors till, wonder of wonders, we were inside, and I swear I could feel him there, sweet Saint Pete, looking at us with a kindly smile and rattling his keys to heaven. I wanted to throw myself down on the ground but even that wasn't easy, as I couldn't find an empty space. No surprise it was such a crush as I saw there were sellers by the dozen even here inside the church. Rome really was a big marketplace and they'd sell you anything anywhere. I found an emptier spot and down I went. Paul was beside me and so was Joan, though she wasn't flat but more sort of crouched. I shouted out loud, 'Dear good Saint Peter, I beg you, ask God to forgive my wickedness and stop tormenting my dear boy,' and it was like I could feel him answer me, 'I'll talk to him, my poor sinner Constance, don't you worry. I'll do my best for you,' and my eyes were wet with tears.

'Hold on tight,' I said to Paul, and to Joan when we got up. 'If we're pulled apart in this crowd we mightn't find each other ever again,' and the three of us went round side by side holding hands. Then it was all waiting. First we were in the throng for mass, though it seemed to take half the morning before our turn came for Jesus' flesh and blood. As we waited I was looking round at good Saint Peter's Cathedral and though it was handsome, no denying, and had very seemly columns in different-coloured stone, I'd thought it would be bigger. I said to Joan, 'It's very fine but Norwich is longer, don't you think?' 'By a good stretch,' she agreed. 'And Norwich has a proper tower and spire,' which was right too.

After mass we joined another crowd waiting to go to Saint Peter in the crypt, and though it was very fine, no denying, I had thought we'd see more of him. Down the steps we shuffled and along an alleyway till we came to a big metal grate with another alleyway leading off. At the end a candle was burning and I could see a red wall with a niche in it, where he'd be. I'd thought we'd be able to see him, or at least see the handsome casket he was in, but no, that was all, and as I prayed with all my strength the ones behind were pushing to get us out of the way. Yet when I got to the altar I still gave him not one but two shillings and I didn't care when Joan cast me a look. I had to give two, couldn't she see? We'd come all this way to get his help, while everyone knew how irked saints got if they weren't honoured rightly.

Finally at long last we were finished. Though Satan wasn't over with his slowing us down even then. We'd hardly got into the courtyard when I heard a voice call out, 'Constance, Joan, thank heavens. Can you come and help us?' It was Sir John, with Dame Alice and Gawayne, all standing beneath what looked like a huge pinecone made of stone. His face was red and I could see he'd got into another altercation. 'You know French, don't you?' Sir John said. 'What's the word for robbery? I need to tell this dirty cassock here,' he said, pointing at a monk standing beside him. 'You'll not believe this. Because he says it'll be a week at least before I can have a script to show I've been here. A week! And he says I must pay for it, too. Sixpence, he wants.'

I'd heard him before then trying to speak French, and getting himself stuck searching for words in his head like needles in a haystack. But though I knew more than him,

I had no wish to wait here for an hour, helping him make his cause. God will understand my saying a little untruth, I thought, seeing as we're here to worship him. So I told Sir John, 'I'm sorry but I hardly know a word,' and wishing him all God's good fortune I led us on through the throng and out into Saint Peter's Square. Finally we were free.

But I wasn't free of my kin. 'It wasn't much of a breakfast we had,' Joan said, 'and we hardly ate a thing last night. The food smells so tasty here.' So we had to stop at a stall for some bread and bean stew, which was good I'll own. Then Paul, who wanted to see the famous things that Father Tim had read about in his book, said we should hire a guide from the ones who kept following us and calling out. 'We've no time,' I told him, but then I couldn't bear to see his sorry little face, and so I took one in the end, for three farthings in real coin, and who said he spoke English though it wasn't much. I told him most sternly, 'You're only to take us to a few places, understand, in between all the churches,' which he gave his accord to.

Some of the things he showed seemed pure truffle to me, like a little pile of rubble that he said was grain that Saint Peter had brought with him to Rome all those years ago, and that wicked Emperor Nero had tried to steal from him so God had turned it into stone to thwart him. But Paul liked Romulus' tomb and I hadn't known Rome was founded by Noah's son just after he got off the ship with all those animals. But the best thing the guide brought us to was a kind of tall cross, which he said was from Egypt and was called an obelisk, and that had a hole near its base. Because if we crawled inside, the guide said, then we'd be cleaned of all our sins. Of course there was a crowd waiting their turn but I thought this was worth a little time. In the end I managed to creep in, so did Paul, and Joan almost did though she couldn't quite fit. And even though I knew it might all be foolish tales, I thought, there's no harm, is there?

After that I told the guide to take us to Saint John on the Lateran Hill, which was the second after Saint Pete's. This Rome's a strange city though, I thought, as we fought our way through more narrow lanes, and I waved my staff to make the Romans give us way. It wasn't like any usual place I'd ever seen, though I'd been to a good number now, from Norwich to here. I wasn't sure I much liked it. Everywhere we went there were more of those giant stone walls that Paul was so curious about, towering over the houses, and which seemed almost like the bones of a huge dead beast. In some there were little doors and I saw someone coming out of one so it seemed he had his home in there. The guide said they were left over from great buildings that had been made by Romans in pagan times, when the city had been much bigger and finer. He showed us a long wall with arches that he said had once carried water, just like the Conduit in London, while in Rome there'd been a dozen of them, though hardly one still worked now. 'It must've been wondrous,' Paul said, which I didn't like the sound of, so I told him, and sharply, 'But it was wicked too, remember, being pagan.' Everywhere I looked there were fortress towers above us, sprouting out of grand houses. The guide said all the great families had them as they were always fighting one another, especially over who among them would be pope next. Which didn't seem very godly to me. Then these Romans didn't strike me as godly, trying to sell us trinkets even inside their greatest church.

We stopped at a big round building that I wasn't sure we should go inside, as the guide said it had been built by the Pagans as a temple where they worshipped their wicked false gods, though he said it was all right now, as it had been made into a church centuries back. But there was a giddy thing, because when I looked up I saw a great hole in the roof. Whoever heard of making a place like that? 'What happens when it rains?' I asked, but then I could see, as it was coming down again and I saw it splashing on the floor. The guide said it drained away through little holes. Still it seemed an idiot notion to me. I said to Joan and Paul, 'You see, those Pagans may have built tall and high and had lots of conduits and such, but they hadn't an ounce of good sense.'

Then I wondered if the guide had taken us the wrong way, because all of a sudden we'd left the narrow winding streets behind and were walking through fields, where I saw folk weeding the land and pruning trees. I was sure we hadn't gone out through the wall again as I'd have noticed, yet it didn't seem like we were still in the city. 'We're still in Rome,' the guide told us. It was just that the city had dwindled so since ancient times that most of the land inside the walls was empty now. Then Paul was pointing at a building up ahead that was a great gogmagog of a thing, huge and round, though one half seemed broken. It had towers growing out of it and was a fortress now but our guide told us that in ancient times it had been the Temple of the Sun and had been topped with a dome with a hole in it, just like the place we'd just seen. 'What a sight that must've been,' said Paul. 'I wish I could've seen it.' 'No you don't,' I told him, 'because it was ungodly, remember.'

Of course he wanted to go inside, which was more of our time gone, but I was glad of it in the end. We were just going in through the arch when I heard a squeaky voice call out, 'So how many have you got?' and there was Hugh with Margaret just behind him. 'How many what?' I asked. 'Years off purgatory, of course,' he said, and when I answered that I didn't know he looked at me like I was a proper fool. 'I've already got five years and two quarantines,' he said. 'At this rate I'll have more than a hundred by the time we leave.' 'And you'll need them all,' said Margaret. I saw she had a shiny new badge in her hat, of Paul with his sword and Peter with his keys. She hadn't wasted any time. 'But you should come over here,' Hugh said, pointing at a big cross at the far end of the flat, grassy space we were in, 'as this is one of the easiest.' If I touched it and prayed, that was worth three quarantines, he said. 'A hundred and twenty days out of purgatory just for touching a cross. Not bad, eh?' Another thing he told me was that this wasn't the Temple of the Sun like our guide had told us, but was called the Colosseum and it was where the emperors kept their lions to eat the Christians. They must have had a lot of lions, I thought, looking at the size of the place.

I walked up to the cross and I swear that just for a moment I could feel the kindly, loving souls of the poor martyrs whom the lions had so cruelly eaten. I put my hand on the cross and I prayed, 'Dear God, I beg you, make my boy well again.' Because I knew it wasn't right, but there were times when I had foolish fears that, even though we'd come all this way and done everything godly like we'd been told, still it would do no good and he'd be no better. It was a thought I could hardly bear. 'Please God, don't let this all have been for nothing,' I prayed. And when I said it, just for a moment, it was like I felt a little warm touch on my shoulder.

After that I got rid of our guide, seeing as he'd been wrong about what this great gogamog had been. He said I was fussing over nothing, as nobody knew what any of these places were, while he'd found that most pilgrims preferred it as the Temple of the Sun. Paul wanted to keep him anyway but I stuck firm and though the guide stamped his foot and said I must give him his full three farthings or he'd fetch the watch, in the end he walked off scowling with two. Nor did we need him, as Hugh had just come from Saint John's on the Lateran Hill and he pointed us down the right road.

In truth I almost preferred Saint John's to Saint Peter's even though it was less renowned. In Saint Peter's all I'd seen was the red wall but here in the main church we saw the Ark of the Covenant that once had Moses' stone tablets in it, and then in the pope's chapel we saw Saint Peter and Paul's heads, which we could look on with our own eyes in their beautiful caskets. Nor was that all, as they had some of the loaves and fishes Jesus had made when there hadn't been enough supper, they had milk from the Virgin's own paps, and they even had Jesus' wrinkly from his member, which Jews cut off their boy babies, as it was one of their strange and wicked ways. And though the priests stopped Joan and me from going into Saint John the Baptist's chapel, as they said women weren't allowed, so only Paul could go in, they told us we'd get the same years off purgatory just by touching the door, which we both did.

By the time we'd done mass there it was already getting late so we only managed two more main churches that Father Tim had told us to see, and then a few tiddlers, which didn't seem much for a whole day, so I felt sour at myself when we went back to the inn and moved our packs to the English Hospital. Another thing that made me ired was that, being the last to move, we got the worst place, in a bed that stank in the corner of the lower dormitory. It was small too, and though we were three and Hugh and Margaret, who were next to us, were only two, theirs was larger. When I said that wasn't right Hugh said yes it was, because Margaret had a sore leg, which was nothing to do with it, I thought, though it was hard to gainsay them seeing as they already had all their things spread out.

Being tired all I wanted was an early night but there was no chance of that with all the celebrating. I was just closing my eyes when in came Beatrix and Warin, who'd drunk a jug of wine by the sound of him. Though I didn't ask him he told me he was merry because he'd found a guide who spoke fair English and who knew an officer of the church who could get them to the pope, so he'd promised. Then he crashed into one bed and another singing, 'We're off to see the pope, we'll tell him what is what, we'll tell him who'll be raised, and who'll be on a pyre, to squeal out as he's braised, and all the flames grow higher.'

They'd just started snoring and left us in peace when all the Dame Lucys came up, not singing but whispering and sniggering. And though I didn't ask her either, she told us that she'd found an advocate who said he'd help get her divorce while Lionel had found a fellow who said he could arrange for them to be married in a fine ancient church, and who knew a famous cook of Rome who'd make them a great banquet. Then Dame Lucy held up her candle and showed us a ring on her finger which, she told us proudly, Lionel had got her. Which didn't seem right to me or to Joan, we agreed later, seeing as by law she was still married to the other fellow. Nor was it much of a ring, I thought, and Joan said the one she'd been given by her Robert was finer, though Joan's was iron while Dame Lucy's looked like good silver. Still it was a poor thing compared to my own, which was gold and had a big, beautiful ruby. Lionel's scarce, I thought. Not that Dame Lucy saw it. Having shown us her ring she told us that after they were wed she and Lionel would go to Monte Cassino to pray to Saint Benedict, just the two of them and their servitors, Brigit and Dobbe. 'It's not the praying she's looking forward to,' Joan said afterwards, and though I know I shouldn't have, I couldn't help but smile. Then Dame Lucy had no shame about her. When they went to their beds I heard her whisper, clear as a bell, 'Come on, where's the harm, seeing as it's as good as done.' Though at least Lionel had some righteousness to him, and I heard him whisper back, 'Then we can wait a little longer, can't we, my sweet.'

After all that crashing about in the night keeping us awake, it was no surprise I had a hard task getting Paul and Joan awake at first light the next morning. 'But it's Christmas Eve,' Paul moaned. 'All the more reason to get up,' I told him, 'as there'll be masses right across Rome.' Hugh, who'd told me it was one of the best days in the year to get indulgences from purgatory, had already left, together with his Margaret. I'd just got mine out of their beds and we were stumbling out of the dormitory when Satan tripped us, like he loved to, and I heard someone whispering behind us, 'Constance, Joan, I was hoping it was you.' It was Ragged Tom. He followed us out to the stairway where he started moaning about how he was worried about the two Jews, Mary and Helena. Hadn't we noticed they hadn't been with us for supper last night? I hadn't in truth, but then it was easy to miss them when they kept themselves so quiet. 'They never came in,' Tom said. 'My bed's next to theirs and I kept watch.' 'I wouldn't trouble yourself,' I told him. 'They probably just stayed the night somewhere else.' 'But then why are their packs still there?' he asked. Then he made us all go back and look, though there was nothing much to see, just an empty bed and a couple of full packs lying on top.

I knew why he was so vexed of course. I'd seen him stealing glances at Helena when she wasn't looking, and I'd seen how he'd been when she taught him his letters, joyed and anguished both at once. He was going a little demoniac with it now, though. He started murmuring to us about an evening in an inn where we'd stayed along the way, where Sir John had been tidying out his pack and Tom saw him take out a long dagger. 'He only took it out for a moment but I saw it clear as day and it looked sharp as sharp could be,' he said. 'Now tell me this, what would a pilgrim be doing with a dagger when the priests say that we're not to carry any such thing? And we all know he hates those two for saying no to Gawayne and for being Jews. He was the first to push them out into the snow.' As if Sir John having a dagger proved anything? 'He'll have brought it in case he meets trouble on the way,' I said. 'That's what he's like.' I told him not to worry. 'Mary and Helena will walk in here in an hour or two, you just wait.' Then, when he started telling it to me all over again, as people do when something gnaws at them, I told him, 'I'm sorry, Tom, but we can't keep here gabbling all day. We've got churches to go to.'

The next thing to slow us was Christmas, because everyone said we must go back to Saint Peter's, as going to mass on Christmas morn was worth seven years and seven quarantines from purgatory. That took hours of course, as the place was crammed right to the walls with pilgrims, much worse even than it had been the last time. Then we had our feast at the English Hospital, which took up most of the rest of the day. Not that it was much of a feast. I'd been so busy with churches that I forgot to get any food till the market was almost closed, and the only thing we found that looked eatable was a big bunch of carrots. Dame Lucy had bought quails and a goose but her cook Jack boiled them too long and the vegetables too, so none of it had much taste. My Paul said it was slippery on his tongue and wouldn't touch anything except the barley bread.

Nor was there much in the way of gifts. That was another thing I'd given no thought to, sorry to say, so all I had to give them was tiny slices from a smoked sausage that I still had in my pack from England. I tried to make it seem more special by saying I'd brought it all the way from Thetford, though that wasn't rightly true, as I'd actually got it on the road near Ongar. The three Sir Johns, who I guessed were no readier with presents than I was, gave everybody a sliver of Roman cheese, Warin and Beatrix gave us each half a little hard biscuit, but Dame Lucy gave all of us a silver penny, which was welcomed by everybody and especially by Ragged Tom. His starved face, which had looked glum till then, lit up like a candle. I thought he'd have nothing for any of us but no, he gave us each a little piece of broken glass. 'It's ancient pagan, of that I have no doubt,' he said, and though they looked like pieces of a broken bottle to me I didn't say so, as it seemed unkind.

That same evening he came pestering us about his Jews again, as they still hadn't shown their faces, so the clerk of the hospital had given away their bed and locked their packs in the storeroom. Tom was so pensive about them that he'd got the clerk of the hospital, who spoke Roman, to go round the nearby shops and stalls with him and ask if anyone remembered seeing them go by on Christmas Eve morning, which was when they'd last been with us. As if anyone would know? One said he'd seen a fair maid with long black hair go by with another woman who was older, though they'd been in a party with two men just behind them, one taller than the other. He only remembered because they'd stopped at his stall and the fair maid almost bought a little icon. That meant nothing at all as far as I could see, but it was enough for Tom. 'Gawayne's taller than Sir John,' he said. 'Don't you see? It was them, following Mary and Helena.' 'Let it be,' I told him. 'I'm sure Mary and Helena just decided to stay somewhere else. They probably decided they'd had enough of us all.' But Tom couldn't stop himself, and he started grumbling about how, bound and low though he was, he had a good mind to stand up in front of our whole fellowship and point his finger at Sir John. 'I wouldn't do that,' Joan said, 'or you might find you get another look at his dagger.'

But after that we had all the hours we wanted. We went to so many churches that I lost count, and to mass so often that I always had the taste of Jesus' flesh and blood on my tongue. Until, for the first time I could remember in many long years, I found I breathed a little easier. Not that my boy was saved yet for certain, but he might be, and there was no doubting that he was a lot closer to being saved than he had been before we'd got to Rome. After another week of churches and masses had passed, and then three days more, I began to wonder if it was time to think of going home. Paul was ready. 'I'd like to sleep in my own bed,' he told me, looking cheerier than he had for a good long while. And though Joan thought we should stay for a few more days, just to be quite sure, even she came round.

Nor was it only us, as it turned out. Oswald was ready to go home too, having done his praying for Damian the tailor. Not that he was glad about it, as he didn't much like going back, so he told us. 'I never know how long it'll be before I find another poor fellow who wants me to go as a pilgrim for him,' he said. 'And it'll probably only be to Canterbury or Durham or Oxford, which will seem a poor sort of journey after Rome.'

The others who were ready to go were Hugh and Margaret. I hadn't been counting purgatory time but Hugh had. 'Five hundred and ninety-three years and twenty-four days I've got now,' he said, 'and I'm sure I won't even need half of that,' though Margaret gave him a sideways sort of look. As for the road back, he'd heard we could take a way that kept to the coast, and though it was longer it would be safer, as we wouldn't have to risk freezing to death on any mountains, which I'd be more than happy with, even if it meant more days of sore feet. So the six of us agreed to set out in a couple of days, when we'd got ourselves ready for the journey.

Dame Lucy was sorry. 'I so hoped you'd all be here for our wedding,' she said. But I was glad we were going and I was all the gladder the next day when sourness fell on her fellowship. The first I knew of it was when we got back from our last day of wandering round the city of Rome. We'd had new soles sewn on our boots, which they needed, being worn down almost to nothing from all those miles we'd walked, we'd got some grain and nuts for the road, and we'd managed a couple more masses too, and when we stumbled back, tired once again from all our walking, I saw Dame Lucy's maidservant, Brigit, was sitting on the steps of the English Hospital, looking sad and sour. When I asked her what was wrong she just jabbed her thumb towards the hospital. 'They'll tell you,' she said. Inside the hall Jack was cooking supper like usual but there was a foul feeling in the air that you could have cut with a knife. I heard Lionel murmur to Dame Lucy, 'You had no choice, my sweet. You had to.'

When Margaret told us what it was all about I wasn't surprised Brigit had looked sour. That morning when we'd been out, Dame Lucy hadn't been able to find her favourite necklace, which was gold, so it was only natural she was troubled. Her party began searching round her bed and then when Lionel was moving Brigit's pack out it fell. Of course Brigit denied it like they always did but then she made it worse for herself by trying to throw the blame on Lionel, saying it was all his doing, and that Dame Lucy shouldn't trust him, as there was no good in him and he was like a sorcerer who had her under his spell. As if her mistress would look kindly on that. Dame Lucy demanded she beg Lionel's forgiveness for saying such a wicked thing about him and, when Brigit refused, Dame Lucy told her she was no longer her maidservant and was no longer in her party, so she'd have to beg her way home.

Still it could've been a lot worse, as I told Margaret. 'At least the necklace was found. And Dame Lucy didn't call in the watch, which would've meant burning on the pyre for Brigit, or whatever the Romans do.' I couldn't help but feel a little sorry for her even after what she'd done. 'They all do it,' I told Margaret, 'so it's like they can't help themselves, though it isn't usually gold necklaces.' Then I told her about one whom Hubert and I once had, who ate a whole cooked partridge from the larder and then said that it had been devoured by mice, though we found all the bones under her bed. 'We sent her out of the house that same day,' I said. And Margaret told me of one she'd had who secretly ate two turnips and half a loaf of bread, though she and Hugh hadn't sent her away but settled with giving her a good, sound beating and then starving her of food for a couple of days, so she paid them back in kind.

Another thing Dame Lucy demanded was that Brigit leave the English Hospital, though it turned out that wasn't up to her but the hospital clerk, who said no, Brigit could stay if she wanted. That made for a sorry farewell feast for us, with Brigit sitting at the end of the table, looking doleful as she maunged on a sad bowl of gruel. But if the air felt murky from her misery at least the food was good. I'd bought some ham and cheese and fruit, including a strange Roman kind of pear that had little juicy red seeds inside that tasted sweet and bitter both at once. We had white wheat bread like gentle folk eat and Dame Lucy had got some eels and sausages, which we didn't let Jack boil but cooked ourselves in a pan with oil so they came out very tasty, and Paul had seconds and thirds. That'll keep him going for the journey, I thought. We said a good few toasts and I was nicely warmed when I went to bed, my head spinning a little but a smile on my face. As I lay down I thought, you've done well here, Constance. You did a wicked thing once but you've made up for it and repented. Now, finally, you can rest easy.

I swear it was as if the devil had been listening. I was just falling into sleep when I heard a groan from Paul in the bed beside me. It's nothing, I thought. He's just having a nightmare. 'Calm now,' I told him in a murmur, not wanting to trouble the others. 'It's only a dream.' But he murmured back, 'Ma, I don't feel right.' 'It'll just be the wine,' I said, because he'd had a few swallows to join in with the rest of us and he wasn't used to it. 'I don't think so,' he said. 'It feels more. . .' 'Then it's the eels,' I said firmly. 'Eels can be trouble. They're so rich.' I'll make it clear, I thought, and then I got up and I didn't care who I woke. 'How are you feeling?' I asked, shaking Hugh awake. 'Not right in your belly after all of those eels?' 'I was fine until you woke me,' he growled. Next I tried Joan and Margaret but they were both right as rain. 'You've got a nasty cold,' I told Paul, quite sternly. 'It'll pass.' 'It's not that,' he said, and then he was wheezing and gasping for breath as bad as I'd ever heard him. Don't ask me why, as I couldn't tell you, but I shouted out just as loudly as I was able, and not once but half a dozen times, 'My boy is sick, my boy is sick.' Joan jumped to her feet. 'Not again, is he?' said Hugh with a groan for my spoiling his night. I could've struck him.

Twice I feared my dear little lad was going, his wheezing was so strong, but in the end he lasted the night. Of course that was the finish of our leaving Rome. The next morning Hugh and Margaret and Oswald went and we stayed. I should have gone down to see them off but I preferred to stay in our bed where I could keep my eye on my Paul every moment. It just seemed right lying there. And it wasn't like I missed them as they all came up to say their farewells. Oswald said how sorry he was that Paul was bad again and that he hoped he'd be well soon. Then they were all sorry, Warin and Beatrix, the Sir Johns and all the Dame Lucys. Which is kind of them I thought, though I didn't love the way they'd crowd round talking so loud. I liked being alone and quiet now.

Joan didn't think my staying in bed was right. 'I don't know why you're still there,' she told me a few days later. 'Your boy's almost himself again now.' She said I mustn't let myself feel cast down. 'No sin is so wicked that it can't be forgiven. You just haven't tried hard enough, Constance, that's all.' I just needed more even than Rome could give. 'Jerusalem, that's your answer,' she said. 'Jerusalem's seven times better than Rome. Here a pilgrim hopes that Saint Peter might get God to show him kindness but in Jerusalem it's a promise made by God himself. Go there and your whole tablet will be wiped clean and you'll start fresh again, like a newborn babe.' Seeing me close my eyes she told me, 'It wouldn't be so hard. We're already halfway there, remember.' It turned out that, just from her own curiosity, she'd been asking about the journey there from pilgrims on the road who'd done it. It wasn't dangerous these days, she said, even though the Saracens held the city, and there were plenty of pilgrims who went. There were two ways we could get there. We could walk on south to Brindisi, which was in the right direction for Jerusalem, and we could take a ship from there. Though the way she liked better was to go back north and go on a Venetian boat.

'Their ships are famously commodious,' Joan said. What was more their voyages included everything in one price, from the meals, which were very tasty, Joan had heard, to the poll tax that had to be paid to the Saracens, to hiring a donkey, to a guide to show you around all of Jesus' holy spots and even to a little journey off to the River Jordan. 'So though you pay more at the start you then have the gladness of knowing you'll not have to give out a farthing more. And the Venetians are safer too. Because the Genoese and Pisans sometimes sell their pilgrims to the Saracens as slaves, so folk say.' As for the cost, Joan knew it would be a good deal more than I had left on my money script from Winchester Fair but that wouldn't matter. 'Thank goodness I told you to bring your jewels,' she said. 'Sell those and you'll easily have enough. And there'll be nothing lost either, because when you're back in Thetford you can sell another house and another shop and then buy some new jewels in their stead so the whole voyage won't have cost you a thing. If you get a good price, you could even buy a horse and cart like Dame Lucy has, for us all to ride in.'

She said if we didn't go then we'd be letting Paul down. 'It wouldn't be right,' she said, especially after coming all this way. 'If you don't go on to Jerusalem then all your travails journeying here will be wasted.' So I agreed we should go, though it was mostly so she'd stop talking so loudly in my ear, and I agreed we should go with the Venetians so we'd not be sold as slaves, which put a smile on her face. 'But not just yet,' I said then, 'as I'm not ready.' Though if truth be told I couldn't have said when I would be ready as the thing that seemed rightest was to keep here in my bed. I dreaded having to get up and go down to the latrine and I'd put it off till I was close to bursting. When I finally went it felt like each step was taking me further from where I should be, and when my purging was done I was famished to get back to my place. Afterwards I'd just lie there for a long while, not moving even a finger or an eyelid, as there was nothing I wanted more than to keep absolutely still, with not a thought in my head.

More folk came to say their farewells to me, as our fellowship shrank ever smaller. Sir John finally got his script though it hadn't taken a week, like the monk at Saint Peter's had said, but almost a month and it hadn't cost him sixpence but ninepence in English coin. 'Now I'll find out how much more land Abbot Simon has stolen from me while I've been away,' he told me sourly on the morning the three of them set off. 'Let's hope there'll be none stolen,' I said, though it was hard for me to push the words out of my mouth, let alone feel much care. A day or two later Warin and Beatrix came up too, looking crabbier even than the Sir Johns had. They'd finally got what they'd sought and met a high cleric of the pope. Just like they'd hoped, God had spoken out from Beatrix's mouth and told the clerk that the end of days were coming, and that he needed to tell the pope that his church was wicked and stinking, especially in Margate, where there were plenty who should be cast out as Satan's chicks. But instead of being full of wonder and taking Warin and Beatrix to see the pope, like they'd expected, the high cleric told them it wasn't God talking out of Beatrix's mouth but the fiend, that Satan had them both in his paws, and that they must renounce everything they'd said and pay a fine for their slanders or they'd be tried for heresy and burned. Warin tried to argue but, not wanting to be burned, he'd paid up in the end, though the fine was so high that he had to hand over all of their silver and sell Beatrix's donkey, Porker, too. No wonder they both looked crabbed. 'I'm sorry to hear that,' I told them, wondering how long it would be before they left me in peace.

The ones who truly wouldn't leave me in peace, though, were my own kin. 'You can't just lie there,' my Paul would say, with tears in his eyes. 'You have to get up.' I was sorry he was anguished, of course I was, but I wished he might be less noisy, as his talking and talking gave me a headache. 'I'll get up in time,' I'd say to quiet him, 'but not today.' Then he'd go on about how I wasn't eating enough. 'You're wasting away,' he'd say. 'You can't go on like this.' Which wasn't right. 'I had some soup earlier,' I'd say, as Dame Lucy was always getting her cook, Jack, to bring something up to me. True I hadn't had much but then I found it hard to feel hungry. 'You don't know how thin and drawn you look,' he'd say. 'You need to eat and get stronger so we can get back on the road. Don't you want to see your dear house in Thetford?' What a lot of nonsense this was. 'Of course I do,' I told him, 'and I will, too. But I'll stay a little while longer here first.'

Or Joan would be telling me to go out to a shop and sell my jewels. She could do it for me if I liked, she said. She'd gone round Rome and found where they all were. 'I don't know what we're waiting for, as you said you wanted to go,' she'd say. 'Selling your jewels is all that's needed as our boots are soled and we have nuts and such for the road.' And though he'd not been eager to go to Jerusalem before, saying he'd rather go home, even my Paul started pestering me to go there now. 'Anything to get you up from that bed,' he said. 'Come on, let's all go to one of these jewel shops right now,' he'd tell me, 'and then we'll have a lovely lunch, something you really like. Remember that bean stew we had on our first day here? You talked about it for days.' And so I had, though it was strange, because the thought of it seemed dreary now, as it was like I knew it wouldn't taste of anything much after all. 'So we will,' I told him, to make him stop being so noisy, 'but not today. I don't feel like it today.'

As mornings mixed with one another and all seemed the same, I couldn't tell you how many had gone by when they brought the little fellow up to see me. I'd been having a doze when I found them crowding round the bed. There was Paul, looking puzzled, there was Ragged Tom, seeming more cheery, there was Joan, who looked sour, there was the clerk of the hospital and finally there was another whom I'd never seen before. He was a curious little body, though. I swear he was shorter even than my Paul and he had a knowing, weary look about him, as if the world had battered him about the head so many times that he hardly noticed any more. 'This man wants to see you,' said my Paul, 'though I wasn't sure if I should let him.' 'You shouldn't have,' said Joan firmly. 'He wants us to go with him,' said Paul then. 'But not me,' said Joan. 'It's you and Paul and Tom he wants and nobody else.' It all seemed so strange and I struggled to get my thoughts around it. 'Go where?' I asked. 'He won't say,' said Paul. 'He says he can't tell us. But he says if we want answers to all the things that are troubling and vexing us, then we must go with him, and we must go straight away.'

All the things that had been troubling and vexing us answered. I lay there for a moment saying the words over in my mind. It was like they made my head spin. A thought came to me, perhaps he'll take me to an angel who'll make everything right, and though I didn't believe it, not really, the notion of it warmed me a little. I looked at the man's face. He didn't seem wicked. Everything that troubled and vexed me answered. Somebody must know something of us for saying such a thing. I tried to think what it would be like for everything to be answered but it was hard even to begin. It was like being in a dark cave for so long that when you step out the light's too dazzling for your eyes. How would it be to get out of this mire that seemed as if it would never end? I glimpsed it now, and it was like I was so starved that I'd forgotten how hungry I was. Even if there was just a tiny hope that it was true, I couldn't let it pass me by. 'You know what,' I said slowly. 'I think I might go.'

'I wouldn't if I were you,' said the hospital clerk. 'I've never seen this fellow before. And it's almost dusk now.' Joan said I was lunatic even to think of it. 'You'll be robbed and murdered for certain,' she said. 'And you're too frail. You've hardly eaten a thing for days.' But strange to say, I didn't feel so tired now. Everything that vexed me answered? There was so much. Mostly, of course, it was the one thing. 'No, I'm going, you hear,' I said and, sitting up and feeling faint, I asked the clerk to fetch me an apple. Tom was glad I wanted to go. 'I was hoping you'd say yes,' he said, 'as I can't think how many troubling things there are that I'd like to have an answer for. For one, why is it that I've not seen Sammy in my dreams for a week or more now, neither in paradise nor in purgatory?' Though Paul wasn't so sure, he said of course he'd come too, as he wasn't letting me go off without him. The clerk, when he came back with my apple, said we should take Jack, being a strong fellow, and Dame Lucy, when she came up soon afterwards, said she'd happily spare him, but we knew it could be only the three of us.

Joan said I must leave my pouch of valuables with her, as it would be plain madness to have that on me through Rome at this hour, so I did and then, feeling dizzy from laying in bed for so long, I got to my feet and made my way down the stairs. Stepping out of the hospital door I found that, even though the sun was down, everything seemed so broad and bright that I had to stop for a moment and rest against the wall. But Paul and Tom helped me and the little fellow was patient and he didn't hurry us. Yet the road he took was a strange one. I'm the kind who usually knows my way but as we turned every moment left or right down another dark, winding, muddy lane, I soon lost all notion. 'Weren't we here just now?' I said to Paul. 'I don't think so,' he answered, though he didn't seem sure. Tom let out a little anguished snicker. 'I hope we won't find Sir John up there with his dagger.' If he'd meant to be funny, neither of us laughed. 'Sir John went home days back,' I said, which had Tom putting up his hands in surrender. 'Of course, so he did,' he said, snickering again.

It was almost dark when our little guide led us into a tiny courtyard and I guessed we were arrived. He pulled a set of big keys from his belt, unlocked a door and pointed us to go in. Looking up I saw it was at the base of a tall, thin tower while from a window on the top floor I could see light gently shining. That filled me with cheer. God's here, I thought. Please, I beg you, help me now and cure my vexations. It was almost pitch black inside and I heard Paul and Tom banging into something, or each other, just behind me. 'I'm not sure I like this,' said Paul. 'It'll be all right, don't you worry,' I said, and when Tom moaned, 'I hope so,' I told him firmly, 'We're not going back now that we're almost there.' The first steps were so dark that I only knew my way from the thump of our little fellow's boots ahead of me, but then I saw a faint glimmering between the floorboards above that grew slowly stronger as I climbed, till I could see my way well enough. Here's light, I thought, with a rising heart. Here's God.

Finally we reached the topmost floor, and I saw that the beacon that had led us up was an oil lamp flickering from a niche in the wall. There was a door, half open, and in the room beyond, getting up from behind a table and giving us a smile, was a man I'd never seen before, with a long white beard. I caught my breath. He looks so venerable, I thought, like a saint, or even God himself. We're saved now all right, I thought. Now my boy will be well, I'm sure of it. But then our little guide opened the door wider and I saw the other two who were getting to their feet beside him. What are they doing here? I thought. Because it was the Jews, Mary and Helena.

Paul darted past me and threw his arms round Mary, while Tom clapped his hands and let out a cheer. Mary must've seen I didn't look much pleased and she stepped towards me. 'I'm so glad you came,' she said. 'I'd have made everything clearer if only I could have.' Then she looked at Tom. 'The truth is, you see, that I need to ask you a favour.'

CHAPTER ELEVEN

Motte

Ever since I was a little girl all I wanted was to be good by God and the world. And the trouble it's got me into.

When I was growing up in Gloucester I sought to be a righteous daughter and a good kinswoman to my brothers and sisters. When my parents said I should please Benedict, who'd come from London to make silver candlesticks for our synagogue, and who I could see had taken a liking to me, I kept his company and tried to show myself agreeable. And when they said I should marry him I did that too. Then I tried to be a good wife to him, though it wasn't easy. Benedict was kindly enough but it was hard to be away from all my family and to live in a big, noisy city that I didn't know. And though I wanted to be a good daughter-in-law I never could bring myself to love Benedict's mother, Licoricia. Then she didn't like me either, and not a day passed without her telling me that her dear son could've married seven times better than he had. But I hardly cared once I'd had my two little boys, Leo and Hame. And I never had to strive to be a good mother and to adore and cherish them both, as I couldn't have done anything else.

When my parents sent my little sister Rosa to stay with us in London to find a husband, I was her protector when

Licoricia complained that she was too sad, always picking at her food, or when she ran away, because she hated being in that house. And when trouble broke out between de Montfort and the king I tried to stay calm, as I knew there was no use doing otherwise. When, in the middle of it all, Rosa ran away once again, I went in search of her, like a good sister should. And afterwards I tried not to hate her, even though it was her fault that I'd been stuck outside the city on that day when the slaughter came, which meant I wasn't able to comfort my two boys when they were taken in the night to be slain, and that I hadn't been killed with them, which was all I wanted, as being spared when they were gone seemed not a blessing but a curse.

I can't say I was good by God and the world after that. I was a bad daughter-in-law, no denying. I couldn't forgive Licoricia for having been spared that day, as de Montfort's folk had thought her too old to trouble with. But what made me hate her every hour, and show it too, was that on that terrible day she'd told my boys they mustn't abjure their faith and declare themselves Christians, which would've saved their lives. And though I tried not to hate Benedict for being her son, I can't say I did well with him either. I knew it was wrong for a wife not to let her husband touch her but I couldn't do it, as the last thing I wanted in all the world was to have another child to be hurt and murdered.

But there's nothing like time to lull the soul. Years passed, my mother-in-law died, not mourned by me, and we Jews were left in peace, mostly. So I tried to be good after all. I let Benedict have his husband's rights and we soon had a little daughter, Mirabilia, my dear sweet Miri. But I swear it seemed like letting myself have hope provoked new trouble against us. Miri had barely come into the world when we had a new king, Edward. I'm not saying any of them had much loved their Jews, but at least some of them had found us useful. And useful we'd been, giving them a way of taxing their own people without seeming to. They'd let us make money from lending and then they'd take it back in the tallage they took from us, which meant they could fleece their folk and put all their hate onto us. But King Edward seemed not to care that we were serviceable to him and he reviled us even worse than any of his forefathers had. He banned us from lending, though there was little else we could do, as we'd long been forbidden from any other converse with Christian English, whether as traders or physicians or anything else. Then he taxed us so high that many had hardly a thing left. My Benedict struggled like the rest, as few Jews had money to buy silver trinkets now, and I tried to be his good wife and give him comfort.

I soon had to comfort him more. King Edward wanted a new set of coins minted and, to stop them being spoiled like the old ones he ordered that anyone who clipped the edges off them – which many had done, Christians much more than Jews – must be tried in the courts. And though hardly one Christian was seized, scores of Jews were and, guilty or not, were hanged. As a silversmith Benedict was just the kind who'd be taken, but I tried to seem calm, not wanting to put more fear into him and little Miri than they already had, though I'd lie awake each night listening for a rap on our door and for his name to be called out. All the while I prayed every waking hour, till finally God heard me and the king ordered the trials stopped. Then he had to or he'd have had no Jews left to tax.

But I should have prayed even harder. Of all the lies told against us in this age of lies, the very worst, and which was first invented in England by English folk, was that Jews loved to steal away Christian children and crucify them, to mock and laugh at Jesus' death. Jews, who venerated all children, whether Christian or their own, and who treated them with more kindness than did most Christians, who scolded and beat their own. Though some had believed it, most hadn't because the kings wouldn't give such a monstrous notion their blessing. That was until King Henry, Edward's father, went to Lincoln to pray to Little Hugh, the poor mite whom Christians said we'd murdered. After that there was hardly a soul who said it was the foul lie it was, and from that time there was nothing Jews feared more than news that a Christian child was missing. Yet when I heard talk that a child had vanished in Northampton I wasn't fearful, as Northampton was far from London and none of us had ever gone there. But it wasn't far enough as it turned out. The Sheriff of Northampton brought some of the city's Jews to London and dragged them behind horses through the streets to die. Afterwards some of the crowd who'd cheered it being done chanced upon Benedict on London Bridge, one of them knew him, and they all set upon him and threw him into the river to drown.

After that there was only one way left to me to try and be good, which was to keep my Miri safe. I couldn't feel right in London any more and so I moved back to Gloucester where I still had kin, including my little sister Rosa, who was married now with three children. I'd worked as a seamstress once before and I set up as a gown maker, and little Miri helped with the fine stitching. But I didn't feel safe in Gloucester either. I saw how our Christian neighbours lost their smiles when they passed us on the street, and would cross themselves and spit. At night I'd have nightmares and I'd wake Miri with my screams.

It happened that next door to my gown shop was a butcher's shop that was owned by a Christian named Edmund, who was a widower with no living children. He was friendly to us in a way few others of his kind were and I saw the way he'd look at me. So my thoughts began to stray where I'd never dreamed they might. My two little boys and Benedict had kept to their faith and what good had it done them? Though I knew it was dangerous, as any doings between my folk and Edmund's were forbidden, I paid visits to him in his shop early in the morning when it was empty, until by and by we reached an accord. One morning I took Miri to the Blackfriars where we learned about Jesus and Mother Mary and all the saints, and we recited our catechism and the Lord's Prayer. I was baptized Mary and Miri became Helena. I paid half of my fortune to the king, as the law said I must, and I ate pork for the first time and though it seemed sweet and chewy I soon grew used to its taste.

If all I'd wanted was to be a good Jew, now all I wanted was to be a good Christian. I never missed church and I prayed to Jesus and God and Mother Mary every day. What's more, I loved Jesus not just when I was with Christians but when I was quiet and alone. And I was set on making Helena a good Christian too. I made her recite her prayers and catechism, I examined her on the saints and the foul deaths each had suffered and the miracles they'd done. And I scolded her most sharply if she said anything that wasn't respectful of her new creed.

Of course I wasn't good by God or the world in the eyes of my kin. None would speak to us, not even my sister Rosa whom I'd watched over in London and rescued when she ran away. If they passed us on the street they'd spit and look the other way just like my Christian neighbours used to do. Even my Helena was angry with me for a long while. Then she'd already hated me for marrying Edmund. Which wasn't right, I thought, as he was a clean and honourable man who did his best to be a good husband, and a good father to her. But most of all she couldn't bear that she'd lost the company of her cousins and her friends. As if it was easy for me? Like her, I missed the turning of the week and of the seasons, which I'd known through the synagogue, where I'd gone each Saturday, and for Passover, Rosh Hashanah, Yom Kippur and the other holy days. And though I tried to love churches, they seemed sorry, grave places, and not warm and friendly like our little synagogue.

Even after giving half my property to the king I still had a good house and my gown shop, while Edmund had a house and his shop too, so we sold it all and bought one of the finest houses in Gloucester, which was on the far side of the town from the Jewry so I passed my old kin less often on the street. We bought a bigger shop for his butchering and for three years we lived well and for the first time in as long as I could remember I felt no fear. Till Edmund did the only thing that I find it hard to forgive him for to this day. One spring morning he was taken sick with a fever and ten days later he was dead.

It was only when he was gone that I realized how much he'd been our shield. I'd known his kin didn't much like Helena and me but I'd never guessed the full truth. We had a Christian neighbour who'd give us news sometimes, and though the way she told us was more taunting than friendly, it was as well she did. She told us that because Edmund had been widowed and childless till he married me, his kin had been looking forward to inheriting his house and his butcher's shop. Now they hated us for taking what they thought was rightfully theirs. They said we weren't Christians but were only pretending and were still Jews in secret. They said I'd used Jew spells to bewitch Edmund and make him fall in love with me so I might have his fortune. Most of all they said that, having got what we wanted, Helena and I had murdered him with poison and magic. And, seeing the hateful looks we got when we walked about Gloucester, I knew that everything the woman told us was true.

After that all my fears came back worse than before. There seemed nothing we could do. We couldn't go back to being Jews again as we'd be burned as apostates. Helena scolded me, saying that we'd turned our backs on our own people and gained nobody in their place. 'You wanted us to be safe,' she'd say, 'and now we're more in danger than we ever were.' I tried my best to be a good mother and not to despair. We're righteous Christians, I told myself. We've learned the Lord's Prayer and our catechisms and all the saints and can recite them better than most Christians can. Surely now that we've given our faith to Jesus and God and Mary, they'll look after us?

I tried to do everything I could to show Edmund's kin wrong. I went to church and I prayed, not only on Sundays but every day. I gave money to the poor of Gloucester and I gave more for the cathedral roof. Whenever I talked to anyone, kin or not, I'd praise and thank Jesus as often as I could. Yet the more I tried the worse it seemed to work against us. Our neighbour told us that Edmund's kin said we made ourselves seem Christian to hide our secret Jewish ways. They said we did magic spells in our house at night, and whenever something bad happened – a neighbour had his head stove in by a barrel falling from a cart, or another was kicked by a horse and died – they'd put the blame on us, and folk believed them. In the morning I'd find our door marked with a Jew star drawn with shit or blood.

Finally I went back to the Blackfriars who'd first taught us Christian ways, and I asked their counsel. They said our sufferings were because God still hadn't forgiven us for all the years when we'd been Jews. They said we should repent our old misbeliefs and seek his forgiveness by going on a pilgrimage. If it was a long one and we went on foot, that would show our neighbours that our faith was true. And then God would see to it that Edmund's kin knew our holiness and we'd find peace.

So, though Helena complained that it would do no good, I had the Blackfriars write a testimonial for us, I wrote my will, I got us both our scrips and staffs and cloaks and pilgrim hats, and I gave the keys to the house and the shop to Edmund's kin to watch over, and I didn't care if they stole half of what was there so long as we'd be let alone when we came back. Then we set off for Rome. Now all will be well, I thought. Now finally my Helena will be free from danger. But then Sir John's boy Gawayne went wooing her. I was pleased at first.

He's heir to a manor, I thought, even if it's a poor one, and though I didn't much like Sir John, if Helena married his son at least she'd escape from Gloucester and be safe from Edmund's kin. And what better way to show that we were true Christians than to marry a good Christian Englishman whose father had fought for his King Edward in wars? But then Helena couldn't abide Gawayne nor his family. So my wish to be good and do the right thing was pulled in two ways at once. I wanted Helena to be safe but I wanted her to be content too. And though I tried to win her round, in the end I had to go with her wishes.

Then we were hated again, and suspected again, and accused again, till that terrible evening came when we were cast out into the snow to die. Yet even afterwards I still tried my best to be good by God and the world. I told myself, yes it was bad but God and Jesus had looked after us in their way, as Tom and the others had come and saved us. If God hadn't watched over us very well, that was probably just because we hadn't yet reached Rome and prayed to Saint Peter. Once we'd done that we'd be safe. But Helena didn't believe me. She'd say to me, when nobody could hear, 'Can't you see, Mother? Whatever we do, it's never enough. It never will be enough. However much we try to be what they say we must be, however much we try to be like them, in their eyes we'll always be Jews, and we'll always be scorned and hated and cast down.'

We kept our counsel and tried not to make ourselves noticed and with time we got to Rome. We moved our scrips from the inn to the English Hospital like all the others, and then we set out for Saint Peter's as any Christian pilgrim would. But then we happened to see two Jews, whom we knew from their clothing, and Helena said, 'I wonder if they're going to the synagogue? Let's follow them and see.' And though I tried to say we shouldn't, she hurried after them. Across the river they went and Helena was right and we saw them go through a door with those familiar letters written above. Helena said, 'Let's go in, just to see. It's so long since we've been inside one, I'd like to go. There's no harm as nobody knows us here.' And though I said no, how can we, dressed as we are in Christian pilgrim gear, in she went and I followed.

It was a fine-looking synagogue, handsome and well furnished with beautiful silver candlesticks that Benedict would have admired. I hadn't meant to talk to anyone but then one of the two that we'd followed was suspicious of us, and he asked us, in French, what two Christian pilgrims were doing in such a place. And though I tried to be righteous and to say nothing, before I knew it I found I was crying, and strongly too, so it was as if the sobs worked right through me from the inside. Then I told him our story. I could see he scorned what we'd done but he looked a little sorry for us too. He said we should talk to the rabbi and though I said no, we couldn't, Helena was eager and so we did. Of course the rabbi scorned us more than the other had, but he said if we still had God in our hearts, as he thought we did from looking at us, then it wasn't too late and we could still come back. As nobody knew us here we'd be safe from being burned as apostates. And though I tried to say no, Helena was smiling like I hadn't seen her in years. She said yes, that's what we wanted, and then I did as well.

I knew it wouldn't be easy. We'd never be able to go back to Gloucester and we'd lose all we had there, the house and the shop. But then, as Helena said, what use would they be if we were murdered by Edmund's kin? Nor would we be able to see any of our family again. But then we'd lost them years back. It would be hard living in another land where we'd have to learn the language and the customs and yet, in its way, this city didn't feel so very foreign to me. It was a mean, grasping sort of place yet somehow it was welcoming too. So it was done. I became Motte once again and Helena became Miri. I'm not saying I'm proud of it. But what else could I do?

We were hidden by a physician, Elias son of Josul, in his house, as the rabbi said we must keep out of sight till all the others in our pilgrim party had left Rome. I didn't dare go back to get our packs for fear we might give ourselves away, and though I felt wrong for leaving without saying goodbye, especially to the ones who'd been kindly to us and who'd saved us that night in the snow, there seemed little I could do. And then I had another reason to feel wrong. One morning when I was talking to our keeper Elias, and knowing he was a physician, I told him about little Paul, and after pondering it he told me what he thought.

Just a few days later the rabbi came to visit us with an anguished look on his face. There was a Rome Jew who had a shop nearby the English Hospital and who'd promised to keep an eye on our old fellow pilgrims and tell us when they'd all gone back, so I wouldn't have to hide any more. Now he'd told the rabbi that the clerk of the English Hospital and an Englishman dressed in rags had been going round asking about two pilgrims who'd disappeared, Mary and Helena. First they'd asked shopmen and people on the street and then they'd tried asking priests and monks. 'This ragged fellow,' the rabbi asked me, 'd'you know him? Is he a zealot? Does he have some reason to be against you?' I said he was a good man and was just worried for us. But the rabbi feared that if he kept asking questions and if he told someone that we'd been Jews before, then, without meaning to, he might put us in danger.

Strange to say, one part of me, the part that always wanted to be goodly, by God and the world, was pleased, as at least now I had a reason to do the righteous thing that I knew I should. Though Miri thought I was a fool. 'You'll just put us in worse danger,' she said, but it was clear as could be that keeping quiet now would be wicked under any god, and she couldn't change my mind. So I asked Elias if he'd talk to Constance and Paul and when he answered yes, I sent out his servant with my message. And though Miri said the ones who'd come up the stairs wouldn't be them but soldiers of the pope, she was wrong, I'm glad to say, and I saw Paul running towards me with open arms.

When I tried to tell them our story it came out jumbled. The more I talked the more I felt like I'd done nothing right in all my days, and that I'd forsaken every friend I'd ever known. 'I'm so sorry,' I said. 'I wanted to be a good Christian, I really did, you must believe me. When I swore myself to Jesus I did it with all my heart, and I wasn't cheating you when we were walking together, as I meant to be as good a pilgrim as the rest of you.' Then I begged them, 'Please, don't tell anybody what I've just said to you, as that will be the death of us both.' Tom and Paul promised willingly, as I'd known they would, but Constance, though she gave her word, looked more careful, so I worried Miri had been right and I had been a fool.

That was when I remembered Elias, sitting beside us. So I told them he was a physician who'd learned his lore at the school of medicine at Salerno, and who'd treated three popes. Then I said how I'd told him about Paul's sickness and that Elias thought he might be able to help. And though Constance watched him suspectingly, Paul was looking at him with wide eyes. Then, with me putting it all into English as best I could from Elias' Latin, I passed on his first question, which was what Paul had eaten the night before he was last taken ill. 'Eels,' said Constance at once. 'I guessed right away that that was what had made him sick, but then it turned out that all the others, who'd had eels too, weren't troubled at all.' 'What else?' asked Elias, and Constance and Paul tried to remember it all, the pottage of leeks and peas, the good white bread that gentle folk ate, and that strange pear with red seeds that were sweet and bitter at once.

'And what about the time before that, up in the mountains?' asked Elias next. 'I had nothing much up there,' said Paul, as they hadn't brought much, seeing as they'd expected to eat at the hospital that night. He'd had some nuts and apples and a little smoked sausage and some honey biscuits that Constance gave him, to give him strength. 'These biscuits, were they pale?' asked Elias, and Paul said yes, they'd been almost white. 'That was the time I grew sick again and again,' said Paul. Finally Elias asked about the very first time that Paul was taken ill, which had been after the funeral of Constance's husband, Hubert. Constance tried to recall the dishes they'd had to honour him, the mushroom with strong powder, the lamb in sauce, the suckling pig and hare and peacock. 'What about bread?' asked Elias. 'We had the very best of course,' she answered. 'Wheat bread like gentle folk have.' 'And you didn't eat that usually?' Elias asked. 'Never,' Constance told him. 'It was the first time I ever tasted it, as Hubert was too humble in his ways for anything but barley or rye. I remember thinking how smooth and soft it was.'

Elias gave a smile then. 'I can't be completely sure, of course,' he said, 'but I think I know what this is.' Then he told us that some people were made sick by things that didn't trouble anyone else, while a few were made very sick indeed. A Saracen physician had written about this kind of affliction. Some folk were struck by spring roses, others by summer grasses or animals. Others couldn't abide rye or barley or wheat, and even small amounts could make them ill, so their bellies swelled and they'd retch and wheeze and fight to breathe. And some were afflicted only by wheat. 'You have no trouble when you eat barley bread or rye?' he asked Paul. 'No,' Paul answered, very quiet now, like he was trying to stop his hope getting too great.

'Then here's what I think you should do,' Elias told him. 'Eat just the tiniest bit of wheat, only half a grain or less, so it can't trouble you much. If you find you feel a little ill then you'll know that's your foe. If it is, as I suspect, then you must take the greatest care to be sure there's no wheat in anything you eat, not even the smallest amount. If you're away from your own kitchen and if anyone offers you bread or biscuits or a pie, then you must ask them what's in it, to be sure. Stay away from fields of wheat when they're ripening if you can. Though with luck you won't have to do these things forever, as if this malady begins when you're young it often passes away when you become grown.'

Paul let out a little gasp. 'You're saying all I have to do is not eat wheat and I'll never be sick again?' he asked. 'That's my guess,' said Elias. Constance was looking at him confounded. 'But what about my sin?' she asked. 'What about it?' said Elias. 'But that's why Paul was struck,' she said. Elias gave a laugh. 'I wouldn't say so.' Then he told us how he knew of the most righteous folk who had been stricken with terrible maladies while others who were wicked to their bones hardly suffered even from a cold till the very day they died. Even still Constance could hardly believe it. 'You're quite sure?' she asked, and then asked it again. 'Paul's sickness wasn't my doing?' Paul was smiling wide now. 'So I needn't ever have come here. I'd have been fine staying at home and eating cheap barley bread. But then I wouldn't have come here tonight and learned what I shouldn't eat. And Aunt Joan wouldn't have been happy, would she? She wouldn't have had a reason to spend our money.' Constance looked like she was about to say something but then she stopped. 'We're not going to Jerusalem, I hope?' Paul asked. A hard look that I'd not seen before during all our weeks of walking together came into Constance's eyes. 'No, Paul,' she said, 'that we're not.'

After that it was time for them to go. Elias' servant, who'd brought them, would see them safely home, I said. It was a sorrowful farewell. We hugged and kissed, and Constance was as warm as any of them, so I knew she'd keep our secret. Miri looked sad when she kissed Tom on his cheek, and three times over she wished him well on his journey home. Then for all his rags I'd seen she was soft of heart for him, and him for her.

So I'd done a little good at least, after all the good that had gone bad. I'd paid some of my debt to Paul who, more than any other, had saved our lives that evening in the snow. And I'd done a little good by God, whom, though I'd never meant to or wanted to, I'd scorned doubly by changing my faith not once but twice. Watch over them on their journey home, I prayed to him when they'd gone. What does it matter what religion they have when their souls are kindly?

CHAPTER TWELVE

Tom son of Tom

They speak strangely up here in Lincolnshire. Instead of saying though they say yof and for shall they say sal, while that's only the start of their odd ways, so there's hardly one word they say right. I already knew their talk a little from hearing Dame Lucy's thralls, Brigit and Alwyn and Jack the cook, and from Dame Lucy and Lionel, but they spoke less strong than most do here, and though I'm growing customed to it, I sometimes have to make a fellow stop and say a thing again four times over before I understand. But it'll come to me in time, I dare say.

It's a wonder to me how the whole world can change on the spin of a coin. It's God's will of course. But then it had been his will that Dame Lucy thought I was the wicked one when Lionel almost let her boy fall to his death by the river. And it had been his will that Dame Lucy thought Brigit was lying over her necklace and that Lionel had done no wrong. But if she wouldn't believe a word that Brigit and I said, she believed what she saw written down in letters.

The first I knew of it was a couple of days after Constance, Paul and I went out in the dark and met Mary and Helena, or Motty and Merry, whichever they were. Lionel and his manservant Dobbe were out and I was in the little hall of the English Hospital, feeling sorry that I'd never see Helena again, as she was so dear and had always been kindly to me. I was getting ready to go out begging once again, which was hard in Rome, where the streets were crowded with pilgrims doing just the same, when I heard a shriek from upstairs. Knowing it was Dame Lucy's voice, and fearing she'd been set upon by murderers, I ran up two steps at a time, but when I reached the upper dormitory the only ones there were her and Father Tim. He looked like he'd been bitten by a snake and she was telling him in a low voice, 'I told you to get out.' Then, seeing me standing there, she turned on me too. 'What d'you think you're gawping at? Get out, I say.' So we both did.

As for what it was all about, I understood better just afterwards down in the hall, when I talked to Father Tim and Alwyn and Jack the cook, and Brigit, too, who'd been begging outside but had come in when she heard Dame Lucy's cry. Father Tim told us that the trouble had all started when he'd been going through the scripts she'd brought, to prove to the pope's court that her husband Walter was her cousin and that their marriage was false. 'I was looking through them for the tenth time, just to be sure I had everything in order before we went to the court, and then I noticed something, there in tiny letters on one of the kin lists. I knew Dame Lucy wouldn't be pleased, but I couldn't keep quiet, so I told her, "I'm very sorry, mistress, but I'm not sure you can rightfully marry Lionel after all."' Dame Lucy had laughed and asked whyever not, so Father Tim had told her it was for the very same reason that she could divorce Walter. She and Lionel were cousins. 'Not close,' Father Tim said, 'but still cousins.' Dame Lucy smiled and said what did that matter, seeing as all the gentle folk of Lincolnshire were cousins, while it only counted when you wanted to divorce one, but she'd asked to see, so Father Tim showed her the script where it said that Lionel was one degree nearer to her than Walter, as he was Walter's first cousin. 'That's when she let out a shriek and told me to get out. I can't understand it.'

If he didn't, Brigit did. 'His first cousin,' she said, clapping her hands together. 'I knew there was something wrong about him. Of course. The whole thing was deceit right from the start. No wonder I never heard thunder that day he came to the house, when he said he'd almost been struck by lightning, or that we never found their horses. I'll bet it was Walter who brought him to us, and who gave him some bruises, so it seemed like he'd been thrown.' I know folk called me Simple Tom but even I could see it then. Walter had known he'd likely lose the fortune he'd got from Dame Lucy once she made her cause in Rome, so he'd sent his seemly cousin, who she didn't know, to woo her and wed her and win her fortune back for his family after all. No wonder Lionel hadn't cared about Peter that day in the mountains. 'So I was right about her necklace,' said Brigit. 'He put it in my pack to get me gone.' That gave me a thought. 'I wonder what he's thinking of doing at Monte Cassino, just him, Dame Lucy and that hulk of a manservant?' We all looked at each other then.

'We'll have to tell her,' said Brigit. Not me, I thought. 'Let's leave her for a little while,' said Father Tim and as it turned out that was the wise thing to do. Within the hour we heard footsteps on the stairs, very slow, and then there was Dame Lucy, looking pale and with her hand raised to us. 'Don't speak,' she said. 'Not a word. When Lionel and Dobbe get back, have them wait here in the hall. Be sure you all stay with them and fetch the clerk, too, and anyone else who's here at the hospital.' Then back she went.

We did just as she'd said and fetched the clerk and some other pilgrims who'd come in, and who were quite puzzled to be asked to stay in the hall. After a time Lionel and Dobbe came back from wherever they'd been, and looked round in surprise at the crowd gathered there. Father Tim fetched Dame Lucy, who came down the stairs with the script in her hand. Those gentle folk have funny ways, though. If this had been my neighbours in Minster there'd have been shouting and punches and clouting with sticks but Dame Lucy spoke in a slow, flat sort of voice, quite as if none of it mattered a fig. 'Is it true, Lionel,' she asked, 'that you're first cousin of my husband Walter?' The way his eyes opened wide I knew the answer to that. 'My dear,' he said, 'what are you saying?' 'Yes or no?' she asked and, smiling like the whole thing was foolishness, he answered yes, as it happened he was Walter's cousin, though it mattered not at all. 'I came here to Rome for love of you,' he said, 'only for you.'

Don't let him coax you, I thought to myself, don't soften, Dame Lucy, but I needn't have worried. Now I understood why she'd wanted a big crowd there. 'Your clothes,' she said. 'Take them off, both of you.' When Lionel stared at her confounded she told him, 'They're not yours, you'll remember? They weren't my gift to you. I lent them to you and now I want them back.' I don't know if the folk all around knew something of Dame Lucy and Lionel or if they'd only guessed, but they were laughing. Lionel tried to laugh too. 'But my sweet, we have no others.' 'That's no concern of mine,' Dame Lucy told him, cold as ice. 'Give them to me now, if you please, or I'll have to have one of the pope's officers called.' The clerk of the hospital was smirking like he'd gladly go out and find one. Lionel looked about him, wondering what to do, but then his hulking servant Dobbe, who'd seen the moment clearer than his master, was already pulling off his boots. So Lionel did the same, still trying to smile like it was all a great sport, till they were both stripped down to their unders. Dame Lucy had Alwyn take the gear from them and then she told them, 'And the same will go for your horses seeing as they were loaned too.' That was when Lionel lost all pretence and looked up at her, beseeching. 'But how will we get home?' 'You have legs to carry you, don't you,' Dame Lucy said, 'and hands to beg with?'

If it was hard on Lionel it was good for me. Dame Lucy never said sorry to me, nor to any of the rest she'd disbelieved, which was no surprise I dare say, as it wasn't for dames to say sorry to their lowers, but she gave me Lionel's clothes, which fitted me well enough and were most handsome, I have to say, and much better than the ones she'd given me before. 'How fine you look, Tom,' Brigit said. 'If I didn't know better I'd think you a proper gentleman.' Another thing Dame Lucy did was to let me eat freely from her food, which meant I wasn't hungry any more. Better again she sold the other clothes she'd bought for me before, and Dobbe's clothes too, and with the silver she got for them she bought a vernicle and a silver cross for Sir Toby, and she said I didn't need to pay for either, which I couldn't have of course. Together they only cost two shillings and eightpence in English coin, and though I said that meant I still owed Sir Toby two shillings and fourpence, Dame Lucy just laughed and said what a funny fellow I was, Tom, as what did that matter seeing as he'd never know?

So she never got her Rome wedding in the end but she did get her Rome divorce. Not that there were many of us left to celebrate. Because of course Joan had gone by then, after the big disputation she and Constance had. That had been on the same night after we got back from seeing Motty and Merry. Paul did as the physician had told him and ate a tiny speck of wheat and sure enough after a time he was itching himself and wheezing, though not badly, as it had been so little. Then Constance told Joan that they weren't going to Jerusalem and after that the two of them were like a pair of boxers landing punches on each other. Constance said she knew it wasn't her sin that had made Paul sick but eating wheat, which she'd learned from a physician who was a Jew, though he'd shown more mind for Paul than Joan ever had. Then Joan said that was nonsense and that God had only given Paul his affliction because Constance had whored herself for her cousin, and that she was a fool just like her husband had been, and that she'd regret her Jew loving when she found herself in hell. Next Constance told Joan that she thought only of herself and always had, and she'd never cared a fart for her or for her Paul either. Finally Constance said she wasn't walking another step in Joan's company, and that Joan could beg her way home alone. Then they each cursed the other, saying all the foul things they wanted the other to suffer, and Joan foretold that Paul would be sick again within the week. I worried that by talking of the Jew doctor Constance had broken her promise to Mary and Helena about not saying anything about them, but then

I doubted it would much matter as, having no silver to stay another night in Rome, Joan set off for home the very next day.

In the end Dame Lucy's divorce feast wasn't quite so small as I'd thought, as we had a guest none of us had expected. The dinner was almost ready and Alwyn had gone out to get some Roman wine in case we ran short, and when he came back he called out, 'Look who I found.' I knew the fellow of course and yet I didn't know him too, as from his face he seemed like a different man. Gone was the sorry, sly look he'd had before and now he seemed proud and knowing almost like a priest. It was Jocelyn the advocate. He'd not come to stay at the English Hospital, he said, as he'd been keeping with an advocate friend who was down here. Though his last parting from us had been sour, that seemed long ago now and Dame Lucy and Constance both made him welcome. When we all sat down to eat and Brigit got merry on the wine, and asked him if he'd found any tree stumps to sit on in Rome and any pretty putains to give his tail a clean, Jocelyn wasn't troubled at all and said no, his every day in Rome had been spent visiting churches and repenting. 'I'm all God's now,' he said. 'In fact I've been thinking of giving up the law and joining the church instead.' We all laughed then. 'You, in the church?' said Brigit. 'And why not,' Jocelyn answered, like he was surprised it was even asked. 'I tell you, there's no folk God has more need of than advocates.' He might work in one of the church courts, he told us, though his real wish was to serve the almighty as a confessor. 'Most of them don't know what they're doing,' he said, 'as they're blind to what sins they should be looking for.' As an advocate he'd know just what unrights people got up to, he said. Including your own,

I thought. 'Why, I might even write a guide for confessors,' he said. He'd stay in Rome a few weeks longer, he said, to meet people who might help him.

But not the rest of us. Now that Dame Lucy had got her divorce and wasn't going to have her wedding there was no reason to keep us any longer, and we all set out on the road a couple of days later. Going home was a much sweeter journey than the one I'd had coming, which was all thanks to Lionel. Dame Lucy decided to sell her cart seeing as it slowed her down so, and she sold it and some of her things that she'd decided she didn't need. Then she told Constance and Paul that they could ride Dobbe's horse and I could have Lionel's, who was a handsome creature, all grey except for a little black dapple on his rump. Every few miles I'd glance at Paul to be sure he wasn't growing sick once again, as Joan had said he would, while Constance looked at him a good deal more often, but no, now that he stayed away from gentle folk's bread he was fine as could be.

Going on horseback being so much faster than walking, over the days and weeks that followed we caught up with our fellow pilgrims one after another. First, when we were coming close to Siena, were Lionel and Dobbe, though I hardly knew either till we got close. I don't know where they'd got their clothes but it couldn't have been much of a spot, as they were hardly better than the rags I used to wear. And something had gone all awry with Lionel's seemly blonde hair too. Whether something had dripped on him or been thrown at him I couldn't have said, but it must have been strong, staining stuff as his head was marked a muddy black on one side. He'd shorn his hair, trying to get rid of the blot as I guessed, so his long locks were gone. 'You look seven times handsomer than him now, Tom,' said Brigit, laughing. 'And I've got his horse,' I answered. When he saw us going by him, Lionel ran up to Dame Lucy and called out to her, 'My dear sweetheart, I beg you, take pity on one who adores you with all his heart and always has.' She just laughed. 'I will if I find one,' she said, looking down from her horse. 'But I don't see one anywhere here.' Then she tugged at her reins and left him behind. Lionel, seeing that I was in his clothes and riding his horse, gave me a burning look. I gave him a little wave as I passed him by.

The next we came to, which was just after Siena, was Joan walking with a crowd of dirty, ragged folk, worse even than Lionel and Dobbe. She and Constance, they didn't say a word to each other, but Constance rode her horse so close that Joan got a good coating of dust from his hooves. After that we didn't see another of them till we met Dame Alice at Lucca. She must've been asking for us, hoping we'd pass by, as we'd hardly set our packs down at the inn where we were staying when there she was, begging a shilling from Dame Lucy to try and get her husband and her boy out of jail. I swear that fellow just couldn't let anything be. He'd gone back to the very same taverner who he'd clouted when we'd come through the first time, saying he'd watered the wine, and clouted him again but worse. So a proper little battle had broken out, with Gawayne and him throwing punches at anyone who came near. This time the Luccans wouldn't make do with tuppence paid to the taverner. Dame Lucy gave her the shilling. 'I just hope I can get him free,' said Alice then, 'and that he won't be sent back to Rome in penance again.' That monk in Saint

Peter's will clap his hands in joy if he sees them all coming back, I thought.

The very next day we passed Warin and Beatrix, sat by the side of the road, and I was sure I heard God's voice croaking out of Beatrix's mouth, saying something about how her boots weren't right, though Warin just told him, 'Put a stop in it, will you,' which didn't seem very reverent, so I thought. Then Warin saw us and grumbled something about high folk perched on their horses. Which made me laugh loud, as never in all my days had I thought of myself as high. But the strangest meeting we had was a good few miles after then, at a town named Nicia that was further along the coast, which we'd kept to so we wouldn't be frozen by blizzards in the mountains. We were staying at a little inn that looked out over the sea. I'd just gone down to the stables with Alwyn to check that the horses were all right and when I walked back out I saw a party of three had arrived and were dismounting from three very fine-looking beasts. I squinted up my eyes for a moment, thinking it can't be, but it was, no mistaking. There, climbing off a beautiful white charger, and wearing a long, white gown, was Matilda Froome. 'Tom, Alwyn,' she called out when she saw us. Then, seeing our surprise, she pointed to the two fellows she was with, telling us they were Flavio and Georgio, who were both messengers of the pope. One was bound for London and the other for Cologne, and as the road was the same for most of the way they were riding together. 'So Cardinal Antonio said I should go with them,' Matilda told us. 'It's so fast and commodious you wouldn't believe it. Everywhere we stop to spend the night there are fresh horses waiting, so we never have to waste an hour pasturing them.'

Cardinal Antonio? It was at dinner that we learned her story. Not long after Constance had met her begging on the street in Rome, she'd gone to a church to pray, where she'd begun sobbing and howling like she did, and though the priest had told her she must leave, as she was spoiling the mass, a woman in very fine clothes followed her out, and instead of cursing her, like Matilda had expected, she'd invited her to her house. 'She has such a beautiful place,' Matilda said, 'just across the river in Trastevere. I stayed there three weeks, in a lovely little room in the tower that overlooks the whole city. And she had a fine table too, so I was never hungry.' I could see she hadn't been, as she was no starveling now, and where there'd been one chin there was a second sprouting out. The lady, who was a countess, gave Matilda money, so did her rich friends, and they didn't care when she gave it all away to beggars afterwards. As for weeping and howling, the more she did it the gladder they were. They bought her not one but two fine new white dresses, and all they'd asked in return was that Matilda should bless them and all their kin, and their houses and their animals and carriages. And they asked for her old dress that was half blanket, which they cut up into little pieces and shared among themselves.

'But why?' asked Dame Lucy, and though Matilda threw up her hands like she couldn't say, the next thing she talked about was a Spanish woman who'd died some years back, and who'd been famous for weeping and moaning and such, and who'd lately been made a saint by the pope. 'So these Romans think you'll be a saint soon,' said Dame Lucy. And though Matilda laughed and put up her palms and told her, 'No, a hundred times no, that'll never happen,' I could see from her smile that she wouldn't be against the notion. After the countess and her friends had shared out Matilda's old dress, they'd made arrangements for her to go home and Cardinal Antonio, who was the countess's cousin, had suggested she journey with the pope's messengers. 'He's such a righteous man,' said Matilda. 'And he's a good friend of the Bishop of Norwich. He's given me a letter to take to him, asking if he might find me a little cell or shed where I can live in holy devotion, all alone.' A dreamy look came into her eyes. 'I'd love that.'

'But what happened to your Welsh friend?' asked Brigit. 'He's in Naples, of course,' said Matilda, like we should have known. She'd brought him to meet her grand new Roman friends and Cardinal Antonio had taken a great liking to him, for his gentle nature and also for his nation, as it turned out Cardinal Antonio was a keen reader of tales of King Arthur and his court, and he was most happy to meet a true Briton, especially one who knew so many languages. He'd helped Iorwerth with the cause he was pleading for his abbey, which was resolved, and then he'd asked if he might work as his secretary. 'I have a letter here to send to Iorwerth's abbot in Wales,' Matilda told us, 'asking his permission for Iorwerth to be let go, and telling his wife and children that they should go and join him.'

But Matilda's best news, she told us, was her last. 'I've got married,' she said joyfully. That puzzled us all. 'But I thought you already were,' Dame Lucy said. 'No, no,' she said, laughing at our foolishness. 'To God, of course.' He'd come to her not long before she'd left Rome, she said, and had asked her to wed him. 'So this was the gift that Jesus promised me in Rome, you see,' she said. And though she'd told God that she'd rather marry Jesus, seeing as he was younger and had more manhood, God had insisted she must marry him and so she had. Jesus had been at the wedding, she told us, and there'd been quite a crowd there, as the Holy Ghost had come, together with all twelve apostles and a good number of saints and virgins, too. 'I worried Jesus might be angry,' she said, 'but no, he was most lovesome.'

We bade Matilda farewell early the next morning, when she rode off with the two messengers, giving us a merry wave and a last howl. I was glad she'd found her feet and the Welshman, too. I'd never minded him, in spite of his spurning us. And though Matilda could be irksome, there were plenty of folk on this earth who were a good deal worse than her. As for the one who we met next, he was hardly less cheery than Matilda had been. Soon after Nicia we turned inland and a week or so later, at the pilgrim hospital in a city named Lions, we met our old friend Oswald. How he laughed when he saw me in Lionel's clothes, pulling off his hat like I was a proper lord. He'd been hoping he might meet us somewhere along the road, he said, as he'd wanted to give us his news. 'You'll never guess the good fortune that's come to me.' It turned out that at a little place not far to the north of Lions Oswald had met an Englishman from Chester who'd been burning with fever and coughing blood. He'd made an oath to pilgrimage all the way to Jerusalem for the soul of his dead wife and, knowing that his life was slipping away, he'd given every penny of his travelling money to Oswald and asked him to go in his stead. 'He didn't linger long either,' Oswald told us brightly, 'and just two days later he was gone. How blessed I am. Because

I've always wanted to get to Jerusalem. Now that I've seen Rome, it's the one spot I've never been to, and it's the best of them all. I felt like jumping for joy.'

After we said our farewells to him and left Lions, Dame Lucy took us on to Paris, seeing as it wasn't far off our route, now that we were taking another road, while she'd heard it was a fine city, and so it was, I thought, with a most handsome cathedral on the castle island in the river. Then we journeyed north to the coast and crossed the sea, which kept calm enough for us. And so I found myself back in England once again, though it seemed like half a lifetime since I'd been there last. I was pleased to be back, of course, but as we rode towards London I was sorry too, knowing that I'd soon have to give back Lionel's horse and say goodbye to my fellow pilgrims, as they'd all be taking the same road together that led north to Thetford and then to Lincoln, while I'd be walking westwards to Minster all alone. And then I'd be back home, tilling the earth in a cold wind. When we came in sight of Southwark I told Dame Lucy, 'We'll be saying our farewells soon. I should give back the fine clothes you gave me,' though I was rather hoping she'd tell me I could keep them, as I liked the thought of stounding the folk back in Minster. Instead of answering me, though, she said something that I could make little sense of. 'Don't worry about those now, Tom, as we'll be on the same road together a little while longer,' and when I asked her how come, and where she was going to, she just laughed and told me, 'You'll see.'

So we crossed London Bridge and reached London, and sure enough it was only Constance and Paul that I said my farewells to. I'd grown fond of them both and there were tears on every face that morning, especially the two little lads, Peter and Paul, who'd become such friends. As to whatever Dame Lucy was contriving, Father Tim and Alwyn and Brigit and Jack all knew what it was, as I saw them smirking as we all rode west, but they didn't give away a word. On we went, through Wycombe and Tetsworth, and how long ago it seemed that I'd been fretting there at having lost all my farthings, sure that I'd be hanged. At Oxford I half expected Dame Lucy to leave me and take another road, to Chippenham or somewhere else west, but no, on we went together and when we got to Witney, where I'd first met Oswald and Jocelyn, she said, 'Would you mind if we go with you to your village, Tom? I'm curious to see what it's like.' Of course I said no, I'd not mind at all.

Then I felt strange, as everywhere I looked there was a tree I knew or a stone wall I'd passed a hundred times. It's been a wet winter up here all right, I thought, looking at the high river. Now I saw the first folk I knew, delving their strips. It was wonderful what being mounted on a fine grey horse and wearing good clothes could do. They looked right through me, not knowing me at all, till I called out, 'Hello there, Ned. Hello there, Susie,' and they frowned and gawped at me, gawped once again and then called out, 'Simple Tom? Is that you? What're you doing up there?' And I told them, 'I'm just back from Rome with some pilgrim friends,' and Dame Lucy and her party gave their hellos.

Next I was at our little house and I'd hardly got down from the saddle when Hal and Sarah were hurrying out of the door. Hal grinned and called out, 'Look at you, my brother,' and then Sarah looked at me with a sorry face and told me, 'Oh my dear Tom, I don't know how to tell you this, but your end of the bed's gone. There's no room as the twins have it now.' So it was twins, was it? I could hear them in there, bleating away. And then, before I could even think of an answer, Dame Lucy cut in, 'Don't worry, he won't need it. He's coming with me.' And that was how I finally learned the reason why she'd ridden all the way to Minster, which was so I might become one of her servitors. 'If you'd like to,' she said, which I did, most certainly I did. 'Then I'll tell you why,' she said. 'You're a good man, Tom, and I trust you.' Which I suppose was her way of saying she was sorry for having disbelieved me when I helped save her boy.

That very same afternoon we went to Sir Toby and I gave him his vernicle and his silver cross, hoping he wouldn't guess it had only cost two shillings and eightpence and not five, which he didn't, and I gave Dame Emma her sewed Mary and baby Jesus. Then Dame Lucy bought me my freedom. In all my years I'd never thought I might see such a day. Tom son of Tom not bound any more, but a free man. How amazed they all were and none was more confounded than my Auntie Eva. 'Who'd ever have thought of it,' she said. 'A useless cluck like my nephew getting his liberty. I'm glad of it too, though, as at least he won't be mine to fret about any more.'

The next morning we set out for my new home. As it was on our road we stopped at Asthall to give our hellos to my first fellow pilgrims, Hugh and Margaret, though I didn't find them in as good spirits as I'd expected. They'd only got back themselves a couple of days before and Hugh moaned that his idiots hadn't looked after his harvest well and that a whole sack had been lost to rats. The grouchiest, though, was Margaret. She asked did any of us have a Rome badge we might sell her, though Hugh said he wouldn't waste a penny on any such thing, seeing as it was all her own fault. It turned out that when they'd been going over the Thames at London in a ferryboat, a gust of wind had whipped up out from nowhere, plucked her hat from her head and dropped it in the river, where it sank in a moment, pulled down from the weight of all those saints.

Two days later I saw my new home of Ropsley manor where I am still. Though Dame Lucy says we'll soon be in a great castle, once she's settled her case against her old husband, Walter. I do like working for her. It's not onerous. I'm the one who does everything that doesn't have a special fellow to do it. I'm not the cook or the steward or the garden keeper, but the one who's sent out to make sure the moat's high with water, or who chops logs or is sent up to Lincoln to bring back French wine or mead or a new gown that's been made for my lady. And I'm to stop her marrying some new rogue, so she likes to tell me. Though that's not really my duty of course, but her gaming me. As if I ever could? I've seen her making pretty eyes at all the young gentlemen she meets. 'I'll find you a good wife soon, Tom,' she tells me. 'I have my eyes open for one, and it's something I have a talent for.' In the meantime, though, another duty I have is my sinning. I know when it's coming up as Brigit has me wash myself from the well and then calls me to Dame Lucy's room to light a candle or move a chair. After that she leaves the room, Dame Lucy pours me a big glass of mead and tells me what I'm to do. It troubled me a little at first but then she told me I wasn't to worry as I could shrive it all to Father Tim and he'd absolve me. And so he does, giving me a weary look and telling me, 'I've absolved enough else so why not you?'

So all in all I'm more than glad that I went on my great pilgrimage. As Sammy's not come into my dreams since I left Rome I reckon he must be in heaven, and though it seems a little unkindly of him not to show me his new home, as I'd love to have a gawp at the place, I don't blame him. He'll be busy up there I dare say, chasing paradise mice if they have them. And I have a new cat now. Mirabel's her name and she's a dear thing, black as a raven and very sweet and friendly. And though she doesn't follow me around like Sammy did, she's a good little animal and sleeps every night on my bed.

All those months of begging and sore feet let me see half the world, filling my eyes with wonders. They won me my freedom and even gave me a tiny bit of rank, as a great lady's servitor, and saved me from delving fields in a cold wind. Often I let myself slip into a merry daydream and remember some hospital or barn where we stayed, and strange to say even the dirty, stinking ones are quite cleaned up in my remembrance and seem sweet enough now. Or I'll recall the folk we met along the way, and how they were kindly to us, most of them, giving me coins and helping us on the road. And I remember our party of pilgrims who I walked with all the way to Rome.

Of course the ones I've thought about most of all just lately are Mary and Helena, or Motty and Merry, whichever they are, though I still think of them as Mary and Helena. They must be glad they chose as they did. If they've learned the news yet, that is. The first I knew of it was when I heard

Jack the cook let out a great cheer from the kitchen. Then the gardener was cheering too, and a delver who was pulling weeds from the field below the manor house. From what folk say they've been cheering all across England. As to what was being cheered, this was the news that King Edward, wanting to make himself more loved, and to get taxes that he wanted, promised to throw every single Jew from his realm never to return. And it's done him well, too. He'll get his taxes, everyone says, and in all his days he's never been more loved than now.

Seeing how glad they all were, I tried to think it must be rightful in its way. But then a couple of days ago we had to go to Lincoln, as Dame Lucy had more business in the courts, trying to get her castle back from her old husband. It was a bright autumn day, just a little warm, much like the day when I set out on the road from Minster one year before. We were passing through a village and the moment I saw them coming towards us, crowded into carts and walking beside donkeys loaded up with packs, I knew who they must be. Some folk by the road jeered but they paid no heed, like they'd become well used to that on their journey down from wherever they'd come.

Then, just as we were going by them, Jack the cook stretched out his head and let fly a gob of spit, so big that I guessed he'd been working it up in his mouth, and it landed on the face of a little maid in the cart, who let out a shriek. That turned the jeers to roars of laughter and the maid's father, as I guessed he must be, had such a face on him that I was sure there'd be trouble, but in the end all he did was give Jack a glare and put his arm round his daughter. 'Really, Jack,' Dame Lucy said, though she had a little smile on her face. The only one who looked sorry was Brigit. In a moment we'd gone by them and when I looked back they were already disappearing down the road. So it wasn't as if anything much had happened. But the maid had long black hair that made me think of Helena. For a moment I wanted to say something and it was like it was there on my tongue, waiting to be said. But it didn't seem wise to make a fuss. So I just kept very quiet.

NOTE OF THANKS

As a relative newcomer to the medieval era, I would like to give all my thanks to the following people, who have kindly offered their expertise, and a great deal of time from their busy lives, to look through and correct the manuscript of this novel: Miri Rubin, Professor of Medieval and Early Modern History at Queen Mary University of London; Marion Turner, Associate Professor and Tutorial Fellow in English at Jesus College, Oxford; and Malcolm Godden, Emeritus Professor of Anglo-Saxon, Oxford University. I would also like to thank Rohini Jayatilaka for her warm support of this project; Patrick Reeve for his wise editorial suggestions; Jean Jones, Head of the Vice-Chancellor's Office of Aberystwyth University, for her help with Welsh language; and Cecilia Trifogli, Professor of Medieval Philosophy at All Souls College, Oxford, for offering an Italian perspective on the subject. I would also like to thank my agent, Georgia Garrett, and my publisher and editor, Will Atkinson of Atlantic Books, for their professional excellence. And of course I would like to thank my family, Shannon, Alexander and Tatiana, for enduring me during the writing process.

I have tried to be as accurate and true to the past as I could. Readers who are familiar with the later medieval era will notice that several characters are drawn from actual historical figures. Lucy de Bourne is based on Lucy de Tweng, a noblewoman from late thirteenth-century Yorkshire who led a highly colourful life and fought a protracted, brutal and ultimately successful case to divorce her husband. Matilda

Froome is based on the mystic and autobiographer Margery Kempe. Kempe lived more than a century after the time when my novel is set and this led me to a little factual invention. The two saints whom Matilda mentions, Saint Truda of Sweden and Saint Sipper of Flanders, did not exist, but are based on two fourteenth-century saints. These are Saint Brigit of Sweden, who persuaded her young husband they should have a sexless marriage, and Saint Mary of Oignies in Flanders, who was known for her weeping and howling. Finally, the character Iorwerth is inspired by a brief claim in the letters of Archbishop John Peckham that Prince Dafydd ap Gruffudd was betrayed to the English by a Welsh clerk, Iorwerth of Llan Ffagan Fach.

NOTE ON LANGUAGE

Language in historical fiction is a dilemma. Ancient mouths uttering twenty-first-century slang can be jarring, if not downright ridiculous. An attempt to write a whole novel in thirteenth-century English will be well beyond most authors' capabilities, and is likely to appeal to a very small readership indeed.

The language of this novel is, not surprisingly, a compromise. Most words that are commonly used in today's English already existed by the late thirteenth century, though spelling could be very different. My main concern was to try to avoid any post-medieval words. I decided to use modern spelling so readers would not be constantly puzzling over the text. Occasionally I have included a word that has long passed from usage, to give a sense that this was a very different era, or to give a word an extra emotional resonance.

When writing this book I constantly referred to the University of Michigan Library's Middle English Compendium, which I had always open on my computer. I would like to pay tribute to this magnificent online resource. Having taken seventy years to create, containing three million quotations, and offering numerous filters to help one navigate through its definitions, the compendium is an example of scholarly generosity at its best – a great gift to the world. Without it I would have struggled to write this book.

As I mentioned, I have tried to be very sparing in my use of Middle English words, and I have attempted to use them in such a way that their meaning should be fairly self-evident.

But in case one may seem unclear, or if readers want to see them precisely defined, I have included a short glossary, and also a glossary of medieval city names I have used in the text (not many, as most city names were much the same then as they are today).

Glossary of Middle English

anoyful   annoying
bairns   children
barnished   pregnant
bordel woman   prostitute
bulk   cargo of a ship
brewster   brewer of ale, male or female
cantred   Welsh area of administration (as English county)
cloisterer   monk
couch   to have sex with
craft   trade, technique, skill, occupation, strength, ingenuity
customed   accustomed to, customary
dotard   fool, imbecile, simpleton
extorcious   extortionate
gogmagog   a misshapen giant
grub   dwarfish person, digger, insect larva
jobbard   blockhead, fool
joyed   happy
loathfully   with loathing
lollerer   (Middle English loller) lazy vagabond, idler, cheating beggar
lordlings   affectionate and respectful term of address
lovesome   beautiful, handsome, lovely, delightful
misborn   deformed at birth
miscomfort   to be disturbed, distressed, a source of anxiousness
to maunge   to eat

noiyous	annoying
nulled	cancelled, annulled
nun treader	seducer of nuns
parage	lineage, family, rank, parentage, nobility
pap	breast
popelot	pet, darling
poppet	youth, young girl
to pretence	to feign, pretend
proudlessly	without pride
putain	prostitute
quarantine	period of forty days
rounsey	a work horse
to scholar	to teach
to scelp	to hit
scrip	leather pouch used by pilgrims to carry their money
scuses	excuses
to shrive	to make a confession to a churchman
slutterbug	(Middle English slotir-bugge) dirty person
sportful	diverting, entertaining, amusing, pleasant
stounding	astounding
to swive	to have sex with
tallage	arbitrary, one-time royal tax, forced levy
thrall	a servant, slave, serf
truffle	nonsense, twaddle, balderdash
uncustomable	unusual
unneedful	unnecessary
unright	a sin

Medieval place names

Besantion	Besançon
Lauon	Laon
Lions	Lyons
Nicia	Nice
Rains	Rheims
San Donen (local dialect)	Fidenza
Taruenna	Thérouanne (then a sizable city, now a village)